PRAISE FOR *THE ~~~~*

"Charming, laugh-out-loud funny, and honest, *The Better Half* celebrates the absurdity and joy in life, and does so with an enviable grace and good heart."

—Mindy Kaling

"The third book from comedy writing duo Alli Frank and Asha Youmans dazzled Mindy Kaling so much that she is publishing the book under her own imprint launched in 2022, Mindy's Book Studio."

—*Entertainment Weekly*, "Best Books of Summer 2023"

"*The Better Half* is a rom-com unafraid to tackle weighty issues, and Nina's narrative voice is a delightfully funny one."

—*The Seattle Times*

"*The Better Half* sizzles with sharp observations and even sharper wit from the first page to the delicious end. Alli Frank and Asha Youmans are a formidable team skewering the culture that forces women into roles while writing characters who both embrace, eschew, and finally succeed in their own powerful way."

—Ann Garvin, *USA Today* bestselling author *of I Thought You Said This Would Work*

"*Tiny Imperfections* is a funny, heartwarming take on finding love in a most unexpected place."

—Anissa Gray, author of *The Care and Feeding of Ravenously Hungry Girls*

"Parents and anyone who's ever been to school will love this peek into the turbulent world of private school, from two women who have worked in it for more than twenty years. Get to know three generations of Black women in San Francisco as they navigate that universe, along with their relationships, motivations, and a heaping helping of drama."

—*Good Housekeeping*

"Youmans and Frank manage to tackle a woman's journey through work, race, and motherhood beautifully in their debut. *Tiny Imperfections* is laugh-out-loud funny and full of heart. I can't wait to see what they bring us next!"

—Alexa Martin, author of *Fumbled*

"Overeager parents are just one of the many things heroine Josie Bordelon has to deal with as head of admissions for a tawny private school in San Francisco. These two authors are brave enough to expose the insanity and hilarity that happen during application season . . . A really funny read."

—Laurie Gelman, author of *Class Mom*

"Humor, charm, and intriguing drama combine in this novel—written by a best friend author duo—about the competitive world of private education."

—*Woman's World*

"Youmans and Frank's deep dive into private school culture sets the stage for a dishy, charming story of West Coast elitism and parenting at its pushiest. But it's the characters, especially the marvelous Bordelon women, who give this delightful novel its heart and humor—and who make you long to be part of the family even after the last page."

—Amy Poeppel, author of *Small Admissions* and *Limelight*

"Perfectly captures the absurdist bubble of San Francisco's tech upper class. A rollicking good read that reminds us that money, power, and influence will never be enough to make someone truly happy."

—Jo Piazza, author of *Charlotte Walsh Likes to Win*

BOSS LADY

ALSO BY ALLI FRANK AND ASHA YOUMANS

The Better Half

Never Meant to Meet You

Tiny Imperfections

BOSS LADY

a Novel

Alli Frank & Asha Youmans

Montlake

Published by Montlake, Seattle

www.apub.com

Amazon, the Amazon logo, and Montlake are trademarks of Amazon.com, Inc., or its affiliates.

ISBN-13: 9781662522918 (hardcover)
ISBN-13: 9781662514791 (paperback)
ISBN-13: 9781662514784 (digital)

Cover design and illustration by Jarrod Taylor
Cover image: © DaHaeHey / Shutterstock

Printed in the United States of America

First edition

For our moms.
For our grandmothers.
And for all the boss ladies out there.
You know who you are.

We often overestimate how much we can accomplish
in a day but underestimate how much we can
achieve in a year.

—A supersmart neuroscientist on a self-help podcast

Confession of two storytellers before you even begin reading. We are fiction writers, not chemists. We are creatives, not capitalists. Any compounds, chemical reactions, formulas, and business lingo we get right in this book is sheer dumb luck. Alli barely passed her corporate finance course in college, and though Asha loves reading sci-fi, she is no scientist. For all the math and science brainiacs who are reading *Boss Lady* for a hit of com-rom, as writers we are showcasing our wordsmithing talents but may botch some of the business and chemistry talk. And anything we get right: we are as surprised and delighted as you.

JANUARY

WEDNESDAY, JANUARY 2

Build-A-Burger sits dead center in San Francisco International Airport's Terminal 3, between Skyline News + Gifts and a questionable ten-minute massage stand. A popular refueling spot for passengers, Build-A-Burger has perfectly crushed ice chips reminiscent of the ones I sucked on at Kaiser hospital for thirty long hours doing my best to push resistant twins into the world. Plus, my friend Zwena is manager-on-duty. I pull my passenger transport cart up to the far corner of the restaurant, hugging the wall tightly. Refilling the ketchup dispenser, Zwena gives me a wave when she sees me out the corner of her eye.

"Hello, there. Small Diet Coke, please," I order with exaggerated formality, so the customer standing a few feet back reading the menu doesn't realize Zwena and I know each other like that. After spending New Year's Day with a raging headache—not from a hangover, but from carbonated caffeine withdrawal—I decided that slowly weaning myself off Diet Coke is a better New Year's resolution strategy than going cold turkey. My friend leans over the counter between us and pretends to pluck a dollar out of my palm before I can hand her a five—airport dining being expensive and all.

"A small Diet Coke it is," Zwena says loudly enough for the customer to hear, then hands me a cup twice the size I didn't pay for.

Nodding toward the fountain drink machine, Zwena walks over to make like she's emptying the liquid drainage tray while I fill my free supersize container.

Under her breath, Zwena reminds me, "I thought you were off Diet Coke." I wobble my head indicating *maybe*, my resolve already waning in the first forty-eight hours of the new year.

"You want a fried fish sandwich? Onion rings? I cannot get you a burger today. Those patties have been sitting in the fridge far too long for my taste."

Even though I haven't eaten since breakfast, I shake my head. I need my carbonated caffeine now, and I can sense Kayla, the new cashier across the concourse at Klein's Deli, watching us like a hawk. For a recent high school grad, she's surprisingly a stickler for employee rules.

Zwena clucks her tongue and then eyes me up and down like I just returned from a trek in the Sierras, not two days off to help my mother paint her kitchen. "Fine, have your Diet Coke, but I'm telling you, you look like you've missed a meal." The graying middle-aged customer is now at the counter clearing his throat to attract Zwena's attention so he can order.

"Excuse you. I'll be over to help you in a minute, sir. You might think about the Bay Area blue cheese and bacon burger. It is very popular," Zwena calls back with no intention of hurrying herself along for this man's order or warning him about the potentially expired meat.

Ding.

Although I am unnerved by Zwena's offer to further rip off Build-A-Burger on my behalf and her comfort level with a potential food poisoning case on her hands, this perfectly timed interruption does give me an out. I hold up my phone, indicating I need to check my texts. Zwena heaves a sigh at my refusal of free food and languidly sashays over to her customer, more confident than any twenty-eight-year-old has a right to be, but she knows her curves make men's necks break. When dealing with the opposite sex, life happens on Zwena's terms.

8:18 p.m. (Sylvia Eisenberg)

Antonia, honey, are you there? Are you getting this? I think I'm doing it right. The nice young man sitting next to me says I'm doing it right. Just landed and the flight attendant informed us we are pulling into Terminal 2 gate D10. See you in a few!

"Gotta go, Z," I say, shaking my sloshy ice. "Mrs. Eisenberg worries when I'm late, and tonight she decided to give Virgin America a try."

"Probably fond of Richard Branson."

I give Zwena a *who isn't* shoulder shrug. Titans of industry are some of my biggest crushes as well.

"Tell her I say she's holding back on details about the fine gentlemen she plays cards with down there in Scottsdale. I'm waiting to hear the truth directly from her. It takes too long to get it from you." Zwena chuckles, amusing herself at the idea of Mrs. Eisenberg making moves in the clubhouse of her gated community.

"Hold on." Zwena ducks behind the counter and jogs over to my cart with an old-fashioned glazed doughnut. Mrs. Eisenberg swears a doughnut a day is her key to longevity and that sugar is the fountain of youth. "She can pay for it next time you two ride by." It's truly a marvel that Zwena can balance the Build-A-Burger inventory at the end of every shift and hasn't been investigated for misdemeanor theft.

"You have your Sharpie?" Zwena asks, pulling one out of her apron and holding it up.

"You know I do," I assure her as I place my drink in the cup holder and the doughnut on the seat next to me. Then I put my cart in reverse and instinctively brace for the beep that, though I've heard it a million times, still gets on my nerves.

There is a predictable rhythm of foot traffic at San Francisco International Airport. Monday mornings are made up of stress-junkie tech types flying south to Los Angeles or north to Seattle for back-to-back meetings, then home, hopefully in time to kiss their children good night. Tuesdays, senior vice presidents who used their Mondays to show their faces with colleagues and organize their week fly out heading east, returning late on Thursdays. When flying first class, Tuesday is a terrible day to try to snag a seat. After a full couple of days on the East Coast, a business dinner Thursday night can morph into Friday morning continental breakfast. The most chaotic time at SFO is Friday after four. Terminals fill with a cross-section of exhausted bicoastal executives returning after a long week bumping up against zealous adventurers racing to their gates for a weekend warrior trip kitesurfing in Cabo, a college roommate's destination wedding, a girls' weekend in Palm Springs, or a testosterone-fueled poker tournament in Vegas. Friday late afternoon is by far the best time for airport people watching, but weaving my transportation cart in and around the hordes whose critical concern is making their flights proves a challenging game of don't clip the commuter.

My favorite time inside San Francisco International Airport is midweek. On Wednesdays, SFO fills with the leisurely pace of poised seniors traveling to visit grandchildren, retirees wanting to arrive a day or two early in Anchorage for an Alaskan cruise so they can "get settled," or folks returning home from a bucket list trip they saved for years to take. From my seat behind the wheel, I wistfully observe devoted, hunched-over husbands and their white-haired wives holding hands, sure to not lose their trusted travel partner. Wednesday travelers are a blend of calm and joyfulness, their faces conveying what I envision are memories of children well raised, satisfying careers behind them, and mutual admiration intact.

I get the sense that when older people travel, they relish the journey as much as the destination, dressed nicely for what their generation considers a luxury. I've never witnessed an octogenarian in leggings and UGGs boarding a plane clutching their emotional support pillow. Button-downs and pantsuits are standard. Midweek passengers who have arranged for my transportation services arrive promptly and chat excitedly as I drive them to their gate or out to baggage claim. If there is a lull in the conversation, which does happen on occasion, I fill it with questions about their itinerary and their own key to longevity. Not having traveled much myself, I view the time I spend with my older passengers as a road map for a future I'd like to have, but so far I am nowhere near that path.

As I pass by multiple United gates, I wave to my friend Krish, the agent on duty for in- and outbound Chicago flights. I keep my distance since he's got his hands full with a canceled route to O'Hare and hundreds of passengers outraged that he can't control a midwestern snowstorm.

In an effort to entertain himself as much as soothe the annoyed passengers, Krish announces over the PA system in his baritone voice, "Ladies and gentlemen, we are gathered here today to get through this thing called flight." He receives a few gratuitous chuckles from the irritated masses for his Prince reference. Krish knows how to amuse a crowd.

He slips his left foot out from behind the counter just enough for me to see. I take in his newest pristine limited-edition Nike sneakers and mouth, *Love them. Me too,* Krish silently responds, licking his lips in leather ecstasy while furiously pecking away at his keyboard.

I make it to Mrs. Eisenberg's gate as the plane from Phoenix is locking in to the Jetway. I open up my bag and rummage around for the Sharpie. Ugh, my hand lotion has exploded all over the bottom. I'll have to head straight to the restroom in baggage claim to clean it up after I deliver Mrs. Eisenberg to her granddaughter, Livy. I rip a blank page from one of the notebooks I carry with me and write in big black capital letters: MRS. EISENBERG, QUEEN OF THE DESERT. I know she'll get a kick out of this one.

I've been carting Mrs. Eisenberg across San Francisco International Airport for two years now. Through grieving the death of her beloved husband, Eddie, a hip replacement, her daughter's second divorce, and discussions over more of my pipe dream prototypes than I care to count, we've ridden side by side. When I was introduced to Mrs. Eisenberg, she was returning from a trip to her second home in Scottsdale for the first time without Eddie. Back then, I thought I was returning to work at the airport for a short stint, six months tops. I had a sign with her name on it to make sure I assisted the right woman. By our second ride we had bonded over our shared love of movies, and now personal signage that relates to our favorite films has become our signature greeting. With each trip the creative bar is raised.

Among the throngs of deplaning passengers at gate D10, I spy the head of a professionally styled dark brunette who I suspect hasn't worn her natural gray in, well, ever. As Mrs. Eisenberg searches for me, I smile and shimmy my paper like I'm standing on a street corner spinning a sign for a Memorial Day mattress sale. Mrs. Eisenberg lights up like a Christmas tree, or in her case a menorah, when she lays eyes on me.

"You got my text!"

"I did," I assure my surprised bejeweled traveler. Last year, I gave out my cell number to a few of my favorite elderly passengers so they didn't have to tangle with the automated terminal transport system. The miracle of technology is a conversation that Mrs. Eisenberg and I often revisit.

"Did you see that awful man walking right behind me? He was wearing shorts on the plane and those terrible shoes that go through your toes!" Mrs. Eisenberg declares loudly enough that the "awful man" can hear exactly what she thinks.

"You mean flip-flops?"

"Yes, those! Just terrible. I don't particularly care to see people's bare feet at my pool club—I certainly don't want to be staring at them on an enclosed airplane." Mrs. Eisenberg scrunches up her nose in disgust as she adjusts the buckle on her purse strap that's likely cutting into her shoulder. I nod apologetically to flip-flop guy as he swiftly maneuvers past us.

"Antonia, is that a new shade of lipstick?" Mrs. Eisenberg stops to ask, blissfully unaware that we are blocking the flow of foot traffic spilling into the terminal. I put an index finger to my lips, trying to remember if what I have on is one of mine or something I borrowed from my girls. "It becomes your coloring. I like that one for you." She wags her finger toward my face and then grabs the crook of my elbow so I may escort her to my cart. *I hope my lipstick is not in the bottom of my bag covered in exploded hand cream and lint.*

"Thank you," I respond, dropping my head, unsure how to receive a compliment from a woman who, I'm guessing, hasn't left the house without an array of Estée Lauder products perfectly applied to her face since the invention of Astroturf.

Settling Mrs. Eisenberg into my cart, I move the attention off me by jumping right to the desert gossip. "So, Mrs. Eisenberg, how's the Scottsdale crew? What do you all have lined up for winter?" We're stuck behind a family spread across the corridor, swinging a toddler wearing a kitty cat backpack. I bite my lower lip to keep myself from informing them this is not a Saturday stroll in Golden Gate Park, and they need to keep it moving along.

"When are you going to start calling me Sylvia?" Mrs. Eisenberg asks sharply, placing a bony fist on her hip to emphasize her point.

"When are you going to start calling me Toni?" I tease, meeting her pseudo-indignation.

"I'll do no such thing. Antonia is a grown woman's name, and in front of God and the doctor, it's what your mother chose for you. All these girls running around sounding like boys on a Little League team. Ridiculous. You're too smart and too pretty to be called anything akin to an outfielder." Mrs. Eisenberg does not hold back on her opinions. A right she claims she earned in the women's liberation movement in the sixties and then fully embraced when she turned eighty. My guess is she's always been liberal with her sentiments.

"Is this a new cart? These seats feel new." Mrs. Eisenberg pats the firm pleather and snags the doughnut with no doubt that it's hers. "If you want to be taken seriously, you have to go by Antonia."

"What *is* going on with the desert crew?" I repeat, guiding Mrs. Eisenberg back to our original topic and off scrutinizing my name and my future. She pulls a miniature boxed water from first class out of her purse, slowly unscrews the top, and takes a drink, no doubt wetting her throat to spill the news she's been holding on to for the two-hour flight.

"Well, we are now down to only two drivers for Saturday-night dance lessons. Me and Patrick. Fred gave it up over the summer. Well, actually, the state took his driver's license. He failed to share the news with the group. Probably mortified since he used to drive race cars for a living. Now Elaine has to ride with me since, you know." Mrs. Eisenberg raises her eyebrows at me, so she doesn't have to repeat the unspeakable. Indeed, I do know. The story is that Elaine, who apparently talks about everything and nothing at the same time, put the moves on Patrick too soon after his wife, Sally, had to be placed in a memory care facility. He declined her advances, and Elaine's subsequent public humiliation at the Vintage Club spring fling brunch last year has forced her to now avoid Patrick at all costs. Mrs. Eisenberg didn't shy away from declaring that Patrick dodged a bullet.

"I should charge like Uber," Mrs. Eisenberg states, nodding once for emphasis.

"You know what Uber is?" I blurt, surprised by the casual mention of ridesharing.

"Well, of course I do. I'll be ordering one every Saturday night for Elaine on my next trip to Scottsdale." Mrs. Eisenberg giggles at her own joke, and I can't help but join her. I've been hearing about what a pain Elaine is for a while.

"Enough about me. What's new with you? It's been almost a month since we've seen each other. Any progress on that frozen food in a coin purse idea?"

"The empanadillas? That idea was four, five months ago, September-ish maybe? When you went down to Arizona this time, I was working through food warmers for lunch boxes. Open them up, shake to create an exothermic reaction, and then set your lunch container on top of them to heat up your meal."

"Right, right. I'm remembering now—sort of. I don't get it, but I recall it. Besides, what if you're having a Nicoise salad for lunch? I always have a salad for lunch."

"Well, no need to remember it. I have no idea what I was thinking. It was stupid." I exhale with defeat. One more busted project has ended up in the landfill of misspent money and time that I don't have to spare.

"Not so stupid," Mrs. Eisenberg asserts, an attempt to comfort me. "Though I don't think I quite understood why someone would use the packets when you can just heat your leftovers in a microwave. Everyone has a microwave."

Exactly, I admit to myself.

"Believe me, Antonia, the process of building something from nothing is miserable and thankless, and there are far more failures than successes. One day when you follow through on one of these ideas you've been sharing with me over the years, it's going to be a huge hit. I know it in my bones. Work hard, and luck will bend your way. It's the answer for anyone trying to get ahead."

I smile at Mrs. Eisenberg's sermon. I know she believes the platitudes she doles out, but hers is a charmed life where dreams come true behind perfectly manicured hedges. Mrs. Eisenberg is as clueless to how hard I work as she is to the financial struggles I face as a single mom from the moment I leave my house in the morning to when I drop dead into bed at night.

"Let's hope you're right, Mrs. Eisenberg," I reply, withholding all the obvious reasons I'm still driving this transportation cart and not hard at work on said "huge hit."

"I'm always right, Antonia," Mrs. Eisenberg confirms without hesitation.

We arrive at the elevator, where a wheelchair waits for us. I hop out and extend my hand for Mrs. Eisenberg to hold on to. She steps off the cart and does a one-eighty to sit down in the wheelchair. Once Mrs. Eisenberg is settled, I push the elevator button and take her down two floors to baggage claim to meet her granddaughter. In the lift,

Mrs. Eisenberg pops a mint LIFE SAVER in her mouth and then holds the roll up to me, her routine gesture that signals our time together is coming to a close.

We exit the elevator, and I push Mrs. Eisenberg over to the illuminated board that lists flight numbers and their corresponding luggage carousels.

"I'm at number six," Mrs. Eisenberg announces before I have even found her flight. Her physical stamina to navigate the length of an airport may be waning, but her eyesight remains impressively sharp.

As we pass carousel four, I scan the crowd for Livy, who is usually standing by a bank of gray plastic seats. I don't see her anywhere. I can tell by the way Mrs. Eisenberg is fiddling with her blouse collar that she's growing nervous not having laid eyes on Livy either. Her fidgeting reminds me of how out of sorts she was the first time she traveled without Eddie, her arm instinctively reaching for his hand that wasn't there, her eyes wildly searching for him. It was heartbreaking.

"Let's take a spin around to the other side, closer to the restrooms. I bet Livy's over there. And if not, she's probably driving in circles, looking for a spot. We both know what a headache parking at the airport can be," I offer with assurance, not wanting Mrs. Eisenberg to become unnecessarily agitated.

"I gave her Eddie's old handicap placard to use for parking when she's running late," Mrs. Eisenberg comfortably shares, as if her granddaughter using her dead grandfather's long-expired placard isn't illegal.

"Look at you going all *Shawshank Redemption* on me." I playfully tap her shoulder, working to alleviate her worries with a shared favorite film reference.

"Just help me find my granddaughter, Morgan Freeman," Mrs. Eisenberg teases. I nearly choke on my LIFE SAVER.

As we turn our backs to the arrivals board, Mrs. Eisenberg stares intently where Livy should be. I look in the opposite direction and see a man whose face is vaguely familiar in a way that I know I've come across him before, but I can't place where. Either way, he's handsome enough for my eyes to linger as my memory tries to work out where this remarkable man may have existed in my unremarkable past. I turn the wheelchair and casually move toward this sorta-stranger, wanting a closer look without seeming obvious. Too quickly, the man's gaze locks in on us, and he starts jogging in our direction, his wing tips not impeding his pace one bit. Imagining he recognizes me, I think the whole scene feels right out of a romantic comedy—except this is my mundane life, not the movies. Startled by his speed, not knowing if he's going to run right past us or run right into us, I pull back on the wheelchair. I don't want to frighten Mrs. Eisenberg.

"Ash! Ash!" Mrs. Eisenberg cries, waving in delight, stepping out of the wheelchair as I continue to pull back to avoid a collision. Our opposing momentums send Mrs. Eisenberg stumbling forward into this mystery man's arms. I lunge over the back of the chair to grab Mrs. Eisenberg's cardigan from behind but miss by inches. The stranger sprints up to Mrs. Eisenberg just in time to catch her in an embrace.

When people talk about accidents feeling like they happen in slow motion, they're mistaken. There was nothing slow about Mrs. Eisenberg tumbling forward as I imagined her new bionic hip shattering into a million pieces due to my recklessness. Seeing Mrs. Eisenberg unharmed and upright in this man's arms, I let out a massive sigh of relief as a trickle of sweat makes its way down the back of my sky-blue polyester shirt.

"Ay Dios! Oh my God, Mrs. Eisenberg, are you okay? I'm so sorry. I can't believe that happened! I was trying to move out of this man's way, but I didn't know you were stepping off, and then you did." I reach for Mrs. Eisenberg's forearm to return her to my care.

"Thank you, thank you, sir," I babble, but I receive no acknowledgment of my gratitude nor for seeming as familiar to him as he does to me.

"Antonia. *Antonia!* It's okay, honey. Take a breath. Calm down. I'm perfectly fine. This wonderful gentleman who caught me is my grandson, Ash. Ash Eisenberg. Livy's cousin."

I stare, speechless. Picking up Mrs. Eisenberg at the airport is not how I know him. It's only ever been Livy to meet us at baggage claim.

"He's never come to greet me at the airport before, he's always flying in and out himself," Mrs. Eisenberg gushes, looking up adoringly at her grandson. "Oh, sweetheart, can you stay for a cocktail?"

You're not the only one who needs a cocktail. I choke it down before it slips out of my mouth.

"My goodness, where are my manners? Ash, this is my friend Antonia," Mrs. Eisenberg introduces us, having tucked herself under her grandson's protective arm. She doesn't give my last name, leaving me to wonder if, after all the time we've spent together, she even knows it.

"Antonia Arroyo," I clarify for Ash and for Mrs. Eisenberg. "But I go by Toni." Mrs. Eisenberg huffs, sharing her annoyance at the shortening of my name.

"Hello," the prodigal grandson says, but his neutral face does not register that there is a person with a name on the receiving end of his disinterested salutation.

"I know, Ash." Mrs. Eisenberg claps, enthused by an idea forming in her head. "You should get Antonia's phone number. She could use some help with her business ide—"

"Grandmother, let's grab your bags and get going. Livy's waiting curbside in the car," Ash answers to his grandmother's unfinished attempt at niceties. Not that I would have given Ash Eisenberg my number because his grandmother suggested it, but he didn't need to make it so obvious that my presence is inconsequential to his day.

"Both of my grandchildren here to greet me, how wonderful!" Mrs. Eisenberg beams, already having forgotten her number-exchanging idea. I smile to meet her enthusiasm, but I keep my mouth shut as the third wheel in this family reunion. "Your being here is such a surprise, I love it!" Mrs. Eisenberg continues to coo as her grandson towers over her in what has to be the most expensive pinstripe cashmere suit I have ever come this close to. A heavy matte steel watch peeks out from under his jacket sleeve, screaming statement piece, annual bonus, or both.

Without a goodbye, grandmother and grandson make their way toward carousel six to retrieve Mrs. Eisenberg's luggage. I'm left standing alone, with my heart rate finally beginning to slow from the collision of events.

Watching them walk away without so much as a backward glance in my direction, it hits me why I remember Ash Eisenberg. I grab the wheelchair to steady myself. "His being here isn't just a surprise for his grandmother," I mutter out loud for no one's benefit other than my own. *I can't believe my past has found me in baggage claim.*

THURSDAY, JANUARY 3

"Lou, Coco, come and see what I have for you!" Zwena knows the way to fourteen-year-old girls' hearts is through consumer goods. I shake my head at her in mock disappointment. Being born on Christmas Eve, my girls are inundated with gifts from the moment midnight mass ends on the twenty-fourth until the last bite of Christmas ham has been consumed on the twenty-fifth. Dry January in our house means buying absolutely nothing for the twins. Zwena, however, doesn't believe my rules of parenting apply to her.

With the grace of a herd of elephants, my twins plow into the kitchen, where I'm frying up a batch of sorullitos. If only they'd travel that fast when the dishwasher needs emptying.

"Whatchoo got for us, Auntie?" Coco asks with the signature *care don't care* tone of a teenager who lives on the cusp of perpetual annoyance.

"What do you have for us, Auntie?" I correct, in what feels like a losing battle against TikTok to keep the English language intact in my house. "This isn't the mall food court."

"These!" Zwena pulls out two boxes, one from each of her back pockets. I'm impressed she could slip them in there, since she likes her jeans two sizes too small with her muffin top slightly rising.

"Baby-pink press-on nails!" Lou whoops, lunging for the box in Zwena's left hand. Louisa's a girly girl, just like my mother, Gloria. When Lou was a toddler and couldn't pronounce her *p*'s, she would go around the house saying, "Ink! Ink!" I'd bring her a pen, thinking I had a future Pulitzer Prize–winner on my hands, and she'd pitch a holy fit that got the neighbors talking until I finally figured it out.

"I'm trying to get these girls into Princeton, not hot pants," I remind Zwena, swatting her now-empty pockets with my spatula. *Whoops, I left a little grease mark.*

"No reason they can't get into both," Zwena counters, pulling the girls in for a group hug and not letting go.

"I'm only paying for Princeton," I reply, pointing my spatula back and forth between Lou and Coco. Currently, I can't pay for either, but I don't fool around when it comes to my daughters' education.

"So, you almost killed Mrs. Eisenberg, eh?" Zwena asks, finally letting go of Lou and Coco so she can open the fridge in search of dipping sauce.

This morning I invited Krish and Zwena over for dinner with the lure of one of my tía Fernanda's recipes and juicy airport gossip. Krish is busy covering a couple of extra shifts for sick coworkers, saving up for yet another turntable, but when I hinted to Zwena that I almost killed someone, she came right over.

"Murder is never good, my friends," Zwena warns in her thick Kenyan accent like she's doling out words to live by. Coco's and Lou's eyes go wide.

"I did not actually almost kill Mrs. Eisenberg," I assure, squashing Zwena's attempt to spread fake news. "I accidentally ejected her out of her wheelchair, that's all." Cooking over a cast iron skillet feels like August in San Juan, but still I shiver from yesterday's near miss fresh in my mind.

"Then tell us what happened."

I hold up a finger to Zwena indicating *one minute.*

"Girls, get out of here and go finish your winter break homework. I know what you have due in language arts, Ms. Martin and I talk." If my wayward husband's parents are helping me pay for Saint Anne, I'm getting our money's worth of teacher time and attention.

"Aw, Mom, when are you going to stop checking up on us?" Coco whines, always demanding more freedom than she's earned. Lou stays quiet, focused on figuring out how the adhesive works on her new nails.

"When you two graduate from college, that's when. Now *out.*" Marking my words, Zwena stamps her foot and swiftly points to the kitchen door, trying on the strict-aunt persona. The four of us double over in hysterics. Zwena doesn't have a stern bone in her body when it comes to my girls, her love for them limitless. And by *limitless,* I mean she spoils them with all the little extras I have to say no to as the family accountant. Lou plucks a couple of sorullitos off the paper towel, hands one to her sister, and high-fives Zwena over the awesomeness of press-on nails on the way to their room.

When the girls have cleared the stairs, I drop a few more sorullitos in the skillet and turn to Zwena. "Mrs. Eisenberg's grandson is *Bahlack,*" I enunciate as if the word has two syllables. Zwena pulls her head back in disbelief. My *doubt me if you want to* expression doesn't crack.

"Are you for real? You're telling me that Betty White has a darkskinned grandson?" I nod, refuting Zwena's doubt. "How exactly does that work?"

"I didn't climb all up in the Eisenberg family tree, Z. What I do know is Mrs. Eisenberg's granddaughter, Livy, is White, but her grandson, Ash, is a full-on brotha." I give Zwena another minute to ponder this fact. I've been pondering it since last night.

"And on top of that shocking truth, right there in front of carousel six, my past and my present collided."

"Don't tell me while you were doing wheelies with Mrs. Eisenberg, you ran into your ex bringing his namaste nonsense back to town. You know I have no tolerance whatsoever for Simon Evans. Plus, I thought we were done with him."

"You know he is not my ex yet. He is Coco and Lou's father, so no, we do not get to be done with Simon."

"Hey, you're the one who started going by Arroyo within weeks of Simon leaving, so I thought we were." Zwena makes a slashing motion at her throat, demonstrating exactly how much tolerance she does not have for my runaway spouse.

"Back on track, Z, this drama has nothing to do with that one. Last night was compliments of my pre-Simon past. Think: young Toni."

As a child, I was a little girl who liked to blow shit up. After school when other kids were at the playground, double Dutching in parking lots or playing kickball in dead-end alleys, I would be mixing up all kinds of concoctions like watered-down dish soap, peanut butter, and iodized salt, keeping detailed notes of my ingredients and their reaction upon interaction.

Every other Friday when my dad got paid, he entrusted me with enough money to grab my twin brothers and walk them down to the corner store to buy candy and soda from Mr. Kim. While David and Gabriel fought over what they should choose in the chips aisle, I always chose the same two things: Mentos and a sixteen-ounce plastic bottle of Diet Coke.

I would put on the safety goggles I'd begged my parents for, drop the packet of Mentos into the open bottle, hop back several feet, and watch the fountain erupt. When the soda settled, I would measure the highest point and the widest width the liquid had splashed across the stucco and record the date and data. And then I'd wash the stickiness off with the garden hose before my mother called me in for chores.

I was the independent, bookish eldest child of the passionate Afro–Puerto Rican pairing of my father, Sebas, who made the living, and my mother, Gloria, who made sure Sebas's life was worth living. Six days a week my dad went to work managing a Safeway across town, where his suave personality made him wildly popular with men and women alike, and my mom ruled the home and, by default, us kids. My parents were secure in their roles and in their marital love, and our home was filled with a solid example of a true and traditional partnership.

I remember sitting on my parents' bed for hours watching my mom get ready for her Saturday nights out at salsa clubs with Papi. When my mom caught a rhythm, my dad's eyes danced like it was the very first moment he had ever seen her. As Mami meticulously put her face together, she would recite her beauty tricks on how to draw a cat eye with black liner, rub in rouge atop cheekbones, and put on nylons without creating a run. I know my mom thought she was imparting the skills necessary to grow into my womanhood, but all I was wondering was if her mascara brush could clean a pipette.

My parents left Las Marías and ended up in San Francisco's Potrero Hill. All they ever heard in church, on the Muni bus, or at Safeway was how attractive I was and what a blessing I would be to a man one day. My caramel-colored skin, smooth like a sucked-on Werther's Original candy, was neither blanquito nor negrito. Soft, loose, dark curls and hazel eyes as large as quarters were compliments of my Black mother and my blue-eyed Spanish father. My beauty was what my parents saw, even when my report cards proved that I was far more than a pretty face.

When I was nearly fifteen, I earned a distinguished California state science student award and was invited to summer camp at the University of California, Los Angeles. As much as my father tried to work the numbers, my parents couldn't afford to send me, and my mother was completely mystified as to why I would choose a college campus over a summer quinceañera.

Undeterred from attending, that spring, while my mom cruised secondhand shops for dresses to mark my "becoming a woman," I nearly put Mr. Kim and his corner store out of business I was slinging candy bars and Skittles so hard in my high school hallways.

I promised my parents a delayed fifteenth celebration, and that summer on the UCLA campus, I found my people and I found my place. Just like me, the other four hundred students from all over California wanted nothing more than to study physics, chemistry, and biology. This was a community of people who, though few looked like me, also liked to blow shit up. When I started my sophomore year in high school, I had a singular goal: earning a full ride to UCLA for college. Nothing but my grades mattered to me. My mom was constantly trying to get me to hang out with at least one of the boys who tried to holler at me, but I was too busy dating the periodic table. When spending time with elements, there's always a spark.

Staying true to myself, while living with parents who pinned their hopes and dreams on my younger twin brothers and only marriage prospects on me, took monumental conviction. I appeased my mother's concern for my lack of interest in boys by spending Friday nights at the movies with her catching the latest romantic comedy. What my mom didn't realize is that while she thought these movies full of meet-cutes and anticipated first kisses in the rain would spark my interest in dating, what they did was make me believe that holding out for a Mr. Right like my dad, versus a Mr. Right Now, was worth the wait.

Once I got my acceptance spring of my senior year in high school, I refused to let anything stop me from going to UCLA to become a Bruin.

My dad did his best to support my academic aspirations by suggesting I attend San Francisco State University and continue to work and live at home. I knew he was worried about money, but I also knew that between my scholarship and a guaranteed on-campus job at Powell Library, I would work hard to not cost my parents a dime. If I focused and graduated in four years with a chemical engineering degree, I could get a job at twenty-two making more money than my dad would ever make on the Safeway management pay scale. I was determined to move my family forward, and by *forward*, I meant *upward*. Financially it would be a lean four years for the Arroyos, but I swore to myself that after graduation I would give back to my family. I was convinced this formula couldn't fail.

"Z, you've heard me say behind Lou and Coco's backs that my two years at UCLA were the best days of my life." When I close my eyes, I can still vividly picture myself striding across Royce Quad, hurrying to class to hang on every word of my professors in the chemistry department and engineering school. I enthusiastically took a course load my adviser was sure I couldn't handle, but I knew I could. "I would wake up before my roommates and go to bed way after they were asleep. I held on so tight to time and facts that I'm pretty sure my roommates thought I was a bore."

"Oh, they definitely did," Zwena concludes, perhaps hinting that I'm starting to bore her right now too.

"There was one class I really loved that I had never even heard of before going to UCLA. It was microeconomics, and I was stuck on the intense baby-faced PhD candidate who was my professor. He had dark skin like my mom's and flawless cheekbones. He wore his hair in a high fade, and if I had to guess, he must have been older than me by six or seven years. I had a serious case of first nerd love and a growing interest in business."

"Okay, now I'm actually listening. I want to hear more about this professor."

"My flirting strategy was visiting his office hours and asking about problem sets I had already completed. Perfectly, I might add. I was sure that in a sea of hungover White student faces, my eager Brown face would stand out. But I never got anything more personal than 'excellent work' while he looked past me to the next person leaning against the hallway wall waiting for help."

"Toni, you have the goods." Zwena waves down my body. "Unless that man was dead inside, I guarantee he noticed you."

"Well, whether he noticed or not, it didn't even matter. Early one morning, a week into the fall of my junior year with Professor Smoke Show, Tía Fernanda called to tell me my father had been killed in a car accident on his way to work." Swallowing, I feel the lump in my throat that arises on the rare occasion that I bring up my father's death.

"That call did me in. But I had to replace my grief with thoughts of David, Gabriel, and my mom's survival. What were they going to do for money? My brothers were in eighth grade, too young to work, and my mother had never held a job in her life. She went straight from her father's house to my father's house."

Even though it's been almost two decades since my father died, Zwena knows talking about it is still challenging for me. Her left arm envelops my shoulders, squeezing me tight. I rest my head against her. "I could barely lift my feet walking to the bursar's office to withdraw from school. I packed up my dorm room and all my potential and caught an overnight Greyhound bus back to San Francisco. With two years of college under my belt, I had more education than both my parents. I knew it was my responsibility to pick up the family's financial burdens and provide for Mami and my brothers."

Remembering the sorullitos, I turn off the stove and pour the hot grease into an empty can. "I balanced lots of low-paying jobs and did what was expected of me. You know how it goes, Z." Without question, in our family, loyalty and survival ultimately reign supreme, even at the expense of individual dreams.

"Sad story aside"—Zwena winks and smiles, letting me know she's redirecting the conversation off childhood struggles before we both burst into tears—"what does your past have to do with what got you so turned around that you almost dumped Mrs. Eisenberg on the cold concrete?"

"Listen, Z, to say I woke up to the opposite sex, *ehrm* . . . on the later side of puberty would be generous," I hint, not eager to dive deeper into my amateur dating history that started with a seismic crush on an economics professor who didn't know me by my student number let alone by my name.

"Like sixteen?" Zwena inquires, picking up a sorullito and blowing to cool it down.

"Sixteen? I'm talking more like twenty. My first crush was on that economics professor."

Zwena drops her snack.

"Let me get this straight, it took a numbers nerd to ignite your lady parts?"

"Supply and demand is surprisingly sexy," I try to convince Zwena.

"Sure, if you're the one in demand."

"Yeah, well, like I said, I wasn't. I promise you, he really didn't know I was alive. The class met in an auditorium that could hold a Rihanna concert."

"Help me out here, because I am not connecting the dots. Your professor has to do with Mrs. Eisenberg's near-death experience . . . how?"

"I saw that professor in baggage claim."

Zwena's narrowed eyes tell me she's still confused, so I spell it out for her. "Mrs. Eisenberg's Black grandson was my economics professor at UCLA, and I almost killed his grandmother in front of him twenty years later."

"I thought you said you didn't almost kill her?" Zwena accuses, completely missing the point she had just been needling me to make.

"Fine, I didn't, but I did almost drop her. This man spotted us and started jogging our way like he was gonna grab us." I mimic for Zwena what I remember seeing—a deliciously handsome guy, albeit older and balder than I recollected, with his arms slightly out to the side like he might be about to take flight.

"Did you think he recognized you, too, and was coming in for a hug?" Zwena assumes every man is out to cop a feel.

"Girl, please. Hell no. Or at least I don't think so, because even though I recognized him, it didn't click for me who he was until after he walked off with his grandmother to get her suitcase. In that split moment, I didn't know if this man was coming right for us or going to blast right past us, so I started to pull back on Mrs. Eisenberg's wheelchair to move her out of the way. And right as I was pulling back, she was stepping off." I act it out for Zwena.

"Oh no, oh no, I don't want to hear the rest." Zwena covers her face with her hands, making a peephole with her middle and index fingers so I can see only the whites of her eyes.

"Yanking her chair back made Mrs. Eisenberg fly forward. Luckily my professor has incredibly long legs and reached Mrs. Eisenberg just in time to catch her. Those open arms were for his grandmother."

"Now, that's impossible. How could this man have known Mrs. Eisenberg was about to go down?"

"I don't think he did, but he did know that his grandma would be excited to see him and want a hug."

"I'm still working out how Mrs. Eisenberg did not end up a pile of broken bones. And how our retired Snow White has a Black grandson. Is he African black like me, or is he more all mixed-up like you?"

"I drive hundreds of people around San Francisco airport week after week—everybody's mixed-up to me." It's not uncommon in one shift for me to see blond people with dreads, Pacific Islanders in fur coats, South Asians with gold grills, and White men covered in head-to-toe tattoos making the argument that they, too, could be called people of color. "But Ash, I'd say he reminds me of *ehrm* . . . polished wood."

"When's the last time you saw wood, polished or otherwise?" Zwena challenges me, holding on to my gaze, daring me to deny her question.

I don't acknowledge her double entendre, nor the truth she already knows. Instead, I get back to the details of the mystery at hand. "Mrs. Eisenberg's grandson is Ash Eisenberg. Ash Eisenberg was once my young, insanely good-looking professor of economics at UCLA. I remember like it was yesterday that his pecs popped in every shirt he wore, especially when he reached up to write equations on the whiteboard." I expect Zwena to give me credit for knowing an exceptionally well-built man when I see one. "Not counting Bill Nye the Science Guy, Professor Eisenberg was the only man I ever lusted after before I met Simon."

"Is *pecs* the medical term Americans use for *pecker*?" Zwena's been considering becoming a medical assistant. She should reconsider.

"It means his chest, Z. And trust me, I spent hours in class daydreaming running my hands all over it."

"I liked it better when I thought it meant *pecker*," Zwena concedes, smacking her thighs in amusement. "So does Professor Sparks still light your fire?"

"Seriously? I just relived the drama of my father being killed, and then me almost killing a rich White lady in front of her grandson, and you want to know if my old economics prof still has it?" I know Zwena questions my definition of *handsome* given my description of Simon's penchant for Birkenstocks.

"Listen to you, eh? You said you only almost dropped her, not killed her. And yes, I do want to know if he's still mrembo."

"English, Z, you know I can't speak Swahili." Amid my humiliation, I did manage to notice Professor Eisenberg had held up well into his midforties. Over the years I've seen my share of men striding through the airport in suits, but none has worn them quite as well as Ash.

"*Mrembo* means *beautiful.* If you're making me learn Spanish to get in on the conversations between you, your mom, Lou, and Coco, then you can make an effort to learn some basic Swahili. It's only fair."

"Fine, that's fair. Yes, he's membo."

"That's close enough for now," Zwena acquiesces, knowing my ear for language lags far behind my skill with numbers. "Did he recognize you? You're looking mighty good, too, these days, even in your uniform."

"Nah. When Mrs. Eisenberg introduced me, he barely acknowledged my presence. It's obvious that outside the walls of SFO, Mrs. Eisenberg and I do not travel in the same circles. Before I could say 'nice to meet you' or 'nice to meet you, again' and tell Mrs. E. I look forward to seeing her in a few weeks, he had checked his watch twice and steered his grandmother away."

"Really?" Zwena asks, yet again baffled by Americans' lack of interest in one another and obsession with time. In Kenya, an introduction is the gateway into an hour-long conversation filled with laughter, back slaps, and discovering mutual friends and family connections.

I pause before sharing the stinging truth of it all. "Z, I don't think a person can have a memory of someone they never noticed in the first place."

TUESDAY, JANUARY 22

"Mom! We got two boxes!" Coco calls as she carries an armload into the living room, where my feet are kicked up on the coffee table. My big toe, painted with Fire Station Flame Red polish, is sticking through a pair of socks worn thin. We are not a family for whom Amazon boxes show up on the daily delivering retail wishes. I'm surprised to be receiving any packages, though I could use some new socks.

"This beat-up box is from Florida. The envelope"—Coco turns it over and around before dropping them both at my feet—"I don't know where it's from, but it looks kinda important."

With my heel, I drag the legal-size manila envelope toward me, so I don't have to lean over to pick it up. I just finished working straight through a busy Martin Luther King Jr. weekend. I'm beat, and my lower back is aching from hours sitting in my cart and pushing wheelchairs with few chances to stretch. If Simon were still here, he'd have contorted me in all sorts of twists and inversions to release what he would claim is bad energy manifested by the stress of other people's holiday travel.

"You know they're both for Mom," Lou huffs, still sore I made her pack food boxes at the Hunger Coalition instead of getting auburn highlights to celebrate MLK Day. While I have no clue what's in the battered package held together by a janky duct tape job, I recognize my lawyer's handwriting on the envelope. Simon's two-year departureversary is coming up next month, and since he left us, I have clung to the sporadic postcards he's sent, even if they have been less than forthcoming about his future plans. For the first year Simon was gone, whenever I drove my cart through the international terminal my neck was craned so my eyes could scan every gate where passengers were disembarking. An average of ten times a day I would hope one of the faces, in a consistent stream of unfamiliar ones, would be my husband's, but it never was.

With the start of this new year, I finally decided to take the first step to considering a life without Simon in it. Eavesdropping on a passenger who was talking loudly into her cell phone about a miracle divorce lawyer who drew up her papers in under two weeks, I wrote down said lawyer's name. The minute my shift ended, I drove to Krish's gate to ask him to ring the lawyer before I chickened out and resettled into my frequent fantasy where Simon returns home, apologizing profusely for his temporary insanity. Krish happily diverted his line of customers over to the gate agent next door and held up his phone between the two of us to make sure I followed through with the conversation. In that moment, I had no idea if I even wanted a divorce, and now that the papers have been delivered two weeks later, I have no idea where I would send Simon his copy. But the singular act of the envelope showing up at my house feels like forward momentum into the new year.

I tuck the papers under my right hip. Coco doesn't need a reminder that at forty-three her father decided the meaning of life was not to be found where his family lived, but instead enlightenment was waiting for him in an ashram in India or a monastery in Myanmar. Without a hint of wavering conviction, Simon packed up the narcissism that he had confused with spiritual awakening and left us "for something bigger."

7:40 p.m. (Toni)

Happy New Year to me, my divorce papers arrived.

7:42 p.m. (Krish)

I'd call them an early Valentine's Day present. And don't even think about using them as fire starter.

I consider Krish's idea. Even though we live in California, Krish knows I love a good fire in winter. January is plenty cold for a woman who has Puerto Rican blood running through her veins.

7:45 p.m. (Toni)

Feels weird having them in my home. To be honest, I'm not sure what to do with them now that I have them.

7:46 p.m. (Krish)

I do. You're going to use them.

I was fifteen when my father turned forty and started surfing again, a beloved boyhood pastime he picked up when visiting his uncle who lived near Playa Jobos. We teased my dad relentlessly that surfing was a young man's fun, but his mornings at Ocean Beach brought him so much joy my mother told us to support his harmless midlife diversion. As Simon inched near the same significant age, my mother reminded me that a wife's job is to be patient and charitable when her husband feels the need to redefine his manhood.

Simon and I met the summer before David and Gabriel entered their senior year in high school. I was twenty-three, lonely, and spending all my waking hours working to support our family. Simon was the older and (I thought) wiser man at twenty-nine. After a couple of years living back at home, working for transportation services at SFO at night and brewing expensive lattes for exhausted technology grunts by day, I finally had something that was all my own—Simon, my best 6:00-a.m.-extra-large-drip-coffee-with-a-splash-of-soy-milk customer.

Simon grew up in a conservative Catholic family that lived in a 1950s time warp where children were to be seen and not heard. Wound tight from existing on a diet of devout Catholicism and an intense job he hated as an associate at a prominent investment bank, it was no surprise that Simon loved the chaos of our rambunctious, overly affectionate Puerto Rican family. We talked loudly over one another and over the background soundtracks of Tito Puente and Willie Colón. Something fragrant was inevitably cooking on the stove, and given what had happened to my dad, it was impossible to leave a room—let alone leave the house—without my mother grabbing our faces with both hands and planting a big kiss on our foreheads like we might never return. Even Simon. The more madness that filled our tiny Potrero Hill two-bedroom bungalow, the more deeply Simon fell in love with me, and though I cared for him, too, what I saw most in Simon was a future filled with security.

Next to the morning my father died, the day we put David on the bus to go to Naval Station Great Lakes in Illinois for boot camp was the other worst day of my life. All David had ever wanted to do was fly planes off aircraft carriers, and I was ecstatic to see him dream big and then to see his dream begin. It was a worst day because I was sick with a stomach bug and couldn't go with my family to the bus station. For four years I had financed David's every meal, and now I couldn't even hug him goodbye and risk him getting sick before basic training started. Simon went in my place, not because I asked him to, but because he had earnestly taken to his role as David and Gabriel's surrogate older brother.

For several weeks Simon moped around after David was off to the navy, and again when Gabriel left on a full-ride academic scholarship to the University of Michigan. I, on the other hand, recuperated and rejoiced in plotting my first step in getting my own life back on track. While returning to UCLA was not in the cards with my mom at loose ends and Simon now a central part of my life, attending classes within an hour's drive of our home certainly was.

When my "flu" continued to rage, Simon ran home, practically yanked his grandmother's ring off his mother's finger, and proposed within an hour of my third pregnancy test. I said yes, because I knew Simon was over the moon about me and my family and I, like my mother, seemed destined to marry the first man I had dated. Even though I didn't have my college degree, Simon's high-paying job could financially support our growing family, and after a lifetime of the Arroyos scraping by, this was a bonus I did not take for granted.

With help from Simon's displeased but duty-bound parents, we bought a small ranch-style starter house on the wrong side of Highway 101 in East Palo Alto, south of San Francisco. Simon was able to cut his time in the office down so he could be home to help with the constant feeding, bathing, and never-ending bedtime routine of what turned out to be our willful twin daughters, no doubt compliments of my family genetics. Then he would return to his computer, banging out emails and fiddling with spreadsheets while I tried to exercise my mind by reading a book, only to end up passing out until the midnight wake-up call from our girls.

By the time Coco and Lou skipped off to Saint Anne for a full day of kindergarten, six years had flown by, erasing our twenties and thirties. Simon and I were a well-oiled parenting machine. With a little more time on our hands, I suggested Simon pick up a hobby. The man had done nothing but work and take care of us for over half a decade. And I was once again ready to dust off my old journals full of half-hatched product ideas and get down to the business of tending to my brain. I was determined not to become my mother, who had relied upon my father for every aspect of her life. I knew I could balance being a good mother to Lou and Coco while pursuing my intellectual interests, my mind and ambition needing more than lunch packing and carpooling.

Given his level of office stress, I suggested Simon give yoga a try. Since our pregnancy-before-matrimony blunder, Simon had grown disillusioned with Catholicism, so I thought yoga would fill his searching spiritual side while lowering his cortisol. My mom had seen a few too many late-night infomercials of Lycra-clad women hawking foam rollers and was worried Simon's eyes and other body parts might wander in a mat-lined studio. I assured my mother that Simon was most likely going to yoga to simply enjoy a nap disguised as savasana. Looking back, I should have listened to my mother and suggested a running club.

As the girls spent more time in extracurricular activities, so did Simon. Hatha, Vinyasa, Ashtanga, and Kundalini yoga classes to be specific. Nightly, Simon would roll through our front door glistening in sweat and spiritual awakening, while I fumed at his missing a fourth family dinner in a row. Simon claimed I needed to "do the work" on myself to discover my divine higher calling. I countered I was trying with my statistics course at San Jose State, but unless Shiva was going to show up on our doorstep to babysit, Simon's obsession with yoga had to stop so that I could restart myself yet again. Someone had to give in, and I was tired of it being me.

While I was aware of Simon's yoga fixation and wasted too much of my limited free time trying to figure out how to tether my enlightened husband back down to this world, I was blindsided by his secret gambling addiction, which stripped bare our family savings. That piece of information came to light days after Simon returned from a literal trip on ayahuasca guided by a world-renowned shaman living in a $4 million treehouse in Malibu. When I confronted him, Simon announced, in the tone of someone who believes they're spiritually superior, that he discovered during his out-of-body experience that our relationship was "suffocating his growth." He revealed that on his trip he had communed with his ancestors, who told him he needed to shed this life so he could move on, unencumbered, to something bigger. It was shitty advice from a long-dead great-grandfather.

With three sarongs, his favorite yoga mat, and a completed exit interview at his firm, Simon went off for an open-ended sojourn to

India to discover his authentic self without a word of when he would return. As Simon headed off to Nirvana, he left me living in hell.

I then experienced an Arroyo legacy déjà vu. Here I was, a single mom with twins, no money, no college degree, no job, and no confidence to stand on my own. Even though Simon had done me wrong, if there's one thing Gloria had taught me, it was to be forgiving of men and their single-mindedness. Shamefully, I left the door open for Simon to come back to me. I needed Simon to come back to me. He was all I had known of men and a stable life since my father had died.

From my early years working at the airport, I was still in touch with my friend Krish. With the lack of empathy of a perpetual bachelor, Krish informed me I needed to get on with my life and recommended the first step was to come back to transportation services. He shared that some of the old crew was still there and would love to see me, which I knew wasn't true as I had flippantly treated my time working at SFO as a pit stop. As well, Krish wanted to introduce me to Zwena, his newest hookup for free airport food, so I could save a few bucks on my grocery bill.

When I resisted going backward, Krish reminded me that public people watching was the best way to make one feel better about one's own problems. And that a lot of people are in jobs they don't like or believe they are above doing, but self-pity does not put cash in the bank.

Dragging my heels, I finally agreed that temporarily returning to the airport might be good for my wallet and my mental health. It would only be until Simon returned home. I called my old boss at SFO transportation services hoping she would take me and my wounded ego back after a decade away.

7:55 p.m. (Krish)

You still there? You get what I'm saying? Keep those papers in a safe place.

I say *"Um-hmm"* out loud even though Krish is twenty-six miles away waiting on my response. Carefully, I tear open the manila envelope along its natural seam. As I pull out the document from my lawyer, I realize an earnest manhunt for Simon is the next logical step. I was sure Simon's midlife U-turn would eventually straighten out and he would come back home. I excused his behavior with well-worn tropes about how we met so young, twins are a lot to handle, and investment banking has a high burnout rate. But resistant as I was, as the one-year mark of Simon's departure passed and marched quickly toward two, I knew the time was coming soon to consider divorce proceedings so Lou, Coco, and I could stop living our life in limbo.

Aggressively riffling through the pages, I realize that what I thought would be elation feels more like anger. Anger that I might be giving Simon exactly what he wants, freedom to traipse around the world unencumbered, his only purpose being personal development. That while he will get to continue building the life he envisions for himself, I will remain at home attempting to shed the part of my heart that is still attached to having him here. With us. With me.

Putting the papers back, I reseal the envelope by pushing hard on the used packaging tape. Looking around my living room, I spy an old chemistry textbook sitting atop my *Day in the Life of Puerto Rico* coffee table book on the shelf next to the TV. I slide the yellow legal-size envelope between the two books, allowing it to stick out just enough that Coco and Lou won't notice, but I will know the envelope is there, a reminder that when I'm ready—if I'm ever ready—the next move is mine.

FEBRUARY

MONDAY, FEBRUARY 4

"I watch those airport smuggling shows on A&E, and this looks like dirty drugs to me," Mrs. Eisenberg proclaims, examining the fat Ziploc bag of powder that looks more like ground cloves than cocaine.

"*Shhhh!!*" I hiss at Mrs. Eisenberg. Three things you do not want to be at the same time: brown-skinned, in an airport, accused of carrying drugs. And even if I were smuggling, Mrs. Eisenberg is the last person I would choose as my mule. She'll give it up to anyone. I brought the bag to work to show Zwena. Given all the spices her mother sends her from home, maybe she knows what the powder is and has some use for it.

"Oh, calm down, Antonia," Mrs. Eisenberg dismisses, waving away my concern like a woman who has no clue what it's like to be racially profiled. Mrs. Eisenberg expertly opens up the bag and dips her pinkie finger inside for a sample. "Doesn't taste like much, maybe a little bitter." She also acts like a woman who has watched one too many documentaries on the Sinaloa drug cartel.

"You're too much, El Chapo," I laugh, pulling my cart up to a drinking fountain to fill Mrs. Eisenberg's water bottle for her flight. She has a faded sticker on it that says, "It's never bad enough to get bangs." I find this decal hilarious because I'd bet Mrs. Eisenberg hasn't changed her hairstyle in fifty years.

"When you grow up in Chicago overhearing horror stories about the Italian and Irish mobs, the world of drug cartels doesn't faze you," Mrs. Eisenberg alleges, pointing onward to her gate as if our conversation were as normal as chatting about the weather. I pass over her water bottle and drive.

"So, if you can't eat it or sell it, why did David send you this stuff?" Mrs. Eisenberg probes, laying the packet down in between us. I don't tell her I have four more like it at home, or about the check that was taped to one of the bags. The package was an early birthday present to me from David and Gabriel, even though they both know I hate acknowledging my birthday. All February 12 does is serve as a reminder that one more year has passed, and I am no closer to fulfilling my potential than I was the year before. To celebrate myself I take the day off every year to hole up in bed and pray the day passes swiftly.

The check came with explicit instructions to sign up for a course or two to get myself back on track to earn my college degree. My brothers also noted the money was not to be spent on another pair of ridiculously expensive leggings for Lou and Coco, that they'd cover those for the twins' birthdays. The funds are still burning a hole in my checking account because though I should consider a biochem or calculus class, there is an entrepreneurial course for non-MBA students at Stanford's business school that I've been eyeing. The course, however, would eat up the whole check, and it would not get me any closer to a bachelor of science. And then there is the nagging reality of my car's bald tires.

"Oh look, Sam's bartending at Yankee Pier. I've been meaning to ask how their clam chowder is." Mrs. Eisenberg waves furiously in Sam's direction. Only Mrs. Eisenberg can take us from the Midwest's mob scene to New England's clam chowder. *I better bring us back.*

"I have no idea what this stuff is. My brother David got it for me in Puerto Rico." Unlike my brother Gabriel, who got my father's gift of gab and is the chattiest mathematician you will ever meet, David is a man of few words. In addition to the check with strings attached, the box of powder came with a brief note that said, "A woman I know in Puerto Rico had this powder. Not sure what it's for, but I picked some up for you." I didn't ask for clarification from David about the powder or the woman he knows, there are too many to remember just one. David has gone against the family grain of marrying young by not marrying at all.

"Was he down there visiting your people?" Mrs. Eisenberg asks, and I shudder imperceptibly. I know Mrs. Eisenberg means nothing by it, but why is it that White people assume, if your skin is brown or black or a blended color like mine, *your people* hail from someplace other than, I don't know, Burbank or Indianapolis? In this case, however, there's no reason to correct my favorite desert dweller since she's mostly on point. My tía Fernanda runs a popular empanadilla shop in La Plaza del Mercado Santurce in San Juan and, even though my mother has been in the United States for decades, she still refers to Puerto Rico as home. In fact, Tía Fernanda is where I got my empanadilla venture idea in the first place. Not that I was passionate about the food industry, but I thought maybe I could expand on her already proven business plan as a shortcut to my own success. Zwena tried to pitch my empanadillas to the district supervisor at Build-A-Burger, but it was off-brand and I should never have allowed Zwena to make the first approach. Her sales skills are more fish market than corporate cutthroat. It didn't help that the dearth of Puerto Ricans in Northern California meant my empanadillas were unlikely to take off in the Bay Area like they did for Tía Fernanda in San Juan, but at least I know where my entrepreneurial spirit comes from.

"David's stationed in Pensacola, Florida, but every so often he and some naval buddies hop over to PR to visit our tía Fernanda. When they visit, our aunt spoils those guys rotten. And just like my dad did, David loves to surf down there. He picks up a little something for me from time to time."

"I know what your brother's like, I listen to your tales. I bet that's not the only thing he's picking up." Mrs. Eisenberg elbows me and points to the bag. The first day I met Mrs. Eisenberg at her gate, her husband, Eddie, had passed away six weeks prior. Though, like my mother, she still wears her wedding ring, Mrs. Eisenberg now loves to dish like the single woman she once was more than sixty years ago. And she, like a lot of women, has a crush on the magnetism David inherited from my dad based solely on the stories I have shared with her.

"Where do you come up with this stuff?" I tease Mrs. Eisenberg. She leans over and pulls out her latest romance novel, a blissful couple entwined on the cover.

"This year I'm trying to spend more time with books than movies. You should really read this one. I'll give it to you when I'm done," Mrs. Eisenberg promises, fanning my face with the book. I suppose if I had a successful six-decade love story like she had instead of a runaway husband, my hopeful self would be reading romance novels too. Instead, I stick to business memoirs written by tech unicorns who made it in America by the time they were thirty. Inevitably, these books make me feel like a failure, but a romance novel would as well.

"What's this?" Mrs. Eisenberg inquires, reaching for the recycled peanut butter jar filled with white cream sitting on top of a napkin in my cart's cup holder. "Oh, heavy." Balancing the jar in one hand, she jiggles it up and down.

I smile and direct Mrs. Eisenberg to unscrew the metal top. Since her arthritis has been flaring up in her hands recently, I purposely left this jar a bit loose so Mrs. Eisenberg wouldn't struggle.

Leaning forward to take in a cautious sniff, Mrs. Eisenberg says, "Smells nice," and I can't quite tell if her head is bobbing in approval or question. Optimism churns in my stomach, overtaking a blanket of exhaustion. I was up late whipping up batches of this lotion, trying to capture the unique aromas of eucalyptus and bougainvillea that are widespread in the Bay Area. Many people in California hate the non-native eucalyptus tree with its blue gum and voracious thirst that sucks soil dry, but there's no denying the smell is soothing.

After observing the numerous bottles of lotions that litter my mom's vanity, a reminder of wasted money and eventual landfill addition, I'm trying to figure out how to make a top-to-toe, one-kind-works-for-all-body-parts cream. Rather than women having one lotion for body, one for dry hands, one for calloused feet, and still two more for their morning and evening facial routines, I want to capture the market share of women who don't have the time or money for all that. I've been at work in my kitchen playing with combinations of water, unrefined shea butter, eucalyptus oil, sodium hydroxide, glycerin, and a whole host of other natural ingredients I have invested in to create a product that addresses every crack, crevasse, and cheek. Basically, my latest business idea is stealing from the one-size-fits-all concept in clothing and applying it to skin care. The only problem is that one size never fits all, and for weeks my efforts have made my kitchen an official disaster zone. My desire to keep at it is evaporating.

"Go ahead and try it on your arms and hands," I encourage Mrs. Eisenberg.

She looks at me suspiciously. "You aren't trying to poison me because I was skeptical about your food heater idea, are you? Remember, I was very encouraging of that nitrogen ice cream experiment. That one I could have gotten behind. If you had really put in the time, you could have been the first to get that concept up and running. Now that stuff is all over the place."

Mrs. Eisenberg's not wrong, I could have been first. For six months she listened to me geek out over every detail as I explored the process of making ice cream with liquid nitrogen, trying to create the smoothest, creamiest texture possible using the freshest ingredients. I read every physics book from the library I could get my hands on and started building a messy prototype in the backyard with parts off Craigslist. Weekly, I would haul a cooler full of ice cream and taster spoons to the airport so Zwena, Krish, Mrs. Eisenberg, some of the United ground crew, and a few of my other trusted regular passengers could sample my flavors. Being part of the invisible workforce at an airport occasionally has its upside. In the chaos of a concourse, no one policed for food safety regulations as I scooped from my cart.

The group enthusiasm for my ice cream venture was high, and Mrs. Eisenberg loved to make the joke that my mind was "churning," but in the end, I didn't have any sort of network to raise seed funding. Between work, parenting Lou and Coco, and worrying about Simon, I never got around to filling out the paperwork for a small business loan. Ultimately, another woman with an MBA from Wharton beat me to the top of the ice cream heap, and now she has four wildly popular shops in San Jose, Oakland, Marin, and San Francisco. I've had a scoop of her balsamic raspberry raisin flavor. It's tasty for sure, but I know mine would have been better. I would have left out the raisins. Still professionally treading water in the exact same place, I'm now applying a few of the principles for creating a smooth, creamy dessert to my lotion and still using Mrs. Eisenberg as my test subject.

"I promise, I'm not trying to poison your pores. Not intentionally anyway. I've been playing around with formulas for lotions since you are always complaining how the drier climate and intense sun in Scottsdale are rough on your skin. And with global warming, skin is crepier now in California too."

Mrs. Eisenberg rolls her eyes at my doomsday commentary before she dips her index and middle finger in for a hearty dollop.

"The texture reminds me of the Nivea cream I used for years." Mrs. Eisenberg massages the cream between her fingers. I slow my cart so I can observe her rubbing the lotion on her arms while still moving safely through the terminal. As she starts at her wrists, I note that the absorption rate into the skin should be much quicker than it is. Lotion shouldn't take work.

We both stare at her chalky hands and forearms. Mrs. Eisenberg says what I can clearly see: "This rubs in too white. Reminds me of sunscreen." I notice with every stroke it's true. Black and Brown women are used to white lotions and sunscreens not rubbing into our skin well, but for a Caucasian woman, even though Mrs. Eisenberg's skin carries a darker Mediterranean hue, there is no reason for lotion residue to settle on top.

"You do have something with the smell, though," Mrs. Eisenberg reiterates. I know she's trying to give me something to keep me going, to not give up, even if the product, meant for the whole body, for now only appeals to the nose. I blow out a huge sigh, one she has heard many times before. I hand Mrs. Eisenberg the napkin in the cup holder to wipe off what won't soak in. "I'll take this jar with me to Arizona to use, but in the meantime, you keep at it, Antonia, and I expect you to have a new and improved sample for me to try when I return."

"Maybe," I appease, deflated, thinking of the wasted gallons of apparently nonabsorbing lotion I have sitting on my kitchen counters. It's going to take some serious research and small-batch trial and error to figure out how to alter the consistency of the product for use on all skin types. Particularly, because I don't have the money to start again from scratch after buying Lou and Coco new dresses for their first school dance this weekend. While their Catholic school touts being in service to others, when it comes to the monumental life moments of teenage firsts, it is all about looking good—better known in the kingdom of puberty as being in service to oneself.

"*Maybe* is for the weak," Mrs. Eisenberg pronounces, dispensing her biting truth.

I drop my chin and don't say anything in response, but in that instant, memories of *maybes* past run through my mind. When my daughters begged to go to Disneyland and I knew we couldn't afford it, *maybe*, I'd said. When thoughts occurred of treating myself to massages when my lower back ached from sitting for hours in my cart, *maybe*, I'd wish. Hoping Simon would realize he'd made the biggest mistake of his life, *maybe*, I'd pray. *Maybe* was often all I had to cling to as a single mother who still had big dreams. Feeling the sting of Mrs. Eisenberg's admonishment, I have to accept that life moves on an upward trajectory for a woman like her. Maybes do not exist. She may think my uncertainty weak, but that single two-syllable word continues to give me hope.

Seeing my face fall yet again in defeat, Mrs. Eisenberg places her lotioned, gluey hand on my forearm. "Antonia, I'd rather you hate me and grow, than like me and stay the same." Mrs. Eisenberg is not at all moved by my pouty face. I nod in wounded understanding, but also with gratitude that at least someone in my life believes I'm capable of growing. That my life can get bigger.

"Oh, stop. Stop!" Mrs. Eisenberg commands, now waving frantically, her face shifting from stern to sweet.

"Mrs. E! Where are you heading today looking so shiny in that lavender getup?" Zwena bellows, striding through a sea of people lining up to board a flight to Washington Dulles, her presence parting the crowd.

Not hiding her girl crush on Zwena, Mrs. Eisenberg blushes. The way these two talk, we are definitely going to be late to the gate now, and I'm still recovering from the harsh words Mrs. Eisenberg just doled out.

"Did that handsome grandson of yours bring you to the airport today?" Zwena casually inquires, followed by a long draw from her Starbucks cup. I bug my eyes out at her, hoping she is picking up my *no you did not and don't you dare make one more grandson reference* warning. I know Zwena—every word she says has veiled intentions, and she doesn't care a lick about the consequences. Both these women should consider investing in a filter before they have no friends left.

Mrs. Eisenberg looks puzzled as to how Zwena might know about her grandson. I take the pause as the perfect opportunity to hit the gas.

"Catch up with you later, Z. We're gonna be late, and Mrs. Eisenberg has a mah-jongg tournament to get to in Scottsdale."

"I'm taking that Elaine down," Mrs. Eisenberg snarls. "She thinks she's so great. Ate half the shortbread cookies I put out at the last game I hosted at my house. Didn't even mutter so much as a *thank you*."

"Listen to petty Betty here," Zwena teases, not one bit surprised by Mrs. Eisenberg's fighting words. "So fierce. I love it!

"I'll talk to you after my shift, Toni," Zwena promises, her palm on the hood of my cart letting me know that she knows exactly what I'm trying to do by hitting the gas—avoiding the line of questioning she was preparing to Ready. Aim. Fire.

THURSDAY, FEBRUARY 14

5:22 p.m. (Krish)

Some chick tried to slip me a hundo to tell her boyfriend the plane is oversold. She doesn't want to go trekking in Patagonia with this dude or apparently date him anymore either.

I'm ten minutes late getting out the door, but I have to acknowledge Krish's text right away. First, I loop in Zwena because Krish is usually stingy sharing any airport gossip, being more a voyeur than a commentator. When Krish puts it out there, we have to keep his verbal spigot open before we lose his stream of consciousness. Plus, Zwena will be so pissed if she finds out I know anything even remotely juicy before she does.

5:22 p.m. (Toni)

Did you take it?

5:23 p.m. (Krish)

Nah. Would you? She seems a little psycho, but she's also kinda cute. I may call her up to the counter in a few and get her number.

5:24 p.m. (Zwena)

I'd take it. The money, not the number.

Of course Zwena would. With a legion of older female cousins from Magongo who were sent off into arranged marriages to lighten strained family financial loads, she does not turn down money. Zwena wanted the same life she saw vacationing tourists enjoying when she accompanied her father on an under-the-table weekend carpentry job at Diani Beach, not one as a city sanitation worker like her father or a laundress like her mother.

Even living in one of the improving settlements, Zwena knew that her chances of being married off were far greater than her chances of learning to snorkel. So she made herself indispensable to the principal of the school her parents scraped together shillings to pay for. It was eventually the principal's sister, who worked as a domestic in Nairobi for the *New York Times*'s East Africa bureau chief, who helped Zwena obtain a visa to come to the United States.

Zwena speaks nostalgically about growing up in the coastal town, rarely disparaging the poverty and desperation that grip much of Kenya, but she also pays forward her good fortune of landing in the Bay Area by rescuing women she thinks may be stuck in a no-win situationship. It's why she's the best possible friend to complain about Simon to, always there to listen and devotedly take my side. I also know right where that hundred would go—in her bra. I've offered to go shopping with Zwena for a wallet, even got her an adhesive money pocket for the back of her cell phone, but she claims storing shillings in her triple-D bra is what got her to California in the first place, and she's not messing with her banking system.

I could spend all day texting with these two, but the clock's ticking, and I know Zwena will be taking it from here with her lightning-fast fingers. Hustling out the door barefoot, shoes in my bag, I catch a quick glimpse of my hair in a disheveled bun, my eyes sitting on pillows of dark circles. I decide to take my hair out of its perpetual topknot and go curls down to distract from my puffy face after three early-morning airport shifts in a row. I realize the T-shirt I have on is one Zwena left at my house, the V-neck hanging too low down my chest, but I've run out of time to change. I adjust the shirt, shifting the neckline back, grab my travel coffee mug to keep me alert in class, and now have only twenty minutes to make it up University Avenue.

Tonight is my second Pioneering Entrepreneurs class at the Knight Management Center at Stanford through the university's extension offerings. Last week, I showed up for my first 5:30 p.m. lecture twenty minutes early, done up in my best magenta wrap dress and platform espadrilles, nervous as hell. Tentatively walking into the empty hall, I was reminded that it had been close to two decades since I had been inside a classroom at one of the top universities in the country. I sat down in the aisle, dead center, and took a few deep breaths to give my brain and my confidence time to warm up before I had to start thinking. As I inhaled, I noticed it smelled smart inside the room, like brain sweat. The second thing I noticed as others began to wander in and find seats was that my fellow classmates, all about a decade or so younger than me, were dressed in business casual, most likely coming from some world-renowned entity of capitalism on Sand Hill Road.

One glimpse of a sockless loafer and tailored trousers and I began to doubt what I was doing there. As these young executives greeted each other, obviously familiar with one another through work meetings and happy hours in downtown Palo Alto, I realized my classmates were here to polish their careers, not find one. They were adding to their elite education to ensure their professional advancement and enhance their networks. They weren't like me, here to get a life. They already had one.

Watching pristine laptops pulled out of buttery leather sleeves, I grabbed my purse and moved to the back of the room so no one would see the yellow legal notepad and Bic pen I was using. With only one laptop at home shared between me, Coco, and Lou, my computer needs always come after their homework. I am one of the few dinosaurs out there who still writes faster than she types.

To calm myself, I popped two Trident sticks into my mouth and went to town gnawing the taste out of them. When the professor walked through the wood-paneled side entrance to the front of the lecture hall, all laptops and tablets lit up and the room quieted. The first class on how to become a tycoon was in session. As the professor began to talk, my feelings of not belonging slowly faded. I was back in a school, the one place I had always shone, and there was no way these suits were going to get a better grade than me.

Unfortunately, that assured outlook was last week. It's only week two, and I'm already on the struggle bus. Having no time to shower after my shift, I did not want to be sweating, running into the Knight Center smelling of stale air, airplane pretzel residue, and lack of planning. I had submitted my first bit of coursework early, and before my shift, I unloaded the dishwasher and made spaghetti and meat sauce to be ahead of my evening mom duties. But during my tight work-to-home-to-class timeline, I unexpectedly had to wrestle the laptop out of Coco's hands before she dived into her first homework essay on Shakespeare's *Romeo and Juliet*, and Krish texted me with work chatter. All the while I was racing to class, I was praying the timing of traffic lights would be in my favor. Turns out I hit every red light, and now I'm sprinting across campus to make it to the Knight Center before the first third of class is over.

Today, a panel of product giants with their deep-pocketed venture capital partners are speaking to my class, and I do not want to miss one minute of it, given my current efforts at building a seedling lotion empire. I haven't had the opportunity to hear in person the *clawing to the top* tale of one, let alone four, victorious entrepreneurs. For me, their stories have lived only on the pages of biographies and *Fast Company* thanks to my public library card.

I am particularly interested in hearing from Libby Starr of No Hurdle Girdle fame, not just because her products keep my waist snatched but because she spent years hawking blood glucose monitors out of the trunk of her car before becoming an industry icon, rather than the more typical shot-to-fame tale of the young tech tycoons who overpopulate Silicon Valley. It's a story I've got to hear. I also like that she hasn't lost her smile and her sense of humor, at least according to what I see on Instagram, where she shows off a great collection of coffee mugs. I feel like we may be soul sisters on this caffeine-infused afternoon as droplets of java jump out of my travel mug and stain Zwena's T-shirt while I hurry across Campus Drive East, bag slung over my chest, pulling on my shoulder.

Breathing heavily, I fall into a front row seat, the only ones that are left since other students have migrated more to the middle and back of the lecture hall after only one class of jockeying for the professor's favor. The panelists and their venture capital sidekicks are already seated, and the professor is introducing each one of them. I don't move a muscle, not wanting to rustle around and risk interrupting the flow of introductions. I can't help but stare at Libby Starr of billion-dollar No Hurdle Girdle, wondering how, with five kids of her own, she doesn't show up at events late with a shine of flop sweat at her brow. After the introductions of the two speakers following Libby Starr, it finally comes to the background of the panelist sitting directly in front of me, who has been perched mostly in profile listening to the bios of his fellow one percenters.

"I am thrilled to introduce Ash Eisenberg. After ten years as the youngest tenured professor of economics at UCLA . . ."

Situated sideways in my new lecture hall, fifteen feet away from me, is my old professor—just as he had been forever ago. I'm in almost the exact same seat I was all those years back, once again ready to hang on Ash Eisenberg's every word. Even with age and fewer hair follicles, he is as attractive now as he was then.

"Ash moved to Menlo Park to launch a boutique venture capital fund focused on investing in consumer product seed-stage start-ups with founders of color . . ."

Ash hastily glances my way a few times, but then he averts his eyes. Does he not recognize me? Maybe not from twenty years ago, but certainly from last month, when we were reintroduced by his grandmother. When his gaze sweeps over the front row, he dodges locking eyes with me. His avoidance is obvious since I'm the only student parked smack-dab in his sight line. Just like at baggage claim, Ash seems bothered that he has to look down from the raised social dais and acknowledge someone like me.

"After successful exits with several companies, Ash has continued to . . ."

Now he's moved to resting his chin on his knuckles and is subtly pointing his index finger at me, while continuing to ensure his eyes don't meet mine. Is this his offensive attempt to address me and wave? Did Mrs. Eisenberg fail to teach her grandson the simple courtesy of eye contact? Seems like something she wouldn't let slip. Nor would his academic supervisors, though I don't remember him coming across as particularly warm at UCLA. I give Ash a slow chin lift and half smile to let him know the recognition is mutual and to mock his ill-mannered salutation. Ash points at me more aggressively, then looks down at his shirt.

I'm confused. Maybe I've misinterpreted his notice of me, so I look down too. And then I see what Ash has been pointing to. And why he's reticent to make eye contact. During my sprint across campus, the strap of my crossbody bag must have pulled Zwena's borrowed, deep V-neck shirt completely under my left boob, leaving my sunshine-yellow bra on full display for the entire panel—but most directly Ash Eisenberg—to see. While I thought Ash was finally responding to me, albeit rudely, he was really trying to warn me that I was putting my best breast forward and publicly humiliating myself in front of America's wealthiest entrepreneurs and one professor who will be determining my first grade in years.

I lift my bag up so fast to cover my chest that I knock my travel coffee mug over, its contents sputtering out as the cup rolls under the panel table. Libby Starr swiftly stops the mug with her red patent stilettos, picks it up, and shoots me a sympathetic look that I interpret as, *Hey, girlfriend, I got you, there's nothing worse than a spilled cup of coffee on a crappy day.*

Oh yes, there is, I think to myself as Ash shifts rigidly in his seat, looking everywhere but right at me, desperate to act like my boobs and I are not there.

SATURDAY, FEBRUARY 16

"Abuelita, they fit!" Lou squeals, securing the buckle of my mom's nude strappy high-heeled sandal onto her right foot. As she kicks her leg out to admire her borrowed footwear, a wad of bloodied tissue stuck to her ankle from a novice shaving accident drops on the carpet. Wrapped in a towel, Coco sneers in disgust as she steps over it, perpetually annoyed at her sister's sloppiness in contrast to her vigilance to detail. Neither of the girls bends over to pick it up, leaving me to do the dirty work of mothering.

"Mi corazón, I tried to give these gorgeous shoes to your mother, but of course she didn't want them." Gloria clucks in disappointment, straightening her silk blouse before handing the second heel over to Lou. I wrap my oversize cardigan tight around my torso to hide the ancient UCLA T-shirt underneath. Frayed at the neck from washing, it's the one indulgence I allowed myself at the campus bookstore freshman year. In my life, I've never seen my mother in a T-shirt.

When I started back working full-time at the airport, I reached out to my brothers and informed them that I was officially passing the baton I had long held taking care of Gloria on to them. As a single navy pilot and a carefree data analyst, my siblings were now capable co-kings of the family.

My brothers accepted the responsibility without pushback, which I appreciated. That was until their first move to build a nest egg for Gloria was to sell her two-bedroom home in Potrero Hill and their second was to relocate our mom into an apartment a few miles away from my house in East Palo Alto. Their reasoning was having her practically next door would make it easier for me to look after her. My mother saw it as an opportunity to parent Lou and Coco right alongside me until Simon returned. A possibility she insisted I stay open to given her constant distress over what we would do without Simon and his salary. It stung with a terrible familiarity to what we would do without my father and his paycheck several years back.

"So, mija, how's that new class you started?" my mom asks offhand-edly, keeping her eyes on Lou. Before I can even decide if I want to share Thursday night's debacle with the Arroyo girl crew, my mother jumps back in with what really interests her.

"They're perfect on you!" Gloria reaches out a hand to help Lou stand and walk our dingy beige carpet, diverting my sharing session, which is just fine with me. I notice Lou is a little too practiced at the heel-to-toe strut it takes to balance on a set of Pixy Stix. Have these two been working the hallway catwalk when I'm not around? Regardless, I make a note to hunt for a rug cleaning coupon when the next value packet comes in the mail.

Because the tornado that is my mother's feminine ways is presently taking up all the air in this small bedroom, and no one other than me really cares about StubHub's growth into the world's largest ticket marketplace, I fall mute. This leads Lou to believe I'm going to let her out of the house in those ankle-breakers for the eighth grade Valentine's Day dance. And she can go ahead and believe that for about thirty more minutes, until Abuela leaves to lead Saturday-night salsa at the Senior Connection. Thursdays my mom volunteers her afternoons painting the nails of the female residents who no longer have a steady hand or the dexterity to paint their own. That's also when she gets the scuttle about who cheated at canasta the night before. Fridays she offers a free wash and set at the industrial sink in the arts and crafts studio for her regulars who are committed to looking nice for the few men without walkers who can still float across the dance floor on Saturday night. My mother imagines herself to be Rita Moreno's much younger sister, and she lives for turning the women at the Senior Connection into *West Side Story* extras once a week. Stereotypical of her, but true. Given her expertise in all beauty-related arenas, Gloria loves her time at the center because she has made herself indispensable to the female residents, not to mention she laps up the compliments tossed her way by men of a certain age who still fancy themselves able to handle a much younger girlfriend.

As the flurry of preparations for the dance continue, I'm reminded that Saint Anne does not subscribe to the progressive Catholic leanings of Pope Francis. The school prefers its social philosophies archaic, and its traditions unchanged. Among the faculty and more conservative parents, I've already got a big scarlet letter *A* for *abandoned* on my chest, so I don't need Jesus falling off his cross when he gets a peek at Lou strutting into the school gym like a streetwalker. While I don't agree with the obsequious message of the school's motto, Women for Others, the math and science departments are some of the best on the peninsula, and we are not getting kicked out on a dress code technicality.

Lou and my mother have been planning a first-dance outfit for ages. In eighth grade, Saint Anne girls and the Trinity School boys across town gather in February and once again in May to iron out awkward pubescent social interactions after nine years of single-sex education and before they enter the high school hormonal melting pot. Coco has gone along with the preparation because she knows it brings her sister and grandmother joy and that I couldn't care less. She's been playing family peacekeeper since the day she uttered her first word, *okay.* But I know Coco, she is me, and I'm pretty sure she'd rather be charting the phases of the moon than prepping for an embarrassing evening warming the gym bleachers. In opposition, her sister will spin the hundreds of hours I paid for ballet lessons into moves she picked up streaming *Dance Moms* while I was working.

"You aren't going to take the girls to their first dance dressed like that, are you?" Gloria asks, standing to fish her compact out of her purse and reapply. *These girls are lucky I brushed my teeth. Not always a guarantee when I have the day off.*

Lou's neck snaps my way, as if realizing for the first time that her mother will be delivering her to this evening's festivities. Giving me a judgmental once-over, she whines, horrified, "Mom! Abuelita's right, I'll die if you wear that to drop us off at the dance! What if someone sees you?"

"Someone will see me, I'm driving. But I don't think the Trinity boys will be checking me out," I joke, trying to lighten the vain mood in the bedroom.

"Ugh!" Lou cringes at my inability to disappear.

"The other mothers will see you," my own mother answers, an expert at maneuvering the ugly side of female-on-female judgment. "Or, if we're lucky, a single dad." Growing up, my family witnessed our Potrero neighborhood morph from guys guzzling forty-ouncers in the park to hipsters swilling their iced lattes alfresco. Since my father died, Gloria has been keenly aware that while she didn't have money or her own credit rating, she did have her looks—and so did I. Since I returned from UCLA to a Bay Area booming with millionaires, my mom has hoped to profit off our beauty. She is still holding on to faith that if Simon is never to return, I will altar up to another husband before she has one toned leg in the grave. For Gloria, on this matter, financial security trumps the Catholic church's stance on divorce.

"I'm just saying, a swipe of lipstick and a brush of mascara on those long eyelashes you inherited from me wouldn't kill you." God bless my mother for believing I own mascara.

Without looking up from her book, Coco chimes in to nobody in particular, "Might not kill you, Mom, but cosmetic testing kills thousands of caged rabbits every year."

"Where do you hear such things?" Her grandmother waves away Coco's nonsense like PETA has no business coming between her and her lashes.

Still in her towel, Coco has curled herself around her latest sci-fi novel. Unlike Lou, who has her finger on the pulse of what Trinity boys her Saint Anne friends are crushing on—we get the download every night at dinner—Coco prefers to do her dating research devouring the social rituals of galactic creatures. She'll get to real-life human interactions in her own time. With a finger saving the place in her book, Coco briefly glances up and pleads, "Do I even hafta go to this dance?"

"No," I insist.

"Yes," my mother voices at the same time, as if Coco is crazy to not want to go.

"*Mom,*" I snap, exasperated. "Coco can skip a middle school dance if she wants. It's not a big deal."

"It's a party, who doesn't want to go to a party?" Mom affirms as Coco and I share a quick understanding glance. "Plus, Toni, this is good practice for the girls' quinceañeras. Lots to do to get ready, and it's never too early to start." I bite my lower lip. *I will not roll my eyes.* Tonight is not the night for us to go to blows over an outdated, centuries-old tradition that marks the female entrance into womanhood, a.k.a. marriage material.

"Come on, sis," Lou joins in, putting out her hand. "I'll make sure we have fun tonight." Always the one to concede, a reluctant Coco takes Lou's hand to pull herself up off the bed and join her sister's grooming efforts.

"Before you get dressed, use plenty of cocoa butter on those legs if you can find it. Ashy is not classy," Gloria instructs, still miffed from last summer, when both girls got terrible sunburns because they refused to apply the sunscreen I begged them to use before heading to the rec park pool. Due to her lack of empathy for how difficult it is to make a teenager do something they don't want to do, Gloria was sure that their skin peeling off in sheets was a result of my neglect.

"Cream is in the top drawer where we always keep it," I direct, owning my passive-aggressive response. Truth be told, we have vats of my homemade lotion stashed all over the house. I wouldn't be surprised if we are still working our way through it all when Coco and Lou leave for college, not a flaky skin patch among us.

When I was three and my parents moved to California, they knew they were leaving their culture behind, first in Puerto Rico, then in the Bronx. What did take my mom by total surprise after their brief stint in New York was how few Black people there were in San Francisco by comparison. Growing up, when I would complain to my dad that Mom was always nagging us to lotion up, only go outside in clean clothes, watch our language in public, not get too dark from the sun, Dad tried to explain it was not because she cared about the wrong things, it was because she cared about the right thing, keeping us safe. She claimed she couldn't get a read on how this place felt about Black people when there were so few of us in her new community. In the Bronx my parents were part of the mix, but in San Francisco my mother felt like our mixed family stuck out. She preferred to keep us safe the only way she knew how, our flawless appearance.

The Catholic church we joined in San Francisco's Mission neighborhood was almost all Mexican and Mexican-American parishioners, and people assumed we were, too, until we opened our mouths and revealed our Puerto Rican accents, or when my mother shimmied into the pew next to me and my dad. Our Spanish did not sound like theirs, and my mother—and eventually my darker younger brothers—did not look like the congregation. Still Mom persisted ingratiating our family into the Mission-Dolores parish because in her mind, this was the closest we were going to get to "home." We attended every confirmation and wedding we were invited to, and in the Catholic religion, that's a lot. I spent more time in a dress, oiled up, smiling politely and offering "peace be with you" to parish members than I care to recall. For me, the only good that came out of it was sidling up to the moms at baptisms and christenings and handing out my homemade babysitting services business cards. For my mother, it was the acceptance into a community that would protect her, protect us, regardless of the color of our skin.

All these years later, she still believes hydrated skin and nice clothes will shield her family.

"Come on, girls—put some care into it," Gloria presses. "Lou, you still need to rub it in more on the backs of your knees. If you sit down like that, the lotion will get all over your dress, and then where will you be?"

Noting that Gloria's observation about my lotion mirrors Mrs. Eisenberg's, I lean over to rub it in myself. I put a little more muscle into handling Lou's legs to help my latest creation blend into her café au lait skin. *F me.* This stuff didn't rub into Ms. Eisenberg's skin, and it's not blending into Lou's either. While the girls are at the dance, I'm going to play with the water-to-oil ratio.

Under her grandmother's critical gaze, dress on, Coco grabs her Converse platform high-tops and begins lacing them up. I see my mother's mouth drop open at the sight of high-tops, and she looks to me, expecting I will say something. In her day there was no such thing as pairing a party dress with gym shoes, but I know which mountains to climb up and die on with teenage girls and this is not one of them. I think Coco being strong-armed into going to the dance by her grandmother and sister is more than enough fourteen-year-old harassment for one night.

"Mami, don't you need to leave for the senior center? I'm sure the ladies have their dancing shoes on and are ready to go," I cut in to distract my mom before she can comment on Coco's fashion choices.

Gloria checks her watch. "Oh, you're right, I do have to go. Time flies when you're getting ready for a night out," Mom singsongs before planting a massive red lipstick kiss on Coco's and Lou's foreheads. "Walk me to the door, Toni," she instructs in that maternal voice that insists I have no choice in the matter. Following my mom out of the girls' bedroom, I turn around and silently overenunciate to Lou, *Take those heels off, now!*

"Promise me, Toni, you won't go out of this house in that outfit. I know all the young women your age are wearing sweatpants everywhere these days, but I am here to tell you they do nothing for your figure." I know that *figure* is code for *prospects.*

"It's called activewear," I interject, as if proper terminology will make an ounce of difference. Gloria slides her jaw back and forth as if she's tasting the term like a rich-bodied cabernet.

"Imagine you run into a successful man on the street, and there you would be wearing that," my mom says, emphasizing her words with a circle of her index finger suspiciously around my pelvis. *Activewear* will not be added to Gloria's vocabulary because she truly believes in Hollywood meet-cutes. In her imagination, the sidewalks are teeming with well-to-do men looking for well-dressed women.

Instead of revealing that not wearing sweatpants out of the house is actually one of my New Year's resolutions, I concede and choose to agree with her. "Okay, Mami, I'll change before I drive the girls over to Saint Anne, promise."

"That's all I ask," she requests, brushing a wisp of hair out of my eyes. I move past my mother to open the front door, but instead of following me, she steps over to the chest of drawers where I stash my purse and picks up one of the five bags of brown powder sitting by my keys.

"Is this what I think it is?" Gloria asks doubtfully, examining a bag and the sticker that designates it's a product of Puerto Rico. "Where did you get it?"

"I don't know what you think it is. I don't really know what it is. David sent it to me last time he was visiting Tía Fernanda. Learned about it from a woman he, *ehrm*, met."

Ignoring my reference to David's promiscuity, my mother claps her hands together with genuine glee. "Then it is what I think it is! I haven't seen this stuff since your father and I left Las Marías. My mami and my tías swore by its magical powers."

"For what?"

Checking her hair in the mirror and then setting down the bag to head out the door, my mother lands her third and final kiss of the night on my forehead. "For nourishing their skin, of course," she replies, her hand lingering on my cheek as if I've asked the most obvious question in the world.

SUNDAY,
FEBRUARY 17

Last night, instead of reworking the lotion viscosity issue like I promised myself I would, I made the mistake of being sucked into the Nuyorican classic film *I Like It Like That*. After vacuuming the living room, I was lost to this edgy tale and the comfort of my couch until it was time to pick the girls up from the dance.

It's now 7:00 a.m. on Sunday as I quietly grab my purse, my keys, a notebook, and the family laptop and tiptoe out of the house. I know the girls will most likely sleep late. Lou and Coco are exhausted from the buzz of their first dance, which Coco reported—before she and Lou devolved into a fit of laughter over their midnight bowls of cookie dough ice cream—was not as awful as she had predicted. I'm pretty sure those laughs were about a night of first slow dances, but they weren't giving it up to Mom.

Searching for a much-needed quiet atmosphere for inspiration paired with a strong drip, I head to the Cracked Cup, valued for its proximity to Stanford and all the brain power that place radiates. Just knowing that this early on a Sunday morning I can settle in at one of the two-tops in the window and look toward the line of trees that flanks Palm Drive leading to the university's Oval gives my motivation a boost. I'm ready to research rare oils like blue tansy, chamomile, jojoba, and lemongrass to tweak my lotion's viscosity rather than falling back on a shea butter base that Black women have sworn by for generations. I want my product to be unique.

Throwing open the door to my de facto office, I'm taken aback by the coffeehouse hum already buzzing inside. My favorite tables are occupied, and the line is a good eight people deep with a slug of a seventeen-year-old boy taking orders. *Who are all these people getting coffee so early, and why are they in my space?* These are most definitely not students. The rabble is more a mix of middle-aged men on gravel bikes and pre-Pilates Gen Xers getting after their cores. Itching to dive into my research following last night's wasted opportunity, I step out of line to assess the coffee queue progress and take note that Mr. Peach Fuzz is working the iPad with a single digit.

I'm going to be standing in line awhile, so I pull out my phone to swipe through the pictures and review the bios of the panelists from my Thursday class and check if the lecture has been posted yet. After giving Ash a full view of my yellow-clad cinnamon tit, I avoided looking at him the rest of the session, and he reciprocated by once again turning in his seat and pretending I didn't exist. I barely heard what anyone had to say, mortification plugging my ears, so I need to relisten to the lecture from the privacy of my own earbuds. Before I focus on the SurveyMonkey the class has been asked to fill out about the value of the panel, I'm resolved to answer from a place of knowledge and critical thinking, not humiliation. Obviously, I will be giving Libby Starr an A+ for rescuing my to-go mug.

"I hope you'll go easy on me. I haven't done many of those things in quite a while," a scratchy morning voice offers from behind my left shoulder. I hug my phone to my chest, hiding it from the peeper. Who could be so creepy impolite as to read over someone's shoulder? "I'm used to leading the class, not being the subject of it."

I turn around and find myself face-to-face with Tiger Woods. Well, not the real Tiger Woods, but a total wannabe. No grown man's pants should be starched that stiff, nor cream colored. And the caramel leather golf shoes and belt are a bit too matchy-matchy for my taste, but I'll give

Ash Eisenberg credit for wearing a robin's-egg-blue sweater that pops against his chocolate skin. I notice him fiddling in his pocket with what I can only hope is a fistful of golf tees.

"Uh . . . rude. Shouldn't you be reading the *Wall Street Journal*, not straining to see my phone?" I snap, pointing out his breach of a commonly practiced social norm when standing in line.

"There's no Sunday edition. The *WSJ* is only Monday through Saturday," is the elitist response I get. *He's on an acronym basis with his newspaper? ¡Qué pendejo!*

"Yep, same as TMZ," I toss back to bring Ash and this conversation down a necessary notch.

"I don't know that news outlet." Ash shrugs, glances at his watch, and then looks past me. I can only assume he's trying to assess how long he will have to make small talk, though he did start it. I begin to turn to let him know that quiet works for me, but then Ash continues, "So, you're in the Pioneering Entrepreneurs class at Stanford." I can't tell if this is a statement or a question since he knows the answer. There's no way he doesn't recognize me from Thursday night, but I certainly don't want to remind him how our paths and our body parts crossed.

"Do you remember me from class?" I ask point-blank, tired of this *does he or doesn't he know me* nonsense. Ash waves a finger to move me up in line, keeping his eyes averted above my head. Ah. The finger and the averted eyes. He most definitely remembers me.

"Why are you taking the class?" Ash inquires, now looking at me with what I think may be a hint of interest—or more likely, skepticism. How much of my history does he want to hear to answer this question? That in addition to being a student in his microeconomics class a lifetime ago, I caught the entrepreneurial bug from another one of my professors who was developing a specialized battery patent back when the Prius was too ugly to consider driving? But then I had to drop out of college? Or the myriad product ideas I had thought up specifically for parents of infant twins, but I was too postpartum blue to do anything about them other than scrawl the concepts down in one of my note-books? Or should I tell him that I have been using his grandmother as a testing guinea pig for my numerous failed products?

"You don't look like the business school type."

Excuse me! Judgmental much? It's early on a Sunday, I'm allowed to be in my sweats when my mother's not around, and not everyone can hit the country club on the weekends. Maybe Ash does remember meeting me at the airport and cannot imagine how someone in trans-portation services at SFO would end up flashing him from the front row of a Stanford lecture hall.

"You don't look like the golfing type," I quickly counter. He actually does, but it's the only thing I can think of to say since I don't know anybody who golfs. I detect a slight smile, the first one I've witnessed. Ash doesn't say anything further. I guess he's still waiting for my answer on why I'm taking the Thursday-night class.

"I've wanted to launch my own product line for a long time. I just haven't landed on what the product will be." I can't believe I just said that out loud. After utilizing my services, many passengers claim it's easier to share intimate details with strangers than with those closest to them. That's why I know way too much about the infidelities, pending bankruptcies, secret side hustles, and surprise engagements of those I shuttle across terminals and never see again. *Great, now I'm the one oversharing with a stranger.*

Ash's interest in me seems to perk up. "If you really want to start a company, then why aren't you enrolled in Stanford's MBA program? One evening course isn't going to get you far." What a funny world this man lives in where admission to a two-year program, let alone having the money to pay for it without working, is a given. And he doesn't even know about the issue of my unfinished bachelor's degree.

"*Ehrm* . . . because I have two children, a mother to take care of, and a full-time job to keep food on the table." *Welcome to the real world full of responsibilities, buddy.*

"What about your husband?" If this brother were not standing here fully dressed for eighteen holes at a haughty private course, I would think it was the 1950s.

Does Mrs. Eisenberg know she has a sexist for a grandson? Irreal! Unbelievable.

"None of your business," I deadpan, finally stepping up to the counter, my back now fully turned to Ash.

"A short two shots, almond milk latte, extra hot," I order, rustling around in my purse for my wallet.

"I'll get her coffee and whatever else she would like," Ash announces over my shoulder to the indifferent barista. He couldn't care less that Ash's offer to pay for my coffee comes with a shot of patronization, but I care enough for everyone in this place.

"I can get my own coffee, thank you," I retort, unmoved. I'm nobody's charity, particularly Ash Eisenberg's. "Just the latte." Unzipping the wallet I have finally unearthed from my bag, I pull out a ten and my Cracked Cup punch card. The baby barista looks undone, like he's never seen such an archaic form of payment.

◆ ◆ ◆

"He did not do that!" Zwena hollers, snapping the nasty towel she's been using to wipe down Build-A-Burger's tables at me.

"*Gross,*" I yell and jump back, missing the germy tip by inches. "And you better believe he did."

"And you didn't stop him?"

"Oh, I thought about it."

"And?" Zwena hates cliffhangers.

"And you know I have a soft spot for Mr. Chen. He's heading back to Pittsburgh for his sixtieth high school reunion, and he's hoping to rekindle the flame with his teenage girlfriend since, apparently, they're now both single. After he leaned in and planted one on me, he defended himself by saying, 'I haven't kissed a woman in a decade.' Turns out there's been no lady on his arm since Mrs. Chen's decision to become a late-in-life lesbian. That could scare any man off touching a woman for a bit. Anyway, he wanted a practice session before he put the moves on the homecoming queen. What was I going to do, shut the man down just when he's trying to get back in the game?"

"I get it: wanting a practice session. How'd he say it was?"

"Like riding a bike. Then he put his hand on my thigh and kept it there until we got to his gate."

"So, he got in a kiss and a feel before boarding his plane? Nice work, Mr. Chen, you should do just fine." Zwena fans herself. Just like me, I know Zwena considers what happened between me and Mr. Chen more community service than sexual harassment. We both try to do our part for our elderly customers.

"Does this mean both you and Mr. Chen are back in action?"

"I wouldn't exactly put the two of us together, Z."

"No, you're right, Mr. Chen is getting after it. You are getting nowhere." Zwena states what she thinks she knows while finishing up wiping down the last two chairs.

I don't admit to Zwena that I had another Simon fantasy the other night. I wish someone else would star in my dreams, but Simon's the only leading man I've known and I just can't shake him. Given what he has put me through, why my brain continues to dwell on Simon is a psychological mystery, but I do have news.

"I got a phone number in line at the coffee shop this morning."

"No!" Zwena cheers, clapping her hands together and hurrying over to her register to hang a CLOSED sign from the chip stand. I'm not sure you can close a restaurant at 6:00 p.m. in an airport, but Zwena can't be bothered by protocol or dinnertime.

"Don't worry about it, Jose and Peter will be happy to take a break from the fry station," Zwena offers as an answer to my quizzical look. "Sit down and don't leave anything out." I'm woman-handled over to the table nearest the soda machine, and Zwena gets us two Diet Cokes, no longer deterred by my New Year's resolution. Maybe I shouldn't have said anything, my brief encounter with Ash may disappoint.

"I ran into Ash Eisenberg at the Cracked Cup."

"Did he recognize your face or your body parts?"

"Thankfully all my clothes were where they should be."

"Okay, okay, that's an improvement. At least for now." We nod in agreement. Zwena was on the receiving end of my phone call after class when I finally got to die of shame in the privacy of my car. "So, who's the guy who slipped you his number?"

"It was Ash," I clear up for Zwena.

"Wait, what?! You didn't ask for it, did you? Girl, you may be dusty, but you are not desperate. Please tell me you kept twenty-year-old Toni quiet," Zwena pleads, only looking for one answer. Zwena has a handful of essential rules when it comes to women going after the opposite sex. The first is that phone numbers should be requested by the man, rightfully keeping the power balance heavily weighted toward the woman.

"No, no, of course I didn't ask for it." This is where I don't quite know how to spin the story for Zwena's entertainment.

After ordering and paying for my own drink, I swiftly moved over to the pickup area to grab my latte and find a table. In the discomfort of the moment, my coffee couldn't come fast enough. I purposely sat down at a cramped two-top with only one chair, my back to where I assumed Ash was waiting on his order. Blowing on my latte, faking being immersed in Instagram, I felt a shadow looming over my morning procrastination.

"Allow me to introduce myself properly. I'm Ash Eisenberg."

I looked up at him, stunned silence hanging between us a beat too long.

"And you go by?" he asked, more like the start of an awkward cocktail party conversation than acknowledgment that we had met twice before. This was the last time I was giving it to him.

"Antonia Arroyo, but people call me Toni," I extended with a hint of attitude.

"Well, Antonia, when building a company, you can't survive on coffee alone. Nor can you do it alone." Ash then placed a stuffed white paper sleeve next to my cup. As he walked off to make his tee time, I noticed Ash Eisenberg's phone number, written in green ink, and a croissant were staring up at me.

Now Zwena's the one staring at me, eyebrows furrowed. "I'm not clear. Does the professor want to have dinner with you or mentor you?" Zwena's tone tells me she's genuinely as unsure as I am. "And are you positive it was his number he was passing along, not the barista boy's, because you do look young for your age, Toni." Before I can react to Zwena's accusation that I'm turning the heads of teenage boys, she winks and calls loudly to a young Delta pilot striding by with his captain. "Hey, Harley!" Mr. Second-in-Command waves, a wide grin plastered across his face, and holds his thumb to his ear, pinkie finger extended, signaling he'll call Zwena from his next destination.

"We'll see if I pick up," Zwena shares, turning back to me. "I laid him out on his last layover here a few months ago, but he's from Salt Lake City, and in between the sheets he kept trying to sell me on the celestial kingdom. I'm not looking for a magical afterlife, I'm working on making magic right here in this life." I'm surprised to hear Zwena mention any life planning or commitment, as she's more a take-advantage-of-what-comes-her-way-today kind of maneater. "But *ummm, ummm, ummm,* for a man who is supposed to wait until marriage, he sure knew what to do. We'll see how I'm feeling the next time Harley passes through." We both watch Harley stride down the concourse, pilot's hat perfectly perched.

"Back to Ash Eisenberg. Did you keep his number, or did you throw it away?" Zwena wants to know.

"I may have tossed it in my purse, or maybe the trash. Honestly, I don't remember. What am I going to do with it anyway, call him? I can handle my business on my own."

Standing to signal to Jose and Peter that break time is over, Zwena places a hand on my shoulder to confirm her profound disappointment in me. "While I don't agree with it, yes, generally that's the idea when someone gives you their phone number—you call them. The first one you've gotten in ages is from a well-to-do Black man and you 'don't remember' what you did with it?" I'm not telling Zwena this is the *only* phone number a man has ever slipped me. "And take it from me, a woman who was able to change her fate to one people back home dream of, none of us gets anywhere all on our own. You need people, Toni." Zwena clucks at me through her teeth. "I should report you to your mother."

"Please don't," I beg, and Zwena lifts a shoulder like she's thinking about it. With intel like this, my mother might head straight to the Cracked Cup and dumpster dive for the paper sleeve herself. The fact is, after I watched Ash exit the coffee shop and clear my view, I slid the croissant out of the sleeve and onto a napkin before any greasy butter stains smudged the numbers. I then got up and shook out the crumbs into a waste bin so I could evenly fold the paper sleeve in half and then quarters for safekeeping in my notebook.

MARCH

TUESDAY, MARCH 5

My phone dings twelve minutes before I've set the alarm. Groaning, I roll over and fumble around for my glasses on the nightstand, knocking Michelle Obama's latest memoir and an empty ice cream pint and spoon to the floor. *Oops, sorry, First Lady.*

I hold my breath, hoping it's an automated text from Saint Anne informing me that while the school applauds my selfless community service on my one day off work this week, today's sorting of hundreds of pounds of donated clothing and home goods for the sixty-sixth annual rummage sale has been canceled. I'm looking to earn parental participation credit for volunteering without leaving the comfort of my own bed.

A month ago, I signed up under pressure from Coco and Lou, who complained that I never participate in anything school related other than emailing their teachers and harassing them about homework. They're too young to hear how being an abandoned working mother on financial aid at a Catholic school in Silicon Valley is a whole other level of loneliness. It's obvious to me that the parents at the school are positioning themselves to make friends with other couples who are higher up than they are on the Saint Anne food chain. The snacks being wealth, power, and fame, of which I have none.

When I'm with other Saint Anne parents on campus, the feeling of being a sinner as well as a charity case is like an itch under my skin,

even if the uneasiness only exists in my head and in what I perceive
are judgmental stares from Father Patrick Egan. Father Egan teaches
the eighth grade life skills class. Lou and Coco insist his features are
frozen in a state of resting dick face, but they think his heart is in the
right place. Still, he makes me squirm like I'm nine at Christmas Eve
midnight mass and in a hurry to get home to see if this is the year Santa
will bring me a microscope before he finds out I nicked a few bucks out
of David's piggy bank.

My pervasive sense of social inadequacy aside, I should probably
invest some sweat equity into the event that raises the bulk of money for
the scholarship Coco and Lou have earned this year. Any mom can buy
cookies at Whole Foods for a holiday party, arrange them on a ceramic
platter, and drop them off in the classroom hoping to pass them off as
her own. I'm forfeiting my day of rest. But now that the morning is
here, my altruism has turned to anxiety at the realization that I will be
trapped in a six-hour marathon of chitchat among women who give the
impression they'd rather be talking to anyone else but me.

The text is from Saint Anne informing me that coffee and mini
muffins will be available at 8:00 a.m. and sorting Saint Anne family
castoffs will begin promptly at 8:15 a.m.

Tucking the covers under my hips to give myself five more minutes
in my warm blanket cocoon, I consider how to send Zwena a persua-
sive text to come be my rummage sale wing woman. Zwena can talk to
anyone. With a roof over her head, cash to spare, and a car that runs,
no one can tell Zwena there's a difference between her and any other
woman. Today especially, I need some of her self-assuredness to rub off
on me.

Before my fingers send out a sleepy SOS, I'm startled by a series
of texts from Sojourn Simon that came in between my deepest REM
sleep and the lure of unlimited caffeine and crullers. *Where's that globe
twatter now?* The last time I heard from him was four months ago from
somewhere in Bali. He wanted me to share with Coco and Lou a blurry
picture of him cleansing himself in a waterfall, arms outstretched like

John the Baptist washing away his sins. It would take a bigger splash than that.

6:18 a.m. (650-726-4100)

Namaste. I'm back in Palo Alto. Every sunrise is an opportunity for a new start.

I shoot up in bed, choked by Simon's saccharine bumper sticker missive and his location. I snap my head left to right, surveying my bedroom as if Simon's hiding in the closet, ready to jump out with a souvenir. Is this his new cell or the number of some guru's phone that he borrowed? And what exactly does *back in Palo Alto* mean? After two years I had come to fully accept that Simon had settled in a meditation cave half a world away.

6:18 a.m. (650-726-4100)

I've returned to launch my next adventure. The joy and purpose I feel for this journey is truly why I was put on this earth. Check me out. www.bestuman.com

6:19 a.m. (650-726-4100)

And I would like to see you, Toni.

I know better. I know better. I know better. *Tap.*
Damn it.

I haven't looked into Simon's green eyes rimmed with heavy lashes since he walked out the front door and I packed up all the pictures I had of him, took them to my mom's place, and had her hide them so I wouldn't cry all over the images as I wallowed in misery. I would have tossed them, but I'm not a total monster, and I knew that one day the girls may want a reminder of what their father looked like before he committed this selfish act that I didn't know how to explain to them. At that moment, though, I needed it to be about me just trying to put one foot in front of the other, so I erased him from our house. Now here Simon is, crisp and clear on my phone, smiling back at me and anyone else trolling his newly launched website, Best U Man. I immediately see the irony that his company acronym is BUM.

Simon is staring back at me, well rested and relaxed, seemingly having taken years off his age. He radiates an enviable energy that I suppose anyone would have after a multiyear vacation doing whatever you want. I mean, can you really call two years of focused breathing "work"?

Expanding his picture, I'm reminded how good-looking Simon is in that slightly burned surfer kind of way. A handful of freckles dance across his nose and cheeks, highlighting a bone structure that should be reserved for women. His jawline is tight, and Simon has ditched the pierced ears he got at Claire's days before heading off the grid. In a perfectly tailored checkered button-down, with his arms crossed, Simon oozes mastery on how to lead a *best life*. His sleeves are rolled up to highlight toned forearms. A billion chaturangas will do that for you. If it weren't for the layers of teak mandala beads, I would swear I am looking at Simon the investment banker.

Life-affirming quotes fade onto and off the screen at a cadence meant to keep people on the page wondering if they read right. Simon's eastern philosophy vocabulary and polished image are working hard to convince his audience that he is a blissful Eastern/Western mash-up of a middle-aged man high on life.

With no reference to any consumer goods he's selling, I realize the product Simon is peddling is himself. If I didn't know better and I was a purpose seeker deep in an internet self-help dive, I would want a piece of Simon's magic. And even though I do know better, I can't deny, staring at his picture, that what Simon is selling is compelling. Simon's website displays a reinvention of himself into an intuitive life coach, business strategist, and inspirational thinker for men searching for meaning. A twinge of attraction shocks my system before I remember I am considering divorcing this cabrón. Who does Simon think he is, dealing in personal success as a deadbeat dad? And where did he find a pile of cash to launch this venture or even pay for a website developer?

At first flinch, all I can think is, How is this fair? Fair to me, fair to Coco and Lou. But I'm also wise enough at thirty-nine to understand that life isn't fair. What I really want to know is how the hell this is possible. How has Simon been able to launch his own company, while all my ideas languish in notebooks and glass jars?

I start on the About page, planning to work my way through to the Power of Yes! tab, but cut my sleuthing short at first sight of a picture of Simon hugging Coco and Lou at their tenth birthday party, right around the time he turned away from engaging with his family and toward individual enlightenment.

Before I can calm my nerves enough to write back and ask Simon what it is he wants from me, because it's clearly not going to be a testimonial, a fourth text comes in.

7:02 a.m. (650-726-4100)

Are you up? I want to talk about when I can see you and my girls.

I throw my phone across the room at a pile of laundry. *His girls?!* Talk about a couple of priceless possessions he will never get his hands on again.

"Mom! Lou put an empty carton of milk back in the fridge! What am I supposed to do for breakfast?!" yells Coco, who has a bowl of Honey Nut Cheerios every morning, her day ruined if her milk-to-cereal ratio is not exact.

"Eat a bagel and get over it," I hear Lou suggest. She is oblivious to things like empty milk cartons, empty shampoo bottles, emptying the kitchen garbage bin when it's overflowing.

"*Mom*, I need you! Can you get up and help me?" Coco continues to whine, ignoring her sister's apathy. "Why am I the only responsible one in this family?!"

I throw my legs over the side of the bed, feet right into slippers, and walk over to pick up my phone. *That's right, Simon, our girls need me. Not you. I'm the one who shared a queen mattress with Coco and Lou for a full year, their fear that I, too, would leave, driving them to my bed to hold on for dear life. The questions about where you went and why and when you would come home were relentless, and I didn't have answers to satisfy their young hearts. Without you, I've been the one ushering our daughters through the transition from childhood to womanhood. Every fever I've snuggled away, every mediocre five-paragraph essay I've edited. I still have to remind Coco and Lou that you didn't leave because you didn't love them, you left because you didn't love yourself.*

I sneak one last look at Simon on my phone. I know that what I should feel is loathing, but instead I feel an aching familiarity. For the preservation of our family unit and my mental health, I detach from my emotions and write back succinctly.

7:04 a.m. (Toni)

I'm up. You can't. Goodbye.

Whoosh . . .

As quickly as Simon has come back into my life, he's just as quickly gone again.

In a frenzy, having had my typical morning routine disrupted by my wanderlust wasband, I leave the house in an attempt to flee my feelings.

After the girls bolt out of the car at drop-off, I park and call Zwena insisting she come meet me at Saint Anne. Before she can ask why, I read my text exchange with Simon out loud. Without hesitation, Zwena promises she will throw on some clothes and be by my side within the half hour.

At Saint Anne's rummage sale setup, I busy my hands folding and refolding with hostility at the winter wear table to keep my head from exploding over this morning's wake-up communications. Plus, I don't want to leave my station of a hundred discarded cardigans and be forced to mingle with the other mothers who are negotiating where to have a late lunch between the taxing work of sorting hand-me-down denim, complimenting each other's hair color, and replaying the adventures of school pickup.

Agitated and waiting on Zwena to show up so we can break down Simon's words, I'm surprisingly soothed by color sorting at the sweater station with the backdrop of organ practice going on in the church attached to the school. As Coco has become more engrossed in the science curriculum, questioning topics her religion teacher deems unquestionable has intensified. I enjoy hearing Coco challenge religion and compare it to what she's learning in the concrete subjects of science and history, usually while her sister does makeup tutorials on YouTube. But at this moment I must give it up to the conservative religion teacher, she can knock it out on the pipes.

"Excuse me, aren't you Antonia?" a somewhat familiar voice asks from behind an armful of barely touched rain jackets. The only voice I want to hear has a Kenyan accent.

I lay down the heather-gray sweater with an imperceptible hole marked by a tiny piece of blue painter's tape.

"Livy, Sylvia Eisenberg's granddaughter," the woman across the mix of wool, alpaca, and cashmere says, pointing at herself. "At first I wasn't sure if it was you, out of context and all, but I thought it wouldn't hurt to ask."

I can't believe Livy is standing in front of me, her auburn hair freshly styled. So far, there is nothing about this morning I would have imagined.

My first day back at work at San Francisco International Airport, I stood fidgeting at the door of Terminal 3 Gate D6, where the airplane and Jetway connect, hoping no parent from Saint Anne would be disembarking the plane and see me.

Uneasy as I was, I had to be present for my first escorted passenger. I knew who she was without having to guess. Mrs. Eisenberg was a woman who looked frail, not from her advanced years, not from illness, but from the all-too-familiar look of heartbreak. Stooped and moving slowly as if wounded, she wore her fragility much as my mother had after she lost my father. Mrs. Eisenberg's brittle countenance matched how I felt with my future hanging in the balance while Simon was out searching for something greater than what he had at home. Pain recognizes pain.

Moving as if the weight of her life was too much to carry, she stirred me to reach over the threshold into the entry of the plane to offer my steady hand, an aircraft safety no-no. We're supposed to wait until the customer has exited the plane to begin our services, but I wasn't convinced this woman I was charged to deliver to baggage claim could take a step unassisted. Without a word, Mrs. Eisenberg grabbed on to me tightly, her grip surprisingly strong.

On our ride to collect her luggage, Mrs. Eisenberg and I didn't exchange a word, nor did she let go of my arm, forcing me to navigate a terminal under renovation with one hand. In continued silence, we met Mrs. Eisenberg's granddaughter, Livy, at carousel nine. Dutifully, Livy helped her grandmother out of the chair, and when Mrs. Eisenberg asked for a tissue, Livy handed her one and assured, "I know, I miss him too."

Livy thanked me profusely for my services. With a squeeze of our hands, Mrs. Eisenberg and I acknowledged our mutual need for human touch more than words. At that moment I knew that, for as long as I would be working at the airport, Mrs. Eisenberg and I would be connected, and I would be seeing her again soon.

Before I can lie and tell Livy it's great to see her outside the airport, she breaks the momentary lull between us. "You assist my grandmother at the airport," she says to jog my memory, as if I don't know. "If it weren't for you, she certainly wouldn't be able to continue traveling as frequently as she does. Thanks again. You're such a huge help to our family." I can sense the moms in the home goods section one table over leaning in our direction. Not recognizing me from the yearly black-tie school auction where Saint Anne's wealthiest bid for a week in each other's second homes, given Livy's proclamations, they are surely now intrigued by the likes of me.

"Livy, hi." I put out my hand to shake hers. I can't help but be struck once again how remarkable it is that this redheaded mother, a Black professor, and a Jewish octogenarian can be related. Adoption is the only plausible answer.

"So glad I ran into you here." Livy looks around at our surroundings like it's one-in-a-million luck that we are both at this school at the same time. "Wait, do you have kids who go to Saint Anne?"

"I do," I answer, suddenly self-conscious of the oversize thick gold hoops I'm wearing compared to Livy's delicate diamond studs. And I should never have slicked my hair up into a bun this morning. I look like Jenny from the Block's younger sister. "A set of twins, they're in their final year. And you?"

"Oh no, not yet. I have an almost five-year-old." That's right. Mrs. Eisenberg has mentioned her ravenous great-granddaughter who is already on her third preschool, excessive biting being grounds for dismissal these days. "I figure volunteering at the different schools we are applying to is as good a way as any to assess the community we want to join." I wonder if seeing me at Saint Anne is going to strike the school right off Livy's prestigious list.

"Since I ran into you here, I'm going to save my grandmother a good half hour of trying to remember, yet again, how to text. Thank God my cousin now lives nearby and has taken over my role as personal

IT consultant. I love my grandmother, but I cannot explain, one more time, how to forward her travel itinerary to family members."

I nod in understanding. The ongoing task of helping our older generations with technology is a universal experience. In the Arroyo family, tech support revolves around my mother's inability to remember how to Dropbox pictures of Lou and Coco to her sisters in Puerto Rico. The steps to success never change, but the imaginary little people that my mom believes live in her electronic devices thwart her efforts. The girls and I have come to call their abuela's imagined phone demons los pequeños. Gloria refuses to admit it's user error.

"Anyway, are you working at the airport early Saturday evening? My grandmother is on her way back from Scottsdale for a couple of weeks." With the mention of a job, I swear I hear a collective *Ahh* of understanding from the surrounding moms as they turn back to their tasks, no longer interested in this conversation. That's how these women don't know me. Not because I am a billionaire CEO too busy running my next-big-thing company to volunteer so instead I write a fat check to the school, but because I have to work a customer service job I never wanted to make ends meet.

"Yes, I'm working Saturday," I assure Livy, stunting our conversation with my brief answer. I don't need the specifics of what I do for a living to come to light for the Saint Anne parent community. Being Puerto Rican, Lou and Coco already feel different among their peers. It's not that being Latina in the Bay Area is any great rarity, but being Puerto Rican this far from the island makes you Latin of a different breed. Historically, Puerto Ricans aren't quite American, but we aren't not American either. People don't know how to place us.

Given our proximity to the United States and freedom to travel across borders, Puerto Ricans are the champs of Spanglish. We enjoy being fluent in Spanish, in English, and in the language of in-between. But our Spanish is one of a different accent than the predominant Mexican intonation that saturates California. At the end of sixth grade, Lou and Coco both received a B- from their Spanish teacher, a native of Oaxaca, because they were apparently not putting in the effort when it came to enunciation. I am not one to make a fuss at school, but it was right around the six-month mark since Simon had left us and my emotions were roiling when I marched right into Ms. Luna's classroom, speaking Spanish in an exaggerated Puerto Rican accent, and got their grades changed to an A. No one is going to tell my girls how to be something they already are.

"Great, well I'm not sure if it will be my cousin or me there to meet my grandmother, but since she will be leaving most of her stuff in Scottsdale this time, if you could just bring her out curbside that would be so helpful. I'll Venmo you a tip for the extra effort." Livy smiles at me, confirming her plan. *Great, now all these moms know I work for tips.*

FRIDAY, MARCH 8

With a first draft business proposal for my entrepreneur class due next week, I should be building a profit and loss statement for my fledgling lotion company, but instead I'm consumed by thoughts of Simon's return. Coco and Lou are having a sleepover at their friend Lily's house tonight, and they're going to spend Saturday with the Antonellis as well—with the promise that they will get their homework done, closet organized, and room cleaned by Sunday-night inspection. When I unloaded the dishwasher yesterday, I noticed half our spoons and a handful of bowls are missing, and I'm fairly certain they are crusted over under the twins' beds. How long they have been there growing mold is too gross for me to contemplate. I don't like the girls overstaying their welcome at other people's homes, but they assured me Mrs. Antonelli, who always compliments Lou and Coco's manners, is happy to have them anytime. And I'd rather have Lou and Coco in the company of another adult than home alone when I am scheduled to work weekends.

Liam, my coworker, agreed to cover the first half of my Saturday shift, and I will go in from 4:00 p.m. to 8:00 p.m. so I can be there to pick up Mrs. Eisenberg. I usually don't bother with half shifts, but Mrs. Eisenberg refuses to ride with Liam—who she insists must have a deviated septum, he wears so much cologne. I've encouraged Mrs. Eisenberg to have some sympathy for Liam—he wants to be married yesterday—but she insists there will be no future Mrs. Fitzpatrick unless Liam switches up his odeur de desperation. I can't argue with her on that one.

Splitting the shift means I'll be able to work on my proposal and products in the early-morning quiet, wash my hair, and figure out how to spice up my airport-issued uniform in case Ash is the chosen grandchild to pick up his grandmother. I still have Ash's phone number inside my notebook but haven't considered calling it. I mean, what would I say? I surprise myself that I even care if I will see Ash at the airport. I guess it's my innate curiosity wanting to find out if his facial recognition and conversational skills have improved beyond the low bar he set at the Cracked Cup.

With the girls at the Antonellis', I invite Krish and Zwena over with bribes of a Friday night drinking cold beer, snacking on quesitos, dissecting Simon's website, and playing spa with the four improved variations of lotion I have been testing. Krish prides himself on being a man with impeccable grooming habits, not one bit afraid of some moisturizing, and offers to pick up a few face masks at Sephora on the way over. Zwena suggests he pick her up first.

Whenever those two go anywhere together, they're at least forty-five minutes late, but eventually they show up full of wine bottles and apologies, so I forgive whoever takes the blame for holding up the other one.

Walking in the door, Zwena announces, "Hey, Toni, did you know Benjamin Franklin invented the lightning rod *and* the urinary catheter?"

I look to Krish and ask, "What is she talking about?"

Krish shrugs out of his coat. "She's been spouting random US history facts the whole ride over."

"Not random," Zwena defends. "I've decided to take my citizen's exam, and these are the types of things I need to know."

"I don't think the invention of the urinary catheter will be on the citizenship test," Krish jokes.

"Maybe not, but it's good to know if I become a medical assistant," Zwena contends.

I pour us each a full glass of wine, and we huddle around my laptop with phones for backup stalking. I pull up the bestuman.com website. Zwena eases into her commentary, announcing she's happy to see Simon has enough self-respect not to wear man sandals online. Though she does remark that his chiseled features could overcome any choice in footwear. Krish calls it as he sees it: "What a douche."

The three of us agree that I shouldn't be the one to sign up for Simon's free weekly newsletter, but someone should definitely keep tabs on him. Knowing how self-involved Simon is, Krish and I determine that he might recognize Krish's name from the years Simon and I dated and the fact that the two men met at least twice. Zwena is the obvious choice since she is from the post-Simon era. After Zwena inputs her email address, I grab her phone. Fifteen seconds later I open the welcome email and read aloud:

> Today is the first day of the rest of your best life! U
> man, are going to become a better human.

"We should sue him for sexist language and gender discrimination," Zwena determines, already bothered. A decade living in America, and Zwena has figured out how things work here. Feelings are confused as facts, and hurt feelings are a foundation for litigious action.

"No," Krish and I decide out loud.

"Keep reading," I insist, thrusting Zwena's phone at her. One line in and I'm already incapable of reading any more of Simon's bullshit, but I still want to hear it.

> You're in a dead-end job that you cannot get out
> of, and you feel like life is passing you by at warp
> speed. You know you're supposed to do something
> wholly different that makes you feel alive and that
> gives your existence more meaning than what you
> are experiencing right now.

I shift uncomfortably on the couch, unable to deny that Simon has nailed my state of living the last two years: a dead-end that he put me in by leaving for that something wholly different that makes him feel alive and full of purpose.

> Or you want to leave your current living situation and move to an uncharted sphere where you can start a new future, start over.

Now that's for sure a topic on which Simon is truly an expert.

> The question you may be asking yourself is, How do you make this dream come true? The answer is you must first say *yes* to exactly what it is you want to do. And when you do that, unequivocally, barriers will start to fade and your world will open to endless possibilities. And that dream you desire? That dream will become your reality.

"Just say *yes*? That's Simon's big solution to getting what you want. You know what happens when you say *yes* too much? Bad credit and chlamydia," Zwena declares. Krish looks at Zwena, horrified, but neither of us want to know if she's hypothesizing or speaking from experience.

"Relax, I'm itch-free," Zwena clarifies, reading our thoughts. "I was making a point. But my credit score could use some help."

> Sound scary? It is. And that's where I come in. Whether you are looking to inspire your company, your team, or yourself, I am the guide you need to walk beside you on this journey from dream to reality. You have already taken the first step, signing up for my weekly newsletters. Read them. Sit with them. I believe, with absolute certainty, that you will know

in your heart the right time to contact me so we can
get to work building the BEST U MAN you can be.

We will connect soon,

Simon Evans

"Do you think Simon came up with the Best U Man himself, or did he spend money he should have been sending your way on a branding specialist?" Krish wonders out loud while uncorking a second bottle of pinot.

My gut twists. When Simon left, I assumed he walked out the door as broke as he left the three of us at home. It never occurred to me he had a hidden stash of cash or was making some while on the road.

"Can we watch one of his Yes, Man videos, and then I swear we're done with Simon," I promise Krish and Zwena. Neither responds. They both know the chances of that being true are nil. "Then we'll be done for tonight," I admit. Resigned, I get the *go ahead* chin lift from my coconspirators. I hit "Play."

Zwena's face registers a mix of whiffing a foul smell and cringing from secondhand embarrassment. "Yesu, Simon reminds me of the European men who used to roam Magongo's streets preaching to save African souls through their religious superiority. Those men were all *praise be* while I was all *please don't.* They did snag one of my uncles, though, and now he's part of their starched white shirt pack, praising the Lord to anyone who will listen. He's irritating as hell." When I reach to tee up a second video, Zwena gives me the same *please don't* glare that I imagine she has given her uncle a time or two.

When Zwena asks me what, specifically, I'm looking for in between Simon's claims, I don't have a solid answer. Sometimes Zwena's command of the English language surpasses mine, having grown up learning the King's English rather than the butchered American version. Matching the conviction Simon has when calling himself a healer,

Zwena identifies him for what he really is, a "right wanker." Krish dramatically yawns, letting us know his attention span for verbal male dismemberment has clocked out.

"Are you two really going to make me forward this self-help-seeking nonsense to you every week?" Zwena asks, holding up her glass to signal she needs a refill. The Western phenomenon of enabling is one that Zwena doesn't get. In her mind, freedom and opportunity are the greatest self-help tools available, so why is there a thriving industry to boost American self-esteem? In Zwena's view, if you want self-esteem, perform esteemed acts and stop whining. Americans are born with all the help they need. "This is the only country where the idea of hierarchy of needs is spelled h-i-g-h-e-r-archy. You all are always wanting more. Looking for what comes next. Let me tell you, you have enough. Right here, right now. Get over yourselves."

Krish and I give each other a sheepish look, schooled once again by Zwena on the simultaneous sins of selfishness and laziness of Americans. We don't want to sweat and suffer, we want a merciful catchphrase and for someone to fix us instead of doing the repairs ourselves.

"Yes, I want it!" I insist, knowing the wrath Zwena will rain down on me, but also owning that I won't be able to keep my hands off the keypad unless Zwena is the gatekeeper between me and Simon's newsletter.

"Yeah, I know." Zwena sighs, conspicuously wiggling her still-not-refilled wineglass. She knows this is not the time I'm going to rise above my anguish over Simon and become my own better human.

After trolling the personal development porn on Simon's website, Zwena shuts down my laptop and turns up her latest Spotify playlist of African rappers as our night takes a spontaneous dance party turn. Zwena loves Sho Madjozi, and the best parts of Zwena come out when she gets her groove on to Lady Sho. Her smile grows ear to ear, turning up as her hips move north, south, east, and west to the rhythm of her homeland. When Zwena dances, I don't see her as the twenty-eight-year-old woman she is, but spy the smart-talking, quick-footed child who was considered the neighborhood entertainer and her family's beacon of light. Her zest for music is infectious, and I hop up to join her. Krish slyly moves the coffee table out of the way to give Zwena and me more room to enjoy ourselves and then sprawls out on my couch to hype up our dance moves while finishing off the last of the quesitos.

When we take a second to catch our breath, Krish puts his hand out for Zwena's phone and his turn to play DJ. She trades her cell for a spot on the couch, and Krish puts his fingers to work. I limp off to the bathroom, my knees not as nimble as those of my young friends. When I return, Krish is busting out bhangra dance moves to rival anything Zwena had pulled from her past or I learned from Gloria. Limbs loose from alcohol and muscle memory, Krish shows us up on our makeshift dance floor, legs flying through the air, briefly touching down only to power back up. All the while doing it with style in stiff denim.

I have only seen Krish in his alter-personality as a sought-after DJ at prominent Indian weddings a time or two that I managed to slip in as his plus-one among the colorful saris and sherwanis. By day, Krish may work as a United gate agent, but at night he comes alive as DJ Sangam, a Hindi word that means *confluence*. The moniker is a nod to his family roots in the land of five rivers in the northwest Indian state of Punjab. While I call him a badass for figuring out how to both hold a responsible job and build a dream, Zwena likes to needle Krish by referring to him as the MCMD because his parents wanted him to be a surgeon. Tonight Krish shares with us that, after fifteen years at the counter, he thinks he has saved up enough money to make a go of being a music producer full-time.

More than once I have marveled that Krish stayed so long in a thankless job. I am guilty of dishing out advice he never asked for—that, without the responsibilities of a spouse, kids, or home ownership like I have, he should have left his job long ago to focus on his love of hip-hop, a far more interesting pursuit. Krish has the freedom to do what I always wished I could, but unlike me, he never complained about his time at the airport. Every shift, Krish showed up to SFO with a smile on his face and a willingness to be in service to, at times, the rudest of humanity. And after fifteen years of humility at the hands of demanding customers, Krish has established a way to gracefully prioritize his music career full-time with both security and certainty. Both of which I wish I had. To say I'm not a little jealous of Krish would be a big lie.

"To your last few weeks at SFO!" I sloppily toast, raising my glass and my voice to honor Krish and his new beginning.

"To me!" Krish meets my green-eyed enthusiasm and puts out his hands for me and Zwena to join him on our tiny, improvised dance floor. While I hop up, Zwena rises reluctantly. I notice her smile fading.

SATURDAY, MARCH 9

8:45 a.m. (Krish)

I don't know how you women drink your feelings and then function the next day. I want to nap on my keyboard, but I have 15 flights to get out.

8:46 a.m. (Toni)

I'll bring you some Tylenol when I get there around 4.

8:47 a.m. (Krish)

I may be dead by then.

8:48 a.m. (Toni)

That would be a waste of perfectly good wine. Go get a cheeseburger from Z, it'll make you feel better.

8:49 a.m. (Krish)

Already tried that.

With last night's spy fest, my Simon curiosity is satiated for the time being and my mind is ready to focus and get to work. I'm only alert because Zwena refused to spend the night, claiming she needed at least forty-eight hours before talking about Simon and his pretentious pulpit again. On her way out the door with Krish, Zwena informed me, "Ukupigao ndio ukufunzao." What beats you is what teaches you. That if I also want my own company, don't waste time fixating on Simon and Best U Man, get busy on my own ideas and make some money. That way if I ever wanted Simon dead, I could afford to hire a hitman. Unusual motivational speech, but it worked.

Today's first order of business begins on my couch, so for added inspiration and some background noise, I search for my favorite reality television show, *Innovation Nation*. On each episode, three ambitious novice entrepreneurs in their first year of incorporation get eleven minutes to pitch their product or service to tech, wellness, retail, and financial titans of industry, or as the show calls them, Iconic Investors. The newbie founders are called Embryonic Entrepreneurs, which I find pretty distasteful, but I get that it's difficult to rhyme with *entrepreneurs*, so the producers had to go with an alliteration that would describe how clueless each contestant is.

At the beginning of an episode there is a bonus recap on how a past participant and their venture is faring in their second year of operation with the infusion of prize money. I realize the show only highlights success stories, not the CEOs who have burned through their capital and are now back working at Chipotle, but the high that the previous seasons' Embryonic Entrepreneurs ride keeps me hopeful that I may get one of my products off the ground someday. I certainly would never have guessed that the world needed a retail company dedicated to holiday aprons, but turns out it did, to the tune of $110 million in sales to date for one of the show's winners.

The high-net-worth innovators turned investors grill each novice entrepreneur who is desperate for their first official seed funding in exchange for a percentage of the company. Seed stage is defined as a fully fleshed out concept, barely any sales, and operating in the red. In other words, being broke as a joke. I'm a third of the way there, living paycheck to paycheck. I love to daydream about what I would wear on the show, and more importantly which one of my products I would try to convince the judges to take a chance on.

If all four investors want in on an idea, often talking over one another on the show to become the first funding partner to the newbie CEO, the entrepreneur receives an extra $100,000 for pitting the judges against one another. It's all wildly entertaining because it never occurs to rich people that they might actually lose at something. When you're poor, the opposite is true: it never occurs to you that you may win. It's why I don't spend too long thinking about what shoes I would pair with my presentation versus how I'm going to afford a new water heater.

Dwayne Washington is my favorite judge on the show. He's the only investor who has swag, and by *swag* I mean **sexy** **with** **a** **g**orgeous nutmeg complexion. I feel like Dwayne and I would be friends, or at least understand one another. The oldest of four boys, at eighteen years old he started the urban clothing company Jus' Dope, slinging cheap fisherman's skullcaps on the streets of Harlem to help his mom make ends meet when his dad split. With a backpack full of hats, he established himself on the corner of Malcolm X Boulevard and West 125th Street to engage customers coming in and out of a popular soul food restaurant. When his signature skullcaps started selling out within an hour of setting up shop, he moved on to logoed three-quarter socks, all while working full-time as a cater-waiter and making sure none of his brothers dropped out of school. Jus' Dope is now a $5 billion business, and all three of Dwayne's brothers are college graduates and vice presidents at the company.

The new season of *Innovation Nation* doesn't come out until the end of September, and I have watched all eighty-two aired episodes of 246 Embryonic Entrepreneurs baring their company's soul for an infusion of cash. I select my favorite one, where Dwayne and another male investor duke it out over a new-fangled, high-speed breast pump while the two female judges look on in amusement.

Fisting a Big Gulp–size coffee to perk me up after last night's dance party ended four hours later than I intended it to, I crack open my notebook. I try to decipher the scrawl of notes I took as Zwena and Krish rolled up their pants and shirtsleeves to slather on the different cream consistencies I had worked out since Mrs. Eisenberg's attempt to moisturize at the airport.

Something Zwena said last night stuck in my head. Chitchatting as she applied a second dollop of lotion to her neck and chest, she commented on how odd it is that, even back home where the majority of people are some sliding scale of black, everyone applies lotion that's white. She casually commented that lotion in Africa should come in various shades of brown to black, since that's what the people are. Shrugging off the random thought, Zwena called it a *no-brainer* before asking me to grab her a beer from the fridge. In my buzzed scrawl I managed to write down, "Why can't lotion be brown?" right below this profound query from Krish: "Can this lotion safely double as lube?"

Considering Zwena's musings, it seems not only obvious for women in Africa, but for women of color everywhere. Why is lotion white? Doesn't have to be. There must be natural products that can tint my lotion various shades of brown without introducing harmful chemicals. Setting my notebook down, I pop open my laptop to get to work researching possibilities. Before clicking on my browser, I already have the answer.

The bags of powder David sent from Puerto Rico are stored with my dozens of backup rolls of Charmin and Bounty. I have an unfounded fear of running out of either, so I'm stocked up at all times Costco style. My mom, Krish, and Zwena have declared they are coming straight to my house in the next great earthquake. But until that time comes, my preparedness is a source of ribbing by all three.

As chatter emanates from the TV about percentage ownership and production costs, I pull out the bags of brown powder and a couple of jars of my lotion. When I peppered David with more questions about what the stuff was, he was little help, only saying he bought it at an outdoor market following an all-nighter and killing time before his flight back to Pensacola. That was some night he must have had with his latest female companion, who, when I got in his business, he grudgingly informed me was not sister-in-law material.

When my mom left my house the night of Lou and Coco's dance, on her way out she did claim that if this powder was what she thought it was, I held an essential ingredient of the beauty regimen of many rural Puerto Rican women from the seventies. At Sunday dinner after the dance, Gloria was forthcoming with a little more insight. She shared that when she and her sisters were teenagers they would take the powder, mix it with drops of water and milk to make a paste, and create some version of a face mask. While she couldn't remember where the powder came from, she did recall stirring it up, caking it on her face, and then lying out in the sun to let it dry. The taste was bitter to the tongue if it got mixed up in your mouth, but older women in Las Marías claimed it kept their skin moist and healthy after long days working in the orange groves. From a young age and with no intention of picking fruit, Gloria confessed that she worked the mask so she could work her magic with men. Clearly it paid off, because Mom remembers she masked up the morning of her eighteenth birthday, and that night she met my dad.

As I open one of the Ziplocs and take a big whiff, the smell is somewhat familiar. It's acrid, but definitely not in the coffee family. At least I don't think so. I recently learned what acai is when, starving before class, I mistakenly ducked into a new quick-eats shop on the Stanford campus. I ordered a bowl thinking it would be easy to discreetly eat in class and was presented with an eighteen-dollar cup of cold, dark-purple mush. I didn't particularly like the taste, but judging by the line dozens deep, eager to Cash App their payment, I wish I had discovered that purple powder rather than sitting here with this poop-brown one.

From the flavor, conferring with David and Tía Fernanda, Gloria's beauty revelations, and a hefty Google search, I figured out that the powder is most likely cacao beans that have been ground up with their shells. Essentially, it's the throwaway beans, or what farmers call *cullage*, that could not be used to make sellable chocolate. While agriculture as a way of life has lost widespread appeal in Puerto Rico given the last several decades of destructive hurricanes and the pull of city office work, the reintroduction of gourmet crops like cacao is drawing people back into farming. Now locally grown cacao is a burgeoning industry with a few island farms and novice chocolatiers popping up hoping to make Puerto Rico a sweets hot spot.

I sample the powder and decide it's too raw tasting to be processed cocoa. It doesn't taste like anything that would be worth a late-night binge session pining over an unrequited love, or Simon. I go back to an article I found and learn that cacao is the term for raw, unprocessed cocoa that doesn't taste good but has superior benefits for well-being. While the information is most likely referring to the consumption of cacao being tied to good health, I'm left wondering what it can do for the skin, a la David's lady friend and my mom. Seems both women were able to capture men with the lure of their luscious skin.

I reread the article a few times and feel my Puerto Rican foremothers sharing their secret to living life under the sun with joy, vitality, and their own versions of riches. It stood in stark contrast to the hundreds of times David, Gabriel, or I misbehaved as children and our antics were met with a stern reminder how lucky we were that our parents saved us from a life toiling under the oppressive sun. While I don't actually *know* much about life on the island, having only visited once when I was a young girl, I have never *felt* more Puerto Rican with five bags of its agricultural history sitting on my kitchen table in California. This powder is meant to be my future.

I take a large jar of the lotion Krish and Zwena confirmed smells the best and divide it into four small bowls. With the first bowl I add one tablespoon of the powder, dump it in my Kitchen Aid, and watch the cream turn a sun-kissed tone matching the shade of the well-traveled tan of Simon's skin. I put it back in its bowl and take a big whiff to determine if the powder has changed my blended eucalyptus and bougainvillea fragrance into something foul. To my growing excitement, the smell is unique and delicious, almost like a chocolate garden. Pleased, I dump the second bowl's contents into the mixer. To this, I add a full cup of powder. While the consistency with the added powder will have to be thinned, the color resembles my Afro–Puerto Rican skin and rubs in with zero residue.

"Women, particularly moms, like things that are natural, convenient, and intuitive," I hear one of the female *Innovation Nation* judges advise Dwayne after he shares a complicated addition he would consider making to the breast pump. *Claro. So true.* Doesn't take an MBA to know that piece of gender intel.

The wise judge is the first one to bow out, claiming the breast pump does not fit her investment portfolio, but she is a champion of women entrepreneurs and loves putting the male judges in their place. When Dwayne starts to debate her assessment, I join in yelling at the TV, "Stay in your lane, Dwayne!" as if he can hear me.

Before I continue to play around with the ratio of powder to lotion to create a rainbow of beige to brown to black creams that dry clear without the risk of staining clothing, I text Frances Antonelli to thank her for having the girls for the evening and much of today. According to what Lou and Coco told me when they called last night to check in, I will be at the airport when Frances drops them off this afternoon, so I won't be able to tell her I owe her one in person.

12:42 p.m. (Toni)

Thank you so much for having the girls over. Can you make sure Lou doesn't forget her pajamas this time? Next sleepover will be at my house. I owe you a night off!

12:43 p.m. (Frances)

Toni, did you mean to send this to someone else? We're in Big Sur for the weekend.

STILL SATURDAY, MARCH 9

"Mami!" I yell into the phone, not even attempting to mask my panic. "Are Lou and Coco with you?" With closed eyes I pray her answer is some version of *yes*. Then I'll know exactly where to go to kill all three of them. What could they possibly be up to that warrants lying to me? Obviously, something I would never allow at home, like those damn highlights Lou won't stop begging me for.

"Are you smoking?"

"No." I blow out my smoke, caught with a Camel Ultra Light from my stress-relieving emergency pack of cigarettes. How can she smell through the phone? "Did you hear me, are the girls with you?"

"No, mi amor. I've been at the Senior Connection all morning. A few ladies paid me to give them one-on-one dance lessons." My girls are missing, and my mom's freelancing. *What the hell is going on?!*

"I gotta go, Mom," I cut in, ending her recitation of what was served for brunch in the dining room in order to text Lou and Coco.

Nothing. Not even three dots.

Before calling the police, I'm going to call Father Egan, who stands out in front of Saint Anne welcoming students on Monday mornings, asking after their weekends and wishing them well when school lets out on Friday afternoons. Hopefully he saw Lou and Coco at the end of school Friday and knows whose car they got into. I can't imagine I mixed up their sleepover invitation, but it's possible.

Fingers shaking, I scroll down to the *E*'s and hope the contact information I have for Father Egan is to his cell and not his office. Or better yet, directly to God. About to select the number, I hear a key jostling in the front door followed by the hinges screaming for WD-40, our version of a welcome bell. I stub out the half-finished cigarette butt in the kitchen sink, wave away the smoke, and pull myself together before heading into the living room to lose it. As I take a shaky, calming breath, I hear a foreign but not forgotten voice announce, "This place hasn't changed one bit, not even the squeak in the front door," followed by a pair of tween giggles.

My jaw locks as I witness Simon walking around my living room, reading the book spines on the shelves, pawing framed photos of Lou and Coco, straightening a throw pillow like he's taking a leisurely stroll down memory lane. All three Evanses stop short when they see me in the doorway.

"Aren't you supposed to be at work, Mom?!" Coco barks, her voice smacking of fear—which, I would say, is an appropriate response.

"Yeah, Mom, that's what the family calendar says, that you're at work." Lou blames me, backing up her sister, like I'm the one at fault for catching these two in a complete lie that was seconds away from an AMBER Alert.

Coco and Lou are home, alive, and that's enough for me. For now. I'll deal with my two little liars later. The silent treatment should be enough to signal to them they ought to be scared, very scared, of their mother. The bigger shock is my adrift husband escorting Lou and Coco home like this is a regular weekend afternoon as a family of four.

"Simon," I announce flatly, buying myself a moment to confirm his presence and think.

"Hey, Toni," Simon responds in an equally measured tone. "Good to see you."

There is nothing good about my husband returning after two years only to kidnap my daughters and then waltz into my house five minutes before I need to leave for a job his actions forced me to take.

"Girls, grab your backpacks and head upstairs. We'll be sitting down to talk later."

"Later, like, *ummm*, in a few minutes or, like, tomorrow?" Coco frets, wanting to know how long she will be living in punishment purgatory.

"Later, like, when I decide I'm, like, good and ready," I mirror back, both girls knowing how much I hate the omnipresent use of the word *like*. Now, in addition to lying, poor grammar will once again be on this mama's path of wrath. Lou doesn't say a word, but her exasperated huffs let me know she thinks I'm overreacting to what is for sure every mother's worst nightmare, her children dragging home her errant husband.

I watch the girls walk out of the living room and wait to hear the predictable slam of the bedroom door from a couple of pissed-off teens. "And don't slam *my* doors!" I yell before I slowly turn my body back toward Simon. I emphasize *my* for Simon's sake. Now that he's here, I want him to know I no longer consider this *our* house. It's mine.

With forced nonchalance I mask my disbelief that he's here, in my house, when I expressly told him over text to get lost. The only thing I want to know at this moment is how he got from receiving my texted equivalent of *drop dead* to sashaying through my front door with Lou and Coco like they were out grabbing pizza. I should have accepted Gabriel's offer to help me sell my house and move when he came to visit shortly after Simon's disappearance. At the time, I claimed it would be best for the girls, given our family's traumatic circumstances, to stay in their childhood home, but what I was really doing was harboring desperate hope that Simon would return, and I wanted him to know where we were. Apparently, that hope wasn't misplaced, it was just mistimed. His actual timing nearly gave me a goddamn heart attack.

STILL SATURDAY, MARCH 9

Let it go already, Prince Harry. I gnaw on the straw of my Diet Coke and judge the wounded prince, whose latest breaking news—and I use that phrase loosely—is once again the cover story of a discarded *People* magazine left in my cart. To my count, Prince Harry has "broken his silence" about twenty-six times since moving to the United States. For famous people who claim to want nothing more than to live a private life, he and Meghan Markle sure work hard to keep themselves front and center in the tabloids.

My on-again, off-again love affair with the ex-royals is dependent on which issue of airport entertainment is left in my cart by passengers who think they are tipping me with their cast-off magazines. I wish I could say there were as many copies of the *Atlantic* bestowed upon me as *Us Weekly*, but realistically the ratio is about one to eight hundred, and as a result I am the addicted recipient of travelers' trashy reading habits. I stay in the know about newly released movies and music, high-profile separations, and who's sporting a baby bump during awards season. All useless information that I store away for random chitchat with my passengers. During my downtime, I should be studying for the exam I have coming up in my Pioneering Entrepreneurs class, but given Simon's startling reappearance, trashy mags are the exact mind-numbing drug my brain needs to avoid implosion. The ex-royals are keeping me preoccupied from journaling a list of possible ways to eviscerate Simon. Spiking his matcha latte comes to mind.

I'm debating whether Taylor Swift really "Wore It Best" when Dieting Donna from JetBlue customer service slides into my parked cart. I don't stop gnashing on my straw to acknowledge her disturbing my foul mood. Right now I prefer to swim, or drown, in the festering sea of me.

"You think you can drive me over to Terminal 1," Donna trills, full of cheer and hopefulness given my obvious lull in driving passengers. "My break's almost over, and you know what a stickler my manager is for time." A waft of Panda Express encases my chariot. I look from Donna's bag full of lo mein to her capable legs and pull a long sip from my crushed straw, the gurgling of my empty cup the only sound between us.

"I'm sore from yesterday's gym workout. Too many squats." Donna rubs her quads for added emphasis, annoying me with jabber I'm not interested in hearing. "Like I told you, new year, new me." There's been a new Donna every year as long as I've known her.

Given my embittered brain, I keep my mouth busy with my straw, so I don't point out to Donna it's impossible to exercise your way into a new you while continuing your old fast-food habits. That's basic nutritional science right there.

"Didn't you tell me you were determined to drop fifty pounds this year?" I finally respond when Donna's eyes look at me expectantly, willing me to fire up my cart so she's not late. With my insult, Donna clutches her plastic bag handles a little tighter. It's not my fault she hoofed it all the way over from Terminal 1 for pot stickers.

"You told me that under no circumstances am I to give you a ride since you invested in a new Apple Watch and you want to complete your movement ring each day." I throw Donna's words back at her, like I'm trying to pick a fight. And maybe I am, but it just happens to be with the wrong person. "I believe your exact quote was, 'sitting is the new smoking' while you marched in place showing off your rose gold wrist coach." God, I wish I could finish my cigarette right now instead of heaping my misdirected anger on undeserving Donna. I almost have the energy to feel sorry for someone other than myself.

"Thought you were my friend, not the resolution police." Donna mopes, grabbing the extra-large chocolate malt milkshake she had placed in my cup holder when she thought she was hitching a ride.

"Just following your instructions," I snipe back, attempting to hide my cruelty behind tough love. Watching her limp away, I do start to feel guilty for taking my rage out on Donna and her sore quadriceps. I turn over the cart key to go after her. Donna's manager really is an asshole when it comes to being late.

Ding.

A text from Coco. I'll apologize to Donna tomorrow with a Kit Kat.

The girls refused to come out of their room before I left this afternoon, so I'm relieved to see Coco respond to the note I left them on the kitchen table. I figured it would be her since Lou is a champion grudge holder.

4:56 p.m. (Coco)

We know you're mad at us for lying. And for seeing Dad. But we're mad at you for not telling us he was home. That was so not okay. You don't get to decide if we see Dad or not.

Ouch. I have to read the text three times, digesting that the biting words are Coco's, not Lou's. Lou shares her emotions the minute she feels them and then holds on until the entire family has been exhausted by her antics. Coco is more reserved with her words, or so I thought. And I do get to decide if they see their father.

4:57 p.m. (Coco)

Dad told me he doesn't have a house key so I gave him mine.

After I sent the girls to their room, the million and one comments and questions I had meticulously customized over the past twenty-four months anticipating Simon's return raced through my brain in garbled language. Unclear where to begin in the grips of alarm and adrenaline, I slowed my internal roil enough to start with the basics. I asked Simon how he was able to contact Lou and Coco since he split long before the girls got their own cell phones. Simon deflected my question by remarking on how well I was taking care of myself. Admittedly, what vanity I do have is small but mighty, and I was relieved that the day my nomadic husband resurfaced, I had put some effort into my appearance. No woman wants to look grubby in front of a former flame, even if the fire's gone out. And given how rarely I do pull it together, I could at least appreciate the timing of Simon's return being today of all days from a revenge perspective.

With curls cascading down my back, a bit of a face applied, and my one pair of work pants that make my backside look lifted, I believe Simon's actual words were, "Toni, you look as gorgeous as always." It felt like a minivictory to hear that Simon recognized what he abandoned until he followed up with, "You've really kept the wheels on the bus." For a reluctant transportation specialist, Simon's added compliment was not much of a bonus.

I was about to respond by inquiring if commenting on someone's looks is considered best practice for a life coach who spouts what's happening on the *inside* is the path to eternal salvation, but I held myself in check with a blank face. I did not want to give Simon even the tiniest hint that I skimmed through his website, let alone memorized every page. In at least two tabs he used the metaphor of keeping the wheels on the bus, so I know the sentiment, genuine or not, was pulled from his quiver of cliches.

"No pictures of me?" Simon observed out loud, confusion in his tone as he perused the bookshelf where a visual montage of our family once lived. As he ran his fingers over my collection of textbooks, Simon's hands looked more wrinkled and calloused than I remembered, like he may have built a school or something worthwhile while he was away.

"Are you surprised?" I had to know if he was really that oblivious. Or arrogant.

"More hurt," Simon confessed, turning back to me with an endearing pout. I softened at his melancholy, but then quickly bounced back to bewilderment. "But not surprised."

"At least your time abroad didn't make you stupid," I clapped back to avoid being pulled into his facade of warmth. It's not that images of reuniting with Simon hadn't occupied my mind, they had, but the scene playing out in my living room was not one of them. I imagined our reunion would be more along the lines of me as a multimillionaire CEO and him scraping by living in a yurt. In my fantasy, my assistant is out for the day, and I have to go to the nearest Target to pick up personal care items for me and the girls. At checkout, as I burrow through an oversize Fendi bag for my wallet, holding a conference call on my earbuds, a faintly familiar voice asks if I would like my items in a large or small bag. Annoyed by the interruption of my very important call by such a banal question, I turn to find out who would be so rude. My pretend scenario ends with Simon bagging my items wearing a company-issued red canvas vest.

"So, did you finish your degree while I was, uh, gone?" Simon asked, picking up one of my notebooks off the shelf and flipping through the pages, completely unaware his knuckles grazed our divorce papers.

"As much as I would love to stay here and discuss what I've been able to accomplish while raising our girls alone, I have to go to work," I quick-fired back.

"Come on, Toni, you can give me two minutes."

"I can't give you two minutes. I don't want to give you any minutes. You don't even deserve a couple of seconds." The truth is, I was afraid to give Simon my time because there is no denying I still see the boyish twenty-nine-year-old I served coffee to all those years ago. Even through my shock and brewing rage I noticed that Simon, too, kept the wheels on the bus on his road to forty-five.

"You can, however, give me the key you used to open my front door." I put out my palm, face up, waving gimmie fingers. "I have to go." Walking out, weighted down by my canvas tote filled with jars of lotion, I used the extra heft I've been carrying to slam that same front door in Simon's face.

"What's all the schmutz under your fingernails?" Mrs. Eisenberg clucks, turning my hand every which way like she's my mother checking my nails before church. Just as Gloria's accent thickens when she returns from visiting Tía Fernanda in San Juan, Mrs. Eisenberg's Yiddish more liberally flavors her sentences whenever she returns from Scottsdale after spending too much time with Elaine. "You're such a shaina maidel, but those hands are a mess."

With Simon waltzing back into my life, I didn't get to scrub up after handling cacao bean powder all morning. Agitated, I dig under my ring fingernail with my thumb. My emotions are riding on the surface of my skin courtesy of this afternoon's shock and awe, and I am feeling Mrs. Eisenberg's observation harshly.

"Relax, Antonia. I just said you're a pretty girl, not some pickle peddler." Mrs. Eisenberg pats my cheek. "Don't think I didn't notice your hair is done nicely today and those cheekbones are a little pink."

I blush, making them pinker. It wasn't Dieting Donna's fault Simon appeared out of nowhere, and it's not Mrs. Eisenberg's either. I need to set the personal aside and settle into being a professional for the rest of my shift.

"My plane landed early, so we have lots of time to catch up." Mrs. Eisenberg squeezes my upper arm as we walk toward my cart. If it were any other passenger, I would remind them I'm at work, I'm not doing this for fun. But it's Mrs. Eisenberg, and we always have a little fun.

"I want to hear about everything that's been going on while I've been away. I've been thinking about your cream the past trip to Arizona. You know we had a bit of rain last week, and the rainbow over Camelback Mountain was exquisite. I really think you're on to something with that lotion, so let's review the progress you've made since I've been gone." I notice Mrs. Eisenberg is moving more slowly than usual, and I can feel her hands trembling, which is new. She smiles as brightly as always, but her face looks a tad more sunken and papery thin. I wonder if anyone in Scottsdale is checking to make sure Mrs. Eisenberg is eating properly, not just picking at a chicken breast or hitting up Krispy Kreme.

"Mrs. Eisenberg, have you been feeling all right?" I ask, trying to be as upbeat as possible. "You making sure to use your monthly food credit at the club?"

"Do you know who's been using my dining dollars?"

"Elaine," we both say at the same time and snicker. But as Mrs. Eisenberg shakes with laughter, I'm forced to hold on to her firmly to ensure she doesn't stumble over her steps. It occurs to me that Mrs. Eisenberg may not have eaten for a few hours as she finds snacking on a plane distasteful. She's shared more than once that she doesn't understand why people pack enough food for a transatlantic voyage. According to Mrs. Eisenberg, no one needs a meatball sub for a two-hour flight.

Even though she comes from a generation of three square meals a day and no snacking, I have a protein bar in the cart to offer her. Hopefully the frailty I feel is only a dip in Mrs. Eisenberg's blood sugar.

"So, where are you on the lotion? I expect you have news to share." On more than one occasion Mrs. Eisenberg has not-so-subtly informed me that in her own life she does not tolerate inaction. Or avoidance of her line of questioning. "What you are working on may be a master-piece, or it may be a disaster piece, but at least you are moving forward," Mrs. Eisenberg says, reminding me of one of her favorite mottos with a finger wag in my face that makes it difficult to see while I drive.

"There is a little bit of progress, in fact," I respond, kindly placing her hand back in her lap.

"Oh, goody. You know I believe incremental progress is the best way to go. Intentional . . ."

". . . steps are best," I repeat with Mrs. Eisenberg. "And yes"—I nod before continuing—"I also remember the best way to eat an elephant. One bite at a time." All Mrs. Eisenberg's favored quips are being lined up like self-help recruits for today's ride.

"Crass, but it makes my point crystal clear." Mrs. Eisenberg purses her lips, admonishing me for stealing one of her favorite sayings. "Don't question Desmond Tutu, the man gives good advice."

"I won't," I promise, not wanting to insult the woman whose company I enjoy and whose random tipping pays for movies and snacks with my family. That said, I can't help but be curious when exactly Mrs. Eisenberg has ever had to dine on an elephant. Desmond Tutu, maybe, but Mrs. Eisenberg? Eddie was clearly successful in some sort of endeavor, though Mrs. Eisenberg has never been specific, and I've not pried. He took care of Mrs. Eisenberg for sixty years and left her with two nice houses, a host of friends, and hobbies that occupy her sunset years. All evidence points to a woman who has skipped more than intentionally stepped through life.

"We have plenty of time before my grandson is here to meet me." There it is. Ash is slated for today's pickup. Zwena's been waiting on this intel. "Unless you have other passengers to take to their gates. Do you? If you do, I want to come with you! Can I drive?" Seated, impatient for my answers, Mrs. Eisenberg seems more her sturdy self.

"No one to pick up right this minute, and no, Ms. Formula One, you cannot drive. Nice try, though."

"You know I drive a golf cart all over my community in Arizona." Mrs. Eisenberg tries to sway me with this logic every couple of trips.

"I do. And it's still not happening. Sit back and relax, Mrs. Eisenberg, I got you."

"What you can get me is a doughnut, then."

"How about this KIND bar instead?" I tap the nut cluster on Mrs. Eisenberg's thigh, hoping to entice her.

"Did Livy put you up to this?" Mrs. Eisenberg accuses, swatting away the plastic wrap.

"No," I lie. Livy did mention at the Saint Anne rummage sale that Mrs. Eisenberg's glucose levels are all over the place and as much as she may beg, could I please deter her grandmother from stopping for a sugar bomb.

"Then you can get me a doughnut. And since Ash is picking me up, what Livy doesn't know won't kill her. Just like a cruller won't kill me."

It's the only snacking she allows herself, I rationalize, and pull a U-turn to head to Build-A-Burger.

"What's with the bag?" Zwena nods at the canvas satchel with navy straps I found at the Saint Anne rummage sale. She grabs the enormous apple fritter Mrs. Eisenberg is pointing to and teases me, "I know you're not heading to the beach."

Mrs. Eisenberg gives Zwena a twenty. With her hand out waiting for the change, Zwena and I are both struck by a ginormous emerald stone, the size of a nickel, flanked by two diamond baguettes spinning around Mrs. Eisenberg's pencil-thin ring finger.

"One of the moms dumped her discarded sweaters from this tote onto my table where I was folding and then just walked off. When I ran after her to give it back, she showed me the dirt on the bottom, said she had three new ones at home from some resort collection she was fond of, and I could toss it out. With a stain stick and a few spins through the wash, I knew this bag could be as good as new," I babble on to Zwena and Mrs. Eisenberg, proud of my refurbishing skills.

"Well, that's a boring story," Zwena concludes, not taking her eyes off the emerald. Mrs. Eisenberg nods in agreement and then clamps down on her first bite of fritter.

"What I really want to know is: Mrs. E, where did you get that rock?! Did you finally agree to marry one of those eligible men who have been chasing you around the golf course?" Zwena comes from around the Build-A-Burger counter to get a closer look at the biggest stone either of us has ever seen. "Maybe I need to get myself to Arizona and find me one of those."

"None of those men are my type," Mrs. Eisenberg insists while holding up the ring for Zwena and me to inspect as if she did, in fact, become engaged. Her face becomes soft, almost girlish. "Eddie gave me this ring for our fiftieth wedding anniversary. Today would have been our sixty-fifth. Or is it sixty-sixth? I'm not sure, but I always wear it on our anniversary." Mrs. Eisenberg inspects the ring herself and smiles, lost in memories of many years past. "I was going to give it to Ash's wife, but now I'm thinking of giving it to Livy."

Zwena raises her eyebrows at me. The hope of rectifying this horrid day with a glimpse of Ash disappears at the mention of his wife. What a waste of my time bothering to shower and shampoo. I grab the ponytail holder off my wrist and pull my hair up into a bun in defeat.

"Hey, if no one in your family wants it, keep me in mind," Zwena suggests, waving her own fingers at Mrs. Eisenberg.

Dropping all the change from her twenty into Zwena's tip jar, Mrs. Eisenberg kids her, "You keep the doughnuts stocked and I'll consider it."

"Can we stop by the ladies' room before we go to baggage claim?" Mrs. Eisenberg asks with a mouthful of fritter. "I want to wash up after the plane." More like wash away any evidence of a half-chowed fritter.

"Absolutely." We still have time to kill before meeting Ash, but if we loiter around Build-A-Burger much longer, Zwena's bound to say something about Ash or Simon or both, and I don't have the patience to get into it.

"Before we go, I have something for you," I inform Zwena, rummaging around in my bag.

"Can't compete with that ring," Zwena chides, winking at Mrs. Eisenberg.

I pull out jars of my lotion in all different tints of brown. I hold up each one to Zwena's arm to see which color matches best. As I thought, the darkest shade is the right call.

"Will you look at who listened to me for once!" Zwena exclaims, turning over the jar that could be easily mistaken for espresso pudding. Unscrewing the top, Zwena opens it up and takes a big sniff. Keeping a straight face, she passes my product under Mrs. Eisenberg's nose for additional inspection.

"Nice," is all I get from Zwena.

"I'm getting a fragrant mix of floral and dark chocolate. What a yummy combination." The sugar is definitely going to Mrs. Eisenberg's brain.

"What's my cut?"

"A cut of nothing is nothing," I retort, explaining to Zwena the most basic of economic principles.

"I'm sensing a masterpiece here." Mrs. Eisenberg's eyes grow wide in a way they never did with my prototypes for fresh-churned ice cream, heating pockets, or empanadillas. Her expressions were always encouraging, but with a side of skepticism. "You have a shade in there for me?" Mrs. Eisenberg asks in anticipation.

"You know I do. You can slick up after we hit the bathroom."

"While you're in there, get after those nails, Toni," Zwena instructs, sharing a disappointed look with Mrs. Eisenberg. "You can't be pushing lotion with your hands looking like that."

STILL SATURDAY, MARCH 9

Even with eighteen stalls, the women's restroom near where the LaGuardia flights depart and arrive has a consistently long line. It's a universal travel phenomenon that in airport bathroom lines there is one impatient woman at the far back of the queue who marches right past all those in front of her when she spies a stall with a partially open door. It's as if the rest of us have not seen the glaring opportunity and are idiots for not heading in and taking a seat.

"She's in for an unfortunate surprise," Mrs. Eisenberg whispers not so under her breath.

"There's always one," I agree. After a superior push of the metal door, the woman recoils.

"Certainly not as smart as she thinks she looks," Mrs. Eisenberg judges, this time not even attempting to whisper. The woman swiftly grabs the handle of her paisley-print roller bag and scurries out into the terminal in search of another line that knows nothing of her bathroom arrogance.

"Yep, there's always one," I repeat, sharing with Mrs. Eisenberg and the women in front and behind us that I have seen this scenario play out plenty of times before. It always ends with a quick exit.

Shoving the saved half of her apple fritter deep into her handbag, Mrs. Eisenberg loses her balance and stumbles backward. Her purse strap slides down her arm, and the bag lands with a thud on the grimy bathroom floor.

"Mrs. Eisenberg, are you okay?" I ask in a lowered voice, feeling all her weight fall into me. The last thing Mrs. Eisenberg would want is for me to make a scene, so I lean my mouth close to her ear to ensure she can hear my voice. As she attempts to respond, Mrs. Eisenberg's answer comes out garbled, and I can see that the left side of her face is not moving as she struggles to form words. Her eyes are having difficulty focusing. As they dart around, I see fear in them when she recognizes what she wants to say does not sound like what's coming out of her mouth.

With all the calm that I do not feel, I shift Mrs. Eisenberg so that both of my arms are securely under her armpits, and I whisper into her ear what I am going to do next.

"Mrs. Eisenberg, I'm not sure what's going on, but I am going to slowly lower you onto the floor." *God, it feels so undignified to rest Mrs. Eisenberg on one of the germiest surfaces known to humankind. But there's no other choice.* "After I set you down, I'm going to call 911." Something that sounds roughly like "please don't" muffles out of the right side of her mouth.

"I have to, Mrs. Eisenberg," I say with as much assuredness as I can fake. My arms supporting her, I bend at the knees and rest Mrs. Eisenberg's upper back and head against my thighs as we go down. Thankfully we land as delicately as possible, and I'm able to keep her head elevated above her heart—I definitely do not want to add choking to the list of terrifying things that are happening.

With a tap on my shoulder, a young woman behind us apprehensively asks, "Is everything all right?" I'm as surprised as anyone that she doesn't have her face buried in her phone, clueless to what's going on in her surroundings.

"Call 911," I instruct, too nervous to let go of Mrs. Eisenberg to fish around in my bag for my phone. With a resolute nod, the young woman dials while I lean forward to check that Mrs. Eisenberg is still breathing. She is. My eyes linger for a moment at the geometric-print signature silk scarf Mrs. Eisenberg has tied around her neck. More than once she has referred to it as her permanent Botox, informing me that before Botox, women of a certain age relied on scarves to hide their necks. I issue an apology to Mrs. Eisenberg as I untie the perfect square knot and slip off the accessory.

"Okay, I called. Anything else I can do?" the stranger offers. I feel all the women lined up for the restroom beginning to shift uncomfortably, unsure if they should take action, step around us into the stalls that are opening up, or abandon their need to pee altogether and leave.

"Yes, in my bag there's a notebook and my phone, can you get them out?" I cock my head at the bag, giving her permission to rummage around in the tote I had thrown to the ground to better support Mrs. Eisenberg.

"Got it." She holds up the notebook, then dives back in for the phone.

"There's a small piece of paper in the front of the notebook." She opens it, and the piece of paper falls out. "Can you dial that number and hold the phone to my ear?" From the corner of my eye, I can see her fingers fumble with the paper, but I stay attentive to Mrs. Eisenberg.

One ring. Two. Three.

"They're coming!" I hear another woman from the back of the line announce. "Move out of the way!"

Come on. Come on. Pick up.

"Hello?" the voice asks, puzzled, most likely due to the unknown number.

"Hi, Ash? This is, uh, Toni from SFO airport transportation services." I try to keep my voice steady. In control.

"Sorry, who?"

Arrrgggghhh! Deep breath. Maybe he can't hear very well from his car with traffic and planes taking off and landing overhead.

"Toni Arroyo. You gave me your number at the Cracked Cup," I answer, my voice wobbling with emotion at the gravity of the situation. "I was in the class at Stanford where you were on the panel."

"Oh right, right. Yes, I remember. How can I help you?" Ash asks with the formality of a work call. The paramedics have now arrived and are bombarding me with questions in one ear while I have Ash on the line in the other.

"I'm with your grandmother at the airport and she's just collapsed," I rush out as fast as I can. "I gotta go, the paramedics are here, and I need to let them know what happened. I'm sure they're going to want to transport her to the hospital. I'll call you back in a few and let you know which one."

"Insist they take her to Stanford Medical, it's the best," Ash commands. "I'll meet them there. And Antonia, tell the paramedics to spare no expense treating her."

Even in an emergency, Ash Eisenberg is a snob.

STILL SATURDAY, MARCH 9

Even though my shift isn't over for another two hours, I can't bear the thought of Mrs. Eisenberg arriving alone at the hospital. A concerned male EMT engages me in a lightning round of twenty-five terrifying questions as the young female paramedic goes through the FAST assessment with Mrs. Eisenberg. Can she make her face smile, raise her arm, say her name? Mrs. Eisenberg is zero for three. Done with notating the events that just transpired, the first responders hook Mrs. Eisenberg up to an EKG machine to check her heart rate and blood pressure. Goddamn that apple fritter Mrs. Eisenberg begged for. Refined sugar on my watch better not be the end of her.

Guiltily, like I ate it, I share one piece of the story I had omitted, that Mrs. Eisenberg did have sugar. Lots of it. The female EMT assures me that the doughnut was most likely not the culprit. Low blood sugar can be a symptom of a stroke, and Mrs. Eisenberg's is elevated, so maybe I saved her by honoring her secret request.

While her vitals are being recorded, I text my boss a cryptic and no doubt confusing *Imfinebutonmywaytothehospital.* On the count of three, the paramedics lift Mrs. Eisenberg off my lap and onto the gurney like she's weightless. With Mrs. Eisenberg's body resting on me for well over ten minutes my legs had fallen asleep, but I didn't move a muscle for fear that my need for relief might incite Mrs. Eisenberg taking her last breath. While the team raises the stretcher and the chatty male EMT speaks quickly into a walkie-talkie to I don't know who, hopefully God, I roll forward onto my hands and knees and shake out my right leg and then my left, trying to relieve the pins and tingles that have congregated in my calves.

6:22 p.m.

Ninety years of age.

Caucasian woman.

Acute stroke.

Complete loss of balance.

Fell in airport bathroom.

Slurred speech.

Left side paralysis. Face. Arm. Leg.

Agitated.

I told them she's eighty-eight! No woman, regardless of condition, wants to be aged beyond her years. I know Mrs. Eisenberg would not be pleased with how she's been described. I would have thrown in classy, sassy, and definitely not happy if this is her send-off to meet up with her beloved Eddie.

"I'm coming with her." My right lower leg is still not cooperating as I try to get up off the floor.

"Are you two family?" the young female paramedic asks while trying to maneuver as quickly as possible out of the bathroom.

"Do I look like I'm family?" I respond, my worry coming out as snark while hobbling after the gurney.

"Sure," she guesses, like I'm the bigot to her woke Gen Zness that doesn't see color. Before I defend myself to someone I will never see again once we reach the ER, I realize she's not wrong. Mrs. Eisenberg's Black grandson is probably already at the hospital, barking out orders, awaiting our arrival. "As long as it's okay with her." We both look to Mrs. Eisenberg, allowing her one small piece of control over her unknown fate.

After a purposeful blink of her watery eyes, I say, "It is," because that's enough of a *yes* for me.

I abandon my cart at the bathroom entrance, and I shuffle alongside the rolling bed as the swath of travelers parts so we can make our way through the terminal and down the lengthy United walkway that leads out the arrivals doors to what I suspect is a waiting ambulance. As inappropriate as I know it is, I choke back a teary laugh. If Mrs. Eisenberg were lucid enough to know what is going on, I'm sure she would be quick with a joke about how she, like Moses, can part a sea. I pray I can tell her about it once she's resting comfortably in her hospital room.

Locked in the back of the ambulance, I point to my phone, asking the paramedic sitting with us if it is okay if I make a call. She nods, possibly sensing this is my first ride with emergency services, and assures me it's fine if I talk. She tells me that, in fact, my voice may prove comforting to Mrs. Eisenberg.

"Hello, Toni." Simon answers like he's not at all surprised to be hearing from me. I should have called Zwena first. Or my mother. But Zwena alluded to a booty call she has going on later this evening, Saturdays Gloria is shaking hers at the Senior Connection, and as I just found out, Frances Antonelli and her family are in Big Sur for the weekend. And Krish does many things, but babysitting is not one of them. I want to call anyone else, but Simon is all I have left.

"Hello? Toni? Are you there?" Turns out his voice grates on me even more over the phone than it did in person a few hours ago.

"I can't believe I'm saying this, but I need you to go back over to *my* house." Again I make sure to emphasize the *my*.

"Do you want me to join you and the girls for dinner?"

"Uh, no," I assure. "There's been an emergency at the airport, and I'm on the way to the hospital."

"Do you need me to meet you there?" Simon panics, doing a stand-up job in the role of recently reappeared and reengaged husband.

"I'm going with one of my customers." Mrs. Eisenberg is so much more than a customer, but at this point I only have time to get out what I need, and what I need is not one superfluous word exchanged with Simon. "I don't know when I will be home, but I imagine it'll be very late. I need you to get the girls dinner and make them do their homework. And if you could help Lou with algebra and her attitude, that'd be great." Lou's simultaneously struggling with math and refusing my tutoring. "Consider it a life coaching session with your kid." *Oh, I didn't just say that, I didn't just say that! I DID NOT JUST SAY THAT!* I pound my fist against my forehead.

You okay? The paramedic mouths when she sees me cringing in pain. I hit mute on my phone.

"I'm wincing from embarrassment," I convince her, pointing at my cell.

"Oh, I'll take bodily harm over humiliation any day."

"Me too," I agree, and take Simon off mute.

"How do you know I'm a life coach?" I hear Simon ask with a touch of amusement.

"Can you go back to the house or not?" I skip right over an admission I am not copping to now, or ever.

"Sure. I'll see you at home."

◆　◆　◆

"Are you with the patient?" We both answer yes from opposite sides of Mrs. Eisenberg's bed. "And you two are . . ." The doctor trails off, her voice hinting at a question.

"Not together," Ash clarifies. "And this is not a patient, this is my grandmother, Sylvia Eisenberg. I expect her private room will be ready shortly so you can get her moved in immediately," Ash says tightly, assuming his wish will be the doctor's command.

"You can expect all you want, but unfortunately, this is not the Four Seasons."

I take note of the name embroidered on her white lab coat. Dr. Tenner Mason. I like her and her smooth sidestep of Ash's demands.

"Your grandmother probably has a couple of hours remaining here in the ER before a bed opens up upstairs, but we will do our best."

"My apologies," Ash backs down. I make a mental note to suggest that after putting Ash in his place, Dr. Mason add *badass* below her name. "I just want to make sure my grandmother is resting comfortably and is well taken care of."

Dr. Mason turns to me, I assume done with Ash's patronization. "I was right there with the stroke team to meet Mrs. Eisenberg when she arrived. We have scanned her head for blood clots, and I am happy to report that there were none present in the brain. We gave her tPA, a clot-busting medication."

"Why did you give her tPA? I read online that not all stroke victims are given tPA," Ash cuts in, not allowing himself to be ignored.

"Well, while WebMD is a source concerned families often cite, I can assure you the stroke team is staffed by exceptional doctors, led by me. I believed it was in your grandmother's best interest to have tPA, so that's what we did." Dr. Mason looks back and forth between me and Ash, making sure we are all on the same page. "Because of her age and the weakness presenting on her left side, when a bed opens up in the ICU, we will be taking her up there to be monitored overnight."

"And if all goes well in the ICU?" It's my turn to cut in, hoping there is more good news. "Being transferred to the ICU sounds scary."

"I promise you, admission to the ICU is protocol for all stroke patients, particularly more senior ones. Totally normal given the circumstances." Ash and I nod in unison to Dr. Badass Mason. "For now, I will be back every hour or so to check on your grandmother up until the moment she's transferred. This is a teaching hospital, so I will have an eager cadre of residents there to provide optimal care for your grandmother as well."

Sensing our need for more, Dr. Mason continues, "And, if there is no delayed bleeding overnight, she's been checked out by the neuro-intensive doctors, has had a round of sessions with the therapy team, and another round of scans comes back clear, Mrs. Eisenberg will be transferred out of the ICU and onto the intensive therapy floor. She may be able to go home sooner than we think, but I would plan on a week or two stay to be on the safe side."

Ash and I can't help but grin across Mrs. Eisenberg at one another. That all sounds less doomsday and more standard protocol.

"We are, however, a long way from that determination," Dr. Mason warns, but with a warmth meant to comfort. "Next step, I will see the two of you within the hour."

After watching Dr. Mason slip through the curtains, Ash turns to me. "So, what exactly happened?" His smile drops, and his question sounds like an accusation.

"I believe Dr. Mason just laid it out pretty clearly: your grandmother had a stroke," I restate. "And she's lucky to be alive, thanks to me," I finish under my breath. Ash looks at me blankly, like I'm speaking a language he's never heard. Was he not listening to Dr. Mason's succinct review of his grandmother? She is one fit woman for her age. A stroke would most likely have been the end for most patients in her peer group. The recovery will be long, but let's rejoice that Mrs. Eisenberg bought herself another spin around the sun.

The patient on the other side of the thin curtain interrupts our conversation with a loud, slurred announcement to the entire emergency room that his balls are en fuego. His friends, crowded around his bed, can't get through the retelling of the story without falling into raucous laughter, high fives, and bro-ish backslaps. What I pick up is that it's the twenty-first birthday of Fiery Ball Boy. When the Stanford basketball game let out, he went to hop a metal bike rack that was in the direct path back to his fraternity and an awaiting tapped keg. As his friends cheered him on, his boozy, blurred mind misread the height of the rack. As a result, the birthday boy's balls crashed onto a metal bar with a force that now has him begging the doctor, in a feverish pitch, to save his testicles. I can't tell if the doctor is trying to teach these drunkards a lesson by scaring the semen out of them or not, but it's sounding like the birthday boy's wish may not come true.

Given the conversation next door, I'm too embarrassed to look over at Ash. When I finally sneak a peek in his direction, I spy Ash fighting a chuckle at our neighbor's expense. I start to crack up too. We look at Mrs. Eisenberg, immobile in bed, wanting her to join in on the absurdity of the situation playing out on the other side of the curtain. I know if she could properly speak, she would have some choice commentary. Probably something along the lines of *stupid is as stupid does.*

For something to do until the doctor returns, I reach into my canvas tote to retrieve a jar of my cream to moisten Mrs. Eisenberg's hands. Ash interrupts my plan. "No. I mean, what happened after the Cracked Cup? Why didn't you call me?" Ash asks and clears his throat to get his laughter under control. I return the jar of lotion to my bag, giving myself a moment to figure out if Ash is actually hitting on me, however ineptly, just as Zwena suspected.

"People pay a lot of money for my advice when it comes to getting their companies off the ground," Ash shares with too much self-assurance. "I was offering it to you for free." Now that I know Ash has a wife, his flirtatious offer of help at the Cracked Cup feels laced with an ulterior motive that he must assume I'll agree to. "You obviously kept my number."

I open my mouth to say something, but nothing comes out. It's true. I have a husband and he has a wife and yet, I did keep his number.

"I'm going to the nurse's station to find out if they have any more information about when we will be moved. Then I need to make a few calls and grab a Coke. You stay with my grandmother until I get back," Ash commands, switching from one uncomfortable topic to another, rather than asking kindly for my help.

I'm just about to retort that in exchange for being with his grandmother at the airport when she collapsed, risking being fired from my job to accompany said grandmother to the hospital, and taking notes when Dr. Mason was talking through Mrs. Eisenberg's diagnosis, his overwhelming gratitude is in order, not his demands. That perhaps

Ash should also stop at the gift shop and pick me up some flowers and maybe a teddy bear. But then, not even trying to hide it, I see Ash wipe away tears that are pooling in his eyes as he searches his grandmother's bedside for tissues. *Great, now I feel like the arrogant ass.*

"I mean"—he softens—"could you please stay with my grand-mother until I get back? I know if she opens her eyes, she will want to see a familiar face."

I give him a *yes, of course* nod.

As Ash fiddles to find the split between the curtains I say to his back, as nonchalantly as I can fake, "Calling your wife to let her know when you'll be home?" I want to let him know that I know he's married.

"No," Ash answers flatly and then turns to look right at me. "I need to call my cousin, Livy. She'll know what to pack and bring to the hospital. And then I need to let folks in my office know I won't be coming in for a couple of weeks."

Leave it to a man to turn the hard work of caretaking over to a woman and beat feet. "Why? Where you going?"

"I'm not going anywhere. I'll be right here by my grandmother's side."

SUNDAY,
MARCH 10

It's 2:30 a.m., and from the 7-11 parking lot to my front door, I have managed to eat around all the blue M&M's. That the blue ones have more preservatives than the other M&M's colors is a falsehood I have lived by since cramming for a physics midterm my sophomore year at UCLA. Or maybe it's a result of the first time I smoked pot and then raided the campus food truck for snacks. I can't remember; they both occurred about the same time. Either way, I rank my M&M's myth up there with the parable of womanhood that if you shave your legs, thicker hair will grow back, or that calories consumed in an airport don't count. I think Dieting Donna started that urban legend.

"I'll take the blue ones," Simon volunteers as he exits the kitchen, surprising the exhaustion right out of me.

"Ack! Simon, what are you doing here?" I accuse, hucking a blue nugget at him.

"You asked me to come back home and be around for the girls. Get them dinner." My confusion turns to recollection of my frantic call to Simon to be with Coco and Lou since I had no idea when I would be getting back. Panicked women can make stupid decisions. "I made them fettuccine with alfredo sauce. I used oat milk. They loved it and didn't even realize it wasn't real cream. There's a cow over in Caliente thanking me right now."

"I bet they noticed but didn't say anything. They didn't want to hurt your feelings and send you running. Again." I collapse onto the couch, spent by the sheer unpredictability of the previous day and the early morning of this next one. "And don't you forget, you left our home."

Simon puts his hands up claiming no blame. "Hey, I'm here at your request, Toni."

I look over at my sorta-spouse, vigorously shake my head, and then refocus on the six-foot familiar foreigner in my living room. Simon's been gone for so long, yet has occupied so much of my thoughts, that his being here seems like a figment of my imagination. Putting on the dutiful dad act by stepping up for the girls this evening makes me wonder what he wants from me. Or worse, from them.

"It's two something in the morning. Why are you still here?"

Simon ignores my time check.

"I had wine with dinner. There's plenty left. Can I get you a glass?" *So, he's drinking wine again. Maybe he was all along in his pursuit of clean living but hid it from me behind his air of Zen zealotry. Either way, at this moment I appreciate his return to hitting the bottle.*

I loudly suck the last of the cheap chocolate out of my teeth and nod. A half glass will quiet my anxiety and prep me to crawl into bed to sleep away the ordeal of my last twenty-four hours.

Simon waltzes back into the living room with two glasses. I should have specified I wanted one glass, to myself, by myself, while Simon scurries off into the night. The mandala beads around his wrist clink on one of the glasses, keeping time as he walks to the couch.

"Here. I can tell you need this." Simon hands me a distinct over-pour. "So, what happened tonight?"

I purse my lips, considering if I want to bring Simon into this evening's events—or any aspect of my life. I take a long sip to buy time to formulate in my head how much talking I want to do, or if now is the time to force Simon to start talking. And if he does talk, am I even ready to hear anything he has to say? I take one more drawn-out sip to allow my slow-firing synapses to adjust and to make Simon squirm.

"Why are you back here?" I press further, my eyes narrow, and I straighten my legs, pushing the heels of my feet hard into Simon's thigh, my body taking up the majority of the couch. He is not swayed by my attempt to shove him off the sofa and out of my house. To speed up the process of unwinding, I take two more big gulps from my glass, as if pinot grigio and my favorite, Diet Coke, are the same refreshment. Almost immediately I realize a single bag of M&M's in twelve hours is not absorbing the alcohol at the rate I am consuming it. I feel a little liquid courage, with a side of lightheadedness, mollifying my mind and—more concerning—my judgment.

"If you don't want to talk about tonight, how about telling me what's up with the dozens of jars lining the kitchen counters? They smell pretty good."

Ah. So, we're both evading. I can keep playing that game straight up. Vamos.

"Nope, we're not going to talk about that either," I state, finishing off my wine and picking up Simon's to pour half of what he's barely touched into my glass.

The grown-up grape juice is loosening the muscles in my neck as I roll my head left and right. My shoulders have been frozen in fear, stuck near my ears since Mrs. Eisenberg collapsed in the ladies' room. Relaxing into the equivalent of an alcohol massage, my shoulders drop back into place as a wash of fatigue settles heavy in my limbs. I may never leave this couch.

With my eyelids closed, my feet sense a disturbance on the other end of the sofa. I crack an eye and spy Simon burrowing into the well-worn cushions. I'm too drowsy to warn him not to get comfy, he'll be leaving soon.

"Thank you for getting here so quickly for the girls," I offer, in momentary truce. "How'd you manage to make it back in such a short time? Your folks are a good forty minutes away," I mumble, with as much vigor and interest as a stoned koala drifting off to sleep.

"I'm not staying with my parents. I'm in an Airbnb only a mile or so from here," Simon reports, reaching over to untie my shoes. "I wanted to be as close to Lou and Coco as possible. And to you too."

Images of Lou and Coco sleeping at their father's aseptic short-term rental when I thought they were at the Antonellis' roll through my fatigued mind. If I had an ounce of strength, I would kick him hard for doing that to me, and then kick him a hundred more times for everything else he has done to us.

Simon continues, "Anyway, it's a week-to-week rental. Seems to me I should be staying here, in my own house." Simon's green eyes bore into my droopy ones. "The place the four of us belong."

My jaw drops open. *What is he getting at?*

Catching my disbelief at his gall, Simon adds, "I mean, I'm happy to stay on the couch. I just want to be under the same roof with you and the girls, like it used to be."

I kick Simon hard, but his body doesn't flinch, and his eyes stay locked in on me.

"Wait, wait, what the hell are you saying?" I question, now lucid, but also confused where this is going. As Simon begins to pull off both my socks, I'm thankful, for once, I let Lou paint my toes Lovely Lilac Unicorn. I told her it is the most Silicon Valley nail polish name ever, but my tech joke was lost on my budding beautician.

"I'm saying"—Simon looks around the four corners of the room—"I should be here, Toni. We're still married. Yes, I lost my way for a while, but I found my way back. And you're still my wife, and I'm still your husband." Simon's claim comes across like he owns something. "And I still own this house." *There it is.*

"Add real estate to the list of things I don't want to talk about tonight. It's been one hell of a day, Simon, and I'm not in the mood to start with you."

"We're dancing around the things we need to discuss, Toni. Us and why you're getting home close to three a.m. You decide where we start," Simon declares, like I owe him any explanation. He's at least smart enough to pour the rest of his wine into my glass.

Or you can leave, I think to myself but don't say out loud, because even if it is the wrong person, for all the wrong reasons, having another adult in the house at the end of this supreme disaster of a day feels better than being alone. Even if it is Simon.

Not having the energy to discuss us, which I know would roll into the hours when Coco and Lou wake, I plan to skim the events of my day, then send Simon on his way. I put my feet in Simon's lap and wiggle my bare toes because, well, the very least he can do is rub them. Without hesitation, he wraps his sizable hands around my left foot and uses the strength of his thumbs to massage my instep. With every pressure point, I appreciate how Simon's touch gained in intensity and confidence when he began his yoga journey. My toes unfurl and my head lolls in the middle of recounting my trip to the ER with Mrs. Eisenberg. I choose not to mention Ash.

By the time I get to the part of my story where Dr. Mason diagnoses Mrs. Eisenberg's bathroom fall, Simon's hands have moved from my left foot to my right, and then they continue up my calves. Now three hefty glasses of wine in, and looser than I have been since I accidentally took two of Zwena's muscle relaxers thinking they were Advil, my guardedness about Simon's presence has eased. He moves his body closer to mine to better knead his way from my calves to the meaty place where my hamstrings and glutes meet. I hear a tiny voice, lodged in that part of the brain no woman wants to listen to, reminding me that liquor and languidness are a dangerous combination. I shut that voice down and abandon my God-given common sense.

Nudging my legs open, Simon growls my name so deeply, it sounds like a lullaby rocking my body into giving in to his touch. "Toni, I'm going to kiss you."

"Hmmm," is all my buzzed mind can manage. The first kiss lands so lightly, I'm not fully aware if it happened or if I imagined it. I'm in that limbo state right before sleep overtakes wakefulness.

Another kiss lands on my mouth, stronger, more intentional, parting my lips to announce that Simon is indeed there. Here. Home. With me.

We come together in a flurry of lips and tongues, familiarity and forgetfulness of all that has occurred before in a momentary dismantling of the guarded walls I have erected since Simon walked out the door. I'm lucid enough to know this kiss can't erase the grief he has caused me, but under the sway of the intimacy of these hands on my body and the recognizable taste of his mouth on mine, I give in to the respite his arms offer.

As Simon's lips move down my neck, my breath quickens and I turn my head left, the full span of my right side exposed, begging for more. It's then that I glimpse the corner of the manila envelope from my lawyer between the books on the shelf, only now there's a bowl with crusted milk and Honey Nut Cheerios sitting on top compliments of a teenager too lazy to make the trek to the kitchen sink.

What am I doing?! That voice in the back of my head alarms, working to halt this forbidden pleasure.

Gettin' some action, I answer the voice back as Simon unbuttons my blouse and slips his hand under my bra strap. I bite down hard on my lip, not wanting to give Simon the satisfaction of knowing how much I've missed this, but also not wanting him to stop.

But what about the girls? The question nags at me. My body has completely disassociated itself, choosing missed affection over rationalization. *This is so selfish. Simon rolls back into town and then what? Really,* then what? *The girls wake up to find their dad back in my bed like nothing ever happened?*

Only twenty more minutes, my libido argues. *Or an hour. The girls will never know as long as Simon is out by sunrise.*

Perfect, I acquiesce as I shift first my left and then my right arm for Simon to slip off my shirt. *Now I'm negotiating hookups with myself.*

As Simon leans back in to lock lips while he toggles with a bra he's unhooked a hundred times before, I push him back to his upright position. I unbuckle the belt around his waist, and Simon's eyes go wide. I give a sly smile, shake my head, and whisper, "Not yet" with a smoothness that lets him know, soon. Simon will get what he wants, and I will get what I need, what I remember.

Starting at his bellybutton, I ignore the Buddha sitting on top of the slogan "Heavily Meditated" on his T-shirt and tug the fitted cotton blend out the top of his waistband. Two smooth muscles peek out at me, urging me to find four more just like them. As my hands roam around Simon's lower abs, he begins to wiggle, simultaneously pulling away from too much pleasure and begging for more. As my hands slide up his sides, bringing the blue T-shirt with me, Simon lets out a guttural moan and impatience gets the best of him as he rips his own shirt up and over his head.

"The *fuck*?!" I cry out and then freeze, praying my voice could not possibly wake two teens deep in sleep. "What are those?!" I hiss, pointing at Simon's chest.

"The nipple rings?" Simon states in the form of a question. Clasping his hands behind his head, he flexes his manscaped chest for my benefit.

"Yes, those!" I emphasize, shock laced with horror in my voice.

"I got them in Bangkok at a twenty-four-hour tattoo parlor all the expats go to." Simon flicks one of them and smiles with pride.

I'm pretty sure when it comes to getting tattoos and piercings, those expats, including Simon, would be better off waiting until they return home and return to their senses.

"Stop flexing!" I insist and shake my head to force my brain back to sobriety. "What are you, twenty years old again? And what kind of health standards exist in Thailand that inspired you to allow someone to mutilate your nipples?!"

"The guy who owns it is British. The Aussies go there too. The owner even offered me green tea while I chose my rings," Simon explains, like he's listing off the amenities of a five-star spa. I throw up in my mouth just a little.

"What? Don't you like them?" Simon asks, genuine surprise in his voice, like we've just met through Tinder, and he knows nothing of the science-nerd germaphobe that I am. "They're a real turn-on when you pull them." He reaches for my hand, trying to recapture the mood. "Give it a try."

"Hell no, I'm not stretching your nipples," I say, and recoil, face contorted and full-on judgy. "What if a ring pops loose or falls out with your skin still attached." I stick my tongue out in disgust. "Not to mention they look terrible."

"On me? Come on. You know I look tight for forty-five."

"On anyone," I assert and cover myself up with the blanket across the back of the sofa. Bad-judgment time is over. Well, obviously not for Simon, but for me.

"So, I guess you don't want to know what I've done below the waist. It's . . ."

"Nope. Nope. No, I don't. That's it, we're done," I declare, handing Simon his shirt.

"Come on, Toni, you have to admit we had fun tonight," Simon works to convince me, redressing slowly so I can take in one last look at his yoga-cut arms and torso.

"Some people are saved by the bell. Tonight, Simon, I was saved by a couple of silver rings," I deadpan and point to his shoes by the front door. "It's time for you to leave."

"I'll go for now, but I'm not leaving for good. We are husband and wife, Toni," Simon vows earnestly, hand over heart and nipple ring, slipping on his Birkenstock clogs as he opens the front door. I have to get up in four short hours to take the girls to a debate tournament, so I am not going to get into it with him that for me, the wife, any vow Simon makes, particularly his marital vow of "till death do us part," means nada.

"Muscle memory, Simon. You've left before. Shouldn't be too hard to do it again," I remind my halfway husband before hopping up to double bolt the door behind him.

APRIL

WEDNESDAY, APRIL 10

"Brown Butter, Baby!" I articulate before my face sets.

"I still like it," Zwena utters stiffly.

"¡Callad, chicas!" Gloria attempts to shush the two of us and taps one of my spoons against Zwena's forehead. "The mask hasn't hardened enough to crack. Stop talking and lay still," Gloria instructs, like she's baking a cake and it needs a few more minutes to cool before serving. "Once it's set, it needs to stay on another thirty minutes, then basta."

"I like the name too." Prideful, I shimmy from the neck down, careful not to move my head. Lying on my living room floor, propped up on throw pillows from the couch, I stretch my arm out straight and poke Zwena's shoulder so she can give me a high five without much movement, fearful of another reprimand from Gloria.

After several weeks of polling Zwena, Krish, Dieting Donna, my boss, and even Mr. Chen to consider a laundry list of possible names for my company, I held a vote last Thursday. We were all working the same shift, and I was picking up Mr. Chen from visiting his homecoming queen. There was only one dissenting opinion among the group, but I'm pretty sure Donna was just in a bitter mood from suffering through her juice cleanse, so I went with the group's vote for Brown Butter, Baby! Now that I have registered the name as an LLC with the State of California, it's official. I'm a company with not one sale to my name and increasing debt. But I love to hear myself say Brown Butter, Baby! out loud any chance I get.

I texted Mrs. Eisenberg with the hope that sharing the list of name options would give her something to focus on during her convalescence, and to engage her greatest strength, doling out opinions. Plus, I figured she would get a kick out of a few of the odder choices, all of them submitted by Zwena. My assumption was that someone would check Mrs. Eisenberg's phone for her, since most likely her hands aren't dexterous enough to do it herself. But I never heard back. When I left the hospital the night of Mrs. Eisenberg's stroke, Ash promised he would keep in touch with me concerning his grandmother's recovery, but the past few weeks it's been quiet. A time or two I've held my fingers over my phone poised to bombard Ash with the extensive list of questions I have on how our desert bird is doing and to investigate the care she's receiving, but I've held back. Ash is surely guaranteeing his grandmother is in the hands of the best healthcare professionals the Bay Area has to offer, and I imagine that in addition to her doting family, Mrs. Eisenberg has loads of friends checking in on her and what I can presume is a team of rotating therapists.

Though I think of her often, I have begrudgingly accepted that I may never see Mrs. Eisenberg again, her stroke most likely ending her traveling days. With the lack of communication from Ash on behalf of his grandmother, I'm beginning to believe that my relationship with Mrs. Eisenberg may not exist beyond the airport. If I'd known our friendship was going to come to such an abrupt end, I would have been more deliberate about writing down all her gems of life advice.

"Has Simon been back sniffing around since, you know?" Zwena asks. Her face stiff from the mask, she points to her nipples in case I couldn't understand her. I shift my eyeballs far left toward my mother, hoping Zwena will pick up my *not now* girl code signal.

"He's been by a time or two," I reluctantly admit, knowing my friend will react with prejudice. Zwena scrunches her nose, unable to itch it or not liking the smell of my answer, I'm not sure which. "For the most part I just have him picking the girls up from school when he wants to see them."

"Pole pole, dada," Zwena says softly.

I hear the loving concern in her voice, even if I can't translate the meaning of the words.

"Go slowly, sister. Forward is the way your feet are pointing," Zwena clarifies for me without having to be asked.

"I hear you." I know, lying next to me, Zwena is unconvinced. "I promise, I hear you," I say with 93 percent conviction.

"Did you know right and left shoes weren't made until 1818 in Philadelphia? Before then, they were the same shape." Glad to know as easy as we swung into the topic of Simon, we have just as easily swung back out.

"You don't need to know the history of fashion for your test," I assert. Since Zwena decided to become a US citizen, Krish and I have been assaulted with trivial American tidbits. Though I was interested to learn that there have been eight presidents who were left-handed like me, Zwena is doing a terrible job differentiating between facts that may be on the test and what might land her on *Jeopardy!*.

"Back to you and Simon." This conversation is making me dizzy. "Have you told Krish what's going on with you two?"

"No, I haven't said anything to Krish, he's disliked Simon longer than you have."

"That's true. Then what about the girls? Do they know?" Zwena is as protective of Lou's and Coco's hearts as a blood aunt would be.

"Know what?" my mom pipes up, trying to get in on our business.

"*Ehrm* . . . know that you are really the brains behind my beauty line." On the fly I come up with an answer that will no doubt appeal to the sweet spot of Gloria's ego.

The past few months, while working through my cacao lotion formula and perfecting the match to my original four skin tones, my mom dropped at least a half dozen not so subtle hints that, in our family, she is actually the one with brown woman beauty expertise. Working against her know-it-all nature to gloat, te lo dije, I believe the last words Gloria chose to plead her case to be involved with my project were, "Trust me, mi amor, it's not just what's on the inside that counts."

My mother was thrilled when I finally called to invite her over and asked her to show me how to use the ground cacao shells as a substitute for clay powder when making a detoxifying face mask. Gloria jumped at the opportunity to play spa director and insisted I have Zwena over as well to get in on the cosmetic counsel she has been waiting her whole life to impart.

Arriving an hour ahead of when I invited her, with the bags she utilizes to transport all the makeup she employs on her Senior Connection clients, Gloria took the invitation a step too far. She thought we were going to have a full-on tutorial into the sacred practices of beautification, not something more along the lines of a lesson in restorative sciences. Zwena was game since she was heading from my house out on a mystery date, probably with an Alaska Airlines pilot she's been eyeing who flies the SFO-Tokyo route. I, however, marched my mother back outside to leave her makeup cases in the car, to both of their disappointments. *One step at a time.* I successfully tempered my mom's efforts and insisted on facials only. Surprisingly Gloria agreed to my terms, pleased, for now, to be included.

While my strategy is set to launch Brown Butter, Baby! with my four foundational lotion shades, face masks may be in the future if all goes according to my Pioneering Entrepreneurs business plan. Gloria riffled through the kitchen cupboards and found my measuring cup to make a ratio of one part milk to three parts water to mix with the cacao powder. I wondered aloud if it would be more nourishing for our skin if the mask base was all milk, or even better, half-and-half, to which Gloria shot me a look of alarm. Growing up in the rural hills of Puerto Rico, for my mother milk was a commodity not to be wasted as it wasn't cheap unless you were milking the cow yourself. Adding water to the milk made the creamy mixture go further, allowing the paste to be shared by more women in the community.

Gloria added a tablespoon of cacao powder at a time to the liquid blend, stirring until the measuring cup was full of a thick paste the consistency of Greek yogurt. Once her concoction had thickened, cayenne pepper was added. Noticing the doubt on our faces, my mom assured us that the heat of cayenne brings blood to the surface of the skin, urging the pores to open up and breathe, creating a long-lasting glow. Just thinking about the heat, I nearly broke out in a sweat.

My mouth and my wallet protested when my mom cranked the thermostat before applying the paste, but Gloria insisted the pumped-in high heat would be the closest thing to relaxing in the Puerto Rican sun, thereby aiding the mask's firming process.

With the concoction applied to our faces and hardening like Magic Shell, Gloria wiggles her body between me and Zwena, reminds us to lie as still as statues, and then scrolls through Amazon Prime until she has found her favorite Jennifer Lopez movie, *Maid in Manhattan*. There is nothing my mother enjoys more than a Puerto Rican rags-to-riches story, and we have watched this one together at least a dozen times. With the mention of J. Lo, Gloria points out that—objectively speaking, of course, given her genes—I'm prettier than Mrs. Affleck. Disagreeing is pointless, since nothing gives Gloria greater pleasure than believing J. Lo is a lesser version of her daughter, but I know this will end up being mocking material for Zwena. I'm annoyed it isn't possible to snack on popcorn with my face plastered into place.

After we abide fortyish minutes in the mask, Gloria stops the movie just as J. Lo considers applying for the housekeeping managerial job in the fake high-end hotel where she works. I usually lose interest in the movie around then anyway, preferring that she be saved by her brains and hustle, not by her dashing costar. Gloria walks us to the kitchen sink, instructs us to lean over, hands both of us a spoon, and directs us to tap, tap, tap to crack our faces like an egg. A few solid knocks allow me to begin to move my jaw and then raise and lower my eyebrows, causing the mask to crumble into the sink on its own.

I hear the distinct ding of my phone on the kitchen table and snap at Zwena to grab it before my mom does. Lou and Coco are with Simon, and I have yet to tell Gloria any details about her son-in-law having returned to town.

I grab a bar of soap to wash the mask residue off my face, and Gloria knocks it right out of my hand. "Only water," she admonishes me. "Let nature's product do the work." My mother is enjoying showing off her experience and bossing me around a little extra.

With my hair pulled up in a terry cloth towel, face mask mud splatters on my white T-shirt. Specks of cacao still sit in the crevices of my nose and ears, and I splash my face with clean water once more. It's Zwena's turn at the sink. I gesture for my phone, but Zwena ignores me, busy reading my texts. As a broad smile grows across her face, her mask cracks from ear to ear and pieces of chocolate bark crumble onto my kitchen floor.

I pluck my phone out of Zwena's hand, hoping to God Simon has not taken to sexting or forwarding pics of pierced body parts.

6:22 p.m. (Ash)

My grandmother has been asking for you.

MONDAY, APRIL 22

Arriving for my visit, I am buzzed in through a set of wrought iron gates that open onto a rose bush–lined driveway that seems as long as an airport runway. Without someone to thank for entry, nor to ask where to park, I decide it's best to hide my car under an ancient redwood tree. Two marble elephants flank the black-lacquered double front doors, and I can't help but reach out and pat one of them on the head. Ash answers the doorbell that rings with the dynamism of Vatican church bells, no doubt having to echo loud enough to be heard throughout the enormous house. Unlike his usual tailored suit, Ash's outfit this afternoon is more understated than I would have expected, though no less fitted. He's wearing a collared shirt open at the neck that hugs his broad shoulders and looks woven for his specific frame. Ash invites me in and motions me through a gaping doorway as I enter the foyer. As I pass, I notice Ash has a fresh shave and that he smells of sandalwood and some other cloying spice that tickles my nose and makes me sneak another glance at him.

I know Mrs. Eisenberg has dough, but I had no idea sweet Eddie, may he rest in peace, had been such a mogul. This house whispers wealth. It shouts refinement. And though, in all our time riding side by side, Mrs. Eisenberg has never been one to hold back on an anecdote, it now occurs to me that her stories are almost always about other people.

Mrs. Eisenberg rarely shares about her own past, and she certainly never shared with me what Eddie did for a living. Walking through the rooms decorated in soft neutrals punctuated by mixed and matched patterned pastels, I'm curious as hell.

"No fucking way! Is this Steve Jobs?" I squawk in surprise, pointing to a framed picture on the fireplace mantel of the young Apple founder with his arm around a middle-aged Mrs. Eisenberg wearing the hell out of a suit with eighties shoulder pads. Too late, I cover my mouth realizing the f-bomb I let slip as a guest in the stateliest house I have ever set foot in.

"It sure as shit is," Mrs. Eisenberg articulates slowly, determined to speak as clearly as possible out of the right side of her mouth, her left still recovering from the stroke.

I love an old lady who can curse, and I'm pleased Mrs. Eisenberg hasn't lost her candor. Cross fingers, when I'm eighty-eight I will have embraced my tempered vices. I'm planning on smoking cigarettes, hydrating with Diet Coke, and cursing like a car mechanic.

"Bring that over to me." Mrs. Eisenberg waves with her right hand. Before I can pick it up, Ash swoops in to grab the photo and deliver it to his grandmother, who is tucked tightly into the couch under several Easter egg–colored cashmere throws. When I tell Zwena about these digs and the type of people and circles Mrs. Eisenberg runs with, she's going to suggest I appoint our desert dame in charge of finding me a new man. Zwena was not impressed I almost slept with my old one.

"He was a good businessman." Mrs. Eisenberg taps the frame. "Not too proud to listen to my ideas in the early decades of his company." On the coffee table within arm's reach of Mrs. Eisenberg is a menagerie of medicine bottles. She's clearly a little high off her pill cocktail, so I'm not going to step on the tall tales Mrs. Eisenberg is lost in telling.

"Terrible father, though, that Steve Jobs," Mrs. Eisenberg concludes, handing the photo back to Ash. "It is possible to be a good CEO and a good parent at the same time, he just never figured that one out." Ah, so she read his eldest daughter's tell-all too. I take note that if Mrs. Eisenberg is stuck at home for several more weeks, I will bring some of my favorite memoirs for her to read, and then we can discuss. *I wouldn't mind spending more time in this house.*

"Hope the traffic wasn't too bad getting here and you found your way without a problem," Ash chimes in, probably to cut his grandmother off from any more prescription-induced anecdotes that may prove embarrassing. *Please, Ash, check yourself.* I have Google Maps and a brain, and while I may not know anyone who lives along the monied streets of Atherton, I can certainly figure out how to get here from my side of the highway.

Ignoring Ash's attempt at small talk bordering on insult, I tell Mrs. Eisenberg, "I brought something just for you. Hold on a minute while I grab my bag from the foyer." I know better than to call the entry into Mrs. Eisenberg's house a *hallway.* My whole house could fit in her foyer.

I clink my way back into the sun-soaked living room, the multiple jars banging around in my tote bag. I'm glad to see Mrs. Eisenberg's eyes light up with a familiar twinkle of curiosity that I feared would be lost forever.

"Ash, could you please get us drinks," Mrs. Eisenberg instructs her grandson, not taking her eyes off me.

"Of course. What would you like?" I spy Mrs. Eisenberg rolling her eyes at Ash's question.

"How about finding out first what our guest would like," Mrs. Eisenberg admonishes him like she's talking to a toddler. "We have everything, Antonia. Except wine. Even though it's after five o'clock, no one in this house will let me have my chardonnay with two ice cubes. Simply barbaric," Mrs. Eisenberg declares while pointing her index finger toward Ash, apparently the accused barbarian.

"What are you allowed to have?" I ask, content to join Mrs. Eisenberg in whatever will bring her a little cheer.

"Club soda with lime," Ash answers before Mrs. Eisenberg can suggest another option.

"Boring but true," she accepts. Then she kindly offers, "But Antonia, honey, you can have whatever you would like. I'm sure Ash will join you in a cocktail."

"None for me, thanks," Ash replies, indicating there is no chance of him partaking, confirming my suspicion that there is not a fun bone in this man's body.

"He's being dull," Mrs. Eisenberg concludes like she has just read my mind. Regardless of her assessment of her grandson, I can see, the way her eyes follow Ash around the room, that after Eddie, he is the absolute love of her life.

"Club soda with lime sounds great," I agree to curtail any family bickering. "I like two limes and a lot of ice," I tell Ash, enjoying him serving me.

"You heard her," Mrs. Eisenberg says to move Ash along so we can get down to the business of examining my lotions.

I'm hopeful Mrs. Eisenberg will be proud of the progress I've made. At least I can provide her a few moments of entertainment outside the hours of daily speech and physical therapy she's endured since coming home from the hospital.

When Ash finally texted to invite me over, I was, admittedly, relieved that my time with Mrs. Eisenberg had not come to an abrupt end. My father, Simon, Mrs. Eisenberg; too many people in my life had suddenly and unexpectedly disappeared. I was missing Mrs. Eisenberg's check-ins on my product progress and her pushing me to figure out the next step, relentlessly urging me toward action, no matter how small. I know she is only one of many elderly women I help navigate the airport, but Mrs. Eisenberg, more than anyone else in my life, has demonstrated sincere interest in my capabilities. She has held me accountable to either moving forward fabulously or failing fantastically, persistent that I not be afraid of either direction.

I figured it was a fair trade. I got a boost of professional encouragement from Mrs. Eisenberg, and she got to complain about Elaine and life in her gated golfing community. But, truth is, with no communication between us for more than a month, I had to dig up my own motivation and personal accountability from my younger days, and it was tough. I missed Mrs. Eisenberg's joke about how to eat an elephant. Her wise maxims help stop me from getting ahead of myself and from sinking too deep into the headspace where all my *can'ts* are housed. If I had a dollar for every time Mrs. Eisenberg told me, *You get what you work for not what you wish for,* I would have no problem financing Brown Butter, Baby! myself. Given Mrs. Eisenberg's regular reminders of my potential, I finally have something tangible to show for it.

When I got the text from Ash, knowing I would be seeing Mrs. Eisenberg stoked my fire. In the week between my invitation to her home and now, I landed on the perfect size of glass jars I wanted to use. I settled on clear glass for its repurposing and recycling potential, but also so customers can see the lotion and determine which shade best matches their skin tone. With the help of Lou and Coco, I designed a Brown Butter, Baby! logo. By pure coincidence, my Stanford professor asked the class to look into the multitude of distribution channels available for new products we were interested in bringing to market. I took the assignment one step further and outlined the dozens of hurdles I will most likely face when trying to launch Brown Butter, Baby! into the world.

I neatly line up my four lotion shades on the coffee table in front of Mrs. Eisenberg, like little soldiers reporting for duty. I can tell she's reserving commentary until after I have presented my all-in-one lotion elevator pitch. As I begin my prepared talk, I spy her biting her lower lip, seemingly holding back enthusiasm. That small indication of advanced praise gives me the spark I need to speak up, even with Ash, a venture capitalist icon, looming in the next room.

"Here I have the first four products of my Brown Butter, Baby! all-natural, all-in-one lotions. I have perfected the specifications for four skin tones, but more will be released down the road." I give Mrs. Eisenberg a moment to take in each jar before I continue. "The first I call Diospyros, which is the scientific name for ebony wood found in East Africa. I named this one for women like Zwena who are lucky enough to walk this world with skin so deeply melanated they barely need SPF." Standing between the coffee table and Mrs. Eisenberg on the couch, I hold up the first jar, label facing my friend so she can admire the font I selected. "Next is called Theobroma for a tree that is endemic to the Caribbean, which I matched to my mom's chestnut skin. As you can see, Theobroma is lighter than Diospyros, but not as light as Nephelium, labeled for the Middle Eastern–grown rambutan tree. This shade is for those with a henna hue to their skin like mine."

I hold the fourth jar up to Mrs. Eisenberg's forearm so she can see how closely the lotion matches her skin tone, typical to those who live near the Mediterranean, even if she has missed the last month in the sun. I share with her that I want to elevate my lotions by using correct scientific names, so I opted for each cream to be named for the genus of a tree. That decision I felt was genius.

"So, last but not least," I proudly proclaim, "is Prunus, which I mixed for White women who have a darker pigmentation, like you, Mrs. Eisenberg."

"I don't know what you mean by *genus*, but it sounds like you named my skin shade after a prune tree," Mrs. Eisenberg concludes after what I thought was a very thorough and professional presentation. The first one I have given about my product line.

"Well, botanists refer to it as prunus dulcis, so I also named you after something sweet," I offer, dismissing Mrs. Eisenberg's concern.

"It's still a prune tree."

"It's actually an almond tree."

"Almonds are wrinkled too," Mrs. Eisenberg insists, not the least bit swayed.

Mrs. Eisenberg doesn't realize that mixing each blend to create the first four hues of Brown Butter, Baby! was easier and caused less brain strain than naming the shades. When I think of Zwena's skin, so rich in melanin, my mind appreciates the biochemistry involved in its creation, the wonder of its power against the sun, the possible efficacy of its chemical makeup to be used to treat skin cancer. The science of it is astonishing to me.

I tried other paths to describe skin colors, but there are people who feel some type of way about being called *fudge brick, nut brown, coffee colored,* or *dark chocolate.* Since starting this labeling endeavor, I've often reflected on the nagging gatekeeping ringing in the back of my head: "Do I look like food to you!?" Finding words to describe Zwena's inky color, or mine that is mixed-race, without insulting customers and inciting cancelers, makes my head spin and has certainly kept me up at night worrying. To stay safely out of the language wars, I decided to stick with the scientific names of indigenous trees for my initial color formulas. Science is proven, methodical, and predictable; the probability of falling under the heel of cancel culture is not.

"Give me that wrinkly hand," I instruct Mrs. Eisenberg with a wink. I place the jar in Mrs. Eisenberg's palm, having observed her right side is by far her stronger hand and luckily her dominant side.

"Nice branding," Mrs. Eisenberg judges, not taking her eyes off my logo design. "Not too trendy or targeted to a narrow age bracket."

I grin listening to Mrs. Eisenberg toss out business lingo. Probably due to a long month listening to Ash talk at her about possible investment opportunities. Maybe I'll invite myself to come back again next week for another Brown Butter, Baby! update and to watch a movie with her for a change in entertainment. There's a new comedy out with George Clooney, who I know for a fact Mrs. Eisenberg fancies. She takes my *People* magazines every time he graces the cover.

Ash rejoins us, carrying our drinks in textured highball glasses on a pretty wooden serving tray with gold handles.

"Ash, the logo reminds me a bit of Maxwell Street Records, don't you think?"

Resting his hand on his grandmother's shoulder, Ash agrees with a gentleness in his voice I haven't heard before. "Sure does."

We are all looking at the jar in Mrs. Eisenberg's hand when she asks demurely, "Would you mind opening this for me, Antonia?"

Turning red, I quickly pluck the container out of her hand. How insensitive of me not to realize that with the jar in her good hand, there is no way her left could unscrew the top.

"It's okay," Mrs. Eisenberg assures me, reading concern on my face. "I'm just grateful to be here. Alive with a bad arm is better than the alternative."

"It sure is," I agree and pick up Mrs. Eisenberg's left arm to massage in a healthy dollop of Prunus cream. Ash audibly clears his throat in uneasiness at his grandmother's allusion to death.

"But the names of your products are terrible."

Ash takes his grandmother's bluntness as his cue to flee the living room.

"No, they're not. They're proper scientific names for the tree that each skin tone represents." I am not going to be the one to convince Mrs. Eisenberg of the consequences of colorization. The topic of racial labels is bigger than body lotion and too big for a Monday afternoon visit.

"It's too hard to remember any of these names. And frankly, who cares what the accurate scientific term is. What you should care about is how anyone, when they go into Walgreens, is going to ask for, for . . . hell, I can't even remember any of the names, and I just heard them. Brand recognition and name retrieval mean everything for retail sales."

I smile along with Mrs. Eisenberg's feedback, but I know that the cream names are just fine. It's her short-term memory that's not firing at her age and that's absolutely normal, particularly after a massive health scare. Plus, age and stroke aside, if it's not Chanel, Dior, or Elizabeth Arden, is someone like Mrs. Eisenberg really going to remember a product like mine anyway? Or go into Walgreens? Women of any age who are well-to-doers like Mrs. Eisenberg are shopping for their beauty products at department stores like Neiman Marcus, ducking aggressive salespeople to reach the counters of their preferred high-end labels. Though I love her input, at the end of the day, I do not consider Mrs. Eisenberg my target market.

"Well, do what you think is best," Mrs. Eisenberg says begrudgingly, tugging one of the piled-on throws over her chest. "But don't discredit my input because I'm old." I drop my head, shocked that Mrs. Eisenberg has read my mind. "I've been around more than twice as long as you've been alive, Antonia. Believe me, I know some things, and I've certainly bought some things."

Taking in this house over the last hour, I can't argue with her purchasing power.

"I know," I say to appease Mrs. Eisenberg, and I make a mental note to get product line feedback from my classmates at Stanford. That's whose expertise I really should be tapping.

"I'm feeling tired. Do you mind keeping Ash company for a bit while I take a catnap? These past weeks all he's been doing is working and taking care of me. I think he could use some company his own age."

Ah, of course. Ash must have himself a trophy wife years younger than him. Típico.

"Sure, I can stay for a little while longer," I promise Mrs. Eisenberg, but her eyes are already closed, indicating taking my leave wasn't a choice.

I stand and quietly pick up our finished club soda tumblers from the coffee table. I lean over to turn off the decorative lamp above Mrs. Eisenberg's head and the ice tinks in the glasses, but she doesn't move. Tiptoeing into the kitchen, I'm met with Ash who, before I can even soap up the tumblers, tells me, "My grandmother's not wrong. Your lotion names won't work on the market. Brand recognition is everything. And if people can't pronounce what they want, let alone remember it, you're sunk."

"Excuse me?" I ask, purposely leaving the glasses on the counter. Ash puts them in the dishwasher without calling me out. As he dries his hands on a dishtowel, Ash's eyes move left to the kitchen table in the lamest invitation to sit down I've ever received.

"Is this an example of the 'free advice' you were so generously offering me?" I do as his eyes suggest and pull out a chair, determined to stay for five minutes tops because that's what his grandmother asked me to do.

"It's as good a place to start as any," Ash counters, clearly enjoying the banter that comes with throwing around business ideas.

"Beautiful kitchen," I observe, stretching to make small talk that has nothing to do with my product line. "I could prepare enough bacalaítos to feed an entire town on that eight-burner gas stove." Mrs. Eisenberg's kitchen looks like an *Architectural Digest* photoshoot with a special sponsorship by Wolf.

"My grandmother's not much of a cook, but I'd love to try your bacala—what were those?" Ash says, butchering the dish's name.

"Bacalaítos. It's a salted cod fritter. Lots of prep and plenty of kitchen space required."

"Sounds tasty," he says, licking his lips and carrying a bag of tortilla chips and a container of salsa over to the table. Of course, because we live in California and I have light-brown skin, Ash makes an attempt to serve snacks from my culture. *Joke's on him, I hate tomatoes.*

"Your grandmother probably has her own cook," I assume out loud.

"A few days a week, but Bubbe isn't eating the food at the rate Emma is making it." Huh, this is the first time I have heard Ash refer to his grandmother by an affectionate name.

"You call Mrs. Eisenberg Bubbe?" I ask. "Kind of an undignified nickname for your grandmother, isn't it?"

"It's common Yiddish for grandmother. It's what I've always called her."

"Oh. My girls go to Catholic school," I say in my defense, placing the blame of my ignorance on Coco, Lou, and their Christian-focused education.

"What does your family call your mom?" Ash asks, appearing genuinely interested—which throws me for a second.

"A busybody."

"Ah. Bubbe can mean that too," Ash jokes, putting me at ease.

"So, what did Eddie do to get all . . . this?" I ask and circle my arms around my head indicating the entire acre-plus property. I realize how rude of a question that may have been to ask and drop my limbs in embarrassment.

"My grandfather? He was a trumpet player in Chicago," Ash answers breezily, seeming eager to talk. Maybe life has been a little quiet for him the last few weeks.

I stare blankly at Ash because a midwestern musician to Silicon Valley mansion owner does not compute. Maybe ol' Eddie made his money the old-fashioned way—he married into it.

"Have you never asked my grandmother about her life?" Ash whispers when we hear Mrs. Eisenberg shift on the couch. I can't tell if there is a hint of condescension in his question or if this is an indictment of my conversational skills.

"Of course, I have," I insist, and too late I hear the defensiveness in my voice. "From what your grandmother has told me, she and Eddie had a beautiful love story."

Ash chuckles and rocks his chair onto its back legs.

"Yeah, they did. Their love story is the stuff of legends. But my grandmother, she's the real legend."

I grab a chip but don't dip it in the salsa. I'm determined to stay for only a few more minutes, but something about the reverence with which Ash uses the term *legend* makes me want to hear the account from his point of view. Pushing the snack bowl closer to me, Ash looks pleased I'm sharing food at his table, but he doesn't continue.

"Well, okay then, are you going to leave me out on this cliffhanger to guess the rest of the story on my own?" I tease. *Whoa, was that flirting? Where'd that come from?*

Ash grins at my eagerness. "Okay then, here goes. At age six, my grandmother was one of the very last Jews to make it out of France. It was 1941, and though many Americans were sympathetic to what was happening to European Jews, they didn't want them here. Her escaping France and reaching the United States was a miracle."

I can sense Ash relaxing into the retold family tale. He taps the two middle fingers of his right hand on the tabletop in a gesture that seems to help him continue. "With the financial aid of some private organization—I forget the name of it—my grandmother traveled by boat with a neighbor lady my great-grandparents paid to take care of her during the passage and then get her on the right train from New York to Chicago. Bubbe's dad pinned a piece of paper in her coat with the name and address of an uncle there. Her mom sewed her engagement ring into the hem. The way Bubbe tells it, the ring was a flawless diamond. The plan was that her uncle Harry could sell it at a pawn shop to help pay for living expenses for the two of them when Bubbe reached Chicago."

"Good thinking," I say while wondering if I could ever send my own daughters off to a foreign land at that young of an age. As a mother, it's devastating to even imagine such a life-and-death decision. I would take Simon leaving over shipping off my girls any day.

"Yeah, smart until the neighbor lady took the coat from my grand-mother at Penn Station and hopped her own train. Bubbe never saw her again. Lucky for her, she had memorized Uncle Harry's address in Chicago and told it to a ticket agent. That address was the only English my grandmother knew." Ash looks right at me, and I can tell we are both willing the tears pooling in our eyes not to fall.

"The agent not only gave her a ticket free of charge, he called Uncle Harry from a payphone to give him Bubbe's arrival time. Then he bought her a sandwich and waited with her at the platform to make sure she got on the right train. Her whole life, Bubbe's been haunted by the fact that she was never able to find that ticketing agent, despite her best efforts, and thank him for what he did."

I push the now-empty snack bowl back toward Ash. I don't even have to ask. He dumps the rest of the tortilla chips into the dish.

"Keep going, tell me the rest."

"My great-uncle Harry was about twenty-two when my grand-mother showed up. He worked days peddling fruit at South Water Market, and at night he played the sax with a bunch of Black musicians in South Side clubs where he lived. He was always gone, and he did not know what to do with a little girl. Luckily, shortly after my grandmother's arrival, Uncle Harry was introduced by a bartender at one of the clubs where he played to a mom who lived a few blocks away and was willing to watch Bubbe. That mom was Evangeline Hubbard, and she had a son named Eddie."

"I may not know much about Judaism, but I remember enough from Sunday school to know the name Evangeline is not Old Testament." I wish my mom were here. I have a feeling this story is about to get better than any romantic comedy we've ever watched.

"No, the Hubbard family was Black. Evangeline was from Mississippi. After high school she came to Chicago to attend an all-Black secretarial school. She was also pregnant."

Ah. I don't need the rest of that part of the story spelled out for me. In those days plenty of girls were sent away from home when they got into "trouble."

"Anyway, Uncle Harry paid Evangeline what he could, in cash and damaged apples, to watch my grandmother. Sometimes he was out all night at the clubs and then would have to head straight to South Water Market in the early-morning hours, so my grandmother had to stay the night at Evangeline's house. Eventually Bubbe and Eddie became good friends."

"In the forties I bet people thought that was strange," I assume more than ask.

"At that time the South Side of Chicago was considered the Black Belt, but poor immigrants had been coming in over the years, and Jewish people were considered the least desirable of them all. On their own blocks it wasn't as scandalous as it was in other Chicago neighborhoods, but you're right—at the time Jews and Blacks intermingling was not at all common. Years later my grandparents did have to fight to be together."

"Which they did," I fill in cheerfully, knowing a few bits and pieces of the story from my cart rides with Mrs. Eisenberg.

"Eventually they did, yes." Ash smiles back, meeting my delight. "First, though, when Bubbe was twelve, things took a turn. One morning, during a particularly bad midwestern January snowstorm, Uncle Harry was driving a produce-delivery truck that slid on black ice and flipped several times, killing him instantly. He was the only family my grandmother had in America. And worse, by that time, every other French Eisenberg that my grandmother was related to had been killed by the Nazis. There was nobody for my grandmother to go back to in Europe. And even if there were, there was no money to send her. Thankfully Miss Evangeline and her new husband, Otis, who played trumpet in the same band as Uncle Harry, took my grandmother in regardless of their neighbors' raised eyebrows."

"Then how is your grandmother Jewish and not Baptist?"

Ash puts his fist up to his mouth to clear his throat, but his eyes give away another crest of brewing emotion. I should probably announce that it's time for me to get home to my girls, and surely Ash needs to go home to his wife. Instead, while Ash gathers himself, I find two beers in the fridge, pop both tops, and pass one over to urge him on.

"Let's just say Miss Evangeline was no fan of bullies," Ash continues after taking a chug of his beer. "She didn't like the ones who teased Eddie because he stuttered, not the ones who beat Great-Uncle Harry to death for wearing a yarmulke, and definitely not Hitler. Evangeline was determined to keep Bubbe's Jewish heritage alive. Otis took Eddie to Monumental Baptist Church on Sundays and Evangeline used her day off on Saturdays to bring my grandmother to the KAM Isaiah Israel temple. Evangeline didn't know it at the time, but she was escorting my grandmother to the oldest reform Jewish community in Chicago. My grandmother loves to repeat the line Evangeline would whisper in her ear when she was the only Black woman at temple and the subject of much whispering, *Same God just different houses to worship him in*, and then she would give my grandmother a LIFE SAVER. Bubbe still sucks on that candy to remind her of Evangeline, her own personal life saver."

My own tears now fall at Mrs. Eisenberg's origin story, and the way Ash retells it with such adoration.

"When my grandmother was nineteen, she followed in Evangeline's footsteps. The two of them took the train into downtown Chicago together, where Evangeline worked for the Board of Trade and my grandmother was the private secretary to the president of Inland Steel. But at night, when Evangeline headed home, Bubbe enrolled herself in evening business courses at a community college nearby. My grandfather decided to follow in Otis's footsteps and become a trumpet player. Grandpa Eddie could play one hell of a trumpet, but he was terrible at getting his new venture, Maxwell Street Records, off the ground. He thought being good at music would translate into being good at making money from other people playing music." Ash chuckles recounting his grandfather's story, and a small grin reaches his lips just before his beer bottle does. I take note that this is the most relaxed I have ever seen my old professor.

"With the promise of an engagement ring one day when they could afford it, Bubbe married Eddie. She left her secretarial job and took her skills from a handful of accounting courses over to Maxwell Street Records to make sense of the finances my grandfather was running into the ground."

"But your grandmother's last name isn't Hubbard," I state the obvious.

"Aren't you old-fashioned?" Ash calls me out for perpetuating a waning tradition. Sharing his family history, which I can see Ash takes great pride in, reveals a sentimentality I would have never guessed he had.

"Turns out people eventually care a lot less about your personal business when you have money lining your pockets. And having the name Eisenberg, my grandfather thought a few more doors in the music industry would open for them. Plus, Sammy Davis Jr. was on the rise, and he was a brother who had also converted to Judaism, and suddenly it became a little more okay."

"But you seem so . . ." I stumble with the right words.

"Handsome? Smart? Entertaining?" Ash offers on his behalf.

"Black. Like, all the way Black," is all I can think of to say.

"Ah. Yeah, that too," Ash agrees with a grin like we're in on a joke together.

"My grandfather was very dark," he explains. "His family was from Central Africa by way of a Georgia plantation. Somehow, he escaped the telltale signs of race mixing over the generations. My father was much darker than his sister. Then my lighter aunt married a blond exchange student from Norway, and they got Livy, a legit redheaded, fair-skinned daughter. My father married a Black woman, and boom, they got me."

"So, wait a minute. Does that mean you and Livy are Jewish? Or are you Blackish?" I stumble through guesses, trying my best to keep it all straight.

"Good question." Ash laughs at me trying to sort out the family puzzle. "Depends on what business deal is in front of me and who's cooking."

This is the craziest story of an ethnic mash-up I've ever heard, and I don't even know what flavor Ash's wife is yet.

"What about you? You don't look like the typical light-skinned sister. You have your own mixture going on yourself." Ash takes his turn to interrogate me.

I've had similar exchanges about my ethnic makeup many times in my life, but I feel a kinship discussing my background with Ash. It's the intent of the question that comes from a person of melanated skin that inspires safety in my answering. I know there is no harm meant. The curiosity of passengers in my cart at SFO who have asked about my cultural specifics is something that inevitably gets my guard up. I don't know what category they are attempting to place me into that might trigger a change in their demeanor, tone, vibe, or all three. The antici-pation of judgment makes me disordered. There's just no grace in being asked some version of "What are you?" when you first meet someone.

"I would guess you are more than Black," Ash hedges. "You look . . ."

"Ethnically ambiguous?"

Ash laughs again at the term I fill in for him, just as Zwena always does.

"I was going to say Filipino. Or no, maybe more Latina."

I put my finger on my nose and point to Ash. "Bingo. But not what you typically think of with a West Coast Latina. I grew up in San Francisco, but I'm from the East Coast." I smile at Ash, inviting him to postulate on my pedigree with a few seconds of silence.

"I'm Afro-Puerto Rican by way of the Bronx. Though we did grow up attending a Mexican-heavy mass, it stuck more with my brothers than with me. The Catholic church's stance on women, reproductive rights, and, well, creationism never sat solid with the scientist in me."

Ash studies my face for a few seconds, and I squirm a bit under his scrutiny. I can't figure out what he's trying to see as he stares across the table, so I add a bit more familial clarification. "I'm the Livy in the Arroyo family, the light one. My brothers are darker like you."

"Ah. Livy's also more Jewish than me." Ash adds to his own story, to relate to mine. "In Judaism, religious lineage passes down through the mother. And Livy's dad was more than happy to let my aunt take the lead on spiritual education as long as they could spend summers in Norway."

"Catholicism is a very patriarchal religion, and I picked apart the messages that had to do with women. My mother claims I was obstinate even in Sunday school when I questioned our teacher about the absence of dinosaurs in the Bible, so she knew what was coming when I heard about Eve in the garden." Ash and I share a grin.

"The teachings always sat better with my father and brothers than with me, but I would argue that Adam came out the hero of that story, so I guess the boys had nothing to complain about." I enjoy another laugh from Ash at my joke and notice how engaging his smile is, a lot like my father's. "Though I do miss going to church with my dad."

"I'd call myself more mixed-ish. I go to temple with my grand-mother for the High Holidays, and Bubbe hosts a Passover celebration every year that I never miss." Ash's face grows somber. "It was supposed to be last week." A weighty silence fills the kitchen, seeming to mark the winding down of our conversation.

At the mention of Passovers past, Ash falls into a sullen mood. It makes me sad after our effortlessly engaging conversation. I know I shouldn't offer him a hug, but I want to. Not only is it awkward, I'm pretty sure his wife wouldn't appreciate it. Maybe putting my hands over his, folded on the table, might offer some solace. Before I can decide, Ash switches the subject.

"Anyway, I've kept you here too long, and your girls are probably wondering where you are."

How does he know I have daughters?

In an attempt to clean up, I sweep chip crumbs off the table into my hand and follow Ash's conversational detour. "So, how does Mrs. Eisenberg know Steve Jobs?"

"This is a good one. In 1980, at the height of its success, my grandmother convinced my grandfather it was the right time to sell Maxwell Street Records. She was ready to be done with Chicago's brutal winters and flat landscape and wanted to move to the warmer hills of Northern California. Like I said, she was the brains of the business, and the marriage."

Mrs. Eisenberg's life story, as told by her grandson, is better than any tycoon tell-all I have ever read.

"Once settled out here, my grandmother invested in a little-known produce company to honor her uncle Harry risking his life selling fruit to put food on the table. That company was Apple."

MAY

MONDAY,
MAY 6

5:18 p.m. (Ash)

At airport. Flight to LA is delayed. Any chance you're here and we can grab a drink?

"Am I here? Is he asking if I'm flying someplace also? Does it weird him out to know someone who works here?" I put my phone screen six inches in front of Zwena's face so she, too, can read.

"Or are you overthinking this text? And what the hell is 'weird him out'?" Zwena asks, pushing the phone away from her nose. I, however, read it again. And then one more time.

"It means does it bother him that this is what I do for a living," I explain in the midst of my overanalysis. "What do I do? I mean, how can it not weird him out? Look at his life"—I point to my cart—"and then look at mine."

"What weirds me out is you letting Simon cook dinner at your house Friday night. Get divorced already." Zwena has had no tolerance for me allowing the Buddha bum back into my life. "What you should do is meet that man," she says, indicating Ash by pointing at my screen. "Text back and tell him to have coffee with you in the international terminal. Your boss never goes over there." Zwena nods down the concourse. "Even I know it's bad to drink on the job. And for you it's bad to drink on the couch too."

"It's Lou and Coco's final Saint Anne's track meet on Friday. They asked if Simon could cook their favorite dinner to celebrate, and he barely has a hot plate at his apartment," I offer as an explanation of why I have not gone full-on, unhinged wife on my half-hinged husband. The last two months Simon has happily carpooled Lou and Coco to and from every practice and track meet, plus he bought them new running gear. Truth is, I haven't presented him with the divorce papers yet because his stepping in without complaint and doing more than his part with the kid load has allowed me time I have never had before to work on Brown Butter, Baby! Dad guilt has really been working in my favor, and I am not quite ready to disrupt our tenuous arrangement of Simon's driving mea culpa and my swallowing my wrath in the name of newfound free time.

"Still weird Simon's coming over."

"Back to Ash," I redirect. "He's married, remember." Sometimes I do have to remind Zwena that marriage is a huge hurdle when engaging with the opposite sex. She's a little less convinced.

"Yes, you have mentioned that to me. And may I point out that you, too, are married."

"It's different."

"Different how?"

"I doubt his wife ran off to an ashram in India."

"This is California, maybe she did too. And anyways, who cares? Ash runs a company that gives out cash to start-ups, and his grandmother is a bajillionaire. You're just having coffee, not sex." Zwena's understanding of venture capital is as elementary as it gets, but this is not the time to give her a lesson in finance. "Here, give me your phone." She grabs it from me while she's demanding.

5:23 p.m. (Toni)

Can't do a drink, I'm working, but can meet you at Green Beans Coffee in the International Terminal in 15. I will take you up on that drink offer another time . . .

Whoosh . . .

Zwena hands the phone back to me. "You move too slow."

"Z!" I yelp. I knew I should have gone straight to Krish on this one, not someone still in her twenties whose idea of a relationship is posting on Instagram about every conquest.

"What?" Zwena says with mock innocence. "He can afford to take you for coffee and a drink. Then sex."

I huff at Zwena as if put out by having to meet up with Ash.

"Toni, you're not fooling anyone. You and I both know you want to go."

◆ ◆ ◆

"Are you going to let me buy your coffee this time?" Ash jokes, which comes off a little stiff dressed as he is in heavy-framed glasses and a navy suit, pulling a titanium-gray hard case. I've now seen sporty, simple, and suit guy. All three are enticing. If I were looking. *I mean, if I cared, of course I would look.*

I decide against coffee to avoid any caffeinated oversharing. "I'll have mint tea, and yes, I'll let you buy." I can't have Ash thinking he knows what to order for me.

Hunting for a table, Ash veers ahead of me to an available space tucked in the far corner. He pulls out a chair, waiting for me to catch up.

"Who's helping out with Mrs. Eisenberg while you're out of town?" I ask, starting with an easy topic of conversation as well as an easy way to casually inquire about his wife.

"Livy is on Bubbe duty. I'm back to frequent work trips to LA over the next several months. Down on Mondays, back on Thursdays."

"Ah. Sounds familiar."

"Oh, do you travel a lot for work?" Ash wonders, looking confused.

"Uh, no. I just spend a lot of time transporting people who work the same commute schedule." I gesture to my cart, which is parked just outside Green Beans, to point out the obvious. "I know your type well. You are usually late for your plane, barking orders into your phone at some assistant cowering on the other end." Ash averts his eyes. I've maybe struck a chord a little too close to home. Backing off a bit, I add, "I love LA."

"You know the city well?" Ash asks, meeting my eyes again and trying to discover a common connection other than his grandmother.

"I went to UCLA for a couple of years. I actually took two of your classes."

"I remember," Ash confirms with a head bob.

"No, you don't," I laugh, not wanting any of his professor pity.

"How could I forget? Student ID 84742-88."

I am dead! I only remember the first four digits myself.

"I have an odd talent for remembering number combinations." Ash pauses, perhaps waiting for me to ooh and aah. Which, as a math and science geek, I would be prone to do if Ash didn't already know he is an exceptional talent. "I'm terrible with names, though."

"And faces," I accuse. Ash cocks his head in curiosity.

"We ran into each other at baggage claim back in January."

"Are you sure? I would have remembered that," Ash corrects me confidently.

"Oh, I'm sure. I was the one who ejected your grandmother from her wheelchair."

"No way, that was you?!" I'm crossing my fingers under the table that he is not about to yell at me like he does his assistant and accuse me of elder abuse. "My apologies. I didn't recognize you. I was distracted.

Too much on my mind that day, but I promise you did look familiar to me at the guest panel at Stanford."

"Ah, so you're terrible with names and faces, but you're good with body parts." My attempt at a little light humor lands flat when Ash responds by checking his phone. Maybe he's more of a leg guy. Or maybe I'm too much.

"Delayed another thirty minutes." Ash sighs, but his eyes dance when he asks, "Do you have a few more minutes to hang out?"

Before I can answer, Ash's phone begins to vibrate.

"Not only am I not going to bark into it, I'm not going to answer it," Ash promises, punctuated with a wink.

My eyes go straight to his ring finger, where there is no ring. I wonder if he put it in his pocket before we met. More than one man has lost his wedding ring out of his pants and onto my cart floor for me to think his bare finger is just a coincidence. It's a sad tactic. Time to let Ash know that I know he's not single.

"So, do you have children?"

"No," Ash responds, and I see his grip tighten around his coffee cup, slightly crushing the paper sides. I take the misshapen cup as my cue not to continue down the kid line of questioning. "What are your girls like?"

I look at Ash confused. I guess I misread his interest in talking about kids.

"My bubbe told me about them," Ash reveals, outing his source. *Aha.* Was Ash asking, or was Mrs. Eisenberg just making random conversation one afternoon between therapist appointments?

"Best twins ever," I brag. "They're in eighth grade."

"Lucky you," Ash offers kindly with a touch of wistfulness.

"Most of the time I feel pretty lucky. Not so much when I'm running late to get somewhere, and I realize one of the two has raided my closet, taking my favorite things. When I can't find my royal-blue cardigan and boot cut jeans, I know exactly where they are, on my daughter Lou. Well, more often on her floor." I laugh, but then roll my lips together hoping I'm not coming across as tiresome with my domestic drivel.

"Whose low-cut shirt were you wearing the night I was speaking to your class?"

"Can we please not talk about Titsgate?" I plead, and Ash concedes with a chuckle.

"Your girls sound great," Ash continues, eyes wide, looking like he's encouraging me to tell him more. "Daughters seem like the best. Especially for a dad."

"Really, you think so?" I question given how forcibly he cut me off when I asked him about children. *Wouldn't Ash rather check his email than talk about my teenage twins?*

"My wife and I couldn't have kids." There it is. I knew the truth would eventually surface the longer I talked about my offspring. Before I can offer an awkward condolence, Ash cuts back in, "I mean my ex-wife. The day you nearly dumped my grandmother on the baggage claim floor was the day my divorce was finalized."

"And I thought I was having a bad day when I almost broke your grandmother. Your day was much worse."

"Yes, it was," Ash agrees, and I turn red with embarrassment.

"I didn't mean to compare your divorce to my clumsiness," I stutter, unsure how to handle this personal information. "I'm sorry to hear the two of you couldn't have a child." And I really am. Lou and Coco may not have come at the ideal time in my life, but I can't imagine never having them at all.

"Me too. I always pictured myself with a big family. Count yourself lucky. You have what I've always wanted."

WEDNESDAY, MAY 8

"Tell me I'm not wrong here," I challenge as Zwena and I look to Krish as the rep for all men.

"I don't know the whole story, and I don't want to dis the guy, but from what you're telling me, yeah, it's kind of a dick move."

"We know that!" Zwena and I yell at Krish.

"Hey, hey, slow the man bashing. I'm not the one who divorced his wife because she couldn't have kids," Krish reminds, hands outstretched, backing up from the two of us before we pounce a second time.

"Z, why are you wearing your uniform from yesterday when you have today off?" Krish teases with a sly smile, working to take the heat off men and, by association, him. Zwena shoots Krish daggers that practically slice his head off.

"Harley back in town for a booty call?" I jump in, wanting to keep our brunch date light and Krish on the right side of Zwena since it's the rare day that all three of us are free. As much as I wanted to text Krish and Zwena right after my coffee with Ash, I knew the breaking wifey news would be perfect brunch fodder.

"Yep, that's it," Zwena answers me and then pushes off Krish's arm that's resting across the back of her chair.

"Must have been some date, Z," Krish continues, egged on by her irritation. "If you're this cranky in the morning, you two must have been going at it all night." Krish loves getting Zwena worked up because her tirades are entertaining, and he knows she can't stay mad at either of us for very long. There is no grudge in that girl.

Surprisingly, "It was okay," is all Zwena gives us, clearly not in the mood to take her turn as the group punching bag.

Krish has the good sense to stop and changes the subject. "Hey, has anyone else gotten an email with a link to Dieting Donna's GoFundMe page?"

"Can you use GoFundMe to raise money for a Spartan Race plane ticket and lodging in Coronado?" I ask the question I've been doubting the answer to since I got the email a few days ago.

"People use it for all sorts of reasons. Darrell at security used GoFundMe for his cat's chemo," Zwena truth tells. "What I want to know is if Donna is really going to do a Spartan race, or is she going down there to find herself a Navy Seal at our expense? She certainly has been high on herself since dropping ten pounds."

"Fifteen," I correct, and we all devolve into laughter. Dieting Donna has made a habit of counting down her pounds to us every week like we are her culpability crew. Though we joke behind her back, I have to give it to Donna: bit by bit she has finally done what she has tried and failed to do before, and I know right where she's coming from. I have a collection of notebooks as evidence of my failures to launch, but I, like Donna, am starting to feel like this time is different. I'm excited for Donna to go ahead and celebrate herself—she'll just have to do it on someone else's dime. All my dollars are tied up in Brown Butter, Baby! and my born babies.

"Zwena tells me Simon's still sniffing around." Krish leans in, stabbing a bite of pancake off my plate. I pull my breakfast closer to me. I don't like to share my food, and he knows that. Krish is really niggling to get under both Zwena's and my skin this morning.

"It's true." Now it's Zwena's turn to lean back and put her hands up in conversational surrender when I reach across the table to take a swat at her.

"Listen, nothing's happened since the night of Mrs. Eisenberg's stroke, when a long, emotional day mixed with alcohol got the best of me."

"You mean when the day and the alcohol got the worst of you," Zwena corrects. "Nothing's happened all right. Your divorce papers are still collecting dust on your bookshelf."

"I moved them to the side table in my bedroom. I didn't want Simon to find them and freak out," I mumble in weak defense.

"So, what I'm hearing is that Ash is the one who should have been concerned about having coffee with someone who's married. He, in fact, is divorced and can get together with whoever he wants. You, on the other hand, are a different story," Krish deduces, twisting the straw from his empty Sprite glass around his index finger.

"Really? You're going to take Ash's side here?"

"I'm just saying, he's divorced. Dick move or not. Your husband is finally back in town and can sign on the dotted line, and those documents are still incomplete," Krish points out. "And as long as those papers stay in the envelope, Simon still thinks he has a chance."

"No. No way he does. I made it clear to him we are not together." And I stand by that statement. Though seeing Coco and Lou blossom in their father's presence has caused me to consider many times whether I could live with Simon as husband and wife until the girls graduate from high school. When Simon left, I did everything I could to keep the girls' bodies busy and their minds occupied so they wouldn't wallow in their grief. I realize now that Lou and Coco knew exactly what I was doing and played along with my frantic need to believe that they were all right even though everything was so wrong.

Observing them with their father again, I recognize that I was deluding myself for my own survival and that Lou and Coco may have been missing their father way more than I allowed myself to admit. I should have let them feel the same lows that I endured. Instead, I forced Coco and Lou to live in the numbed space of fake smiles, overscheduling, false enthusiasm, and acceptance that being just okay and making it through the day was good enough. Only it wasn't.

"One, Simon doesn't know about the papers. Two, he comes and goes from the house with Lou and Coco. And three, he's making dinner for you, his daughters, and his mother-in-law on Friday. Let me repeat, he still thinks he has a chance. And no, that is not just my perspective, that is one hundred percent the male perspective." Krish counts off his evaluation authoritatively while buttering his toast.

I open my mouth to protest, but Krish isn't done.

"Maybe with Simon away it was easy for you to talk a big game about dumping his ass. Now that he's back, you're not sure you want to do it because you feel guilty about how miserable Lou and Coco really were with him gone, and it's nice to see them happy again. Come on, Toni, admit it. Staying with Simon for the sake of the girls feels . . ."

"Lame," Zwena fills in the blank.

FRIDAY,
MAY 10

From the garage the aroma of garam masala hits me, and my mouth waters. Simon is inside preparing what was one of our favorite family dishes, tandoori chicken with a sweet chutney and short grain rice. While my mom usually pushed the food around her plate, never having developed a taste for cuisines outside her treasured Puerto Rican staples, the girls and I gobbled it up whenever Simon made this dish. Once he left, we tried every Indian restaurant in a ten-mile radius until we found a close second to Simon's.

"Abuelita is on her way over," Coco announces from the kitchen when she hears me open the door from the garage. It's as much a warning as imparting information as I carry in the bag of last-minute groceries Simon asked me to pick up.

"Hey, Toni. Did you hear the news?" Simon calls from the stove, acting way too familiar with my pots and pans. Lou and Coco willingly peel onions on either side of him, eager to do the dirty work of prepping family dinner for their father that they dodge doing for me when requested. I recognize what they're up to, being yes women to keep their father happy and home for the foreseeable future. Being agreeable to the whims of men is far too generationally ingrained in Arroyo women for my comfort, and I cut directly into this domestic serenity.

"Girls, why don't you go shower? It was hot at the track meet today," I direct, handing Simon the butter and mango he asked me to pick up along with the cookies.

"Hot in more ways than one," Lou pesters Coco, causing her sister's face to bloom into cayenne red. Turns out that first dance morphed into Coco having her first boyfriend. I would have bet one hundred to one that Lou would have been the first to fall for a Trinity boy, but if it was going to be Coco, at least she chose someone who is a star on the track and in the classroom.

"Oh, Dad's staying for a movie after dinner," Coco announces, like this is what we do as a family every Friday night. "He says the new *Avatar* is on Hulu." I look at my girls, confused. Arroyo women don't do blue creatures living in fabricated worlds. We fawn over formulaic rom-coms with guaranteed storybook endings in Central Park.

Before I can protest the plan, the girls skip out of the kitchen, and Simon and I are left alone with a pan of sautéing onions. "Did I hear what news?" I ask, wondering if Simon's gotten himself a bigger place so he can spend less time at mine, or if Best U Man is actually making money and he's ready to pay his accumulated back child support. I've kept receipts and know exactly how much he owes me.

"Your millionaire TV boyfriend Dwayne Washington is being replaced as a judge on *Innovation Nation* for the new season," Simon ribs, making the assumption, two years later, Dwayne Washington is still my CEO crush. He is.

Even through Simon's early phase of searching for some esoteric spiritual utopia, we still enjoyed curling up on the couch with a bag of OREOs and watching eager upstart entrepreneurs vie for funding on *Innovation Nation*. In retrospect, Simon's willingness to watch the show with me and debate which newbie founder we would bet on if given the chance should have served as a clue that his yearning for the pious life would be short lived. Sitting next to me he'd fantasize about taking the cash and traveling the world while hogging the cookies. The girls and I were never mentioned as globe-trotting companions, nor were the rules of the show, that the money is to be invested in the product, not the president. I could have saved myself a lot of heartache with some earlier analysis of Simon's viewing behavior.

"Where'd you hear that?" I ask, breaking into a case of cold sparkling water, a luxury that rarely occurs in our house. Simon is really going all out for the last track meet celebration. I think about the divorce papers in my bedroom and Krish and Zwena's constant needling about them collecting dust. Maybe after dinner I'll send the girls to their room to finish their homework and finally give Simon the papers. *He has to be expecting them.*

Simon points with the spatula he's wielding to his open laptop. "Check out CNN, it's top right."

"I wish they'd replace Dwayne with Libby Starr, she would kill it on the show. But they'll probably end up replacing him with any one of a million dull White tech dudes." The carbonation soothes my throat following an afternoon of cheering on Lou and Coco in their final middle school races. Though I hollered like my babies were competing in the Olympics, let's just say I'm certain track and field is not going to be anyone's ticket to a college scholarship.

"Go ahead and read. They already picked the guy." I sit myself down in front of Simon's computer to the headline **Congress Gridlock, Again**, with a picture of four angry politicians barking at each other and one in the background who looks like he's napping, or dead. *Again, is right.* As if dysfunction in Congress could be considered headline news anymore.

"You're half-right about the new judge. The guy's a venture capitalist from Palo Alto, so he's definitely boring."

Well, before you decided to drishti your way to dharma, you would have been working side by side with said boring banking bro. And we all would have been better off for it. I'm dying to say that out loud, but I don't want to sour Lou and Coco's special night.

"But at least he's Black, so the show can keep up appearances."

Okay then, move over Dwayne, maybe I will have a new on-screen boyfriend.

"Guess he used to be a professor at UCLA, but recently he's made a name for himself investing in companies with founders who are not, as you say, *dull White dudes.*"

This résumé sounds unnervingly familiar.

"Though his last name sounds kinda Jewish." Simon speaks into the open fridge before I get to that part of the article.

I freeze with my right index finger over the scroll bar. "Eisenberg?"

"Maybe. I've never heard of him, have you?" Simon holds up a half lemon from the back recesses of the refrigerator in triumph, like he's struck gold. "Show nailed it with the double diversity. Network probably felt the pressure to find another smooth-talking Black guy more than someone well known."

"You probably weren't reading Bloomberg News on your personal pilgrimage, but lots of venture capitalists are investing in people of color," I dig, feeling oddly defensive of Ash. "And yes, I've heard of him. Youngest tenured professor in economics at UCLA, so obviously smart." Simon comes up behind me and scrolls the page down to a picture of Ash leaning against a white oak standing desk, a requisite piece of abstract modern art hanging on the wall behind him.

"I don't think it's his brain that's going to keep viewership up." We are both staring at Ash's self-assured demeanor, one ankle crossed over the other, shoulders rolled back, hands in his pants pockets, radiating a *master of the universe* smile. This is what Ash must have meant when he told me he would be traveling back and forth to LA the next couple of months. I think he was wearing that same tie when we had coffee at Green Beans the other day.

"I recognize a ratings magnet when I see one. He's a good-looking dude," Simon admits, like he's either expecting me to counter that Ash isn't nearly as handsome as he is or comment on how highly evolved Simon has become. *No toxic masculinity here.* Either way, though rusty,

I'm schooled enough in male speak to know Simon's aiming for me to make it all about him. I'm not playing along.

"Well, I'm going to give him a chance. I like what his work stands for. We need more CEOs of color." I close the laptop, hoping Simon will pick up the hint that this is the end of our conversation. After the night of our near miss sex-up, I've been attempting to only small talk with Simon over text or when the girls are with us. We have returned to the low-hanging language of our marriage, only discussing logistics as pertains to our girls. Safer that way, while I figure out what we are and if I want any part of it.

"I was thinking, for Christmas, maybe we could all go on a trip somewhere. We never did take the girls to Disneyland. I think it will be good for us."

My mouth opens to jump all over Simon that we were supposed to take them to Disneyland for Spring Break of seventh grade. Instead, I treated them to a school-free week bingeing Disney+ when Simon headed to his own version of Neverland the week after I made our reservation at the Grand Californian. Luckily, I was attuned enough to Simon's shifting sense of family commitment not to pay in full up front for a 15 percent room discount.

"Toni, did you hear what I just said?" Simon nudges my shoulder, I assume looking for validation of his generosity when I don't immediately react to the offer of a long-awaited vacation. *Good for us, or good for you, Simon?* Does he really think a couple of days with Mickey Mouse can assuage his guilt for leaving his daughters and fix what has been broken between us? Walking down Main Street with churros in our hands, will Simon miraculously grasp that I was not heartbroken that we didn't go on vacation? I was heartbroken that Simon so flippantly discarded our life partnership for his solo adventure when all I ever tried to relay to him was that what I needed from my husband was support to restart an adventure of my own.

Or is it that, down deep where no one wants to excavate, I am angry at the both of us for not listening closely to one another about what we needed to flourish in our marriage and in life? Our interactions had devolved to reacting to each other's words and actions, not proactively supporting them. In my feelings of lack—lack of time, lack of support to grow into the person I wanted to be, lack of Simon really understanding who I am—I lashed out at him and where his interests were gravitating. With every lash, rather than having a conversation with me, Simon spent more and more time away, until he chose to completely walk away—for two whole years. While there is a possibility of us being some sort of family again, I don't know if our marriage can be repaired. What I do know is that I have people in my life now who will listen to me and help point me in the right direction of my dreams.

"I need to go make a call," I say, rather than remind Simon of exactly why we never made that trip, which might send him into defensive mode. Lou and Coco will come in swinging to shield their dad, and I will be the one to blame for destroying dinner. I point toward my bedroom, nipping the perfect family vacation planning fallacy in the bud.

"Make it quick, your mother will be here in a few and dinner will be ready in ten."

When I finally told my mother the G-rated version of how I discovered Simon had returned, she did not look up from washing the dishes in her sink. I had taken her out to buy a second curling iron and new set of blush brushes for her client friends at the Senior Connection, and she repaid me for the ride by forcing me to sit down and try out her new twist on arroz con dulce. Turns out the twist was a tablespoon or two of rum.

Wiping her hands on her apron, she faced me, taking time to compose her thoughts. Her usual MO is to think after she speaks.

"Bueno," was all she said.

"¿Perdón?" I replied in shock. While my mom and I talk in English, we fight in Spanish, and I was gearing up for an all-out battle of words.

"Las niñas necesitan a su papá."

Rolling my eyes, my sense of self-preservation shot up. "No, they do not need their father. I've been doing it all just fine the past two years."

Gloria took my words into consideration with another round of tense silence. She had to admit the girls are healthy and thriving in school, and while we don't have much money or time for the extras in life, Coco and Lou are never short on love.

"Mija, there is no substitute for a father. It's best Simon is back. For everyone." There it was. Falling back on that tired cultural patriarchy, my mother wants me to sweep Simon's selfish behavior under the rug. There was no misinterpreting Gloria's sentiments that we all needed Simon.

"Don't doubt me, mi amor. You'll see I'm right," my mom stated, summing up her thoughts on my current marital affairs. In response, all she saw of me was my back as I stomped out her front door.

Pick up, pick up, pick up. From the privacy of my bedroom, I will Zwena to find her phone.

"Enjoy your pulled pork sandwich, it's one of my favorites." Zwena doesn't eat pork. "And be sure to stop by again next time you're in San Francisco." I cannot even begin to estimate how many times I have heard Zwena call out that line after a male customer who, she assumes, is hungry in more ways than one.

"Are you regretting dinner with Simon before you even sit down?" Zwena muffles without so much as a *hello*.

"Bring the phone closer to you, Z, I can barely make out what you're saying."

"I can't pick it up," Zwena articulates louder. "I have on latex serving gloves. They're the last pair here, and they need to survive until the end of my shift. I think Peter or Jose have stolen the backup box to make water balloons, and now I can't mix phone germs with the garlic fries." I hear the metal scooper scraping the bottom of the fryer basket.

"Forget it, I'm calling Krish."

"He's working an engagement party at the Four Seasons, some billionaire on his fourth wife," Zwena's yelling continues after taking another customer's order. "He went over a little early to take advantage of the prime rib and crab stations. He goes on in an hour. I will talk to you later."

As the mother figure in our threesome, I'm used to being the one who keeps track of everyone's comings and goings. Zwena is usually only interested on a need-to-know-because-it-will-make-my-life-better basis. Her awareness of Krish's whereabouts momentarily throws me off our triangular social equilibrium.

I hear Simon open the front door for my mom. I roll off my mattress to scrunch onto the floor between my bed and the wall where no one can see me, and most importantly, no one can hear me.

"Dinner in five!" Simon bellows as if my house is huge and the sound needs to carry far. I faintly hear my mother give her *isn't it great to have a man back in charge* giggle even though absolutely nothing in Simon's directive is remotely funny.

"Krish?" I whisper when he picks up on the first ring. I can hear a boisterous crowd behind him and, according to Zwena, he hasn't even started spinning. Knowing Krish, his body is vibrating in anticipation of stepping behind his turntables to do the thing he loves most in the world. I'm so swept up in his hype I temporarily forget why I called.

"You okay, Toni?" Krish asks loudly when I don't speak up immediately. He's likely pressing one ear against the phone with his finger plugging the other so he can hear.

"I'm good, I'm good," I stutter, but then I pause again.

"Toni?"

"Do you think I should try out for the show *Innovation Nation* with Brown Butter, Baby!?"

"Whoa. That's out of left field. Hold on." I hear Krish shuffling through the crowd to find someplace semiprivate.

"There. Okay," Krish exhales. In the minute it takes for him to find a quiet spot, I realize how ridiculous my question is. "You want to try out for *Innovation Nation*? Like, the show?"

"Never mind. It was stupid."

"Maybe not, something gave you the idea." Krish actually sounds encouraging, and he wears the title of Mr. Cautious out of the three of us.

"Ash Eisenberg is going to replace Dwayne Washington as a judge on the new season. He's the—"

"Hot grandson!" Krish interrupts. Apparently, he does listen when Zwena and I yammer on about nonsense and we think he's wrapped up in Wordle.

"I think you have two choices here, Toni."

Oh, I like choices. Krish is really good at thinking things through and coming up with reasonable options and outcomes.

"You can either try to get money out of this Eisenberg guy, or you can go ahead and sleep with him. What I've heard from you and Z, either is possible."

"What?!"

"Or do both. Though getting the money first, then sleeping with him, is the safer way to go. You don't want to feel like he's paying for sex if you win on the show and Brown Butter, Baby! gets funded. Or if the sex is *meh*, you don't want to have to see him again."

"He's not interested in me like that," I insist. I think Krish may have hit the open bar a little too hard in addition to the surf and turf tables.

"Of course, he is. You flash him your boob in class, and the next time he sees you he gives you his number to 'talk business.'" I can feel Krish's air quotes over the phone. "Then, at his grandmother's house, he pours out his family history and invites you to coffee soon after. He tells you he's not married and—for a dude—shows an abnormal amount of interest in your kids, but he doesn't tell you he's now on your favorite show." The timeline of events Krish repeats back to me is true.

"I'm a guy, he's a guy. I'm telling you it doesn't track that he just wants to mentor you." Krish says *mentor* with a hard hit of sarcasm. "He's more interested in getting in your pants than he is into your business plan. But sure, go ahead and try out for the show."

"Toni, what are you doing on the floor?" My mother stares down at me quizzically. I didn't even hear her traipse into my room, which I'm pretty sure was intentional. "Simon and the girls are waiting for you downstairs." I can hear her accusation that I'm the one holding up the Rockwellian family portrait waiting for me in the kitchen.

"Just think about it, Toni," Krish says in my ear. "You're not the only one who understands chemistry."

"Krish, I think you're making this up."

"No, I'm telling you the truth."

SATURDAY,
MAY 18

When Ash texted earlier in the week that he was on his way back through SFO, and would I like to grab dinner after work if I was free, I lied and said that it was my day off and I had plans with Lou and Coco. I made sure to be nowhere near the United terminal when his plane landed. In fact, I hid in a Hudson News way over by the Delta gates downing a share-size bag of Skittles. I scuttled out when I knew for sure that the baggage from Ash's United flight had been delivered and all the passengers had most likely cleared the airport. For the thirty-five minutes of occupancy, Sharon, who was working the register, made me scroll through dozens of pictures of her recent trip to El Segundo to meet her first grandchild. I'm happy for Sharon, but all newborns and all palm trees pretty much look alike. It's also fascinating how many people have to buy emergency toothbrushes at the airport. Isn't that an obvious item on every traveler's pack list?

Reviewing Krish's words in my mind, I decide it's not that I'm opposed to going to dinner with Ash, but rather that since learning he's a judge on *Innovation Nation*, I'm not sure what I might ask from Ash Eisenberg the next time I see him. Once we got past the awkward hellos and small talk the few times we've been together, Ash did ease into conversation I found interesting. Over coffee, he told me about the high-speed battery charging station company for electric cars in rural America that his firm is considering investing in. And the science behind a new sealant they just funded that decreases the glare of solar roof panels is exciting. Ash generously answered all my questions about stored energy and how utility companies can incentivize homeowners by offering rebates. With Ash, I can nerd out with my sciencey questions about the products and their viability, and he enthusiastically answers all my probing without a hint that he has somewhere better to be.

Regardless, mentioning *Innovation Nation* may come across that I am after Ash's money, and that is not the case. *I think.* For every small business loan I've applied for, the *nos* and *best of lucks* have become the soundtrack to my life. As a trade in kind, my boss has reluctantly agreed to give me Saturdays off to attend the Alemany Farmers Market if I keep her Samoan skin lubricated with a bimonthly supply of Theobroma lotion for her and her sister. They are not small women, so they power through a lot of lotion in a short time. To make up for my boss's freebies, I am counting on selling out at the market. My success there is all thanks to Zwena's skills at strong-arming people who walk by my booth.

"We've been here a couple of Saturdays, and I still can't remember the names of your lotions, let alone pronounce them. And there are only four," Zwena complains, juggling three jars from my perfectly curated display I've designed to look like a molecular structure. Her fanny pack full of ones, fives, and coin change bounces against her hip, keeping time with her tosses. I'm in charge of Square and Cash App sales, since Zwena decided it's not as fun as handling real money.

Though the fog is rolling through, bringing with it a damp spring chill, Zwena is rocking a cropped hoodie to my puffy jacket. She swears the more skin she shows, the more product people will buy, but looking at her makes me shiver. This morning alone, Zwena has lured a half dozen men in, misleading them on what they were getting, but, as she is always able to miraculously do, they leave with a smile and a couple of jars of lotion for their girlfriends or mothers. Zwena is for sure Brown Butter, Baby!'s number one employee. Even better than me if sales are the ultimate measurement of success. Too bad 50 percent of our gross goes to paying for a prime spot at the market, 50 percent to supplies, and Zwena's only cut is my continued gratitude, friendship, and reliance on her saleswomanship. If this thing ever gets funded, stock options and a paid job as my number two are hers. Zwena thought stock options meant she gets the pick of any of my products. I assured her she already has that.

"Can I get you two anything?" Simon asks, looking from me to Zwena. He arrived at the market with Coco and Lou, but it's clear they dropped him the minute he parked the car and gave them each a twenty. I'm disappointed the girls didn't come by to see my booth and say good morning to me and Zwena before setting out to get breakfast. They could have at least feigned interest in their mother and then left, taking their father with them.

"Would you like a hot drink or a croissant?"

"Go away, Simon, we're busy here," Zwena demands, grabbing an innocent passerby and pulling them into our currently empty stall. I apologize to the customer we just lost for being woman-handled by my best friend and give her a free sample as she scurries away. Zwena initially met Simon when I asked her to pick up Lou and Coco from his place one day when I knew, if I saw him, I would rip into him for buying the girls' forgiveness with Nike Air Force 1 sneakers. I didn't want to know where he got the money, and I didn't want to hear the girls gush about their generous father compared to their miserly mother.

Since that afternoon Zwena has not softened one bit toward Simon or our current state of marital limbo. At her age, I probably would not have had any patience for it either. Without the addition of kids, home-ownership, joint credit, and shared history, it's easy to draw definitive boundaries when it comes to relationships. In your twenties a relationship is between two people. In midlife it consists of multiple characters, including your mortgage officer, shared friends, and Catholic mothers.

"Nice to see you, Zwena," Simon says flatly, making it clear his interest in my friend is mutually nonexistent and that the offer of a hand-delivered breakfast was not aimed at her. Lucky for Simon he's mature enough to recognize he needs to keep it civil because he is still working hard to get back in my good graces, and Zwena is already and forever there.

"On second thought, I'll take a large macchiato from Blue Bottle, a baguette from Rolling in the Dough, and some sharp cheddar from Foggy Bottom Creamery. Oh, and a few apples from whatever organic farm stand looks the most expensive. I'm starving," Zwena orders, not handing over any money to pay for her grocery list. Simon looks to me to stop Zwena's snack bullying, but I shrug. It feels good to have Zwena act out the aggression I often feel toward Simon but have to keep in check due to our daughters.

As I'm grabbing more lotion from under the table to fill in my molecular structure, I hear Simon say, "Here you go. Oh, and you too." I look up, confused.

"What's that?" I point at my table to a pile of cards where a jar of Nephelium should go. I recently sold the two display ones to a nice mother from Brisbane with three boys under four. She looked in need of some self-care. Zwena picks a card up, reads it, and promptly tosses it in the trash can with an unamused huff out her nostrils.

"Since you have the booth here, I thought I could leave a pile of Best U Man cards." I look at Simon quizzically. "Listen, you're already here selling self-care, so why not help me out? Plus, let's be honest, there's way more financial upside in Best U Man than your couple of bottles of"—Simon picks up one of said bottles—"how the hell do you even pronounce this?"

I grab the jar out of his hands, my eyes stinging. Simon sees that he's struck a nerve and that Zwena looks about to throw a punch. Backtracking, but still with an air of arrogance, he says, "I'm just saying, if you look at spending trends and financial analysis of wellness products, mental health is where people are spending their money these days, Toni. Desperate for help, folks are throwing cash at anyone who can guide them to find their purpose and get them on the road to becoming their best self. The market proves it, so why shouldn't some of that money be thrown at me? At us?"

"What does it even mean to become your 'best self,' as if anyone knows what that is?" Zwena cuts in. "I mean, how do you even know if you ever get there? Is there a bell that rings and confetti falls? And once you are there, how long can you stay there? It's only a matter of time until someone like yourself comes along and kufanyika, done!" Zwena claps her hands together for emphasis. "You just can't help but tell them to bugger off, and then you are right back where you started, an average human doing what they can to get along in this crazy world."

Ignoring Zwena's analysis of his business pitch, Simon continues, "If you want to have a successful company, Toni, you have to follow the money. Remember, I worked as an investment banker all those years you were home with the girls, I know where the money is and who has the purchasing power."

Is this Simon's way of saying there is no value in my products? Or is he saying that I am not the person to lead this enterprise?

"Look at you, Simon. You had two whole years to find your best self, and you came up short," Zwena concludes, stepping in between Simon and me, not allowing herself to be excused.

"In those two years I came up with a company that is already on the verge of turning a profit because of its low overhead. It's just me I have to sell. And people are buying my combination of inspiration and aspiration," Simon flexes. "Outside investment in hard goods is near impossible. It's all about selling a growth mindset. I challenge you to find me one person who doesn't want to become their Best U Man."

"You, man, are a dumbass," Zwena concludes, but I know Simon is not all wrong. There are now monks making millions from their book deals and meditation apps. Alcoholics turned athletes hosting transformative podcasts with Fortune 500 sponsors. It's not enough to look good on the outside anymore, you also have to make over the inside, which, I know, is a much harder job. That I have allowed Simon back into my life because it benefits Lou and Coco is yet another testimonial for a flawed person trying to be her best human. No potion or lotion is going to help me forgive Simon—that is 100 percent an inside job.

"Not so dumb," Simon responds with a confidence that is at an all-time high this morning, even for him. "I found out yesterday afternoon that I made it past the initial screening for *Innovation Nation*. Each year ten thousand people apply, but only a hundred make it to the next step. I got in early applying for this season, and I already found out I beat the odds. I'm in the second-round consideration pool. Next week I have a call with one of the associate producers."

I'm knocked off balance, stunned speechless.

"When I go down to shoot my segment, you and the girls can come with me. We'll hop over to Disneyland to celebrate. Finally get our turn on the Matterhorn."

Coming to stand by me, Zwena corrects, unimpressed, "If you get picked." She grabs my hand to steady me behind my janky fold-out tables pushed together with a worn white bed sheet over them and a Puerto Rican flag hanging on the front to hide the boxes underneath. The flag being Gloria's contribution to building my brand.

"Oh, I'll get picked. America loves a transformation story."

"Even when it's in reverse?" I find my voice to question.

"From spouse to louse," Zwena adds, her winning smile back for the first time since Simon showed up.

JUNE

SUNDAY,
JUNE 2

For over a week, I stewed on Simon's announcement that he and Best U Man made it past the initial screening for *Innovation Nation*. Since my Pioneering Entrepreneurs class ended in May, I've rewatched sixty-eight episodes of the show and tallied how many services won funding versus hard goods. I wrote down every new business term I heard come out of the judges' mouths and cross-referenced it with what I learned at Stanford. If I didn't know a concept, I looked it up and committed the terminology to memory.

I kept track of how many men versus women were selected for investment and how many people of color made it on the show, let alone earned their first cash infusion. Occasionally there were some on-air dramatics. I noted that thirteen presenters cried, either from nerves or emotions, and that there was one full-on snot bubble blown on national television. I created a contestant chart of who earned funding and tracked who received more. Not surprisingly, on average women were offered 22 percent less funding. Was it the viability of the product? Was it the contestant? Or maybe the marketplace? I don't know, but I would have to work out my own odds before I considered applying. I was earning my MBA one *Innovation Nation* episode at a time.

I watched the show while I cooked dinner and folded the laundry. I brushed my teeth with the *Innovation Nation* theme music stuck in my head. And at work I perched my phone up on my transportation cart dashboard with my notebook open on the seat beside me. I viewed with one eye on my phone and one eye on the foot traffic as I drove between terminals, pulling over whenever I needed to jot down something relevant to my chances of gaining placement on the show. There had to be an explanation why this program, which I had long admired for its talent and foresight into what would take off in the free market, would consider someone like Simon. If I was going to apply, I didn't want to only make it on the show, I wanted to beat Simon. I wanted to prove to him that I, too, had evolved in his absence.

With my eyes fried from an overdose of screen time, but my statistics exact, I texted Mrs. Eisenberg under the guise that I would like to bring my mother over so the two of them can meet. And, as a bonus, my mom could do her hair since Mrs. Eisenberg hasn't been able to get out of the house and to a salon in quite some time. As suspected, Mrs. Eisenberg was giddy for the company and the coif. She insisted I bring a couple of jars of Prunus Dulcis for her and a few Nephelium for her speech therapist. While she's being rinsed, I plan to dig to find out if, as a new judge, Ash has any pull on *Innovation Nation*.

"Mi amor, Simon brought the girls over to see me the other day after school. He also brought me a vase of long-stem tulips. My favorite." I don't bother responding as Simon's tactics are so obvious, and we are late getting out the door of my mother's apartment and over to Mrs. Eisenberg's. Simon is working my mother, as well as our girls, to get me to agree to let him move back in the house. I believe he genuinely wants to come back home, but I also know he gets kicked out of his Airbnb at the end of the month. "He adjusted the screen door off the kitchen, so it doesn't catch anymore. Very handy, that Simon."

"Yep, he's handy," I agree as a neutral answer since he did fix the rattle in my garage door recently.

"He seems happy to be home," my mother persists, not letting the conversation end with Simon's skill with an Allen wrench.

"If by home you mean the Bay Area, your guess is as good as mine." I do not want to reveal any of the conversations I have had with Simon about him moving home nor the considerations in my head about us staying married.

"I'm not guessing, Toni, I know these things."

I'm sure she does. The two of them are most likely scheming behind my back on how to get him through my front door, for good.

Recently my mother has taken to lecturing me on two items: my disinterest in having a quinceañera for her granddaughters and, as Lou and Coco march toward womanhood, their need for an example of a healthy grown-up relationship like I had as a girl. She bugs me about how they are going to learn what love looks like, let alone feels like, if they don't observe it at home. I want to tell her the chances of Simon and me ever returning to a shining example of marital harmony are slim. With regularity, Gloria takes the opportunity to point out that every woman in her granddaughters' lives is single. Their grandmother, their mother, Auntie Zwena. When I suggest to my mom that she is free to date and be the image of domestic bliss for her grandchildren, she gives me the sign of the cross and dismisses such nonsense, reminding me she has had her great love. And then she holds up her ring finger, pointing to heaven to show she still wears her wedding band.

For my mother, marriage continues beyond "until death do us part." Given my marital situation, she has extended that to "until runaway husbands return." The conversation inevitably concludes that the reason the girls like to spend so much time at the Antonellis' house is because both parents are around. It takes every ounce of my being to not go nuclear on my mother when that argument arises. Lou and Coco like to hang out at the Antonellis' house because they have a PlayStation, a Ping-Pong table, and a brooding teenage son who plays the guitar and is captain of his lacrosse team. I'd hang out there, too, if I were a fourteen-year-old girl.

On the way to Mrs. Eisenberg's, in the waning early-evening light, the houses along the serene streets of Atherton look even more exclusive behind their manicured hedges and expansive old-growth trees. There is no sense that behind these facades are people organizing for the work-week ahead, tidying up, and making meal plans. These are tasks of their past before financial windfall came their way and made every day a weekend. My mom quiets as we roll through the neighborhood at the required twenty-five miles per hour, real-estate gawking and not wanting to call any attention to our out-of-place secondhand SUV. With each driveway we roll up to, I can see my mom get her hopes up that this is the house we get to visit, and as we pass her expectations drop until we reach the next grandiose driveway much farther down the block.

"I think they filmed a movie here once," my mother comments, leaning forward in her seat as Mrs. Eisenberg's pinkish French-inspired chateau with white shutters and dozens of black-lead windowpanes comes into full view. "You know the one I'm thinking of. It's got that cute Kate Hudson in it."

"Kate has three baby daddies, none of them her husband." I spoil my mom's admiration for the actress by dropping this fact.

"But Kurt Russell and Goldie Hawn are the grandparents," my mom answers, pleased with herself for responding with her own pop culture knowledge.

"They never married."

"¡Ay, Dios mio! Antonia, give it a rest." My mom sighs and flips down her visor, exhausted by my less than charming habit of needing to have the last quip.

"You look great, Mom," I offer by way of apology for my brattiness. She smiles, cleaning up the lipstick in the corners of her mouth with a fingernail. In Gloria's world, a compliment is an acceptable stand-in for *sorry*.

"You, too, mi amor," she replies, which is her agreement to stand down. In fact, I don't look great, having forgone a shower for braids, a baseball cap, and swipe of deodorant so I could have time to read the fine print on the application for *Innovation Nation*. I also had to run Lou and Coco to buy glue sticks and pipe cleaners for the final project in their elective engineering class. I was sure last-minute runs to craft stores would end with elementary school, but turns out, even with all the technology at students' fingertips, trifolds and handmade 3D models are still a teacher's favorite form of presentation and every parent's hassle.

"Con mucho gusto." My mother beams upon meeting Mrs. Eisenberg, who is propped up in a beautiful hummingbird-print upholstered wingback chair. Her color has returned to her cheeks since the last time I saw her.

I have witnessed it at the Senior Connection and now one-on-one with Mrs. Eisenberg. My mother has the magic touch of being able to make a person feel like the most important one in the room, just as my father was able to do. Gloria is one of the few people whose heart expands for those who are older than her when other people fail to acknowledge their presence, let alone their value.

"Look at me," Mrs. Eisenberg shows off, lifting both her arms and legs at the same time, her left side only slightly lagging behind the right.

"Someone's been acing her daily workouts." I put up my right hand so Mrs. Eisenberg has to high-five me with her left for an extra rep.

"And I got my physical therapist set up so she can do Zoom workouts with Elaine and Patrick in Scottsdale. Next, I'm going to have her record her sessions with me so she can start a subscription service online for seniors. That's how you really start making money, auto-renewal. I've been meaning to talk to you about that when it comes to your lotions."

"So, what you're telling me is you're a fitness model now?" I chuckle a little too long, needing a few more seconds to get up the nerve to ask Mrs. Eisenberg about Ash and *Innovation Nation*.

"I'm going to go viral," Mrs. Eisenberg says, holding up her phone.

"How do you know what viral is?" I laugh again, unable to imagine Mrs. Eisenberg spends her time on anything as trivial as social media.

"Back in 2009 I was one of the original investors in Instagram's Series A round of funding. You know I don't believe success is ever instant, but the 'gram proved me wrong." Mrs. Eisenberg lifts a finger at me. "But that's a one in a billion exception. The norm takes a ton of slow and steady work that goes unrecognized."

"Speaking of work," my mom says, running her fingers through Mrs. Eisenberg's hair. "Where should I set up so we can remind your roots what color your hair really is?"

"Eddie used to tease me that while I was living in the twenty-first century, my hair was stuck in the eighties. It was a bold claim coming from a man who went bald before we had our first baby."

Ahhh. That could explain Ash's shiny head.

"The eighties were my favorite decade." My mom grins, and I know it's true. That's when my parents fell in love and started our family.

Feeling extraneous in this conversation, I inelegantly butt in with the real reason we are here. "Before you two hold hands down memory lane to the shampoo bowl, I need to ask you about something, Mrs. Eisenberg."

"Sounds serious." Mrs. Eisenberg straightens up in her chair and looks to my mom to see if she knows what I'm about to pry into. Gloria's face indicates that she is as clueless as Mrs. Eisenberg is. Feeling like I'm going to chicken out, I grab the jars of lotion I promised Mrs. Eisenberg from my bag. She waves her hand for me to put them on the coffee table where her finished lunch plate still sits.

"Would you like me to clear that for you?" I ask, picking up the plate, surprised there isn't help in the house taking care of such things, but happy for a moment more to procrastinate.

"Antonia, you are not here to clean up after me. You are here to ask me something. So go ahead and ask. You know I believe mood follows action, and you look absolutely terrified."

"Last time I was here, while you were resting, Ash told me about your past. Your history," I begin, but don't offer too much more in case Ash overshared in the emotion of the afternoon.

"Ah," is all Mrs. Eisenberg replies.

"How come you never told me anything about your childhood and career before?"

"You never really asked. Your generation is obsessed with learning from the rare young Zuckerbergs of the business world. It's true, they made it in their twenties or early thirties, but there is even greater wisdom and depth of experience that surrounds you all." Mrs. Eisenberg points back and forth between herself and my mother.

"Success does not come fast for the majority of people, Antonia. If it comes at all. But when it does come at record speed, well, that is sheer dumb luck. Building a company is a slow process full of small steps forward and immense setbacks. But that's not what you young entrepreneurs want to hear, is it? The minute things get hard, and failure is nipping at your heels, it's easier to quit than dig in and deal with the outcome. It's possible to come out the other end of a mess better than where you started. Or maybe not, no guarantees." Mrs. Eisenberg leans forward with a wry grin.

"This may be hard for you to believe, but the pants-on-fire risk is the most fun aspect of being an entrepreneur. Once you achieve what you set out to do, well, honestly, it's kind of ho-hum." Who knew Mrs. Eisenberg was such an adrenaline junkie?

"I think we both know my past ideas were all failures. You were with me on those adventures to nowhere," I lament.

"I didn't know that for sure. You didn't give any of them enough time to play out. You decided they were flops before they even had a chance to become anything tangible."

"You didn't like them," I insist defensively. My mom shoots me a familiar *be respectful in someone else's home* look. Her glare is reminiscent of those she gave me during all our years sitting side by side on hard pews in God's house.

"I was dispensing critical feedback so you could make your products better. That's how much I believe in you. My observations were not criticisms meant to cut you down. You are the one who confused the two and then abandoned ship."

As true as this may be, I really wish my mom didn't just hear what Mrs. Eisenberg said. I can feel her filing away the term *critical feedback* for the next time she hassles me about my appearance.

"And the lotions. Do you believe in Brown Butter, Baby!?"

"The question is, do you believe in them?" Mrs. Eisenberg presses me. "Stand up straight and own your answer when speaking, because if you don't believe in you, no one else will either."

"That's what I'm always saying!" My mom is thrilled to have a partner in commentary concerning my posture.

I look over at the freebies I have put on the coffee table. The beauty industry is littered with companies with all sorts of claims: wrinkle erasers, skin neutralizers, remedies for rosacea or eczema. Some promise to not just moisturize, but to turn customers dewy. And my favorite, those that claim to be age defying, as if anyone can cheat time. But Brown Butter, Baby! does something different. It recognizes that the skin of Black and Brown people is just as valuable, just as beautiful, as White skin. And products should match people. Match the customer. Yes, my products are all-natural and moisturizing, but they don't treat the customer as skin, they treat the customer as a person. And for that Brown Butter, Baby! is unique.

"Mrs. Eisenberg, do you think I should apply to be on the show *Innovation Nation*?" I ask timidly, not wanting her to think I am trying to get to her grandson through her.

"That won't do, Antonia. What do you want to ask me?" Mrs. Eisenberg insists again, locking eyes with me so intently I can't look away.

I clear my throat and ball my fists as my arms hang firmly down my sides. "Mrs. Eisenberg, you have built and sold a lucrative record company. You had vision not once but twice in the tech field. That's more than just luck, that's a sharp sense for business and investment. In your expert opinion, do you think I should try out for *Innovation Nation*? I'm not looking for a shortcut for Brown Butter, Baby!. I'm simply looking for the next step forward for my company."

"I don't know, I've never seen the show." Mrs. Eisenberg shrugs cavalierly, as if I just asked her if she'd rather have tacos or lasagna for dinner, not if she could help me chart the right direction for my fledgling beauty empire. "You know I prefer movies to network television."

"What?" I groan, realizing I summoned all that courage for nothing.

Mrs. Eisenberg cocks her head toward the kitchen when the door slams.

"Ask Ash. He just walked in the back door."

"Ask me what, Bubbe?" Ash saunters into the living room carrying a hand towel. As he pulls the cloth down his face to take in the two of us, my mom minigasps at the sweaty hunk of man standing before us. I reflexively grasp her hand to shut her up, and to tamp my own physical reaction to being face-to-face with sporty Ash.

"Hey, Antonia. Nice to see you," Ash draws out as he throws back his left leg to grab his ankle for a quad stretch. His upper thigh muscle spreads like a giant bar of irresistible chocolate, thick and smooth. I assumed Ash was the quintessential business dude, only trading his weekday suit for eighteen holes in saddle shoes, but here he is, back from a weekend warrior basketball game looking like he just walked off the cover of *Men's Health*. I focus my eyes on the white stitched Michael Jordan silhouette dunking on the left leg of Ash's blue mesh shorts. If I don't gaze somewhere neutral, I'll be caught staring at the arms I admired all those years ago writing formulas on the whiteboard. In a tank top, his biceps are jacked and glistening from shooting hoops.

"Hi, I'm Ash Eisenberg," the Air Jordan wannabe introduces himself to my mother, then looks at me, eyebrows raised, calling out my rudeness.

"Oh right, this is my—"

"Gloria. You can call me Gloria." My mother drops my hand to shake Ash's, doing her best to come across as a peer, not the woman who birthed me.

"—mother," I finish my sentence, clarifying even the slightest chance of misreading the situation. My mother huffs her disapproval just loud enough for my ears.

"Pleasure to meet you, Gloria." Ash tips his head in deference to his elder and plops down in the other wingback chair directly across from us. My mother's palm covers her heart in a small swoon. A perfected move from her hours of rom-com watching. "What are you two doing over here this afternoon? Keeping my grandmother company?"

Before I can come up with a cover story, Mrs. Eisenberg spits out, "Antonia here wants to be on your show. Can you help her out?"

MONDAY,
JUNE 24

The three of us are huddled over my phone screen. In the tense silence, I can hear Krish and Zwena breathing.

4:32 p.m. (Ash)

It's all arranged. I worked with the producers to get you on the show. The rest is up to you.

I look up expectantly. When I meet eyes with Krish and then with Zwena, both are hesitant to be the first to react. I have been sitting on this text since Friday afternoon because Krish had a twenty-first birthday that night to emcee, and over the weekend he was headlining on the main stage of the Folsom Street Fair in San Francisco. Ash's twenty-word text couldn't compete with the dozen or so pictures Krish sent me and Zwena from the DJ booth. There were folks walking their partners in studded neck collars, naked women teetering on stilts, and delicious-looking penis popsicles that Krish reported sold out by noon. Merchants at the stall next to his turntables offered open-air body waxing. And not of legs and eyebrows, Krish was quick to report. Zwena, who is rarely fazed by words or images, explained away the popsicle popularity by responding that it was unseasonably warm for

San Francisco's typical June gloom. I couldn't take my eyes off the guy juggling XL-size dildos in various skin shades. Maybe Krish was right and my hued lotions could be used as lube.

Zwena was also unavailable over the weekend. She had to bail on working my table at the farmers market to pull three sixteen-hour shifts to cover for Peter the fry guy's last-minute elopement to Vegas. I waited anxiously for their busy weekends to end in comparison to my slow one spent side by side with Simon purging garbage bags of baby paraphernalia from the garage, a task we were meant to accomplish before our now teens had become tweens. I spent six hours with Simon reminiscing over all the milk-stained bottles, worn blankets, miniature shin guards, and dog-eared school yearbooks, as if every moment of Lou's and Coco's lives he was present for and yearned to relive. Later, I called an emergency Monday-morning meeting at Krish's apartment to occur immediately after I dropped Lou and Coco off at YMCA camp. Zwena must have recognized the urgency in my voice when I insisted the three of us had to get together first thing Monday. When I showed up, Zwena was already at Krish's place ready to throw water on another one of my dumpster fires.

"For the record, I didn't ask him to do this for me," I offer as an explanation and a conversation starter. A flush of embarrassment rises from my chest to my cheeks. Even in front of these two, who know that I detest asking for help under any circumstance, I can't quell the heat.

The afternoon at Mrs. Eisenberg's house had gone from casual and effortless between three women to uneasy and frankly a little demeaning once Ash walked into the room. While Mrs. Eisenberg had coached me to own my worth by asking for a raise at the airport and Christmases off to be with my girls, I figured she was mentoring me to stand up and ask for what I want even if it went against my nature. It never occurred to me Mrs. Eisenberg would do the requesting for me.

Masked as a question, Mrs. Eisenberg all but insisted that Ash figure out how to get me a spot on *Innovation Nation* without going through the regular channels. Ash had just sat there adjusting himself in the chair, either from social discomfort or from an irritating jock itch. Either way, Mrs. Eisenberg's query hung in the air like dead mistletoe. No one stood to pucker up with a response.

It was my mother who cut the tension in the room, saving my dignity by bringing us back around to the other reason we were there, to give Mrs. Eisenberg a wash, color, and set. Not waiting for Ash's answer, Gloria slung her bag of hair products and styling tools over her shoulder and suggested I help get Mrs. Eisenberg on her feet and into the bathroom so she could wash the desert queen's crown. My mother, usually the last one to leave the presence of a striking man, was astute enough to know that I needed an out, pronto.

With the two of us flanking Mrs. Eisenberg, we shuffled out of the living room. Ash continued to sit in silence. My fear of his answer was met with something much, much worse. No answer at all. And I hadn't heard a word from him since. Until his text Friday night.

"Girlllll!!" Zwena finally jumps to her feet, whooping and clapping, her hips swinging from side to side, slicing the contemplative air around Krish's kitchen table. "You got on the show. You. Got. On. The. Show. Yougotontheshow! You've been telling me to watch these past few years, but you know I can't stand watching those pinch-faced wabenzies throw their money around. But," Zwena asserts with a finger pointed at my heart, "if they want to throw money your way, that I will watch." Zwena rubs her palms together, indicating her zeal at the idea of my windfall.

"I didn't get on the show," I correct her enthusiasm, acutely aware I did not earn a spot. A spot was given to me. "Somehow, at his grandmother's direction, Ash got me on the show." This is the first time I have articulated the truth out loud, and the words sound just as bad as they do in my head. "As a new judge, that's risking a lot." *I know he loves his grandmother, but why would Ash cash in this chit to help me?*

"*Pft.* Nani anajali. Who cares? You're going to be on TV!" Zwena waves away my need to express the difference without a second thought. Krish, however, exaggeratedly moves from hunched over my phone to leaning his chair on its back two legs. With each passing moment of Krish's silence, my internal temperature rises a degree. I'm pretty sure I know what he's thinking, because I'm thinking it too. For years Krish has pulled forty-hour weeks at the airport and dozens more on the weekends working on his music and hustling for any gig he could get. While his one indulgence is his sneaker collection, Krish hasn't been back to India to visit his extended family since he was nineteen. For as long as I've known him, I can't recall a time he has so much as taken a three-day weekend. Krish has stayed true to himself, making endless sacrifices to chase his dreams while squaring his parents' disappointment in his choices with the life he desires and has been stubborn enough to prove he deserves.

Krish's parents left everything they had known in India after earning full scholarships to Rutgers University in New Jersey. Growing up in Sherman Oaks on a heavy diet of famous quotes from captains of capitalism and open web browsers to America's top medical schools, Krish, without the blessing of his parents, left for San Francisco to build his music-production empire one intentionally scratched record at a time.

I can see, before Krish opens his mouth, that he is working out in his head how to balance his bitterness at my boon with words of wisdom on how I should proceed. I can't stand his quiet a moment more and interrupt his deliberation so he can hit me with the truth.

"Trust me, I'm aware that a primetime slot that I didn't earn was given to me. I'm not someone's charity. I didn't want this handed to me, I wanted to earn the spot. But here I am." At least that is what I'm working to convince everyone, including myself. Truth is, over the weekend I kept thinking back to January and Mrs. Eisenberg's prophecy that one day "luck will bend my way." At the time, I thought those were musings of the elite. However, now that I have more knowledge of Mrs. Eisenberg's background, I understand her words came from her own experience, not just mah-jongg tournament table talk. What I don't know yet is if Ash's effort to get me on the show is luck finally bending my way or an offer with strings attached.

Zwena reads my mind. "Is Ash expecting something in return?"

"I don't know." I cringe.

"Well, do the producers know you and Simon are married and he's a finalist to be on the show?"

"I don't think so, but this is all I've heard from Ash since we last saw each other at his grandmother's house. And there's been nothing from the show."

Krish jumps in, "How did you respond to his text?"

"I haven't yet."

"Then I stand by my original answer. Who cares?! You are on the show!" Zwena celebrates.

"Wait, you haven't texted him back yet?!" Krish presses, his eyes popping at my inaction. "Or called?!"

I thought Krish of all people would be supportive of my steadiness, of not jumping at the opportunity without marinating on it, and at least asking for input from my small but devoted panel of life advisers. These two. Krish must realize I needed time to consider what I may have to do to return Ash's favor, though perhaps that is something that would only cross a woman's mind. And most importantly, lying wide awake at night, I needed the dark, undisturbed hours to weigh the pros and cons of accepting an offer I didn't earn on my own merit. From the days of securing my spot at UCLA's high school science camp to sweeping Mr. Kim's store aisles to waking up at 5:00 a.m. to study for college exams to piecing my life together when Simon deserted me, I've been relying on my sweat and skills to earn my own way. I loathe the idea of pulling strings for my benefit, and the thought of slighting the system makes my stomach feel like it's unraveling.

"Krish, you more than anyone know I didn't earn this. I will be down there filming with other entrepreneurs who came by their finalist position honestly. Founders who are financially strapped supporting their business ideas." It pains me, like a screw to the temple, that one of those founders could be Simon. That would just be weird if we were both on the show. "They all went through the mandatory steps to make it on the new season."

"No one has to know," Zwena cuts in sharply, annoyed that we are even contemplating what my answer to Ash's offer should be. How nice to be in your twenties with a rubber-banding interpretation of right and wrong.

"Toni, maybe you didn't *earn* the spot on *Innovation Nation*, but you have more than *earned* a break. You have *earned* a little luck in your life," Krish insists.

"That's true, that's true," Zwena clucks, tiring of a discussion she believes is a closed case.

"You remember my first big gig over a decade ago? I got to DJ a Stanford fraternity lawn party, and it turned out that the social chair of the house was the son of some Houston oil magnate." I nod, remembering being impressed by the story. Krish floated through the airport the two weeks leading up to the party piecing together tracks in his head. "And the next thing I knew I was DJing the kid's graduation party on his dad's yacht in Mykonos." *That's right, Krish has had one vacation in the past ten years.*

"What I never told you was that it was the daughter of that oily Houston tycoon who got me the gig. Her younger brother was the frat brat at Stanford. I met her in SFO when she was flying first class to London, and she was a big-time flirt. From her ticket class and her last name, I figured that it might be worth my time to flirt back." Krish shrugs, feigning innocence.

"In less than fifteen minutes, she asked me to be her date to her sister's Southern society wedding. I didn't have to connect too many dots to figure out she wanted to take a working-class Indian dude to piss off her parents. Did I tell you she asked me if I could wear a pagri? She had no idea that I am Hindu Punjabi, not Sikh Punjabi. I could have been insulted. I could have gone to HR claiming I was suffering from the effects of microaggression and asked for paid sick leave for my bruised mental health. Instead, I saw an opportunity. I made a deal. I would go with her to the wedding, but she had to get me a DJing gig before I went as her date. She kept her word, and that night at her brother's fraternity party my career skyrocketed."

"Do you still talk to the trust fund baby?" Zwena questions Krish, her level of interest in our conversation rejuvenated. It also allows her the opportunity to use one of her favorite American expressions, *trust fund baby*, that for years she thought was *trust fun, baby*, which she took to heart every moment she wasn't at Build-A-Burger.

"I see her from time to time in the airport. These days she carries a puppy in a purse and has a barrel-chested, big-buckled husband about twenty years older than her. Doesn't stop her from giving me a little wink, though. Trophy wife was definitely her calling."

Later, I'm going to have to explain *trophy wife* to Zwena too. I don't want her thinking you earn a trophy just for getting married in America. From my experience, it's quite the opposite.

"So, you would take the offer?" I clarify with Krish, desperate for his honest answer. I don't have to reconfirm with Zwena, we all know where she stands.

"I would take the offer. And when you land the deal and turn your first profit, let's use some of the money and fly to Mykonos for market research and moussaka. I've always wanted to go back," Krish affirms with a heartening head tilt.

JULY

SUNDAY,
JULY 7

Pouring a second cup of coffee, I hear the slow churning of the garage door. One of the clickers is on my car's driver's-side visor, and the spare is in the kitchen junk drawer. It's 9:00 a.m., and Lou and Coco are still asleep upstairs after a night helping their grandmother host a post–Fourth of July dance party at the Senior Connection while I capitalized on time-and-a-half holiday weekend pay at the airport. The girls came home bragging on their abuelita leading residents in a slow but enthusiastic conga line. The retiree romp even included the curmudgeonly old diabetics who only attend the dances for the free cookies since the nurse who monitors their blood glucose levels has Saturdays off.

I pick up the frying pan left in the sink from late-night tostones and press my ear against the door between the kitchen and garage. I can't imagine anyone would risk stealing my 2002 Ford Explorer in broad daylight, especially when the car pickings across Highway 101 are infinitely better, but I guess when you're desperate, a ride's a ride.

I barely make out a low scraping sound, like a raccoon is pawing through leftovers in my garbage can or something heavy is being dragged across the concrete floor. Fridays are garbage day in my neighborhood, so I know the plastic bin is empty and a raccoon certainly did not open the garage door. I see my phone on the kitchen table, 911 a quick dial away. But if I called, what would I say, *It sounds like nails scratching a chalkboard in my garage, send someone quick?* Now that Simon is back, if something happens to me, will Lou and Coco live with their dad, or stay with my mother? In Simon's absence I let the decision of guardianship lapse, along with selling the house and changing my phone number.

I close my eyes and instinctively make the head, heart, left, right sign of the cross before raising the pan above my head with one hand and cracking open the back door as discreetly as I can. The scraping sound grows louder, accompanied by huffing as I reach right to flick on the overhead light.

"Ahhhh!!" Simon yells. Surprised by the sudden fluorescence, he drops an enormous cardboard box with an earth-shaking thud. To smack him with my frying pan now, I would have to leap over the multiple IKEA boxes littering my recently cleaned-out garage. Sweden has saved Simon.

Instead of hitting him with it, I point the pan toward Simon. "How the hell did you get in the garage?" I strain through tight lips.

"Is that what you wear to bed these days?" Simon replies, taking me in from top to bottom. I look down without recollection of what I slid into at midnight. My worn-thin plaid pajama bottoms have shrunk to floods, and I have on Coco's discarded Saint Anne's debate team T-shirt. Inside out and backward. Even though it's supposed to climb above ninety degrees today, the concrete floor is cool on my bare feet.

"The garage, Simon. How did you get in here?" I repeat, taking the frying pan off Simon and pointing it to the metal rolling door. Simon doesn't take his eyes off me.

"Last night I swung by and got the extra clicker from the junk drawer in the kitchen. You really haven't changed a bit, Toni."

I know Coco and Lou are loving that their dad comfortably comes and goes from our home, able to swing by at a moment's notice and be there when I can't. His attention is something they crave, and I'm happy for them that they are getting it. Also, with the possibility of break-ins like this one, it does ease my concerns a bit to know the girls are home alone less than they used to be when I was single parenting.

However, Simon's invasion of my privacy when the girls aren't home, even if it is into a house he co-owns, is not okay with me. It strikes me as I stand here ready to strike Simon that this house has become more than a place to rest my head. In two years, I've claimed both sides of our marital bed. I hand-wash my bras and hang them to dry wherever I please. I am highly tuned to the sounds the girls make as they go about their daily routines because there is not another voice demanding my attention. And the only schedule I have to work around to invite friends over to the house is mine. My vagabond husband is an intrusion in this garage and a stranger in my sanctuary.

"How many lint rollers does one person need?" Simon mumbles to himself while pawing through my stored items. Exhibit A right here: our lack of established boundaries since Simon's return. Not that it's any of his business, but my uniform sweater tends to pill, so in the winter I give it a good once-over before I leave for work, otherwise I'll just pick at it all day.

"What's this, Simon? You trying to boost Sweden's GDP?" Between my entrepreneurs course and my blinding hours reviewing *Innovation Nation* episodes, business terminology has crept into my vernacular. We both turn our heads around the garage to take in the half dozen IKEA boxes where the bins of the twins' childhoods recently resided.

"I know we are taking things slow," Simon begins with a pout. "But my new apartment is tiny, and I need a proper office to work and see clients." Other than mutually enjoying the spark that has returned in Lou and Coco since Simon came home, I wouldn't label our relationship as moving at any speed, slow or fast. The divorce papers are still in their envelope, and Simon is out of his Airbnb and settled into a short-term rental. He does have a key to the house, and apparently now access to the garage. Fewer nights to cook has been a bonus, the increase in tempeh and tofu to my diet has not. We are semicomfortably living in marriage limbo until I figure out what I want. Simon got to decide to leave, I get to decide if he comes back.

"I hear office sharing is a popular option. There's a 'for rent' banner hanging on the side of the building on El Camino Real near the Menlo Park Safeway," I say, kicking my big toe on the side of the box that looks to be a desktop.

"I need something more private to meet with clients. A secure space." The way Simon keeps saying *clients*, like he's still an investment banker and not a charlatan shaman, grates even my dark brew caffeinated patience.

"They need to feel safe in order to open up to me," Simon pleads, and I can see that he has perfected an expression of empathy mixed with concern, likely in his bathroom mirror. "What better place than our cozy home. Plus, we can write off the square footage of the extra bedroom as a business expense." I had promised Lou and Coco that the week before high school starts, one of them could finally move into that extra space. They have been nagging for their own spaces since they were ten and Coco wanted to use their bedroom to read while Lou preferred to blast music.

When Simon left, I thought it was best for Lou and Coco to continue sharing a room for consistency and company being minus one person in our family. I wanted no doubts in their minds that while their father may have cut out, sisters are forever. They do not leave. In my mind there would be nothing more reassuring than being able to roll over and stare into your mirror image. That level of comfort I could assure them. And for me, their sharing a room ensured Lou and Coco remained young and innocent a little longer. If I allow Simon to use the extra bedroom as an office, it will keep the girls together, preserving the childhood that I am not ready to let slip. Bonus, I could blame the change in plans on their dad.

"If I use the extra room, then we can trial run my being back in the house on a more regular basis." Simon delicately wades into rough relationship waters as I am still lost in the thought of tucking the girls into their matching twin beds for the foreseeable future.

Sensing a genuine opening, Simon steps into my sight line and continues. "We can try it for six months. If I get funding from *Innovation Nation*, then obviously I will need to hunt for a professional office space in Palo Alto by the start of the new year. Best U Man will be exploding, and I'll need a business manager. You love numbers, so you could leave your airport job and come work reception and deal with the quarterly books." Simon's voice speeds up in fervor for what he thinks is a brilliant idea, and he rubs my arms to warm me up to it. Until recently, as far as I knew, Simon was wrapped in Tibetan prayer flags chomping on chia seeds. Now he's back predicting that in six months' time Best U Man will be the next California maleness rage and I'll, once again, passively relinquish my forward momentum to his latest project. Simon still believes that as long as he is advancing spiritually, professionally, whatever, the family will thrive, and I will be content standing still.

Content my ass. He has no idea about my own advancement, let alone my contentment.

"You seem pretty confident you're going to make it past the final selection for the show." I shake Simon's hands off me and place the frying pan on top of a box. I cross my arms under my boobs to hold them up where they used to sit.

"I'm not confident, I know." Simon throws his shoulders back and grins. I swear he grows an inch taller. "Found out Wednesday. The producers let all the selected contestants know before the holiday weekend."

Oh my God, this hit show will turn into a shit show if Simon and I compete against each other. Hopefully the producers really don't know we're married, we do have different last names. And even if they do, they'd never put us on the same episode.

"Congratulations. Sounds like prioritizing yourself has really paid off," I remark with a backhanded compliment Simon doesn't pick up on.

"Thanks. I think I have a good shot."

Following Ash's text and the Monday-morning table talk with Krish and Zwena, I rushed to upgrade my website and set myself up with a Brown Butter, Baby! company email. Should I accept Ash's generous, if not wholly above-board deal, I want my company to look legit. Only thing is, I have completely forgotten to check the new email since I set it up. I must have gotten the same email Simon did.

"I have a ton of work to get pitch-ready between now and then, so I really do need a quiet place to work, to focus. A normal business pitch is around forty-five minutes, but on *Innovation Nation* you only get eleven minutes before going to commercial, so it has to be tight." Simon explains the obvious like I haven't studied every aspect of the show. "I'll probably have to cut back on my time with Lou and Coco to get it all done." Simon sees my facial muscles tighten, just not from what he thinks. "Though if you let me back in the house, I can keep being a star dad."

Oh, how convenient it is to be a father who believes he can float in and out of parenting duties based on where he lays his head at night. *First time, shame on you, Simon. Second time, it's a pattern.*

There's no way I was going to tell Simon that I made it on the show. That intel was too formidable to share on a random Tuesday daughter drop-off. It's perfect ammunition for I don't know when, but I'm withholding it for now. I haven't even told Ash yet that I'm accepting his generous offer. I'd been struggling to receive it for exactly what it is, charity, but Simon has pushed me over the hump. *It's on.*

"Trust me, Toni, this is going to be great for our family. Just great," Simon states definitively and reaches into his pocket, pulling out a Swiss Army knife. He's readying himself for a day building a home office set with the assistance of overly complicated directions despite having a disgruntled wife with one foot planted on his desk box.

"Think about it," Simon continues with his professional daydreaming. "When I get funded, Best U Man will take off, the money will be rolling in, and we can go back to how things were. You can take care of the girls, help in my office, and if there's time, pick up a class or two."

I can see Simon is proud of himself for mentioning I have intellectual interests as he spins what he believes is a pretty convincing vision of our future. "Disneyland this year for sure, a new house in two. This is our destiny, Toni, we both know it."

So, in this version of our destiny Simon gets to move forward with no repercussions for his vanishing act, and I get to go in reverse, scarred and embittered. I may not have made substantial progress on myself since Simon left, but I certainly have no desire to backslide to the way things were. Simon looks up from cutting through packing tape to see if my facial expression has shifted to match his enthusiastic three-year plan. It hasn't.

"Excuse me." A raspy but authoritative voice accompanies a knock just outside the garage, interrupting Simon's fantasy that I don't want, now or ever. If only the girls didn't want it either. Unfortunately, they do, so here I am, again, standing still.

"Ash," I gasp, and my arms drop to my sides in shock. So do my boobs. Simon turns away from his cardboard box to take Ash in. "How do you know where I live?" Sensing my piqued interest and shift to a friendlier tone than I had been using with him, Simon leaps over the boxes to stand by my side, two against one. I take a big step to the left, unsure where to place myself between the two men.

"You left your information on a piece of paper at my grandmother's house," Ash says, shielding his eyes from the morning brightness so he can catch my gaze. "Right after your mother and Bubbe decided to make the hair house call a standing weekly appointment."

Indeed, I had left my address. The following day an exquisite bouquet of peonies showed up with a card with no name thanking me for bringing my mom over to do Mrs. Eisenberg's hair. The day after that was spent driving my cart past Build-A-Burger at least two dozen times to ask Zwena if she thought Mrs. Eisenberg sent the flowers or maybe it was Ash. Each time she told me to go ahead and ask one of them. And each time I waved away her advice as ridiculous before returning twenty minutes later to ask for it again. On my final drive-by, Zwena informed me that Albert Einstein claimed that the definition of insanity is doing the same thing over and over again expecting different results. She clocked out of her shift before I could tell her one, Albert Einstein was not a founding father, therefore he would not be on her citizenship test, and two, leaving me to stew in my own thoughts is in violation of our friendship code.

"I wanted to give you space to consider my offer, but time's ticking, and frankly I'm surprised I haven't heard from you." Ash waves his index finger back and forth like a metronome keeping time to make his point. Dang, I should have listened to Krish. He warned me that if I waited to respond, Ash would think I was not only ungrateful but also an idiot. "Anyway, I thought I'd stop by.

"I also wanted to let you know my grandmother has been loving her hair appointments with your mom. I'm not sure she will ever head back into the salon now, and she has had a long-term relationship with her hairdresser, so that's saying something." I giggle under my breath listening to Ash talk about his grandmother's grooming habits. It's really attractive for a man I initially considered to be short on emotional intelligence.

"Space to consider what?" Simon asks, interrupting my focus on Ash. Simon sounds perturbed that a man is here, towering over him, to see me. I'm enjoying observing Simon's internal angst as he tries to parse out if I'm juggling two men in my life.

"I need to know what you've decided," Ash says, moving into the garage to step out of the rising sun. His eyes stay fixated on me, not acknowledging Simon's presence or his question. "More importantly, the producers need to know."

Clearing his throat to be noticed, Simon reaches across the boxes to take my hand and ownership of me. "Hey, aren't you the new judge on *Innovation Nation*?" Simon furrows his brow and squints his eyes in an attempt to place Ash. I avoid Simon's hand by clasping my own behind my back. I'm now acutely aware of the inside-out shirt I'm wearing in front of Ash with the tag sticking out like a tongue at my neck.

"I am," Ash states matter-of-factly.

Realizing who's standing in front of him, Simon tries for a formal introduction. "I didn't get your name," he says with a *man of the house* tone that makes me gag. Simon spreads his legs to appear bigger than he is, adding to the protective vibe he is working to send Ash's way.

"Ash Eisenberg. I'm a friend of Antonia's. And you are?" Ash continues straightforwardly, taking one step closer into Simon's space. I can't help but swallow a snicker. *Is this about to be a cock fight?*

"I'm Toni's husband."

"Didn't realize she had one. She's never mentioned you," Ash responds unremarkably, knowing full well I do have a husband. Or did. Or I don't know.

Ash's disinterest in Simon is made apparent when he turns his back to him and fully faces me. "The producers are finalizing the cast list for the second half of Season 18 right now. So, what will it be, Antonia?" Ash's tone is one of finality, telling me he is not asking again. I cross my ankles, trying to hide one ratty pajama–clad leg behind the other. Simon is looking at me profoundly confused, so I move my eyes to avert his gaze.

"Mom, you used up all the eggs and I want to make french toast!" Lou yells from the kitchen to wherever she thinks I might be in the house.

"Yes, I'll take you up on your offer," I answer Ash. I lift my chin assertively and more than a slight bit competitively with Simon standing there trying to expand his own presence and diminish mine. Today is not the day 610 Andrews Street will become a communal office space. I, too, have a company to launch. The extra room will not be Simon's. It will not be Lou's or Coco's. It will be mine for Brown Butter, Baby!.

"Yes, you will go get more eggs?" The girls bounce into the garage following my voice.

With the three of us in our Sunday-morning pajamas, I gather Lou and Coco under my arms, most proud of these two products that I have funded and raised. This time, happy to make introductions, I look first to Lou and then to Coco. "Ash, these are my daughters, Lou and Coco."

"Our daughters," Simon corrects, his tone a mixture of irritation and injured manhood.

For the first time since Ash walked up to the garage his face, like the summer sun, warms up and radiates an inviting smile toward the three of us. "It's so nice to meet you two." Ash slowly turns his head back and forth, taking in my twins as if teen girls are the most miraculous invention he has ever seen. "Your mom is one lucky woman."

"I am," I agree, and give both girls a squeeze.

TUESDAY, JULY 23

It's a little over six weeks until I go to LA to shoot my segment for *Innovation Nation*. The result of a decade of mothering girls who were wide awake at the stroke of 5:30 a.m., my circadian rhythm is trained to the first sign of dawn. My boss was so excited at my news and to have a reality TV personality as an employee that she rearranged the personnel schedule and put me on the 3:00 p.m. to midnight shift through September. Now, if I hop right out of bed when my eyes open, I am able to optimize the peace in the house for a solid five hours before my sleep-drunk teens rise to ask for food, cash, and rides. I can then return to manipulating my pitch from 10:00 p.m. to midnight from the quiet comfort of my cart, when the need for airport transportation services is relatively sparse. As a general rule, older customers tend to be early travelers, not wanting to navigate airports, car rentals, taxis, or hotel arrivals in the dark. Their need to be settled in early is serving Brown Butter, Baby! well right now.

12:36 p.m. (Gloria)

Niña, come rápido!

12:36 p.m. (Gloria)

And bring mis nietas.

12:36 p.m. (Gloria)

And azúcar. I'm out.

My mother thinks slower than she types, so what should be one communication hovers around four on average.

12:37 p.m. (Gloria)

Ven acá. I'm doing Sylvia's hair soon.

12:38 p.m. (Toni)

Unless you have a broken bone or a leaking roof, can I come over tomorrow? I only have a little time before I have to be at work.

12:39 p.m. (Gloria)

My bones are bien. Come ahora.

When Gloria leans on Spanglish, I know she's flustered. She uses her native tongue to socialize with her Spanish-speaking friends and with David, Gabriel, and me in casual conversation so she can check that we haven't lost our accuracy or accent. English is mostly reserved for the grocery store, her volunteer time at the Senior Connection, and begrudgingly her granddaughters. She loves to remind me that I have failed at building their authentic Spanish fluency to her standards since

Lou and Coco entered kindergarten, and I was no longer their primary source of conversation.

"Girls, grab your shoes, we're going over to Abuelita's," I holler, gathering up our shared laptop that has become all mine in the summer months. I'm not even met with a rustle of movement at my request. My house isn't that big, and I know Lou and Coco heard me. I also know they're awake, because there's an empty box of cereal and a wilting blueberry muffin wrapper on the kitchen counter.

The floor creaks, broadcasting one of my lazies is creeping from the bathroom back to her bed. "Be ready in five, or I'm not taking you to meet your friends at the Stanford Shopping Center tomorrow." This will push them along. Lou and Coco have been working as assistant camp counselors for the six- to eight-year-old group at the YMCA, so for the first time in their fourteen years they have money to burn, and they want to light it on fire at a shopping mall that is outside of our budget. I can't wait for them to return home with the realization that they can purchase a full-length pair of leggings for every day of the week from Target for what it costs for one capri pair at Lululemon. Some math lessons are best learned in the real world.

"Be down in three." My upstairs suddenly sounds like a couple of recruits scurrying to tidy their barracks before rack check.

"What does Abuelita want?" Coco asks, the first to make it downstairs. I hand her a barely-been-used brush out of my purse. She looks from me to the brush. "Hypocrite much?"

I look in the mirror behind me. My hair is twisted around two chewed-on Bic pens holding the bun in place. I grab the brush, pull out the pens, and take a few swipes through my knotted waves. "Better," I admit out loud, and then give the brush back to Coco.

"That just saved us five minutes of you bickering with Abuelita," Coco concludes as she brushes her own hair, not taking her eyes off me. She's not wrong, but I don't like that Coco recognizes that her mother and grandmother squabble over such trivial concerns.

"Mom, can we stop and get a latte on the way?" Lou asks, saunter-ing down the stairs like stopping at Starbucks is something we do on the regular, and so is fourteen-year-olds drinking coffee.

"*Ehrm* . . . when have you ever had a latte?" I probe, hinting to Lou she just made a request that landed with a thud.

"Dad takes us to get one on the mornings he drives us to the Y. We get a latte and coffee cake."

"And then you jitter yourself into camp?" I snap, misplacing my annoyance at Simon.

"You can't start work with little kids without caffeine." Lou speaks her truth like a mother who's been parenting on interrupted sleep for years. In what world does Simon think this is okay? And with what money is he dropping a twenty on breakfast twice a week? I make a mental note to text Simon about this when I get to the airport. Then I make a second mental note that I will probably forget by the time I get there.

"Well, I hope you enjoyed yesterday's lattes, because those were your last ones," I update the girls and point toward the garage.

"Always the funpire, sucking the life out of anything cool we do with Dad," Coco slings under her breath, perfectly timed as she walks past me.

"Excuse me?"

"You're not even giving Dad a chance," Lou accuses, eye to eye, which I note is a new development in her growth trajectory on her way to pass me by. I'm tuned in enough to know that Lou's comment has more to do with me not allowing Simon to live in our house than it has to do with specialty caffeinated drinks.

"You don't give anyone a chance," Coco follows up with a punctu-ated jab. That snippy remark is coming right from Coco's desire to paint the extra room aqua before moving in. Needing only two seconds to consider the mess and shoddy workmanship of it all, I gave her decor plans a hard pass. I know Coco, and after one wall she would cry bored and we would be left with half a job done crappily and three cans of pointless paint. Plus, I hate aqua.

◆ ◆ ◆

There's a pristine black Range Rover with beige leather seats squeezed tightly into my mom's carport. That's usually where I pull up right behind Gloria's Toyota so as not to piss off Mr. Aberdeen next door. The girls and I run our fingers along the driver's side of the car, hoping, I don't know, maybe that a life of luxury can come through osmosis.

Using my key to let ourselves in, Lou yells, "Abuelita," to announce our arrival. "We're here!" And then the girls head right into the kitchen to see if there is any sweet majarete.

"Here, here, let me help you up," I hear my mom offer from behind her bathroom door.

"You know I'm much steadier these days. I've been working hard with Sophie on my balance and strength. We just might be able to pull this off." The voice behind the door is so muffled in comparison to my mom's insistence of help that it's hard to tell if Gloria is in there with a man or a woman.

"Are Abuelita and her apartment building buddies planning a robbery?" Coco jokes, cuddling a large bowl of majarete she's found in the refrigerator. She's been influenced by a summer of reading bank heist novels from the library and dessert for breakfast with her father.

"I bet Abuelita can run pretty fast in heels," Lou says, jumping in on the ribbing over the capabilities of senior citizens.

"Just the opposite," Abuelita corrects, cracking open the door to the bathroom just wide enough for us to see her eyes. "Go make yourself comfortable on the couch, we'll be in in a minute." The girls and I look at each other. *We?* And then they dig back into the pudding.

"Oh my God, Abuela has a boyfriend," I lean over and whisper into the ears of the girls who've decided to sit on the floor with their snack, backs against the couch.

"Do you think she called us over to tell us she's getting married? Is he here?" Lou and Coco turn and ask me at the same time. They've never seen their abuela with a man, let alone heard her talk about dating one.

"We all know Abuelita has better skills with boys than any of us do," Lou giggles, having witnessed her grandmother sweet talk her way into discounts all over the greater Bay Area. The trick, Gloria has instructed them, is to always get in the line where a man is working as the checker. Never a woman, they won't fall for the game. Gloria's life advice about seeking support from other women has gone against what I have drilled into the twins, that is to walk through the world as women who boost other women up. One of my favorite economic policy aphorisms is the belief that "rising tides lift all boats." It works for female empowerment as well as economics.

"Hey, I had a boyfriend," Coco protests. She's not sure she wants to be associated with her sister's or her mother's lack of experience with the opposite sex.

"For about a minute," Lou reminds Coco. Coco's first boyfriend traded her in for an older woman of fifteen and then proceeded to ignore her. When I wasn't consumed with wanting to throttle his pencil neck, my heart broke for Coco. Her desperate attempts to put herself in the twerp's sightline at interschool events brought me back to Ash's microeconomics office hours and me hoping that this time, unlike the last dozen, my perfect problem set would be the thing that made Ash notice me.

"If she is getting remarried, that must be one secure man because Abuela still wears Abuelo's ring," I blurt out. *I should have probably kept that thought in my head.*

"Shame on you, Toni. I am not getting remarried," Gloria disciplines me from behind the bathroom door, her hearing as healthy as a horse's.

"Then come out of the bathroom and tell us why we had to come over here so fast. The girls are about to make themselves sick off your majarete," I report, the minutes ticking. I need to get to the airport, and I still have no clue what my mother's texting desperation is about.

"And for God's sake, let out whoever you are holding hostage in there with you."

Gloria strolls out of the bathroom in tailored black pants, a polished cream silk blouse, and the most sensible shoes I have ever seen her in, a low pump that doesn't give toe cleavage. A simple gold chain is around her neck, her wedding ring now accompanying the cross. *So, she isn't wearing her wedding ring anymore.* There definitely must be a love interest in the bathroom, and from the looks of my mother's conservative outfit, he's likely a strict Catholic. She would never go for a Protestant. I thought I had shed devout Catholics when Simon left, and with him went the mandatory attendance at Sunday mass with my in-laws. I fear Gloria may be bringing piety back into my life with this new person.

"*Ehrm,* either you are dating an evangelical, or the apartment complex is having a costume party. Which one is it, Mami?" I can't think of any other reason Gloria would be standing in front of the three of us, who know her best as a woman in a waist shaper, disguised as an insurance broker.

Ignoring my petty humor, with a clearing of her throat Gloria announces, "I have something to give you," and reaches into her pants pocket to pull out a folded piece of paper. She extends her arm to hand it to me. I'm terrified my mother has either been sued for negligence by the family of Richard Harris, who threw his back out at Saturday night's salsa lesson last week, or she's gone loca and is asking me to proofread the ransom note for the person she's holding under duress in her bathroom.

I unfold the heavy paper carefully, realizing it's perforated a third of the way down. "Last month the Senior Connection hired me as their arts and activities coordinator." My mom claps her hands together, giddy with her news. I can't believe it. At sixty-five, when most people are looking to retire from their very last job, my mom has accepted her very first. "I'm no longer a volunteer! I have a job with a salary and benefits." Gloria puts her hand up for a high five from her granddaughters. Being employed and high-fiving are two things I have never seen Gloria do. I look at her in disbelief.

"Damn Abuelita, you're killing it!" Lou cheers. I shoot her a look to watch her language around her grandmother.

"I am killing it, sí?" My mom nods in agreement.

"Open it, open it!" I'm commanded as my mother does a mini cha-cha across the carpet. A check for $948, after taxes, stares back at me.

Ah, I'm beginning to see. Gloria is playing the part of an employee donning professional attire. That's what gives with the black slacks and pumps. "Now that I'm a working woman, I would like to be your first official investor in Brown Butter, Baby!.."

"Did you tell her yet?!" a familiar voice calls out loudly from behind the bathroom door. "Can I come out now?"

"Yes, yes, come out," my mom calls and walks over to the bathroom door to open it. A walnut wood derby cane reaches over the threshold first, its tip confidently placed so the hand may follow. A leg with a shoe equally reasonable to my mother's follows behind. And then I see a smooth brunette helmet perfectly hair sprayed into position.

"Hello, Antonia." Mrs. Eisenberg beams, pleased with herself. She's standing tall, chin held high, her hand gripping the ball of her cane for security and wearing a suit I recognize.

"Mrs. Eisenberg, is that the—"

"It sure is," Mrs. Eisenberg confirms, patting the shoulder pads with her free hand. "If it was good enough for having an investment meeting with Steve Jobs, it's good enough to have a business meeting with you. Plus, it still fits!" The three of us at the couch are graced with a little shimmy from our stylish blooming cactus.

"What's going on here?" I move myself forward from my relaxed schlump into my childhood couch. I need to shake my head to perk myself up from what I thought was going to be a casual visit to restart my mom's Wi-Fi. Scraping the bottom of the bowl like she's never been fed, Coco glances up, finally interested in what is going on in front of her.

Gloria shifts to stand next to Mrs. Eisenberg. "Well, after a couple of times going over to Sylvia's house to do her hair, I could tell she was getting restless spending every day in her own four walls." There are more than four walls in Mrs. Eisenberg's home. If you have to be on health house arrest, that's the house to do it in.

"So tiresome," Mrs. Eisenberg adds for emphasis. "I'm Sylvia, by the way," Mrs. Eisenberg introduces herself to Lou and Coco.

"I love your earrings, Sylvia," Lou says, staring wide-eyed at the biggest diamonds she has ever seen outside of social media.

"Mrs. Eisenberg!" my mom and I correct Lou in unison.

"So old-school," Mrs. Eisenberg retorts in mock exasperation and winks at the girls.

"We have called this surprise meeting because the two of us have been talking," Mrs. Eisenberg continues. *Feels more like a hostile take-over.* "We would like to join you on *Innovation Nation.*"

Gloria picks up with a well-practiced, "We believe that with our range of ages and skin colors we could really help you . . . *ehrm.*"

"Pitch," Mrs. Eisenberg not-so-whispers in my mother's direction to help her out.

"Pitch Brown Butter, Baby! to the judges," my mother finishes.

"You want to be my wing women on the show?"

"Sure?" the two women claim, puzzled, clearly unfamiliar with the term.

"I will triple your mother's contribution, so you have absolutely no incurred costs for the trip to LA."

"Have you even been cleared by your doctors to travel?" I ask Mrs. Eisenberg with concern. I can see by the turn down of her mouth she takes my question as an insult.

Shaking her cane at me, she says, "Of course. I'll just have to find someone new to drive me through the airport since you will be busy. And no, it won't be scented Liam." Dismissing any misconstrued offense, Mrs. Eisenberg laughs at our inside airport joke, and I join her with a giggle of my own. I can tell my mom is a little miffed she's not in on it with us.

"We do have one more request," my mom says, getting our conversation back on track by plucking her paycheck out of my hands. I'm not sure these women get that there is no offer on any table to negotiate, but I humor them and listen.

"We've got the eighty-, sixty- and forty-year-old women covered right here." Reflexively I want to correct my mother that I am, as she surely knows, not yet forty, but I choose to withhold the trepidation of my looming decade milestone in exchange for brevity.

"We need Zwena to join us for our model in her twenties, and her skin tone as well. Kenyan, Afro-Puerto Rican, ethnically ambiguous—that would be you," Mrs. Eisenberg says as she points to me, clearly proud of herself for recalling lingo that Zwena and I bat around. "And of course me with my olive complexion. The four of us are the complete package of your product rainbow."

"The show only pays to fly me down and put me up in a hotel, and Zwena's saving up to go back to Kenya to see her family next year. There's no way she can afford a trip to LA."

"I talked to her this morning," Gloria cuts me off from coming up with more excuses. "Zwena is going to travel as Sylvia's guest, and they will share a room to make sure nothing goes wrong."

"Nothing will go wrong," Mrs. Eisenberg affirms, keeping her ego intact. "I just have a bit of trouble with my shoes and buttoning my blouse, so Zwena will be there to assist me." Both elders in the room nod their heads in unison, informing me that the three women have it covered and come as a packaged deal.

"What do you say?" my mom presses, a little too needy.

"There is nothing to say, Gloria." Mrs. Eisenberg bangs her cane like a gavel on the faux hardwood floor, not allowing further deliberation. "All the pieces are in place. The deal, done." I have now experienced a crystal-clear glimpse of the unyielding and decisive lady boss Mrs. Eisenberg must have been all those years ago running Maxwell Street Records. And I am smart enough not to say no.

AUGUST

THURSDAY, AUGUST 22

After nine years of going to school with the Father, the Son, and the Holy Spirit, but no boys, Lou and Coco begged to pursue the nonsectarian academic path otherwise known as public high school. I couldn't argue against the free tuition, and with Simon's midlife penchant for praying at the altar of Hindu deities, it seemed more than justified that the Evans girls be allowed to step off the Catholic conveyor belt.

It's just over two weeks until the taping of my *Innovation Nation* segment and, instead of being at home choreographing my pitch that integrates three willful women with competing visions for the most important eleven minutes of my life, I am skirt deep in school orientations. Tuesday and Wednesday Lou and Coco had their introductions to Palo Alto High School. While they perused the multitude of club tables, from Model United Nations to Girls Who Grill, I was introducing myself to their counselor as the mother she won't be able to shake until graduation. My first order of business, right there in the high school hallway, was how I could get the girls out of the California state requirement of speech class. The twins have been to the middle school state debate tournaments the past three years. In my opinion they have nailed eye contact and cadence, so the class would be a waste of their time on the path to an AP-packed schedule. Counselor Greenberg looked at me with complete indifference and shared that, in Silicon Valley, she has been up against the grizzliest of parental demands, and I do not scare her. Then she yawned in my face and informed me that Lou and Coco will have sixth period speech fall semester.

Following high school orientation, today I am back in the auditorium at Saint Anne, a school and its accompanying judgments I was ready to leave in the rearview mirror. Graduating at the top of the eighth-grade class and recognized as Saint Anne's first Puerto Rican American alumni, Lou and Coco had been asked by Father Egan to speak at the incoming families assembly. The twins were coached to thread the rhetorical needle by championing their academic and religious experiences at Saint Anne without mentioning their decision to cut their Catholic education short in favor of free dress and Darwinian instruction.

The Sunday morning Ash showed up in my garage ruined Simon's hope for a threesome with me and IKEA. I had been juggling around a few ways to tell Simon that I, too, had been offered a slot on Season 18 of *Innovation Nation*, but the news being personally delivered by Ash Eisenberg was not one of them.

With my "yes," Ash gave me an unexpected toothy grin and thanked me for keeping the executive producers happy with him in his first season on the show. I assumed this relief was so the showrunner didn't place him in one of the outside panel seats. From my detailed episodic research, I discovered the two judges sitting in the middle chairs had their offers accepted 18 percent more times than the two judges sitting on the outside. The reason for this phenomenon I can only attribute to the contestant sight line.

Immediately following my acceptance of Ash's kindness, the atmosphere in the garage palpably shifted with Simon's darkened mood. In the moment, I wasn't sure if his brooding was because I would be in direct competition with him for seed funding or because he learned Ash Eisenberg is a friend and therefore might choose to invest in Brown Butter, Baby! over Best U Man. It's possible Simon concluded his odds of gaining funding dropped by 25 percent before he even set foot on the show. I was beating Simon before the contest had even begun.

To add to our already strained relationship, a week after Ash's visit, Simon and I were informed of what I thought would never happen. We were two of the three founders slated for the finale of Season 18. I couldn't disagree with Simon's incessant reminders that I got on *Innovation Nation* without having to do the same amount of hoop jumping as he had to. But his claim that Brown Butter, Baby!'s success at the farmers market could in no way compare to Best U Man's growing cross-country clientele teetered on haterism.

The final blow to our tenuous partnership comes while sitting elbow to elbow in the Saint Anne auditorium waiting for Lou and Coco to be called to the stage to speak. Scrolling our phones at the end of Father Egan's opening remarks, we land on the same email from *Innovation Nation* confirming our filming date for the finale and exact contestant lineup for the show.

Simon complained for weeks that he drew the short straw by filming on the last episode of the season. That while he didn't want to be called to the studio first when the new season and new judge were working out the kinks and investing conservatively, he did think Best U Man deserved to be on the third or fourth episode. As he cooked a Friday night family dinner, Simon worried loudly about investor fatigue and shifting market trends over the course of recording the show. Then just as loudly he attempted to convince us that Best U Man is an evergreen opportunity. Becoming your best self is a timeless endeavor, therefore who doesn't want the opportunity to build a company that is investing in personal perfection. The rationale sounded perfect to Simon.

I nudge Simon, and he removes his elbow from the armrest to avoid being touched by the enemy. I elbow him again so he can't ignore me. He reluctantly looks at me, and I point to my phone screen. There it is. I confirm with Simon he is the first CEO on the episode, I am the last.

More than once since finding out I, too, would be joining the show, Simon, looking to secure an advantage over me, has implied that while filming in the last episode is not ideal, a worse fate is being the third out of three contestants. The first slot, judges feel like they have full pockets to spend. By the last slot, more than likely their money has been depleted. The coffers are empty and you, which now means me, are sunk. No longer espousing the awakened philosophy of there being enough positive vibes to go around, Simon has become a karma hog.

The Gods shine on those who are righteous and live an honest life, Simon types into his Apple notes section, fingers tense. He turns his phone to me, keeping his eyes locked on the stage. Of course. Simon is convinced that I am appearing on the show thanks to a favor rather than worthiness.

Righteousness comes with a great vacation plan, I type back, not missing my own opportunity to point out to Simon that there is nothing honorable about abandoning your family.

Bitterness is not a good taste on you, Simon jabs back, now typing right in front of my face. *Really, this is where we are going to do this?* All our ugliness from Simon's selfish sojourn is being displayed on a yellow-lined screen to the soundtrack of Father Egan trying to sell the virtues of participating in the PTA.

Thinking of the cacao cullage serving as the secret ingredient in my lotions I bang out, Funny because bitterness is working well for me with Brown Butter, Baby!. So good in fact it got me on Innovation Nation. It's going to be hard for Simon to argue with my forward momentum.

It's not the viability of your company that got you on the show, Simon thumbs angrily, knowing that nothing will hit harder than calling my merit into question and doubting my intelligence.

Not caring about disrupting Sutton Fisher, the new Saint Anne PTA president stepping to the mic accompanied by jarring feedback, I grab my purse and shuffle out of the row away from Simon. Lou and Coco are still backstage. There are three more agenda items to cover before alumni are marched out for Q and A. If Lou and Coco had spotted us in the audience, I wanted them to see Simon and me as a supportive, loving united front, but I can't do it today. I'm moving up close where they will for sure see me, their mother, who has been here, cheering them on, every day of their lives.

Retreating from Simon, I plop down in the aisle seat in the front row, my bag slamming against the gentleman settled in next to me.

"Sorry," I whisper behind my hand.

"It's okay," my row mate answers, turning to give me an accompanying *no problem* half grin.

"What are you doing here?!" I yelp, and Sutton Fisher shoots me a scowl from the stage before launching into the benefits of collecting items for the yearly rummage sale now so funding can be secured for the refurbishment of the playground later.

Ash points to the other side of him and there is Livy, beaming up at Sutton. I guess minicannibals add to diversity numbers these days. And then I remember Livy's daughter is also a quarter Black, Jewish, and soon to attend a Catholic school. A Black Jewish biter makes two half Puerto Ricans look downright dull.

"Livy's husband couldn't get out of work, so I'm subbing in," Ash whispers once Sutton's eyes have moved off us. So, this brazen brother leaves his wife because she can't give him a baby, but he's willing to cram his tall, toned body into a rickety wooden auditorium seat for his five-year-old niece? Ash being here demonstrates both questionable judgment and a lack of hobbies.

I lean over and wave at Livy. Her face registers the same surprise to see me here as it did over the sweater table months ago. She mouths *hello*, and we both reach over Ash's lap to squeeze hands in a friendly gesture. My fingers accidentally graze Ash's crotch when I let go of Livy's hand, and he inadvertently gasps. I instinctively drop my head between my legs in extreme embarrassment and for self-preservation in case I start to hyperventilate from the faux pas.

Ash taps me lightly on the shoulder, but I don't move. I prefer to keep my head buried until the orientation is over and everyone has exited the building. Hopefully Simon will record the twins and I can watch them from the privacy of my hiding spot, under the covers in bed. Ash pokes me harder, letting me know I can't ignore him after what he can only assume was a freebie dick grab. Cringing, I tilt my head halfway up, and he nods to the back of the auditorium. Ash stands and whispers, "Follow me." Without question, I stumble after him to get my scolding about inappropriate touching over with.

Ash deftly pushes against one of the double doors, avoiding any creaking, and once we are on the other side, he gently closes it behind us without an audible click.

"Just so you know, every year the airport makes all the employees take a three-hour sexual harassment course online. They even pay us for our time," I babble as a way of apology and an excuse for my unintended pants skimming.

Ash laughs and puts up his hands. "I'm not going to take you for all you're worth, Antonia. Promise."

"Trust me, I don't have anything you would want," I say, blowing out a breath of relief that the only documents I will be needing to file will be my divorce papers.

"I'm not so sure about that," Ash says with a wink, cagey. "I'd like you in a dress."

A dress, huh? Maybe I wouldn't mind paying him back for that favor.

"Now that the balls game is over as quickly as it started, what are you doing here, Antonia?"

"Ha, I get it, balls game," I giggle.

"I thought Lou and Coco were heading to high school."

I cock my head and look at Ash curiously. It's so sweet he remembers their names, but odd he knows things about my girls that I never told him.

"Your mom talked my ear off when I was waiting at her house to pick up Bubbe and take her out to lunch." My mom will talk about Lou and Coco to anyone who asks, or who will listen. *Pobrecito, Ash.* Gloria has not mastered the art of polite but brief answers when it comes to her granddaughters.

"The girls are speaking during the Q and A as Saint Anne alumni," I explain. "What else did my mother tell you?" I'm prepared to be mortified for a second time in four short minutes.

"Are you here with your husband?" Ash questions directly.

Yep. That's what else Gloria told Ash, that Simon and I are together. "Technically, I'm here with Simon, yes," I answer honestly, unsure how to explain to Ash what Simon and I are other than husband and wife. "We're only here together for Lou and Coco," I clarify.

"I know," Ash responds, not at all bothered.

He does? How?

"Listen, of all people I understand that marriage is complicated. There are lots of reasons to be together, children being the most compelling reason of all," Ash says like it's a conclusion he's come to believe himself.

Is it? Is raising children together more essential to a marriage than deep, loyal love? I wonder standing in front of this man who, albeit slowly, has begun to grow on me.

"Is that why you and your wife got divorced? Because it got complicated when she couldn't have kids?" My mouth takes off before my brain can think through my words. Ash was the one who told me over tortilla chips in his grandmother's kitchen that he wanted nothing more than to have a family. Standing in Saint Anne's hallway, I wonder if I am being an emotional bully picking on Ash because I want him to spill his sad story so I feel better about mine.

Ash stuffs his hands in his pockets and bites his lower lip, appearing shut down given my line of questioning. I don't know what my purpose was deflecting the conversation off me and my unraveling marriage and onto Ash's, which has already unraveled. But maybe together we can deconstruct the muck of our tangled ties.

"I didn't divorce my wife because she couldn't have kids," Ash states, ruining my assumption. "If my ex-wife had been on board, I would have loved to foster and ultimately adopt a house full of kids in need of a family. If Evangeline hadn't done that for my grandmother, I wouldn't be here talking with you."

"*Ehrm . . . ,*" is all I say, trying to sort out in my head what must have happened in Ash's marriage. Though now I take a beat to choose my words more wisely, I can't control my face giving away that I desperately want to know more.

"My wife wanted to experience pregnancy. She left me because I was the one who couldn't have kids and she wanted to be pregnant. Ultimately, I wasn't enough, so she went out to find someone else," Ash says, practiced, like it's an anecdote he has delivered too many times, but he still hates the sound of it coming out of his mouth. "She is twelve years younger than me, and I couldn't stand in the way of what she wanted for herself, so I let her go."

I chew on Ash's words as he stares down the row of royal-blue lockers lining Saint Anne's main hallway. Stories of female infertility litter middle-aged women's social media. There are fertility doctors making TikToks on how to talk to friends struggling to conceive. I've seen numerous stories on Instagram on how to tiptoe around the dicey Mother's Day celebration with a sister-in-law who wants nothing more than to be a mother when all the other mothers in her family are dying to be celebrated by being left alone. As far as my scrolling shows, there is nothing that mentions the personal pain of a man who cannot do the thing society assumes all men can do.

"She's expecting in January," Ash admits, though I'm not sure if it is to me or to himself. *She certainly didn't waste any time.*

I think about what I can do, in this moment, to help Ash under-stand he is not alone in feeling that he wasn't enough. "Simon left us. Just got up one day and decided to walk out the door. For him, I guess, having a wife and kids was not enough of a reason to stay."

"I would never do that. You, Coco, and Lou would have been more than enough for me."

SEPTEMBER

WEDNESDAY, SEPTEMBER 4

"Who are you, and what have you done with my friend?" I nudge Zwena with my shoulder to get her attention. We are at gate D6 sitting four across, sandwiched in with my mother and Mrs. Eisenberg, on fixed pleather seats waiting to board a plane for Los Angeles. When I saw the man directly across from us with his hoodie pulled over his eyes and his body contorted over the immovable armrest to catch a few winks, I angled for us to take the wheelchair accessible seats near the window. Mrs. Eisenberg feigned insult and shrugged me off when I tried to steer her in that direction. There was so much commotion about who should sit where, taking on and off coats to contend with the air-conditioning, and back and forth roller bag comparisons, I feared the motionless man was not actually asleep but faking death to dodge the four of us.

Encased in a thick blanket of fog, the airport has closed a runway due to visibility concerns, resulting in our flight being delayed until the inbound LAX plane can land and its passengers disembark. Zwena ignores my nudging, and she ignores Patricia on the intercom, who is overly peppy with her intermittent updates—which is never comforting when your flight is postponed for weather reasons. I wave my fingers up and down, signaling to Patricia to tone it down a notch. She has only been a gate agent for a month and has yet to learn that raising passenger hopes inevitably crashes into pissed-off people when travel expectations are not met.

Settled in for our extended wait, my mom and Mrs. Eisenberg are exchanging favorite age-spot serums and Hollywood leading men, unconcerned with our deferred travel plans and my wrecked case of nerves. Every hour of this past week has been earmarked to ensure perfect preparation for our filming tomorrow at 11:00 a.m. Call time on the lot in Studio City is 9:00 a.m., which means I must be in the hotel lobby coffee shop for a double espresso by 7:20 a.m. to perk myself up to just north of wakefulness but south of the jitters. For this afternoon, though, before Zwena is allowed to go in search of the five-star food truck with the best Nyama Choma in greater Los Angeles, the four of us need to do a final run-through of our Brown Butter, Baby! presentation in the Hilton business center. Then Zwena can go grilled-meat hunting, and my mom and Mrs. Eisenberg can order room service and a hotly anticipated Kevin Costner rom-com made for the AARP crowd. I will be checking for the fifth and final time that the studio received all my lotions and display cases, and then I want to be tucked into my hotel bed by 7:00 p.m. to ward off under-eye dark circles. Except now it looks like we won't be taking off until close to 5:00 p.m. Good thing I made a trip to Sephora to buy puffy-no-more eye patches in case of this exact scenario.

Since we got to the airport, Zwena has had her nose in the recently updated US citizen's test prep book that Krish ordered for her. With our growing intolerance of Zwena's near constant insertion of random North American facts into our conversations, for the preservation of our friendship with Zwena, and to increase her chances of passing the test on the first try, Krish bought her the tome. The hope is it will narrow her history knowledge down to exactly what she needs to know to nail the exam. No more. No less.

I rolled my eyes as she started on page one, thinking I was going to have to relive the dry, uninspired lectures of my twelfth-grade government teacher. It all felt oddly new to me, with only a few familiar tidbits here and there. I couldn't answer most of the practice test questions, or even offer a best guess. As it turns out, Zwena from Kenya knows more about the three branches of our democratic government than I do. It's not a great feeling to know you are too ignorant to become a citizen of your own country.

I slurp the dregs of my drink extra loud and then stir my straw around the ice, intentionally trying to break Zwena's concentration so she will pay attention to me. If I have to spend one more minute alone with my thoughts questioning every word I've selected for the presentation tomorrow, I may have a mental breakdown today.

"Subiri," Zwena instructs, holding her right hand up to my face. Her left index finger follows a sentence in her book to the end of the paragraph. "Hey, hey, look at this. Did you know your mom can run for president of the United States?"

I glance over to the woman who is pulling an eyelash curler out of her purse. "No, she can't, she was born in Puerto Rico," I respond, gnawing on my straw. "You have to be born in the US to become president. And you have to have the slightest interest in politics." *Whew, there is one fact I remember from second period senior spring.*

"Ah. Wrong." Zwena looks up at me from under raised eyebrows. "As of April 2000, any Puerto Rican who has lived in the United States for at least fourteen years and is over the age of thirty-five can run for president," she corrects me, licking her index finger and marking an imaginary point in the Zwena column of our ongoing US history scoreboard.

"Did you know that not one, but at least four attractive men between the ages of twenty-two and fifty have strolled past us, and you have not noticed one of them? Not one. And that guy"—I point down the concourse toward a fading man with a pair of Bose headphones warming his neck—"was trying to get your attention, and you didn't even bother to look up!" With pursed lips, Zwena throws me a scowl like I must be mistaken. I meet her lips with a huff and give myself an imaginary point in my own column.

"Points are for facts, not fiction. Trust me, I can multitask. I saw that brother in the red Adidas tracksuit. He's too lanky for me, plus he reminded me of my cousin Gathii." Zwena shivers, sticking her tongue out at the thought. Then she dives back into her catalog of facts, leaving me alone with the ping-ponging disastrous scenarios that could occur tomorrow taking up residency in my brain. The most recent scenario being the possibility that I am filming dead last in the season because including me on the show was solely a favor to Ash and the network has no actual plans of including my segment in the final cut. *Of all things that could happen, please don't let it be that.*

"Hey, ladies!" Krish saunters up, greeting the four of us with a warmhearted grin that, of course, captivates my mother. Zwena's neck snaps to meet Krish's voice with an equally affectionate grin. *She can tear herself away from her studies for Krish, but she couldn't bother with a moment of eye contact in my time of need?*

My surprise delight in seeing Krish in street clothes at the airport mixed with my nervous anticipation for the next twenty-four hours comes out as an interrogation. "How'd you get past security since you don't work here anymore?" On more than one occasion, Zwena and I have lamented that we miss having Krish as our workday sanity check. Just as an airport has a center with limbs that extend from its heart, Krish often felt like our center, tethering Zwena and myself to earth, or at least insisting we be tolerant of Dieting Donna and her weekly wellness check-ins.

"Albert at security owed me a favor. My last week of work, I gave him a bunch of happy hour coupons for Hayes Street Grill." Krish points behind him, and we look over his shoulders to a handful of guys drinking beer and watching a game, their carry-ons littering the bar area. "He loves their cheese curds."

"Then are you going someplace?" I continue, searching for Krish's own carry-on. Krish had finally saved enough money to take a three-week trip to Jalandhar to see his relatives, but I'm fairly certain he's not leaving until November.

"No, I have an anniversary party tonight at the Old Union at Stanford."

"The Patels', right?" Zwena chimes in, looking proud to have memorized this fact too. Krish is right, she really is holding on to way too much useless intel.

Nodding to Zwena's fact-checking, Krish brings out a cloth bag he's been holding behind his back. "I wanted to surprise you ladies and wish you the best of luck in LA. You're going to crush it, Toni." Krish opens his free arm, inviting me in for a hug. "I know it."

"Plus, he's schtupping Zwena," Mrs. Eisenberg deadpans.

"No, he's not." I laugh, entertained by the Yiddish of an old Jewish woman from an era when it was assumed men and women couldn't be just friends. Releasing Krish from our embrace, I glance back and forth between Krish and Zwena, looking to them to confirm this foolishness.

"I'll bet you a maple bar they are." Mrs. Eisenberg meets my doubt and puts her hand out to shake on our wager. Livy drove me, Mrs. Eisenberg, and my mother to the airport. Under her breath, Livy made me swear to monitor her grandmother's sweets intake over the next two days to keep her blood sugar stable, since this is her first trip away from her doctors. My guess is that Mrs. Eisenberg knows about our—apparently not so subtle—exchange, and this is a bet she would only place if she was certain to win. I keep my hands at my sides, but my eyes return to my friends studying their shoes.

"Antonia, if you are going to be a CEO, you really should be more in tune with the lives of your coworkers," Mrs. Eisenberg advises, disappointed with my lack of awareness. "Go ahead, ask them."

When Krish and Zwena peer up, I shoot them a face that says, *Can you believe this lady?* If there was something between these two, I would know.

"I saw them walk into the airport together, for heaven's sake," Mrs. Eisenberg heaves, exasperated by my cluelessness. "I bet he's been waiting over by Compass Books for an acceptable amount of time to pass before sashaying over here as casually as possible for a man head over heels in love."

Zwena howls at the absurdity of being caught by Mrs. Eisenberg, then gives Krish a wet kiss on the cheek and an *okay* nod. I watch my best friend comfortably settle herself under the arm that Krish just hugged me with, her textbook—the sole focus of her attention the last thirty minutes—discarded to the ground.

"Yes, I'm schtupping your best friend," Krish announces, like he won the prize of a lifetime. Which he has. "And have been for quite some time."

"Good for you." Mrs. Eisenberg beams, loving being right. "You know, the most fun Eddie and I ever had was the months we were sneaking behind Evangeline's back, stealing kisses when she was at the stove frying fish on Fridays. Or when we offered to do the laundry so we could have a few hours alone at the laundromat. How Evangeline and Otis never figured that one out is beyond me. Left to his own devices, Eddie would have worn the same drawers until they fell off him."

"Sebas and I used to love to . . ."

"No, no, no, Mom. I don't want to hear about you and Dad. I heard too much as a child."

"I was just going to say that the orange groves in Las Marías worked in our favor so we could . . ."

"Yep, yep, still don't want to hear it, Mom," I stop Gloria.

"I do." Mrs. Eisenberg elbows my mom. "Later, of course."

"Since when?" I question Krish and Zwena, not willing to believe their getting together got past me. *What free time did these two have that they weren't spending with me?*

"Since January?" Zwena's voice wavers, and she glances at Krish for confirmation.

"That can't be. What about, what about . . ." I catch myself before blurting without thinking, *What about Harley?*

"Exclusively dating, since right after that night at your house in March when we were cyberstalking Simon and we toasted me quitting working for United," Krish interrupts. My mind has temporarily switched subjects from running through my own schedule to putting the Zwena and Krish timeline together. "Remember, we showed up almost an hour late to your house?"

"But you two are always late," I remind them.

"Exactly," they both say. Has it really been so long for me that my nose doesn't recognize the scent of love? *Wow, muy triste.*

"Zwena was so upset I was leaving the airport she wanted to lock me down." Krish laughs and Zwena flutters her eyelashes, letting us all know *as if* while squeezing Krish a little bit tighter. I do remember celebrating Krish's plans that night, and in this case Krish is on the right side of history. Zwena had become unexpectedly sullen with his announcement.

I learn the story of Krish and Zwena's first kiss, which apparently happened after I made them both come to Coco and Lou's painful middle school interpretation of *Grease* nineties style, that they both wanted something positive to come out of the bust of that Friday evening back in early December. My mother sits quietly through the tale, enraptured by a real-life rom-com where she knows the lead actors. At the end of the back and forth telling of the Zwish love story, Gloria hops up, planting kisses first all over Zwena, then Krish. The red of my mother's lipstick looks like welts from an allergic reaction, but neither of my friends move to wipe the love nor their smiles from their faces.

"Good news for gate D6," Patricia interrupts, singsonging into her intercom with what I swear is a drop of *I told you so* directed at me. "The inbound flight is approaching, and as quickly as we can get the plane cleared and cleaned, we will begin the boarding process."

"Look who I found meandering through the airport," Dieting Donna yoo-hoos, arm looped through Mr. Chen's right elbow, his homecoming queen holding on to the crook of his left.

"Hey, hey, Mr. Chen," Zwena booms, taking the attention off her and Krish. "No ride today?" Mr. Chen's broad smile meets Zwena's, and he strides the last few steps into our growing group with the vigor of his younger self. I spy Dieting Donna quickly tucking a roll of SweeTARTS up her sleeve when she thinks no one is looking.

"Everyone, this is Helen," Mr. Chen introduces his new/old flame to the group, holding out her hand so she may step into the assemblage. I swear I catch Mr. Chen eyeing my mother from behind the homecoming queen's back. With his reinvigorated manhood, maybe Mr. Chen is not as much of a one-woman guy as he previously thought.

"No need for the cart, Zwena. Helen has me resistance training three times a week," Mr. Chen brags, lifting his carry-on from his side to above his head. "Don't even need help getting it in the overhead compartment anymore."

"Any passengers needing extra assistance may begin boarding in five minutes," Patricia announces. I look at Mrs. Eisenberg.

"Okay, okay, I guess that's me," Mrs. Eisenberg agrees, blowing out a defeatist puff of air.

"You should start resistance training too," Mr. Chen advises Mrs. Eisenberg.

"Oh, I've been met with resistance my whole life," Mrs. Eisenberg lets Mr. Chen know. "Don't need any more of it. Besides, Antonia and I have been training for this moment long enough. Right, Antonia?"

"Right," I answer, mustering the confidence Mrs. Eisenberg wants to see in me. *It's true, we've both been in the trenches.*

"Well then, you probably don't need these, but"—Krish reaches into the cloth bag he's been holding—"put your palms out." Krish looks at Zwena, Mrs. Eisenberg, and my mom, then lingers on me. We do as we are told.

An intricate wooden carving of an elephant is placed in each of our hands. "For Indian people, an elephant is associated with the deity Ganesh." The four of us nod but say nothing, as Krish rarely talks about his roots. He is proud yet protective of his culture and avoids inviting careless comments from strangers. To be singled out in this moment feels intimate even in the middle of this bustling terminal.

"An elephant, or Ganesh, is a symbol of strength, wisdom, and general good luck." Mrs. Eisenberg gently picks up her elephant, looking at all sides. "And when an elephant's trunk is facing upward like this one, it means success," Krish enlightens us, brushing the tip of my elephant's trunk. "Ganesh is also a protector of women."

Taking in the gathered group, a pang of guilt hits me, and I swallow over a lump in my throat. Here I am, headed to the most important professional moment in my life, surrounded by supporters I have come to love in the place I most wanted to avoid. This airport was a symbol that I had failed and retreated to an ordinary job to save my ordinary life. Now I appreciate this gathering of odd but beloved characters who have cheered all my crazy ideas and picked me up after, one by one, they were tossed aside. I rub my Ganesh with my thumb and wish for success, not just for me, but for my collective airport family too.

"We feel the strength, Krish. We feel it," Mrs. Eisenberg confirms, patting his forearm. Mrs. Eisenberg smiles at the whole group and then tips her chin to me. "Let's go make our luck, Antonia."

STILL WEDNESDAY,
SEPTEMBER 4

"I like the Hollywood you, Toni," Gloria compliments me, inspecting the cotton fabric of my sundress and checking for quality. I cross my white leather sneakers under the airplane seat before my mother can comment that unless I am going to the gym, sandals go with a floral outfit. As I tuck my free-flowing hair behind my ears to distract her from my feet, my mother gasps, "My wedding pearls!" Her hand leaves my dress to secure my curls away from my face so she can admire the earrings for the entire flight.

"Claro," I respond and clasp my mother's hands inside mine so she will stop fussing with me. My father's family gave my mother the earrings as a wedding gift, and she had worn them with her simple white dress that had been handed down from Tía Fernanda's nuptials five years earlier. Gloria wore the earrings every day of her life until she gifted them to me for continued health and happiness on my wedding day, since they had brought her and my father many prosperous years. Unfortunately, the earrings didn't prove magic for my marriage, but I am still holding out hope that with them, and with Sebas's voice in my ear, tomorrow I will be counting my blessings.

Also, not that I've been tracking, but I haven't laid eyes on Ash since the Saint Anne's new families orientation weeks ago. The past few days, however, I have received plenty of advice from him via text on how best to escort Mrs. Eisenberg through the airport on her first trip since the stroke, as if I didn't already do exactly that for a living. Livy was included on the communication thread so there wasn't room for a witty comeback, just compliance to Ash's appeal to please arrive with plenty of time in case Mrs. Eisenberg needs to use the restroom before boarding the plane. And to remind her to carry her purse on her right side since her left is still rebuilding its strength. My personal favorite was Ash's request to make sure she has plenty of LIFE SAVERS for the trip. Then Livy thankfully spoke up and told her cousin to shut it down.

The last directive was sent this morning and did not include Livy. Ash asked that I text him if our plane is on time or if it is delayed because he would be picking the four of us up at LAX. I paced around the house, wondering if I should send a chatty response now that it was only the two of us on the thread, or if I should just send a double thumbs-up emoji. On my sixth trip down the hallway, I typed:

10:42 a.m. (Toni)

Will do. Looking forward to seeing you. I will take good care of your grandmother and again, thank you so much for helping me get on the show.

I blew out five forceful breaths like I practiced in the one Kundalini yoga class I attended with Simon and hit "Send."

10:42 a.m. (Ash)

Looking forward to seeing you too.

With Ash's immediate response I bounded upstairs into Lou and Coco's bathroom, tearing through their drawers until I found a watermelon and lychee hydrating facial mask shoved behind the Q-tips box, the packaging unopened. Looking like Freddy Krueger while my face soaked in fruit salad, I pulled out my favorite yellow flowered sundress with smocking and tie shoulder straps that hung crumpled in the back of my closet. It hadn't seen the light of day since Lou and Coco's middle school graduation. I turned on the shower and hung my dress on a towel hook and then also ran a scalding bath so I could wash my hair, shave my legs, and steam out the outfit. My goal was to use the heat to lower the stress-induced inflammation my body was carrying due to the next twenty-four hours determining the rest of my life.

While I was slathering myself face to toe with Nephelium, my phone rang. I saw Simon's name. I let his call go to voice mail. Part of my preparation strategy for the days leading up to the show was to not let Simon get in my head. And by not getting in my head, I mean not speaking to him or seeing his face until our paths crossed on the studio lot. Instead, I confirmed with Frances Antonelli the plans for the next two days.

11:50 a.m. (Toni)

Double-checking that you will be picking Lou and Coco up from their last day of work at 3. They have their overnight bags with them. I get home tomorrow night and will come directly from the airport to pick up the girls. Crossing fingers I will have good news to share even though my NDA says I can't.

11:52 a.m. (Frances)

Yes, that's the plan, don't you worry about a thing. We'll say an extra prayer for you at tonight's grace.

11:53 a.m. (Toni)

AMEN.

I haven't abandoned all Catholic rituals.

After some bickering with myself, I opted for clear polish for my fingers and toes. If I am going to be selling natural beauty to the Iconic Investors, I can't do it lacquered in Friday Night Out Fuchsia, particularly on a Thursday. Plus, I would also have to find a lipstick to match. Allowing time for my nails to dry, I hit my phone's voice mail icon with my knuckle. Lou and Coco were screaming good luck over and over, filling my bedroom with their electronic voices. I sure hoped the sweet message was sent on their lunch break, not when they were supposed to be hawkeyed watching their little charges in the pool at the end-of-summer-camp party.

I used my knuckle again to close out the voice mail screen, but accidentally hit "Play" on Simon's message.

"Letting you know I'm already in LA and went to the studio today to scout the scene. Ninety-nine percent of success is preparation, you know." With Simon's attempt at intimidation, I was pretty sure Thomas Edison rolled over in his grave at the butchering of his famous quote. "I heard from a reliable source that a natural beauty products company in an earlier episode was funded. I assume you know it's a saturated market, so I don't want you to get your hopes up. Best if you just think of tomorrow as your eleven minutes of fame. See you on set."

Since the afternoon of the girls' alumni speeches at Saint Anne when Simon insinuated I should forget about a positive outcome on *Innovation Nation*, I had felt an even greater loosening of the ties binding me to him. Alternating between aching for him to come back and going easy on him when he returned had only resulted in painful bruising on my heart. Simon was my first love, the one I swore vows to, and the only man to share my bed and my body. That history had become like the San Francisco weather, a rolling fog obscuring my sensibilities. After hearing that voice mail, I decided no más.

I thought giving my daughters everything I could meant accepting their father back into my life. But it's them who needed him, not me. It's possible that what I was feeling was not a loss of my bond with Simon but an acceptance that my love had shifted. I now knew that I had a responsibility to love myself, and Simon's message had finally freed me to fulfill that long ignored duty.

I listened one more time to Simon's voice mail. Anger could be powerful fuel.

The Toni of last year would have let this voice mail confirm the fear that I was not enough, sending me in retreat. I would have chosen safety and sticking to what I know, shorting myself new opportunities. Change was something I had avoided because, in my experience, what lay on the other side of a life-altering event was something to be feared. My father unexpectedly dying, my college career cut short, surprise pregnancy, being ditched by Simon—all were scenarios where I had no control, and loss of control gave me anxiety, and anxiety obscured opportunities that may blossom from change.

Today's Toni, however, with a team of women who collectively had over 180 years of life savvy, was ready to step into the newness, even with all its discomfort and unknowns. If I had given myself the time to reflect on the life mutations that happened to me, not because of me, I could have seen that I was competent and more adaptable than I had ever given myself credit for. In fact, I was quite practiced at newness, at working through the unfamiliar. Today I was stepping toward my forward. *Innovation Nation* was my big break, and I was done looking back.

Delete.

When Livy picked me up and I slid into the back seat, Mrs. Eisenberg commented that she sensed a shift in me. That—in addition to my appearance, which she was happy to see did not include a sweatshirt—I wore the air of conviction and industry well. Her approval of my demeanor and my dress came with the reminder that women have had to use every advantage they possess to get ahead in what is still, to Mrs. Eisenberg's bewilderment, a patriarchal society. Over the past couple of months, Mrs. Eisenberg had proven to me that she was a ruthless businesswoman, and I was not going to judge her methods. Mrs. Eisenberg opened her mouth one more time to say something, but then shut it again. I couldn't help but wonder if she knew what I knew. My appearance was less about impressing all the judges tomorrow and more about impressing one specific judge today.

As the flight attendant announces to the cabin that we should bring our seats to their upright position for landing, Mrs. Eisenberg peers over her reading glasses at me and says, "I'm looking forward to seeing my grandson." I flush tomato red under the air-conditioning of our row. "That's what I thought," Mrs. Eisenberg concludes and pushes her glasses back up the bridge of her nose to return to her hyped *New York Times* bestseller. I can see her fighting to keep a smile on lockdown, and I can't help but think that Mrs. Eisenberg's interest in standing beside me on the show is less about facilitating the next step in the Brown Butter, Baby! journey and more about directing her grandson's love life.

"Hey. *Hey.*" From the row behind, Zwena pokes me through the gap in the seats. I turn to look at her through the opening between my mom and me, not wanting to have to face Mrs. Eisenberg and her astute observation. "You haven't said anything about me and Krish."

"What should I say?" I ask, poker-faced. My bogus indifference will torture Zwena, and I want to have a little fun with her since she and Krish iced me out for far too long.

"I . . . I don't know." Zwena pulls back to think for a second, flustered by my withheld opinion. "You're happy for us. You think we make a cute couple. You hope it works out because you love us both." All these things are true, but I am not giving in to Zwena just yet. "Hell, I'd settle for a thumbs-up."

"Why Krish?"

"Why not Krish?" Zwena jumps to his defense. "He's driven. He's thoughtful." She dances the miniature wood elephant across my sight line. "He's—"

"Good at, you know," my mom butts in, and clicks her tongue twice, not taking her nose out of her *People en Español*.

"Do you want to know if the sex is good? Or better than good, the best I've ever had?" Zwena searches my mom's words, sussing out how much she should share, not at all bothered by the strangers flanking her middle seat, who I am sure want to hear the answer to this question less than I do.

I rise out of my seat and crank my head to look at Zwena's row mates. Thankfully, their ears are covered by headphones and their minds are engrossed in whatever shows are playing in miniature form on their phones. "I've never thought of Krish that way, and until earlier today, I figured you never had either. I don't think I'm ready to hear about the sex, Z," I admit to my best friend.

"We're ready to hear," my mom and Mrs. Eisenberg cry in unison, cutting me off. Zwena shoves her arms between the seats and gives us a double thumbs-up as an appetizer to her review. Chemistry surely is not an issue between my best friends turned romantic couple, and I am genuinely happy for them. I just don't want to become a third wheel to my two favorite people.

I riffle through my satchel and hand out the finalized scripts for tomorrow. The four of us can snicker about Zwena and Krish after celebrating my hopeful windfall. Each person's lines are highlighted in their own color. Subconsciously, I must have known something was up with Zwena because her words are framed in hot pink. "Do not lose these, we will use them to practice a few more times before the show," I instruct, lowering my mother's magazine to make sure she is listening to me.

"Has anything changed from the other two copies you gave us this past week?" Zwena bellows from behind. "Am I still here to represent the motherland as the foundation of all skin on this planet? Wait, what you really should do is reveal that I am the one who planted the seed for Brown Butter, Baby!!" Zwena lays it on thick, knowing she's speaking the truth.

"Pipe down, African queen, nothing's changed. I just want you all to have a fresh copy."

Zwena puts her gum on the front page, crumples it up and hands it back to me. "I'm good, sis. I have the lines in here." Zwena taps my head to indicate she's got it all down in hers.

"Are you sure you want me to say, 'Esta fórmula es de las islas de nuestras antepasadas'? If you only have eleven minutes, shouldn't it all be in English so not one second is misunderstood?" Gloria asks. "I can just say, 'This formula is from the islands of our foremothers.'"

It's a gamble for sure, but one I have considered. I want Brown Butter, Baby! to come across as more irresistible and inclusive than any product *Innovation Nation* has ever been pitched.

"I see you haven't changed the names of the lotions," Mrs. Eisenberg mutters under her breath. I shoot her a look that says *I don't need you to start questioning me too.* "What? It's elder abuse to make me associate myself with the word *prune* on national television."

"Don't even play that, Mrs. Eisenberg," I scold, and as Ash insisted, check her seat belt when the flight attendant announces we are about to land. "You've never been in better shape, and you are rocking the hell out of that coral pantsuit."

"Don't forget to mention that I also walked from the curb to our gate in SFO all by myself. Didn't even hold on to you, Antonia."

I am impressed with Mrs. Eisenberg not only working hard to reach her recovery goals, but proudly surpassing them. I am also sad that she may soon surpass the need for my airport services as well. She will be heading back to Arizona in early November, and I sure hope, even if Mrs. Eisenberg doesn't need me, I will still be included in the first leg of her trip.

"I love my cane. I should have gotten myself one of these years ago." Mrs. Eisenberg pats the stick that is replacing my wheels. *Is it possible I'm jealous of an inanimate object?*

After the plane touches down, my mother leans across me to lock eyes with Mrs. Eisenberg. She gives my mother a barely perceptible head nod that concerns me.

What are these two women up to?

"We're about to deplane, Toni, would you like to borrow my blush?" my mother offers.

STILL WEDNESDAY,
SEPTEMBER 4

"Go, go, go." Mrs. Eisenberg pushes on Zwena's shoulder, hustling her and my mother out of the back of the car as quickly as she had maneuvered them into the rear at the airport. Looking straight ahead, Ash rolls his lips together and keeps his hands at ten and two on the parked car's steering wheel. I open my mouth, intending to call them out on their lack of stealth, and Ash shakes his head. He's content to witness this multicultural *Golden Girls* reboot play out their obvious attempt to get me and Ash alone. As Zwena shuts the door behind her, I clearly hear Mrs. Eisenberg proclaim, "Well done, ladies, I don't think they suspect a thing." It's fortunate Mrs. Eisenberg was a hell of a businesswoman because she never would have made it as an undercover agent.

"I should probably help them check in," I suggest, watching Zwena pull three roller bags while my mom and Mrs. Eisenberg head into the hotel locked arm in arm. "I need to remind Zwena that she can't raid the minibar just because the room is under your grandmother's name. There is only one place Pringles are more expensive than in an airport. A hotel."

As I elbow my door open to step out, Ash reaches across to close it. "Let my grandmother have a little fun with her friends, she's been pretty miserable stuck at home rehabbing."

I'm touched that Ash considers Zwena and my mom his grand-mother's friends. Mrs. Eisenberg is a woman used to living large at the Vintage Club, and I can imagine these past few months at home have been hard on her.

"God knows Livy has taken her job as health warden too seriously," Ash claims, attempting to throw his cousin under the bus. I let out a bluster of a laugh. Does Ash not recall his endless hovering the first few weeks Mrs. Eisenberg was home from the hospital?

"What?!" Ash cries, incredulous.

"Let me read back to you the ten-point action items for safely transporting your grandmother, from Arrivals to boarding the plane, that I received at 11:49 p.m. last night. My personal favorite being the one asking me to have her blow her nose before the plane takes off, so her ears don't plug."

Ash drops his head to the steering wheel. "I did do that, huh?"

"You are an exceptional micromanager."

"You think so?"

"Takes one to know one." I fan my multicolored script in his face and catch a glimpse of my watch. I am two hours and thirty-eight minutes off my scripted schedule. I can give Ash six more minutes, and then I have to go. "I am curious, though, how is it that you and your grandmother are so close? I mean, there is close, and then there's you two." I genuinely am interested, at least for the next five minutes and forty-five seconds. Having grown up without grandparents, that bond is one I didn't experience. I only met my abuelos once when I was ten and my parents scrimped and saved to take the five of us to Puerto Rico to meet our extended family.

"I love my mom and dad, but they did not follow the child-rearing tip to parent the kid you have, not the kid you want to have. While my parents were busy trying to make me into a genius musician like my grandfather, my bubbe saw me for what I was, a nerdy kid who loved numbers and had no rhythm. I would tell my parents I was at jazz band practice, but really I was at math club or the robotics league, and eventually president of my school's investment club. All that time my parents were sure I was a Miles Davis in the making."

"Your young love of numbers just may have out-geeked my love of science," I rib, understanding what it's like to be raised by parents who don't truly see you for who you are.

"And you haven't even heard the whole story yet. My grandmother covered for me and paid my private trumpet teacher hush money to not rat me out to my parents when I skipped lessons for investment club. That is until my parents were called into the head of school's office when I was a junior in high school. The whole idea of the investment club was to play the stock market with pretend money and see if we could make a profit from our fake investments. Instead, I collected real money from the club members and started my own hedge fund to manage. I promised great returns. Completely illegal by the way. Bubbe and I both got in trouble from my parents on that one," Ash chuckles, lost in the memory. "But, once the yelling was over, Bubbe and I strategized how I could build a big life rooted in numbers during our Sunday afternoon ice cream dates at Baskin-Robbins."

Ash's childhood trajectory was not so different from mine, he just lived in a different zip code and income bracket. Mami and Papi chose to parent me based on who they believed I should become. They did not prioritize the path I was demonstrating I wanted to be on as a curious scientist staining the side of our house with sticky Diet Coke. Gloria wanted my quinceañera to be the pivotal moment in my teenage life, but instead my summer at UCLA with other academic-minded kids was. On campus, alongside students who had their parents' blessings and perhaps a handful, like me, whose interests were foreign to their families, I absorbed the learning that made me feel alive.

"Well, your grandmother did right by you, so I have high hopes for me tomorrow," I respond, looking for even the tiniest indication in Ash's expression that I may have an edge over the competition by including his grandmother. Ash's face reveals nada, which I take as my cue to get out of the car.

"I need to go gather my team," I tell Ash, reminding us both why I'm here. "I'll see you on set tomorrow." I rush out of the car without any last words from Ash. It's best for my psyche to believe that since he has had a hand in getting me this far with *Innovation Nation*, his altruism will continue through tomorrow's filming.

Checking in at the front desk, I hear my phone ding as I root around in my purse for my ID and credit card for incidentals—of which my mom and I will have none, we can't afford it. I hand my license and Visa to the bored-looking young man initiating my room card, then swipe over to text with a quick prayer that all is fine at the Antonellis'. I have no bandwidth for a teenage meltdown over a boy or a perceived sister slight, and definitely not an unexpected trip to the emergency room. Tonight's plan is pitch review, book, and bed. Exactly in that order.

7:31 p.m. (Gloria)

Sylvia ordered me something called an arugula salad.

7:31 p.m. (Gloria)

We are sharing an order of papas fritas.

7:31 p.m. (Gloria)

I'm going to try a dirty Shirley. Es una bebida.

7:32 p.m. (Simon)

The show has us staying in the same hotel. With no kids, tonight is an easy time for us to talk about what's next for us. Meet in the lobby in thirty minutes?

7:32 p.m. (Gloria)

Sylvia is in room 642 and Zwena has already left for the evening. We might treat ourselves to a chocolate lava cake for dessert.

7:33 p.m. (Ash)

You need a margarita. Meet me at Cantina Pequeña two blocks south of the hotel.

THURSDAY,
SEPTEMBER 5

"Your mom's in there, worried sick over you." Lost in my own thoughts, I am startled back to reality by Zwena's claim moments before I trip over her. "You said we'd meet sometime last night in the business center to practice, and then *poof*, you disappeared." Zwena's sitting on the maroon and red geometric hallway carpet, legs outstretched, ankles crossed, head leaning against my hotel room door like she's been resting there for a long while. Two venti Starbucks cups are tucked next to her hip, closely guarded. I'm assessing what's the least amount of explanation I have to give in order to get her to hand me one of those iconic white cups.

"Couldn't sleep, so I got up early this morning to take a walk in Griffith Park and practice the pitch out loud to the hummingbirds since the three of you scattered last night." Placing the responsibility for not calling an evening rehearsal on my team's shoulders seems like the shortest distance between me and the coffee she's hoarding. I need the caffeine to keep my crooked tale straight.

"Didn't know hiking in yesterday's dress was a thing in Southern California. Formal wear Thursday in the great outdoors, eh?"

"I only packed a change of clothes for the show, *ehrm*, and I didn't want to sweat in it, *ehrm*, so I had to go with . . ."

"The same thing you had on when Ash dropped us off?" Zwena finishes my lame attempt at spin-doctoring my absence the last twelve hours.

"Yep." I nod once to demonstrate my conviction. "The light cotton of my sundress is actually quite breathable," I stammer out, an impromptu justification for my walking attire. With no quick-witted response lobbed back to me, I figure Zwena has dropped the subject and we can get a move on with our morning. Having run out of time, I've convinced myself we are ready for our eleven minutes leading to a financial foundation, but I do have one important change to our pitch that I wanted to share with the team last night. But then Ash enticed me with a better offer than spending the night in a business center. Now I'm hoping we can arrive at the studio lot early and have a handful of quiet moments together for review. I need everyone's attention before we set foot onstage.

It's three hours and five minutes until we are due to check in at the studio lot gate, and I crave the endorphins that were pumping through my body last night to rev back up. I lean over to pick up the cup without lip marks on it and get my engine going for the day. I'm met with a swift slap to the hand.

"First of all, this is for Mrs. Eisenberg, not you. She and your mom had a late night waiting up for you." Zwena crosses her arms, protecting the coffee and our two elders' beauty sleep. "I finally put them to bed with the promise I would make sure you got home okay." She takes a long, slow draw from her cup and smacks her lips together to let me know it's tasty.

"*Ehrm*, you've been here all night?" I ask, feeling a warmth and genuine love well up in my chest given my sweet, selfless sister friend's concern that is tempering her refusal to share.

"I thought Krish warned you to get the dough before being a ho."
Okay, maybe not so sweet.

"Zwena, do I hear Toni out there?" From the other side of my hotel room door, we both hear my mom bellow with a wash of relief. Her butting in has saved me from a coerced confession.

"You sure do," Zwena responds, not taking her eyes off me.

"¡Gracias a Dios! I've been worried sick!" I hear my mom shuffling across the floor, most likely to find her robe and slippers. She was never one to parade around in her nightgown, let alone open the door to a public space wearing it. "Where was she?"

Why are they talking about me like I'm not here?

Zwena cocks her head, an all-knowing expression resting on her face. I bite my lower lip, smoothing out the front of my dress to maintain my composure and find solid ground to counter Zwena's assumption that she has something to hold over me. "She fell asleep in the business center. Passed right out practicing for today. You know your daughter, always working it hard, hard, hard." *Really?* I mouth to Zwena. "Yep. *So* hard." Her pursed lips challenge me to claim otherwise. "The concierge found her practically spooning the printer. She's a little scruffy, but nothing a cold shower and a few Hail Marys can't fix."

"Toni, I'm hopping in the shower quickly, then you can have the bathroom all to yourself," Gloria announces to me, Zwena, and the Lycra-clad couple heading down the hallway hand in hand dressed for an actual early-morning walk. Zwena and I listen to their sneakers squeak toward the elevator before either of us continues.

There is nothing quick about Gloria showering, both Zwena and I know it. With some time on our hands and Zwena serving as the bouncer to my room, she pats the worn carpet next to her. "How about a seat," she suggests, turning a question into a non-negotiable.

"If I sit, can I get that coffee?" I counter.

"You can get the coffee if I get the details of your night with Ash." Zwena knows she has the upper hand.

"How do you know I was with Ash? Could have been Simon," I assert, blowing out a heavy breath, trying out my acting skills in La-La Land. Zwena points her finger down her throat like she's gagging.

"Well, Ash called Mrs. Eisenberg right after he dropped you off this morning." I check my watch. That was less than five minutes ago. "She called me right away, thinking I might have caught up with you.

I was actually in the elevator about to deliver Mrs. Eisenberg her coffee when I got the call. She insisted I hurry here knowing you were nearby."

I fidget from side to side, my anxiety about withholding details of last night from Zwena making me dance. Or is it nerves that I don't know how much Ash shared with Mrs. Eisenberg about our evening? Or is it reality setting in that the next time I see Ash face-to-face, the four of us will be on air trying to convince him and his fellow judges to take a chance on Brown Butter, Baby!?—and hopefully on me.

"Your panties in a bunch getting caught in the act?" Zwena accuses, watching my little shuffle back and forth.

"Nope."

"You sure?" Zwena laughs at me, pleased by her role as sex sleuth.

"I'm sure because they're in my purse." I open my bag, and Zwena peeks inside looking for evidence. I snap it shut inches away from her nose and throw a juvenile *"Ha!"* in her face. The only thing interesting in there is a spare pack of LIFE SAVERS Ash gave me. He figured we all might want one to wet our throats before our presentation. I hope we don't need them to save ourselves from drowning onstage.

Now that I have the upper hand, I ask, "What did Mrs. Eisenberg tell you?" and slide down the door next to Zwena, trying to sound as uninvested in the answer as possible.

"What you really want to know is what Ash said to Mrs. Eisenberg."

I shrug at the differentiation, knowing I'm doing a poor job convincing my best friend I couldn't care less one way or the other. Zwena knows me too well. She understands I'm a stickler for correctly reported facts.

"You sure you want to hear?" Zwena teases. She's having too much fun at my expense to recount the details easily.

"You know I do," I concede.

"Ash told his grandmother he just had the best night of his life." Zwena smiles and raises both eyebrows at me, indicating she's proud of me and to spill it.

"Is that so?" I beam. "Was that it?" I cross my fingers on my lap hoping there is no *but* to follow.

"Is that it?! What more could you want? That was a great review!"

"I don't know, he could have shared the specifics."

Noticing my intertwined fingers, Zwena pats my hands. "Well, I know they are close, but let's hope not that close. I'm not sure Mrs. Eisenberg could handle all the details."

"No, I'm not sure she could," I brag and chuckle as last night's highlights flash through my mind, triggering a light sweat to form at my hairline.

"But I can," Zwena insists just as we hear Gloria turn the water off.

"Time to get ready," I announce and pop off the floor. "We gotta get going, Z—big day ahead of me."

"And apparently a big night behind you," Zwena heckles and reluctantly rolls over to stand up and let me off the hook. For now.

"You go ahead and take that coffee to Mrs. Eisenberg. I think this is going to be a quadruple espresso shot kind of day for me."

"It's gonna be some kind of day for sure," Zwena calls over her shoulder, striding down the hall, two coffees in her hands.

For sure, I admit to myself, sliding my key through the card lock and heading inside to get ready for the rest of my life.

◆ ◆ ◆

"I don't think I can watch. I thought I could, but I can't." I peek through my index and middle finger long enough to catch a glimpse and then quickly hide my eyes again.

"Turn it down. Turn it down!" With my hands over my face, I can't cover my ears. Purposely, I turn my body away from the monitor in our dressing room and into the corner by the air-conditioning unit.

"I can't find the remote," Gloria panics, and I hear my mom riffling through the green bottles of Perrier and bowls of every imaginable salty and sweet snack littering the coffee table in our small but well-appointed holding stall. I hate to be a diva, but when I walked into the windowless room on zero hours of sleep and there was not a Diet Coke in sight, I begged the scattered intern giving us the history of the studio to find me three cans and a bucket of ice immediately. She spun on her heels at my request and sauntered off to fulfill my order at a less-than-hurried pace.

"Do you want the volume off or just down?" Mrs. Eisenberg asks, weighing the options calmly from the love seat. She is not at all pressed by Simon walking onto the national stage to spew some nonsense about how he stands before the judges as his truest self, living at the intersection of wellness and wokeness. I'm not sure she fully appreciates that this is the exact stage we will be occupying in under an hour and that we are not solely in LA for a girls' getaway. Behind my back, I can hear Mrs. Eisenberg's hand fondling the bowl of Raisinets when she thinks everyone is focused on me and my reaction to Simon opening the final episode of Season 18 of *Innovation Nation.*

"*Innovation Nation* welcomes Simon Evans, founder of Best U Man, incorporated this March in Palo Alto, California. As a former investment banker and current life coach . . ."

"Sound down, but maybe not off. And keep the screen on," I direct from my chosen corner. "Z, how does he look? What's he doing? Does he seem nervous? What are the judges' reactions? Is he waving his arms around? Simon's always talked too much with his hands." Not wanting to rely on my own eyes, I bother Zwena with a new question before she can answer the last one.

"Oh, so you want *me* to give *you* the play-by-play when it comes to Simon, but you get to stay quiet about what went down with Ash last night?" Zwena finally gets a full sentence in, and it is not the one I was looking for. Mrs. Eisenberg's fistful of Raisinets tinkles back into the bowl, and I hear my mom plop down in a seat, ready to listen.

"After fifteen-plus years as an investment banker, working hundred-hour weeks, missing out on my daughters' soccer games and spring breaks, I knew I had to *do the work* to turn my life around so I could live it authentically as well as in harmony with humankind. I needed to drastically reevaluate my lifestyle, and how I view my role in society, my purpose on this earth, my passion in this complicated world." I can barely make out Simon's confession to what will eventually be millions of viewing Americans, so I take three steps backward to be closer to the monitor without having to turn.

"No, he didn't. He. Did. Not," Zwena emphasizes at the top of her lungs, her attention quickly swinging from Ash back to Simon.

"What'd he do?" I whip around, desperate to see how Simon just blew it on network television.

"He used the term *do the work*. Do the work!" Zwena's body tightens like she's ready to throttle Simon and his idiocy for including too many trendy idioms in his opening remarks. I shudder, triggered by Simon's words as well. Nothing raises Zwena's, Krish's, and my cynical hackles more than hearing people wax on in books, podcasts, talk shows, and health-o-mmercials that what we as a society need is more people willing to dig deep and *do the work*. It's repeated so often and definitively that one would think every American ascribes to the same definition of what *the work* is when, in fact, there are innumerable claims. Is it a dedicated three-hour morning routine, complete with meditation, journaling, mushroom tea, and perineum sunning? Or is it cognitive behavioral therapy? Microdosing psilocybin? Maybe you can just get yourself an anxiety alert dog and call it a day? With all the people out there with *Dr.* in front of their name, why any investor would back Simon's unfounded pseudoscience is beyond me.

"And yes," Zwena recounts with a huff, "his mandala beads are waving at the audience from his wrist while he explains all the ways he feels years younger from practicing his Best U Man rituals."

He feels years younger because he got to skip his daughters' middle school years, I think to myself. *That drama will age any parent.* When sneaking a peek at the monitor, I take note Zwena has turned back to the mirror, done with Simon but not her false eyelashes. Now that I've lost my commentator, I am forced to face the screen.

The camera closes in on Ash as he listens attentively to Simon's pitch. I feel heat rise from my stomach, and I exigently begin to fan my armpits. My mind flickers too fast, back and forth from last night to this moment, from the comfort of my past relationship with Simon to the anticipation of what could be with Ash, from the years driving a transportation cart to launching my own company. The life whiplash makes me lightheaded.

Ash and I shut down Cantina Pequeña last night. We polished off a pitcher of margaritas and a plateful of loaded nachos between us.

I'm unbothered by the nosy antics of Zwena, my mother, and Mrs. Eisenberg. Because I rolled in at 6:30 a.m., the trio has become obsessed with their own narratives about what happened last night. All of them include innuendos of a rom-com-worthy first kiss under the streetlights and rolling around in the frothy surf, unable to keep our hands off each other.

Hello, ladies, I came home dry as a bone.

The truth is, Ash and I talked all night. Never have I experienced a man, or anyone, listening so intently and showing such admiration for my simple, mundane life. His reserved body language of encounters past—set jaw, steely posture—gave way to loose limbs and a booming laugh that made my body hum. While I tried not to bore Ash with descriptions of the daily deeds of me, Coco, and Lou, that's what he wanted to hear. Working to recount stories that ensured I came across as an outstanding mother and daughter, I rambled on as Ash drove us from Cantina Pequeña to the beach at the Santa Monica pier. I told Arroyo tales as we took in the darkness of the ocean lit up by an almost full moon.

Ash grew concerned during my story about Coco and Lou giving each other goose eggs on their foreheads from falling over one another when attempting their first steps. He was in disbelief when I disclosed that Simon is the only man I've ever dated. When I asked Ash how many people he's dated, he teased with a wink, "I can't incriminate myself to you so soon. My body count could get me arrested." His answer left me no choice but to call him out on his slick evasion of my question.

When Ash cupped my hands in his, I felt safe enough to relive the day I got the call at UCLA that my father had died and with him my dream of graduating a Bruin. Ash's presence, along with the comforting blanket of an inky sky, was calming. The setting opened the floodgates of my experience that for my whole life I have lived for other people's come up, while sidestepping my own. I felt myself oversharing like some of the passengers I transport between terminals, but Ash didn't interrupt. He listened until I had my say.

As we dipped our toes in the ocean, it was Ash's turn to storytell while I took a breath. Although he already seemed to me like the ultimate success, I asked Ash what he was looking for next. He revealed that as he passed forty-five and marched toward fifty, he was determined to have a family and had broadened his vision of how that might look. Ash disclosed that over the past few months he'd been looking into surrogacy and adoption on his own. To that surprising news, I blurted, "You and late-night feedings?!"

Without missing a beat, Ash assured me, "Don't worry about me, I can stay up all night long."

Taking him in as our toes sank in the sand, I thought to myself, *I bet you can.*

I was gathering myself after that suggestive response when Ash leaned in and whispered, "I'd also welcome a couple of stepchildren." I didn't presume he was talking about mine, but the thought did make me smile.

Ash added that he hoped this plan would play out while his grandmother is still alive. He aspires to show Mrs. Eisenberg that he can be as devoted a parent to his children as she has been to hers, and to her grandkids. At the mention of stepchildren and the familial dedication that we were both raised and enveloped in, we reached for each other's hands and stood in quiet understanding.

While my lips craved a kiss in the fortuity of having the beach to ourselves, I was content simply sitting in the sand tightly next to Ash, our shoulders, arms, hips, and legs touching. We were so close not even a breeze could blow between us. As we told our stories, sad and joyous, side by side, we were two melded into one. As the sun began to rise and the weight of the coming day loomed ahead of me, Ash cut into my dreaminess with, "I can't have spent the night on a beach with a beautiful woman without—"

"Kissing her?" I finished his sentence.

"Kissing you." So he did.

Ash dropped me off at the hotel when the sun was high enough in the sky to insist a new day had arrived. He pressed his lips to my hand. The one he hadn't let go of for hours. Not knowing how to say to Ash that he had given me the gift of an incredible night without sending him running for the hills, I simply breathed, "Thank you."

"This is just the beginning, Antonia," was Ash's response as his eyes met mine with the perfect mixture of care and conviction.

Given the magic of the last ten hours and feeling like the opportunities of the next ten were limitless, I could only respond with, "I believe you." And in that moment, I did.

Now, I can't tear my eyes away from Ash in his judge's seat. He's sporting a crisp khaki suit, and I know his lavender button-down is a nod to his grandmother's favorite color. He bites the end of his reading glasses, then puts them on to jot down notes on a pad of paper as Simon talks. Having met Simon in my garage, and then listened with care last night as I revealed the details of my marriage journey, I suspect the words being scribbled are *what a loser*.

I glance over at the love seat in our dressing room and notice Mrs. Eisenberg is staring as intently at her grandson as I am, a loving gaze settled on her face. She meets my eyes momentarily before returning to the TV, and a simple, knowing "Uh-huh" releases from her lips.

"He's doing well," Gloria informs the room, as if rooting for Simon even in the slightest is acceptable. I don't want to believe Gloria is pulling for Simon, but maybe she is.

Zwena steps next to me, wrapping me under her arm. "These judges are going to rip his phony ass to shreds, I can tell." I get a big side hug to calm my indignation at my mother's comment. "Neither of the female judges are falling for his tall talk. He's a sham. Transparent as tissue paper. Any woman can see that." I lean in to Zwena to show my appreciation for words I could not have delivered myself without catching an attitude and putting on a whole other kind of show.

Ash asks Simon the first question: "What's your revenue to date?" As the person who knows his body language best, I can detect Simon bristling at what he perceives as Ash launching a direct attack on his early financial success. I have to give it to him—Simon has managed to exploit the American penchant for silver-bullet fixes in order to achieve the latest wellness standard du jour.

Ash's question serves as a warm-up, and soon the other three judges pelt Simon with challenges he seems ready to catch and then return with data-infused answers like a fast-paced game of spreadsheet dodgeball. I soon realize that when watching the edited version of *Innovation Nation* from the comfort of my own home, the show seems to move at a tolerable pace, the participants having a moment to think and then respond. In the studio, the show moves at hyperspeed. Each question, each interrogation, each proposition comes at Simon before he can fully address the last, but he remains calm, losing neither focus nor form in the eye of the storm. Watching him take the verbal hits in stride leads me to believe that maybe he did get something out of his personal pilgrimage other than an impending divorce.

With an imperceptible press of Simon's thumb on a gadget I didn't realize he was holding, life-size images of the four judges appear on the screen behind him. All four are clad in apparel that relates to their favorite pastimes, serene smiles on their faces, and not a wrinkle among them thanks to Photoshop. In the case Simon is making, these lifestyle goals are thanks to the services Best U Man can provide. Ash is on television in his full golf getup, welcoming watchers to become as blissed out as he's been made to look.

"I think Simon looks nice and is well spoken. He did always present his best side," my mom voices, Zwena's alliance with me having washed over her like water off a duck's back.

As I'm about to not so delicately lay into my mother, Simon gets his first rejection in the form of a big red buzzer when one of the two female judges claims, "I'm not sold." *Eat it, Simon. Ash isn't going to invest in you either.*

Simon's first offer comes from the female judge who's still in play. The offer is drivel compared to the $400,000 for 20 percent of the company Simon pitched. Seems both women know Simon's self-care services are bunk. I bite my lower lip, sitting in smug satisfaction that one of the female judges has valued Best U Man at nothing and the other as not being worth much of her effort or finances. A pity deal. My guess is that as a revered manufacturing magnate, she's only willing to invest a paltry amount in Simon so her portfolio proves entry into the mental health industry. The four of us watch Simon's eyes desperately dart back and forth, anxious for more bids.

As a lull of indifference for Simon's services settles on set, an offer is lobbed for $425,000, cash, more than Simon wanted, but for 30 percent company ownership. The offer comes from the eldest investor and resident bully on the show, the only judge who has held his seat since season one. I grab my notebook of *Innovation Nation* statistics out of my purse and quickly run my index finger down the investment numbers I have recorded from the past three seasons. Simon just received one of the highest cash offers on record. He looks unfazed that he has made reality TV history. I know there is no way he is giving up that much ownership of his company. Hell, all he offered his own wife was a glorified secretary position.

On the heels of the veteran's deal, a third offer is made. By Ash. Same amount of cash but only 20 percent ownership, exactly what

Simon is seeking. Zwena gasps and covers both our mouths, silencing me before swear words start flying. Ash is telling all of America that he wants to be in business with Simon. Even after all he heard from me last night, Ash still considers Simon a founder worth investing in and Best U Man a solid company capable of decent returns.

I think I'm going to be sick.

The female judge who started the bidding war, knowing she can't compete and doesn't actually want to, hits her red buzzer indicating she withdraws her offer. The now-angered veteran and Ash are the only two left vying for Best U Man. The OG waves his fingers above his buzzer, pulls his hand back, and hovers it over the buzzer once more, then pulls it back a final time. He matches Ash's proposal of 20 percent ownership plus raises his cash investment to $450,000. Ash throws up his arms in defeat, then slams his right hand down on his buzzer and announces, "I'm not sold!" It all makes for great television.

As I take in Simon's elation at his deal, my knees buckle. Simon immediately accepts the offer before the seasoned judge realizes that he may have had a senior moment and overbid. The veteran investor gingerly rises from his chair and advances toward Simon. Going in for an embrace, their puffed-up chests bump first. Ash and the female judge to his right shrug and offer one another an *oh well* conciliatory grin. In this absurd moment, even my mother is wise enough to keep any commentary to herself.

The screen goes black for the twenty-minute break between segments to tear down Simon's set and organize for the next founder, who is hawking a ten-year tattoo concept. A decade is just long enough to commit to an image on the body in the present, knowing it will fade and ultimately disappear before the skin sags and an affinity for Chinese characters is lost. It's absolutely brilliant. If I had two bucks to rub together, I would invest in that company—quickly. I also wouldn't lose so much sleep at night as a mother freaking out over the possibility of permanently stamped poetry on my daughters' shoulder blades.

Ding.

I've been hoping Lou and Coco would wake up early enough to reach out to me on my life-changing day and give me a "get it, Mom" for taking the steps to finally chase my dreams. It's wonderful when your daughters can look to other women to motivate them in their pursuits, but knowing that I'm now one of those inspirational women and my babies are texting to tell me so is next-level motherhood success. When I get home, we are going to celebrate big-time.

10:26 a.m. (Simon)

I told you everything would work out, Toni, I knew I had a unicorn company on my hands! With Best U Man's infusion of money, we can go back to the way things were, but flush with cash. Whatever happens with your lotions doesn't really matter, I'm going to be all right.

I huck my phone across the room into the cushions of the love seat. I was counting on Best U Man bombing and Simon walking away with zero investment, ensuring that the last episode of Season 18 would build in excitement and intensity to culminate in a rousing four-judge fight for Brown Butter, Baby!. My only hope now is that investor fatigue is not affecting the judges, nor are they running out of money.

"You will be on deck to check your displays in forty," the Diet Coke fairy sticks her head in the door to tell us. "I'm going to walk you to the side stage waiting area in ten, and you can watch the second entrepreneur live from there. Cross fingers your segment goes as well as the first guy, he's set for life." She throws us a double okay sign and closes the door behind her, completely unaware of how unwelcome her cheerleading is.

STILL THURSDAY, SEPTEMBER 5

"Is it *Dulce* or *Dulcis*?" Mrs. Eisenberg asks me for the hundredth time. "Don't worry, I have the *Prunus* part down just fine." The question is delivered with a salty eighty-eight-year-old side of continued disapproval.

"You only have to say *Prunus*," Gloria reminds Mrs. Eisenberg, looking pleased to guide our contrary teammate to the profit promised land minutes before our segment starts.

The four of us are now stage left, out of camera sight line, watching the tattoo guru's head whip back and forth as all four judges yell and fight over one another to be considered for the best seed-stage investment opportunity that may ever have come across their portfolios. For sure the ten-year tattoo concept will be the opening "look where they are now" company featured for the launch of Season 19. Even I predict the patent on the specialized fading ink will be worth billions, the way people use their bodies as a canvas to fill when they think they have something to say.

In a matter of moments, the judges will clear the stage for their second break, and it will be my turn to head onto the set to inspect my four plexiglass displays that are quickly brought out by a couple of stagehands dressed in black.

"I'm with Mrs. E. There's still a chance my tongue will get turned upside down over pronouncing *Diospyros*, even though I've been practicing for weeks in the mirror," Zwena complains, linking her arm through Mrs. Eisenberg's in solidarity over my lotion names. I take Zwena's complaint as the perfect time to let my sales squad in on a new development.

"Change of plans." My three sidekicks look at me, panicked. I am not a woman known to make last-minute adjustments, particularly when the stakes have never been higher.

"Relax, this is an easy one," I assure my team. "I will introduce the name of each lotion—the three of you are off the hook." A look of relief washes over my crew, no one more so than my mother. I guess she, too, was unsure if the judges would hear *Theobroma* correctly in her lingering Puerto Rican accent. "When you hear your name, step over to your assigned display case. Next, open the lid to the lotion at the top of the pyramid and show the color of the cream to the judges. The assistant director tells me the camera will pan from your face to your lotion, then to the judges' reactions. And last, they will zoom in on the jar you're holding on the screen."

"The same screen your golf pro boyfriend was on during Simon's presentation?" Zwena ribs.

"If we don't get to say anything, then basically you've turned us into Vanna White, minus the White," Mrs. Eisenberg jokes, ignoring that she's White too. Our group's elder is more relaxed now that she does not have to compare herself to a shriveled plum on network television. We all chuckle—except for Zwena, who has no idea what we are laughing about. I guess *Wheel of Fortune* was never syndicated in Kenya.

"Well, that's good news for me," Zwena responds, also now more at ease, her face lighting up to complement her sunshine-yellow, pink, and orange kanga dress with matching dhuku. I love that Zwena has chosen to bring Kenya with her on our shared adventure in Los Angeles.

"That's good news for all of us," Mrs. Eisenberg confirms, pulling on the cuffs of her lavender blouse so they peek out of the sleeves of her power suit. "Though I don't like not having a talking part. Antonia, you know I always have something to say."

"Yes, I do, but today let the product speak for itself. And me." I make eye contact with all three of my assistants, checking that everyone understands there is no room to argue or deviate from the new plan.

"Also, I want us to walk onstage holding hands," I announce, shifting directives, with one more sweep of my eyes to hold my ladies' attention. "Mrs. Eisenberg, you will be on the right side of me. Mami on my left. Zwena, you will be to the left of my mom."

"You sure you don't want me on the other side of Mrs. Eisenberg?" Zwena offers with an exaggerated bug of her already wide eyes. I know what that look is asking, and so does Mrs. Eisenberg.

"I can walk out on that stage holding only Antonia's hand just fine, thank you very much." Mrs. Eisenberg waves a scolding finger at me and Zwena. "Do you know how many keynote speeches I've delivered? More than once I saw Bill Gates on the edge of his seat, hanging on my every word."

"Okay, boss lady." Zwena backs away, hands up in surrender to our resident tycoon.

"We are in this order, from darkest to lightest, to represent the color range of my cream collection. When I say your name, you step forward, smile at the judges, and head on over to your display case. That's all you have to do. Z, I want to start with you to honor the beauty and depth of your skin color. That sound okay?" I know exactly how it sounds to her seeing the tears well up in Zwena's eyes. She has often commented on what, at times, feels like the singularity of her deep, blue-black skin among West Coast people of color and wondered if she would have felt a bit more at home in New York, Baltimore, or Washington, DC, where African immigrants historically have been more likely to settle. My reaction is always the same—*What would I do without you in my life?*—but I also make sure Zwena knows I hear her. While the Bay Area is not as ripe with the African diasporic glow as other parts of America, similarly, not much has changed since my parents arrived in

San Francisco and had their Puerto Rican heritage lumped together with the dominant Mexican culture. I more than understand Zwena's sentiment, but I am thankful, every day, that Zwena's visa sent her to the Golden State and that I was here too. Despite oceans between our ancestors, destiny ensured our paths crossed.

"It's go time, ladies." Our assigned intern's peppiness is waning now, perhaps the result of shooting eighteen episodes on a rigorous schedule, or she just found out there isn't a paid assistant producer position waiting for her at the end of this gig. Either way, no double okay sign this time, so I give her one of mine.

"Mi amor, of all the people watching today, you know who is most proud?"

I'm still irked at my mom for her play-by-play commentary of Simon's turn on television, and I am not in the mood to play twenty questions.

"Gabriel?" I throw out quickly. I had run my projected numbers by my data analysis dork of a brother before submitting them to the show, and he was pleased with my work. My mother shakes her head while running her hands over the skirt of her cherry-red belted A-line dress with a scoop neck. A little *too* scooped for an abuela on network TV in my opinion.

"David?" It has to be David, he's the one who sent me the mystery powder in the first place.

"No." My mother points to the sky. "Your father. You and your brothers have become the success stories he always wanted his kids to be. And it all started with a Puerto Rican import."

"The cacao bean," Mrs. Eisenberg agrees.

"No, my parents." I smile at my mom and touch the cross and the wedding ring resting on her heart.

◆ ◆ ◆

"MynameisToniArroyo," I rush through my introduction as I see the time start to tick down on the teleprompter directly in front of me. I feel moisture forming in my armpits and curse my decision to wear an orchid-pink silk button-down primed to show pit stains. When I saw the shirt paired with a pencil skirt—also pink but two shades darker— in the Bloomingdale's window, I couldn't resist. I swear that mannequin waved me inside and asked for my credit card. She also insisted I buy the slingback gold heels to complete the look.

Mrs. Eisenberg squeezes my hand hard. I swallow, and my voice catches on the peach pit–size lump now in my throat. "Excuse me, excuse me, can I start over?" I shake my head vigorously and take an enormous inhale and exhale to steady my nerves. Three of the four judges are looking at me expectantly, their wrinkled foreheads telling me to get on with it. Only Ash speaks up, encouraging me to take my time and noting that *Innovation Nation* has a whole slew of editors for this exact reason. I nod and will the tears I feel pooling not to drop. Creatives are emotional, entrepreneurs are not, and though you need to employ both to make it as a founder, today my tough, resilient side must lead the way.

"I am Antonia Arroyo, founder and CEO of Brown Butter, Baby! a lotion company dedicated to meeting *you* at your *hue*." I pause for dramatic effect and to let the tagline settle into the hearts of the judges. I notice the two women write the motto down, or add to their grocery list—it's never been revealed to the audience what the judges actually scribble on their notepads. Of the roughly thirty-two catchy taglines I came up with and collected from my airport family, this one was the unanimous winner. Turns out Dieting Donna is quite the clever wordsmith. I haven't told her that out of all the entries, I chose her catchphrase. I want her to be surprised when the show airs.

Feeling a wind catch my confidence, I blow wide open with my most endearing grin and announce, "Brown Butter, Baby! is a lotion company with inclusivity in mind." All the judges nod in approval of my mission and hopefully of me.

"Today I am here seeking three hundred thousand in investment for 20 percent of Brown Butter, Baby!. I have with me the first four of my signature shades to help women of all ethnicities celebrate their skin color because contrary to centuries of history, white is not always right." I had worried a bit about using that line, but Mrs. Eisenberg assured me of the importance of making bold statements when presenting to investors. She insisted this is how a fledgling CEO comes across as assured in the future viability of her company, particularly for women who tend to undersell their worth. I see one side of Ash's mouth turn up at the corner in approval, but the other three judges sit stone still. The poise I am working to project starts to waver, and I flex my leg muscles to solidify myself on the stage.

On episode six of last season, Dwayne Washington said to the entire country that retailers are looking for Black female company founders, so while I may have botched my opening line, I have that ace in my back pocket. Simon and the tattoo guru don't. I look right and then left down my row of women. Zwena, my mom, and Mrs. Eisenberg are my true winning hand, my dream team. The squad that got me to this stage. Zwena who, with youthful enthusiasm often reminds me that I can do anything I set my mind to and is the first to wave away my excuses. My mother who, though taking on her first full-time job at sixty-five, has finally learned to honor her brain and mine. Me, who has taken note from Gloria that it's a beneficial bonus that my smarts come wrapped in a well-groomed package. A little lipstick never hurt any woman's cause. And finally, Mrs. Eisenberg. A woman who taught me that forward momentum is a superpower. Whether I walk through fire, a forest, or the walls I have erected around myself, I just need to keep walking. One foot in front of the other. One bite of life after another. These three women are responsible for getting me here, and thank God I was finally at a point in my life where I was sharp enough to listen and follow their lead.

"The first lotion I would like to introduce you to"—I pause to let my words sink in—"is called Zwena." I turn my head left to see Zwena's mouth open enough to trap flies in surprise. "Go ahead," I encourage with a lift of my chin, hoping she will catch my drift to walk over to her display case with the newly labeled lotion. This morning while my dream team was settling into our dressing room and speculating about my evening, I pulled our assigned intern aside to appeal to her "can do" attitude and asked if she could quietly print new labels for me. Five minutes later she returned with what I asked for. I then crept to where my product was staged and slapped the new labels onto the crowd-facing Brown Butter, Baby! jars without letting on to my ladies what was to shortly be revealed. I tick off a list of sensuous adjectives to describe the hue of Zwena as my best friend unscrews the top, beaming with pride. I tilt and turn my head just enough to spy her image on the screen holding the open jar, and even I'm impressed with how well the cream matches Zwena's rich skin, still smooth from only twenty-eight years on this planet.

"Next is *Gloria*," I say, releasing my mom's hand so she knows it's time to take her walk across the stage. Mrs. Eisenberg squeezes my hand again, and this time I know it's in approval. She sees what I've done renaming my skin shades and, as my mentor, I sense she is full of pride. With a twinkle in her eye, my mom glides across the stage like it's the Miss Puerto Rico pageant runway that she was always meant to walk. The slow sway of her hips and swing of her arms takes up valuable seconds, but I am more than happy to let her have her moment in the spotlight. I know, between the four of us, she is enjoying it the most.

"Then we have *Antonia*." I look to Mrs. Eisenberg to confirm with her that I have to let go. She nods, letting me know she is steady with her cane, and drops my hand.

"Now *that's* a Boss Lady," Mrs. Eisenberg declares to the judges and the entire nation before giving me a little push toward my own display case. The judges chuckle, allowing for a moment of levity since my botched introduction.

Standing firmly in place, Mrs. Eisenberg is the only one left center stage, in a purple power pantsuit and pressed lavender shirt to match her grandson's. Her eyelids droop closed and my stomach flutters, the scene in the airport when Mrs. Eisenberg fell into my arms racing through my mind. I'm about to hurry to her side when her eyes pop back open and her smile grows wide, embracing the whole room. Before I can say my next line, she announces to the panel of judges as she saunters over to her display case, "And this is the *Sylvia*." As practiced, Mrs. Eisenberg rests her cane against the case, picks up her lotion, and unscrews the top without a hitch from arthritis or hint of her recent stroke. "And you all would be idiots not to invest in Brown Butter, Baby!. This here is the future of the beauty industry, and you do not want to miss it." I should have known Mrs. Eisenberg would not go quietly across that stage, particularly in her position as the punctuation to my product presentation. Standing by our designated display cases, there is not much more for me to say that would enhance Mrs. Eisenberg's final words. We are a skin rainbow, representing the first dedicated lotion company to celebrate just that, and it is an honor to have done it with my mom, Zwena, and Mrs. Eisenberg.

◆ ◆ ◆

The taped moving box of my jars is weighty on my legs, but I rest my cheek on top of it, my head too heavy to hold up as we crawl through Los Angeles traffic on the way to the airport. My mom is rubbing my back, and Mrs. Eisenberg is dabbing at my eyes with her embroidered handkerchief. Zwena is in the front seat with the Uber driver carrying on an inane conversation about the weather, I'm sure to distract him from chatting with the three of us in the back seat about where we are from and what we were up to in LA. Though Zwena knows little about meteorology, she is informed enough to bring up the troubling threat of drought, and I'm relieved we'll be conversationally safe until we reach Departures. My phone buzzes in my pocket, but I have no interest in answering it. Most likely it's not Lou or Coco, so it's either Simon or Ash, neither of whom I have any desire to talk to.

"If we have time after we check the box as luggage, let's go to a bar near our gate. I'm thirsty," Zwena says as we inch toward the first

United sign, our Uber driver jockeying for a place to safely pull over and unload us.

"I think that would be wise," Mrs. Eisenberg concludes, placing one of her hands over my mother's that hasn't left my back, both seeming to make sure my heart is still beating.

I added a few stats to my company spiel about future projections after Mrs. Eisenberg's proclamation that the judges best make the smart move and invest in me. The four of us stood like warrior statues by our display cases, me ready to answer, deflect, or lob back any challenge that came my way. While I was excited at the prospect of negotiating, all I really cared about was walking away with a deal where I retained at least 75 percent ownership of Brown Butter, Baby! coupled with a somewhat decent cash infusion. I know I don't know what I don't know when it comes to scaling a consumer products company, and that I am at the beginning of my journey, therefore I need a lot of experienced guidance. I have skin in the game, but no ego. Any of these four judges would help me accelerate Brown Butter, Baby! tenfold and I wanted all of them, but only needed one of them.

Instead, the studio had fallen silent. I looked side stage for our intern to check that I didn't miss a signal to stop filming on set, hence the quiet of the judges. As I searched for her, she was nowhere to be seen. I turned back to make eye contact with the female judge directly in front of me. As she cleared her throat, I said a silent *thank you God* for being saved by a sister in spirit, and then she hit her buzzer and proceeded to give a thirty-second monologue on why she was not sold on Brown Butter, Baby!. The veteran followed with nothing other than, "I'm not sold either," and the pound of his buzzer stung my ears. He then fussed with his tie, not even paying attention to what played out in the remaining minutes of the season finale.

Ash flung what felt like a couple of softball questions my way about research and development and end-of-year projections. I answered earnestly, but his possible investment in Brown Butter, Baby! died after his mild line of questioning as he averted his eyes and hesitantly pressed his buzzer. My future was now left in the hands of the one remaining female judge who had yet to speak. I could only pray this moment was scripted to ensure a tension-filled season finale.

With the clock running out, the last judge took on the persona of a compassionate albeit condescending patron and wished me the best of luck, but that my company was *too, too* early-stage and I was *too, too* inexperienced for her level of comfort. And the last buzzer of Season 18 shook the studio.

The flight passed in a blur, and right on time, Krish is curbside to pick Zwena up from SFO. Seeing us, he inches his car forward and parks under the sign that says ANY UNATTENDED VEHICLES WILL BE TOWED AT THE OWNER'S EXPENSE and hops out to jog over and give me a hug. I don't need to ask if Zwena has filled Krish in on what happened. From the strength of his embrace, I know she has, and I leave my head resting on Krish's chest for a couple of long, reassuring moments.

When I finally let go of Krish, Zwena asks him for the keys so she can take the wheel of his unattended vehicle. She directs him to retrieve my heavy box of lotions spinning around carousel twelve. I would have left the box, my interest in taking my lotions home being zero, but Zwena informs me that a single, unclaimed cardboard box with a raggedy tape job would likely set off an airport-wide alert. The last thing I need on this day is to add the moniker *terrorist* next to *loser*.

Mrs. Eisenberg had been uncharacteristically quiet when nursing her chardonnay at the LAX bar, resting her head on the plane with closed eyes, and greeting Livy mildly at SFO. Twenty-four hours ago, the four of us chatted lively on our way to the airport. In contrast, this evening as Livy pulls into my driveway, barely a dozen words have been exchanged in forty minutes, none of them from Mrs. Eisenberg.

Without my having to ask, my mom gets out of the car with me to spend the night. She takes my phone to text Frances Antonelli a lie that our flight has been severely delayed and can she keep Coco and Lou until morning. Mrs. Eisenberg reaches her right hand out of the passenger-side window and grabs on to my sleeve. With all her strength she pulls my upper body over to her, our heads now face-to-face through the open window. Mrs. Eisenberg's expression is serious with a resolve I have never witnessed before.

Waving her fingers, pleading for me to put my hands in hers, she grasps me tightly. I'm concerned she may never let me go, and my achy, tired brain is desperate for Advil.

I can feel Mrs. Eisenberg is anxious to transfer every ounce of conviction and faith she carries in her body through her hand and into me. I hate being the one who has created such palpable worry in a woman whose only concern should be getting her health back in shape so she can return to her beloved Arizona this coming winter.

"This is not the end, Antonia." Mrs. Eisenberg's eyes beg me to believe her. "I promise you, this is not the end."

SATURDAY, SEPTEMBER 7

Somewhere between the dark of Thursday night and burying my head under the pillow on Friday morning to avoid the new day, my mom slipped into my room and whispered that she was taking my car to pick up Lou and Coco from the Antonellis' and bringing them back to her place. She insisted that I needed the quiet to sleep. Other than a few restless nightmares reliving what transpired on the studio lot, sleep is exactly what I did until Lou and Coco sneaked into my room this morning.

Propping pillows against my headboard, I sit up and open my arms for a double hug. Both girls barrel into me, and we stay that way until Coco pulls back to inform me my breath stinks and quite possibly my scalp as well. Fair enough. I haven't brushed my teeth or showered since Thursday.

Lou and Coco present me with homemade cards, reminiscent of the ones they constructed and brought to my room in the weeks following Simon leaving us when they were desperate to do what they could to turn off my waterworks. The drawings on the front of their cards haven't improved much. Their genetic art code is hardwired to not evolve beyond daisies, sunshine, and stick figures, but the heartfelt notes inside prove their emotions have deepened, as has their empathy. I'm warmed by their sentiments concerning what transpired my last forty-eight hours as described to them by their abuela. I hold the cards to my heart. Both Lou and Coco snuggle up as if shielding me from the harsh world that exists outside my bedroom door.

I think of the multiple child psychologists I have read over the past fourteen years who report that it's often easiest to talk with teenagers about difficult topics when you are either driving and they are in the back seat, thus avoiding eye contact, or any scenario where mother and daughter are staring straight ahead. Apparently, truths are most easily discussed without having to witness one another's reactions. Our three sets of eyes fix on the maple tree rooted outside my bedroom window where a familiar blue, black, and white bird is twittering around hunting for the perfect branch to land on. It seems the Steller's jay is looking for a guarantee that her chosen twig won't break beneath her. I know exactly how that bird feels. I, too, desperately want assurance that all will be okay when I land, but my wings are tired of flapping, and that type of certainty only occurs in the movies. It's time for me to land regardless of the outcome.

"Girls, you know your father and I love you both more than anything," I begin, pulling Lou and Coco in tighter, but not taking my eyes off the bird. My opening line sounds like I plucked it from a *What to Expect When You're Divorcing* script, and I bite my tongue to keep myself from adding my own flavor: *Though obviously I'm the one who loves you more. Moms don't leave.* "But your father and I are getting divorced. I'm giving him the papers tonight." I have cried out all my tears the last twenty-four hours, and I am now present and ready to wipe away theirs. I'm totally fine with Simon being the last to know my decision. I have been last to learn of plenty of his life decisions. Simon will have about thirty-two pages worth of nighttime reading this evening to help him grasp that our marriage is over and that I will be moving on without him and his seed Best U Man financing from *Innovation Nation.* However, since California's a community property state, any Best U Man income earned beyond the initial funding from the show, I get half.

"Obviously you're getting a divorce," Coco chuffs as if what she really wants to say is *no duh*.

"We can't believe it took you so long to decide. We were beginning to think you were actually going to take Dad back," Lou adds. "That would have been so dumb."

Huh? Maybe their Saint Anne Catholic education was a little more progressive than I gave it credit for.

"Wait." I push the girls and all the expert child development advice to the side and look directly into Lou's and Coco's faces. "What I hear you saying is you want us to get divorced?" I question, my voice suggesting disbelief.

"No kid *wants* their parents to get divorced," Coco affirms. I knew it. I knew they would prefer that Simon and I stay together. And up until Thursday, I may have been able to pull the marriage off until the girls graduated from high school, but Simon's messages that suggested I diminish while he expands solidified the end of us. "But we do want you and Dad to stop being so strange around each other. It's weird . . ."

"We're happy Dad's back," Lou cuts in.

"We also know that was a total dick move leaving us for a couple of years," Coco finishes off her twin sister's thought.

"Hey, language," I remind the girls. But Coco certainly did use *dick* in the right context. Krish must have instructed her swearing skills.

"Okay, but seriously, Mom, you need to get on with your life," Lou declares.

"We want you both to be happy, and Dad seems to be doing a better job at making it happen for himself than you are. If you get divorced, then maybe you can focus on something else. Maybe someone else, someone more like all the stories about Abuelo," Coco analyzes. "It's got to stop being us, Mom. We're too busy, especially with high school starting."

I can't help but let out a huge howl of laughter, the exclamation point to my truth-telling teens.

"What about that guy who stopped by when you and Dad were in the garage? He seemed into you," Lou dishes, wading into the water of what is now, officially, my post-Simon life. I don't reveal that "that guy" is the reason Brown Butter, Baby! has no funding and their mother has a musty stench. That "that guy" could have set my life on a whole new trajectory and he didn't. "That guy" has also left me several voice mails and texts since Thursday afternoon, all of which I've ignored.

"He was kind of good-looking," Coco ekes out, acting like she's choking down a horse-size pill. "I mean, for an old, bald guy. It was sorta funny watching Dad get jealous."

"He was a little jealous, wasn't he?" I giggle, and the girls join me.

"Leave him jealous." Gloria falls into my room, blowing the ruse that she has been in the kitchen cooking pollo guisado rather than listening at my door. "There's no greater position of power for a woman to walk away from in a relationship." The surprise counsel keeps coming, and for once I believe my mother is spot on.

"But Mom, you believe that marriage is forever. That it's a woman's job to stand by the man she married, to keep the family together."

"No. No. No. I never said that." Gloria waves her index finger at me, and I notice that in my forty-eight hours of grief she has had time to change her nail polish. "I said stand by true love. That true love is forever. If Simon isn't that, then, mija, you don't settle for less. I didn't."

TUESDAY, SEPTEMBER 10

Aside from the terrible decision to spend three stress-inducing hours in Target shopping for school supplies on the Sunday afternoon before the Arroyo family Labor Day cookout, life is returning to normal. Over the chai lattes that I ran out to the Cracked Cup to get the girls for a first morning of ninth grade surprise, Lou and Coco informed me that today would be the one and only day I am allowed to drive them to high school clear through graduation. Starting tomorrow they will be taking public transportation. Before I could protest, the rules of etiquette for parenting high school girls continued between slurps. I had to give my solemn promise that all kisses, hugs, and requisite first day of school pictures would be done within our property lines. There could be no more lunch box love notes. And then Coco brought up, for the hundredth time, moving into the extra room. I told her I would genuinely consider it, to which she replied, "Well, that's progress."

With the girls tucked in to their new academic year, looking the high school part in matching Lululemon leggings their Uncle David and Uncle Gabriel bought them, I have two hours to myself before I return to the airport after my week off that aged me a year. Even with the NDA that Mrs. Eisenberg, my mom, Zwena, and I had to sign saying we would not reveal what happened on the show until it airs, Zwena still made sure our shifts aligned this week in case Dieting Donna, Liam, or any other of our airport family gets up in my business wanting specifics. If I crack, Zwena's there to have my back.

Reheating my chai, I hike up my joggers and sit down to be a grown-up. With Lou and Coco's blessing, I delivered the divorce papers to Simon's apartment on Saturday night. He was much more gracious and conciliatory than I was expecting. Maybe it was because I came around when he was emailing with a property manager for a three-year office space lease and was distracted. Maybe our kindhearted daughters had given him a heads-up. Or maybe he was content to be married to a noncompetitor, but he certainly didn't want to be married to a loser. Who knows, but Simon took the papers from me without much fanfare and offered that he was free to pick the girls up from school on Tuesday and take them to their orthodontist appointments. I said that would be great since the days of our girls wanting to be seen in public with us are waning. We both let out a laugh, awash in the pain of knowing that with each passing day, our children, like all children, need their parents less and less.

Walking me to the door after my five-minute stay, Simon blandly offered his condolences that I didn't get the outcome I was hoping for on *Innovation Nation*, and I met his lukewarm sincerity by inviting him over to the house for our Monday night cookout. If all Lou and Coco are asking for is that their parents work on their own happiness, then the four of us can gather as a family from time to time to enjoy each other's company, remember what was, and celebrate with one another all that is to come. Maybe not me, but Simon, Lou, and Coco will certainly have new adventures as the weeks and months pass by.

While I have used up every ounce of my maturity with Simon these past few days, I have yet to face the endless stream of voice mails and texts from Ash that I have left unheard and unread. I place my phone face up in front of me, the screen saver of Coco and Lou laughing wildly on the swings when they were five egging me on to find out what's behind their ecstatic faces. I take one more sip of chai and then swipe up and see that of the sixteen texts from Ash, four are from this morning alone. Figures a single guy with no kids wouldn't realize that moms are busy the day after Labor Day, the most common date in the United States for the first day of school.

I stretch my fingers across my forehead and massage my temples, warming up my mind to face reliving last Thursday's debacle clear through Ash's waterfall of thumbed communication.

Ding.

Livy. Not sure why she would be texting me. Maybe Mrs. Eisenberg has received the all-clear from her doctors to consider a trip to Scottsdale, and Livy knows I will do everything I possibly can to assist. By any account, Livy is an easier Eisenberg to warm up with. *Wait.* I stop myself from swiping. I can't imagine Ash would resort to having Livy do his bidding since I have refused to respond to him on my own. Not possible. Livy loved the concept behind Brown Butter, Baby! and claimed her cousin was a complete buffoon the entire ride home from the airport while her grandmother sat silent in the passenger seat. I understood. Mrs. Eisenberg couldn't and wouldn't speak ill of her adored grandson, but while Livy freely railed on Ash, I detected Mrs. Eisenberg's subtle nods in agreement.

8:42 a.m. (Livy)

Ash has been trying to get ahold of you this morning, but he's having difficulty. I am so sorry to be the one to tell you this, but our grandmother passed away in her sleep last night. I guess it's kind of fitting she died on Labor Day, the original working girl. She had eighty-eight wonderful years on this earth, but that doesn't make it hurt any less.

Oh no. Oh No. OH NO! I move to Ash's texts, starting with the most recent one from this morning, and read backward.

8:35 a.m. (Ash)

I want to let you know she loved you, Antonia. I guess this is goodbye for both of us.

8:08 a.m. (Ash)

She's gone. She's really gone. The person who understood me most in this world is gone.

7:52 a.m. (Ash)

I just tried to call you, but you didn't answer. My grandmother passed away in her sleep last night. I thought you would want to know, and I wanted to be the one to tell you.

7:48 a.m. (Ash)

Please, Antonia. It's clear you're angry with me but you need to pick up the phone. Now.

Yesterday 9:01 p.m. (Ash)

Thinking of Lou and Coco on their first day of high school. I wish them the best.

Sunday 4:14 p.m. (Ash)

My grandmother has advised me to give you space. I hope in time you will let me explain.

Saturday, 11:06 a.m. (Ash)

I know I wasn't the only one who thought Wednesday night was special. You wouldn't have forfeited sleep the night before the show if you didn't see me as important to your future as Innovation Nation. Come on, Antonia, tell me I'm not crazy and I'll leave you alone.

Saturday 7:14 a.m. (Ash)

I'm headed to the Cracked Cup for coffee. Please meet me there.

Friday 8:19 p.m. (Ash)

I flew home this afternoon and had dinner with my grandmother. She laid into me for leading you on in more ways than one, but I swear, that's not what I was doing. You are as smart as you are beautiful. I thought I was doing the right thing on the show.

Friday 11:56 a.m. (Ash)

I don't understand why the other judges didn't invest in Brown Butter, Baby! I was sure they would. You have to know I think it's a brilliant concept, otherwise I would have never vouched for you to be on the show.

Friday 5:58 a.m. (Ash)

That's the second night in a row of no sleep. Wednesday night was one of the best nights of my life. Last night, one of the worst. Have you been getting my texts and voice mails?

Thursday 9:02 p.m. (Ash)

You have to know I couldn't invest in Brown Butter, Baby!. Contractually I'm not even supposed to talk to participants on the show prior to filming, but I lost all judgment when I saw you in that sundress.

Thursday 5:06 p.m. (Ash)

I just talked to Livy and told her what happened. I know she's on her way to the airport to pick you guys up. Call me after you have dinner with Lou and Coco. We have to talk before you go to bed tonight.

Thursday 3:38 p.m. (Ash)

Obviously, you're gone. My grandmother isn't picking up her phone either. You have to let me explain. Call me when you land at SFO.

Thursday 1:22 p.m. (Ash)

I don't want you to leave the studio without my seeing you.

Thursday 1:18 p.m. (Ash)

Antonia, where are you? I'm trying to find you. Don't discount last night because of what just happened. Last night was real. The show . . . that's all an act.

DECEMBER

TUESDAY, DECEMBER 31

I have at least three dozen strips of packing tape expertly torn off and lined up on the edge of my dining room table like soldiers reporting for duty. Hair up in an all-business bun, I'm sitting cross-legged on the floor, garbage bags of compostable corn packing peanuts surrounding me like a fortress.

"Abuelita, I can't believe you gave your red heels to Zwena and not to me," I hear Lou whine from her upstairs bedroom.

"I know, they look great on me, eh?" Zwena gloats.

On a Wednesday in mid-October, Simon and I surprised Coco by moving her bed, stuffed bookshelf, and clothing into the extra bedroom off the kitchen while the girls were at school. I made Coco's new digs feel familiar and homey by throwing her T-shirts and jeans all over her floor just like her formerly shared room. Simon did splurge for new linens for Lou and Coco, their twin bedding no longer matching one another, but complementing their individual personalities. As I predicted—because while a mother might not know all, she does know her daughters—for the past two months Coco has only used her new room to sleep. All waking hours are spent with Lou on the floor where Coco's bed used to be, working out the trials of being teenagers at the bottom of the high school social totem pole. I've never worked so hard not to say *I told you so*.

"You know how conservative your mami is when it comes to you dressing up for a party—she would have never let you out of the house in those red shoes." Gloria blames me to get her off the hook with her granddaughter. That's rich coming from the woman who didn't allow my knees to show in church.

"But you can wear these, just don't tell her. Put them on in the car and don't forget to take them off before she picks you up," my mom instructs Lou, thinking I can't pack a box with my hands and hear with my ears at the same time. "And if you're a good niña, maybe your mom will let you borrow the red shoes for your quinceañera. Miracles can happen, mi amor."

I don't know exactly what *these* are, but I have an experienced guess so I yell up the stairs, "I can hear you! And if 'these' are hoop earrings, it's a definite *no*." I'll consider allowing Lou to wear the red heels; they do match her quinceañera dress perfectly. And she is fifteen. I have two weeks until the blowout party to decide how ready I am for my baby girls to become women.

Not wanting to shoulder all the parenting faults, I add, "Your father would agree with me." And lately that's true. Simon and I have fallen into a congenial coparenting pattern over the past couple of months. On Sunday afternoons we log on to the shared family calendar and enter what we each have scheduled for the coming week on top of the girls' schedules that I manage, a parenting responsibility I don't want to give up until we deliver them to college. Simon puts an *S* next to the rides he can cover for Lou and Coco and the events he can attend. I fill in the rest between me and my mom.

Since high school started for the twins, Zwena has evolved from passing out press-on nails to dispensing cool aunt counsel. I appreciate the complementary perspective Zwena offers Lou and Coco, her having been a teen who did not grow up in the trappings of American culture. The girls need a person they love and respect who can show them there are alternative paths to wading through the hormonal hordes of the next four years, including finding a job, believing kindness is cool, and holding a dream in their hearts. With each year I have less sway over Lou and Coco, so I am hopeful Zwena will keep them off the materialistic track with tales of her teen years spent in an under-resourced school vying for any job she could get.

Listening to the chatter upstairs, I realize I have miscalculated who should be teaching the twins that life lesson. Zwena's voice fluctuates like doppler radar, vacillating between stories of surviving profound poverty and the ecstasy of mall shopping after receiving her first US-earned paycheck. I have no clue what the twins will glean from these divergent messages, but I do know that young people benefit from positive adults in their lives. A strong family is one thing, but Zwena is that credible outside influence for my girls. And though I am far from my teenage years of angst, I can see that Mrs. Eisenberg served as that same support for me.

I miss her terribly.

"That's because both of you are no fun when it comes to fashion," Zwena hollers down the stairs to me. None of us are willing to change locations to negotiate over New Year's Eve outfits. "You know who else was no fun? James Madison. He may have written the first draft of the US Constitution, but all the founding fathers considered him Father No Fun." Krish and I had misjudged Zwena's interest in US government as a temporary fixation in her efforts to become a citizen. Turns out she finds the men who established the United States fascinating and doesn't miss an opportunity to inform me that I should, too, since they established our legal and banking systems. Also turns out Zwena's no longer interested in medical assisting; instead she wants to be a court stenographer.

"Have you girls packed?" I'm determined to switch the subject off the me-versus-all-of-them fashion mediation to something more pressing. Coco, Lou, and Simon are leaving at the crack of dawn for Disneyland. I may never make it to the Magic Kingdom, but I am pleased Simon has stayed true to his promise to take our girls to the happiest place on earth to kick off the new year. It's a destination they have long deserved to visit. Best U Man is doing so well that, as Simon predicted, he has hired a receptionist and established a subscription model. He has also been depositing money into my checking account the first and fifteenth of every month without any influence from me. Turns out, after the Iconic Investors do their post-show due diligence examining founders' personal finances and detailed business plans, 90 percent of the entrepreneurs fail to withstand the scrutiny. After all the probing into his background, Simon's deal was actually sealed.

Additionally, I learned there is something called the "Innovation Nation effect," where even if a founder doesn't secure funding, the company still experiences an increase in sales. After selling out at several farmers markets in a matter of hours, I set up an Etsy shop, and I'm spending my New Year's Eve packing lotions to fill a recent order for a bachelorette party gift bag in Boca. I like to imagine Simon's deposits are at least one instance where my not taking the initiative to change our coupled finances when he went on his sojourn is paying off. Literally.

"And no booty shorts! Show some respect for Cinderella," I insist, knowing there is a minimum of two pairs of those straggly denim shorts packed into their shared duffel. When Lou and Coco head out with my mom to assist with the New Year's Eve party at the Senior Connection, I will be double-checking their packing job and sneaking in a few skirts with their volleyball shorts to go underneath.

After first searching unsuccessfully in my junk drawer for a Sharpie, I finally find one in the bottom of my purse. It's covered in lint and dried out, but I hold it tight. The last time I used it was Mrs. Eisenberg's final trip home from Scottsdale. I remember I had written, "the desert already misses you (and so does Elaine)" and that had given Mrs. Eisenberg a hearty laugh. She asked that I take a picture of it with her phone and send it to Elaine, an action I had taught her to do at least a half dozen times, but she still insisted I do for her. When I wrote that sign, I had no idea what a prophecy it would turn out to be. If I could go back to that day, I would have written, "this desert queen reigns supreme."

Other than a few snapshots from our time on the set of *Innovation Nation* that I still haven't had the stomach to upload from my phone onto my laptop, this pen and a notebook full of scribbled life advice are all that remains of my friendship with Mrs. Eisenberg. Right at eye level are textbooks from my multiple efforts to earn a degree and come up with the next big thing to pursue. I tap the pen down the spines of each textbook and think of the ideas and subsequent conversations that passed between me and Mrs. Eisenberg as we rolled through SFO together. At the very end of my shelf is the spiral-bound book of case studies from my Stanford entrepreneurs course. I hook the Sharpie to the plastic cover. Mrs. Eisenberg is now the most recent source of knowledge in my quest to ultimately reach my destiny.

"You sure you don't want to come with Krish and me?" Zwena asks, leading my four favorite women down the stairs, each one as beautiful as the next. Over the past week, Zwena has invited me multiple times to join her and Krish for their New Year's Eve celebration, believing spending the evening alone is bad luck for the coming year. She doesn't like the thought of me by myself, and I can't share with her that this is the one night where I don't mind us not being a friendship thruple. Krish and I have been busy secretly planning the perfect engagement without a hint of suspicion from Zwena. Not the only stealthy one in our group, Zwena thinks she's attending a New Year's Eve party Krish is DJing for a tech icon's fifth fiancé, and she wants me to come join her on the dance floor. I reassure Zwena she will definitely have someone to dance with while fighting with myself not to say anything more. At this moment there is a new East African restaurant not too far from here with a beautifully set table for two. When Zwena was swiping through hair tutorials with Lou and Coco last week, I sneaked her phone to find her parents' and siblings' contact information. I gave it to Krish, and he has arranged for her entire family to be together in Kenya to celebrate with the two of them over FaceTime, which is no small feat since it will be early morning New Year's Day half a world away. Krish has promised me that after Zwena's family, I will be the very next call.

"Well, enjoy your time with me, 'Gloria,' 'Sylvia,' and yourself," Zwena instructs, taking in my stack of jars. Meanwhile I take in my radiant girlfriend in her last moments of singlehood. "Although I'm way more entertaining in person."

"You are," I agree as Zwena plucks a "Sylvia" and drops it in her handbag.

"Wrong one, Z," I correct, handing over her signature shade.

"No, she's the right one," Zwena says with a wink. She misses Mrs. Eisenberg too.

"She really was." I can't argue otherwise.

"Zwena, you ready to go?" my mom asks with an extra check of her face in the mirror by my front door. Zwena is dropping Lou, Coco, and my mom off at the Senior Connection, and I am picking them up at 11:00 p.m. *A late night for old folks*, I had teased my mom, and she had schooled me that since the residents all take late-afternoon naps, the party would and could go into the wee hours if there is enough staff on hand to help everyone back into their beds.

I envelop Lou and Coco in big New Year hugs and then step back to admire the young women they have become. Their hair lies smooth and soft down their backs, and they wear just the right amount of gloss and mascara to highlight the pink lips they got from their father and round espresso eyes they inherited from their abuela. Converse low tops with their minidresses is the perfect style for a couple of kids who are in constant negotiation with their mom over their efforts to become women. I appreciate Coco and Lou appeasing me by staying young for one more night.

Knock. Knock.

"So, you're willing to spend New Year's Eve with Uber Eats, but not with me, eh?" Zwena scolds as my mom, Lou, and Coco put on their coats. I don't have the heart to tell Zwena I have been looking forward to having my Philly cheesesteak, waffle fries, and Diet Coke to myself all week. There's a formulaic winter wonderland in Vermont rom-com on Netflix that has gotten terrible reviews, and I can't wait to dig into it and my meal.

"Hope the delivery guy is at least cute." Zwena crosses her fingers and waves them in my face before opening the door.

"Oh, he's cute," she guffaws, embarrassing the delivery boy for sure. I grab the door from Zwena to take my food and rush these women out and on with their night. Only the boy on my front stoop is not a boy. He's a man. And that man holding my order is Ash Eisenberg.

"You drive for Uber Eats?" I spit out, confused. Zwena smacks me hard on my backside, disappointed that these are my first words to Ash since September.

I had sobbed uncontrollably from Livy's text of Mrs. Eisenberg's passing clear through Ash documenting his feelings for me. Through blurry eyes and shaky hands, I had thumbed Livy and Ash back how shocked and sorry I was and would they please let me know when the memorial was scheduled, I would be there. A brief message was returned by Ash that it was his grandmother's wish that her remembrance of life be kept to family members with a recording of Eddie playing the trumpet in the background as she was laid to rest next to the love of her life. I was so upset that I wanted to write back that if his family was so expansive to include Jewish people, Black people, and a Norwegian, couldn't they make room for one Puerto Rican, but instead my last words to Ash were that I understood.

Gloria steps forward toward Ash, takes the bag out of his hand, and places it on the entryway table where my purse usually goes. "There, your food has been delivered. Now you two can talk. Let's go, ladies." With the same insistent wave she used to get me, David, Gabriel, and my dad to scoot down the pew at the Mission-Dolores church, Gloria ushers Lou, Coco, and Zwena out the door. "Have a good night, Antonia. We'll see you around eleven."

Ash peeks into my house to see if anyone else is inside as I say goodbye to my girl posse. Zwena turns around to mouth a dramatic *OMG* in my direction.

OMG is right, I mimic back because she, too, is about to get one hell of a surprise.

"Hi," Ash says sheepishly, leaning against the doorframe, a cozy plaid cashmere scarf framing his handsome face.

"¡Que cojones tienes! What are you doing here?" I ask, cautious of his random appearance. I have packed away my emotionally tumultuous year with the Eisenberg family into a compartment in my head and in my heart that I do my best not to visit.

"Enough time has passed. I had to come see you." Ash pauses, his eyes imploring me to say something, but I don't. "You're right, Antonia. It took me a lot of nerve to come here."

"So why did you?" I'm having a hard time believing Ash didn't have a better New Year's Eve plan than this.

"I want to talk as freely as we did that night in Los Angeles. Before everything that happened on the show." The tremor in Ash's voice doesn't come close to the level of trepidation I feel.

I consider his proposition, but I don't move to invite him in. "Okay then, I'll go first." I straighten my posture, shoulders back, feet firmly planted like his grandmother taught me. Ash stands to meet my comportment, not backing down one bit.

"You wanted to invest in Simon, but not in me." My cheesesteak and waffle fries are getting cold, and my Diet Coke is warming, so I don't have time to mess around.

"I didn't want to invest in either of you."

Ouch. Eso duele.

"Are you kidding me!?" I bark through bared teeth and jab Ash's chest with my index finger. "¡Eres un comemierda!"

"Did you just tell me to eat shit?" Ash asks incredulously.

"No. It means you *are* a shit." I poke him one more time. "Obviously, the night we spent together in LA was a joke," I accuse.

"It was no joke," Ash says, defending himself.

"Oh, really?" My juvenile side comes out, and in an instigating voice I let Ash have it. "What about all that, 'Antonia, you're so talented the investors would be fools not to back you. I believe in you. Lou and Coco will be so proud of you. All the judges are going to fight over you.'"

I run out of breath and my blood is pumping from my racing heart to the fists formed at my sides.

"I looked like a fool on the show. A complete idiota!" I want Ash to know it was all his fault. "You didn't do a whole lot while I bombed in front of those cameras, but you sure were there paving Simon's way to investment."

"My tactic was to push Simon on another judge," Ash asserts.

"That makes no sense," I challenge Ash, not accepting his answer.

"I knew the other male judge would do whatever was needed to invest in Simon. The guy's portfolio is full of companies that have done significant damage to this planet. He's looking for a fast track to save his soul for all the poor choices he's made. And he's made a lot. Best U Man is his silver bullet to redemption."

"That may be true, but it doesn't explain why you got in on the bidding." I catch a big flaw in Ash's semiplausible explanation.

"I figured the more money I could get Simon by engaging in a bidding war I intended to lose, the greater the chance that he would move on with his life and leave you alone. Leave you for me."

"So, you set Simon up for success, but allowed me to bomb in front of my mom, my friends, and America, so you could have me all to yourself?"

"I did," Ash admits without a touch of remorse, and damn if it's not a little bit sexy. "It was a strategic move."

"How was you buzzing me a strategic move?" I scoff, but feel my iciness start to melt.

"I really thought the remaining female judge would invest in you. I was sure it was a done deal."

"You thought wrong."

"And I feel terrible about that, you have no idea." Ash's eyes plead with me to believe him. "Listen, Antonia. I was going to invest in

Brown Butter, Baby!, but that night in Santa Monica made me realize just how much I was invested in you."

"*You buzzed me, Ash!* The least you could have done was help me save face by keeping your hand off the buzzer and throwing me a low-ball offer."

"I couldn't!" he asserts. "Early on the producers figured out you and Simon were married, and they wanted to take advantage of it. They insisted that before I made any kind of offer, I ask about Simon and your relationship with him. The producers were looking to drum up some drama for the finale. That's why they were so willing to put you on the show and slated you last. They had this whole scenario planned to boost ratings."

"What?! Why didn't you let me know?"

"I didn't even know ahead of time! During the break when the stagehands were setting up your displays, the producers pulled me aside and laid it all out. When I balked, they suggested one of the other judges could air your private business since you and I are friends," Ash explains.

"That's still to be determined."

Ash meets my contention with an eye roll.

"I didn't want anyone creating drama at your expense, so I told the producers I would do it," Ash says, contrite. "And then I didn't."

"Oh, so you're a hero now?" I retort.

"No," Ash answers, hanging his head. "I'm not a hero. And I'm not a judge anymore either. They canned me right after the show."

I'm shocked that my ordinary life created such an extraordinary outcome on *Innovation Nation*.

"And I don't care that they fired me. I would have quit anyway. People are more important to me than money, Antonia. They always have been."

"I-I get that," I stutter, not wanting to come across as callous but knowing valuing people over money is easy for someone who has always had both.

As if he has read my mind, Ash adds, "It is possible to have both."
I hope to one day find out for myself that the two are not mutually
exclusive. "Listen, I know you're pissed, and I am sorry about that. But
can you give me one more minute?"

That better not be my apology.

Ash unties his scarf and reaches into the inside pocket of his jacket.
"I wanted to hand-deliver this. It's for the start to your new year." He
holds out a standard white business envelope but keeps the box with a
simple lavender ribbon tied around it.

Catching me looking at the present, Ash urges, "Read the letter."

September 6

I don't even get past the date without looking back up at Ash, awe-
struck. The letter was written the day after filming *Innovation Nation*. A
shiver ripples through my chest, accompanied by a hitch in my throat.

> Dear Antonia,
> Over the years I have shared with you many of the
> abiding aphorisms that kept me going in challenging
> times. I know they often went in one ear and out the
> other, written off as trite clichés from an old woman
> of a generation long past its prime. But I noticed you
> wrote one or two down in your notebook. I hope
> when future circumstances call for it, you will pass
> them on to your girls compliments of a dear friend.
>
> There is one last gem I want to leave with you. It
> has been my north star since my father whispered it
> in my ear as a six-year-old girl in France, getting on a
> boat alone, to sail into the unknown. Roughly trans-
> lated he said, "Have the courage to live a big life even
> without a safety net."

In the time I have come to know you, I have learned that when you stumble, Antonia, you get back up again. And again. Please trust me when I say that that is what it takes to stay the course, become your own success, and enjoy a big life. It's not the safety net of a degree, the support of a husband, children graduating, or the blessings of a couple of self-aggrandizing judges that you need to become the person you are meant to be.

If you are reading this, I have stumbled for my last time, but you have not. Use this money for the Brown Butter, Baby! journey as it stumbles toward triumph. I believe in you, Antonia. I always have. And, if you are up for it, maybe take my grandson along for the ride. I know he wants to join you.

Keep eating that elephant one bite at a time.

All my love and luck,

Sylvia Eisenberg

Tears are rolling down my cheeks, and I wipe my nose on my sleeve before I speak, afraid I will blow a snot bubble in front of Ash. "Did you know about this letter?"

"I did," is all Ash says in response to the question I can barely choke out. He hands me the box, in exchange for the letter. I carefully untie the lavender ribbon, intending to save it to wrap around my Sharpie, another reminder of my dear, beloved friend. I wiggle off the top of the box and lift out a square carefully wrapped in multiple layers of tissue paper. I let the top and bottom of the box fall to the ground. The tape lifts easily, and I peel back layer after layer until a silver corner peeks out at me, followed by Steve Jobs's face.

Taking in the photo, Ash explains, "She wanted you to have it." We both chuckle in unison, the photo of Sylvia Eisenberg and Steve Jobs staring back at me, daring me to believe in myself too.

"She also wanted you to have this." Ash gently takes the framed photo from my gripped hands, flips it over, and returns it to me. On the back is taped a check, made out to Brown Butter, Baby! for $300,000. The exact amount I sought from the judges on *Innovation Nation*.

"And you retain one hundred percent ownership."

"Wait, wait . . . What?" Trying to process Mrs. Eisenberg's generosity, my mouth stumbles over my brain.

"As executor of my grandmother's will, it took me a bit of time to work through her estate, but this was an amendment she insisted I help her make when she returned from taping *Innovation Nation*. When I explained to her why I did what I did, she was not happy with me, but she understood my long-term goal. She was always a visionary."

I nod in agreement. She was.

"Her plan was to give you the first half after you had picked yourself up from what happened on the show, the second half upon her death." Ash chokes up, unable to continue. Without hesitation, I grab Ash's hand and squeeze tight, just as his grandmother had done to comfort me many times before.

"I had to get it to you before the new year," Ash says, willing himself back into control. "I wanted, no, I needed to make this year right before we both head into the next."

I, too, understand the need for closure and new beginnings.

"You've come a long way from almost dumping my grandmother at my feet at SFO to this." Ash gestures over my shoulder to the shipping and receiving center set up in my living room. I turn and take it all in myself.

"All thanks to your grandmother, not to you," I remind Ash, but this time with a flirty tease and a hope he can sense my shift in demeanor. Ash glances over my shoulder again at the Brown Butter,

Baby! inventory, and then he looks down at my left hand, clearly checking there is no ring in sight.

"You look like you're doing all right."

"I am doing all right," I assure Ash, because it's true.

"Where do we go from here?" I question the universe as much as Ash. It still stings that he did not invest in me, but I'm blown away by this gift from my new silent business partner, Sylvia Eisenberg. Women-owned businesses are all the rage right now. "The truth still stands that you chose not to invest in me."

"That's because I didn't want you to need me. I need you to want me," Ash says with his full chest. "I told you, I'm already invested in you, Antonia Arroyo. For the long term."

"I'll need a couple of weeks to do my due diligence on you, and then I'll want that timeframe in a binding contract," I haggle, straight-faced, but then I can't help but break into an enormous smile.

"Until then, would you settle for a handshake?" *Look at Ash being the coy one now.*

This is a negotiation I will not back down from, and one I'm determined to win.

"No handshake," I counter. Ash looks surprised at my refusal given the delight on my face. "But I do want a kiss."

"Right here?"

"Right now." I pull Ash into my house and close the door behind him. "Happy New Year to me."

"Happy New Year to us."

ACKNOWLEDGMENTS

As comedic writers, we absolutely love the remarkably talented Julia Louis-Dreyfus. Elaine was brilliant, but oh do we wish we could vote for Selina Meyer for president. On January 18, 2021, Julia appeared on the podcast *Smartless* with Will Arnett, Jason Bateman, and Sean Hayes. During the interview, the hosts asked Julia what she would do if she wasn't an actor. Julia responded that she would work in an airport and that she "would drive the go-cart that takes the old people to the gate," that *that* would be a cool job. (Can't you just hear her saying it?) We doubt Julia imagined her offhand comment at the end of an hour-long interview with three silly men would be the ember that sparked the idea for Antonia Arroyo and *Boss Lady*. In fact, it did. We owe you one, Julia Louis-Dreyfus.

Now four books into this partnership of ours, we have had the most dedicated women walking alongside us since our first written words became our first book. Luck bent our way when Liza Fleissig and Ginger Harris agreed to represent us in late 2017. In 2018, Tegan Tigani joined us as our developmental editor and has been critiquing our work with a joyful spirit ever since. Amid the publishing upheaval of 2020, Alison Dasho became our acquisitions editor and our most enthusiastic champion at Amazon Publishing. This, along with the many hands and eyes of our painstakingly thorough editing professionals at APub, is our dream team. Our supportive ranks continue to grow with friends and family pitching in to be extra eyes of accuracy for this book, including early readers Larry Frank, Shilpa Shah, Emille Marie Torrens, and Deborah Zipser. To the Cohodas and Frank families: this one is a nod to all of us and the almighty apple. And flowers of honor and respect to the Hughes sisters of Cambridge, MA, who together raised a dozen children and dozens of grandchildren in a beautifully loving blend of Afro–Puerto Rican culture.

Without formal training as writers, we left accomplished careers in education to take a chance on ourselves and fulfill a shared dream: making people laugh with our stories. It was daunting. It is still hard. But if we can make boss moves, so can you.

BOOK CLUB QUESTIONS

1. Upon Simon's return, Antonia is hesitant to serve him with divorce papers. In her place, how would you have reacted to Simon's midlife betrayal?
2. Zwena and Krish are successful keeping their relationship a secret. If you have ever engaged in a clandestine workplace romance, how were you able to keep it under wraps?
3. What are some examples in *Boss Lady* of sacrifice of self for loved ones?
4. In what ways would Mrs. Eisenberg have faced hurdles to her business success in her day? How are Antonia's hurdles similar and/or different?
5. What are the disparate and/or analogous lenses on America that guide Antonia as the child of Puerto Ricans and her best friend Zwena as an immigrant?
6. In what ways does the fear of judgment shape the relationship between Antonia and her mother, Gloria? Are they specific to this mother and daughter relationship, or is this a common experience?
7. In contrast to the trope of male assertiveness, Ash is restrained in his romantic approach to Antonia. What is attractive about his persona in *Boss Lady*?

ABOUT THE AUTHORS

Photo © 2018 J Garner Photography

Alli Frank has worked in education for more than twenty years, from boisterous public high schools to small, progressive private schools. A graduate of Cornell and Stanford University, Alli lives in the Pacific Northwest with her husband and two daughters. With Asha Youmans, she is the coauthor of *Tiny Imperfections, Never Meant to Meet You,* and *The Better Half* and is a contributing essayist in the anthology *Moms Don't Have Time To: A Quarantine Anthology.*

Asha Youmans spent two decades teaching elementary school students. A graduate of the University of California, Berkeley, Asha lives in the Pacific Northwest with her husband and two sons. With Alli Frank, she is the coauthor of *Tiny Imperfections, Never Meant to Meet You,* and *The Better Half.*

For more information, visit the authors at www.alliandasha.com or @alliandasha.